THE OBSOLETE TRUTH

Scott Davis

This is a work of fiction.
While it has not actually happened,
if men don't get their act together,
soon,
much of it will.

Published by
Obsolete Publishing
Contact:
scottybsharp@gmail.com

ISBN:979-8-218-00987-8

THE OBSOLETE TRUTH

Bryan Bowman

Edited by Gaia Alt

EDITOR'S NOTE: Bryan Bowman recorded his story with voice memos, videos, selfies, and some old-school pen and paper. He posted during a three-month span in the fall of 2032. Memoirs bore me to tears—even ones that include me (I'm his oldest friend)—so to spare you sifting through thousands of posts and videos, I converted his words and images into prose. His complete archives can be found at theobsoletetruth.com and hundreds of YouTube videos are available.

I hope I have retained the essence of his story. After all, isn't essence what really matters?

May his story, and over four billion others like his, never be forgotten.

THE CAVE

A man is just a woman's strategy for making other women.
                              - Margaret Atwood, The Handmaid's Tale

EDITOR'S NOTE: I start with one of Bryan's last posts, Dec. 13, 2032:

Don't know how much longer I can hold out, hiding here, trembling, the rock face all around me radiating cold like blocks of ice. The steam of my breath, the beat of my heart, the twitch of my left leg, are my only company. Miguel is out there somewhere, maybe surrendered, maybe captured, maybe dead, I don't know, and it's only a matter of time before they find me. I can't remember the last time I've shivered so hard. I don't know how cold it is, can't check my weather app, it would give away my location. Drones would be on me in a moment. I crouch in this wannabe cave, the size of a walk-in closet, inhaling the damp smell of mossy rock and drenched leaves. The falls spills over a cliff above me, tumbling in a curtain of water onto fallen trees and boulders leaning against each other at the bottom.

I dig into my pants pocket, pull out my amber bottle, raise it to my lips, tilt it upside down just to verify it is indeed empty. I'm out of my golden tincture. I hold the glass dropper under my tongue like a toothpick. It gives me comfort.

A familiar buzzing comes on, pricking my ears. I gaze out through the shimmering curtain, watch a sparrow-sized drone weave in and around trees, searching for me.

Shit.

The flying spy hovers and then soars beyond the bare limbs of maples, elms, and sycamores that twist like veins against the gray Ohio sky. The drone moves on, vanishing, thank goddess. I listen for the snapping of twigs under the bootsteps of Sister Deputies, feeling like a terrorist-in-hiding. The forest, my usual muse, now feels claustrophobic. I whisper into my cell—perhaps my last thoughts?— while my heartbeat is screaming, the throbbing in my forehead spreading down my neck, splaying out to my fingertips. I dare not move. I clamp down on my left leg that twitches like little earthquakes underneath my sore, cold ass.

I hear dogs barking in the distance—they say even the tracking dogs are bitches—coming steadily closer. I'm gonna have to make a run for it but where do you run when you've got nowhere to go?

WELL, HOW DID WE GET HERE?

EDITOR'S NOTE: Bryan's first posting was dictated at home on Sept. 29, 2032, almost three months prior. From here on out, I will structure his posts into a narrative.

I turn forty in a few weeks. I will soon become an obsolete. Who would've guessed we brothers would end up like this? Some feminists hoped for it, dreamed of it, but even they had to be surprised how quickly we got here.

    I blame science.

    I blame Sisters.

    I blame us brothers the most.

    It's early autumn and I've been reflecting on the chilling changes and wondering where the hell we go from here. So I decided to record my story, a creation myth, like the Hindu Vedas, the Garden of Eden, the Great Spirit stories. And like all creation myths, this one involves epic destruction. Yes, we should've seen it coming, this near-extinction of half the world's homo sapiens, which I recently learned is Latin for wise man. Ironic. If we were so wise we wouldn't be in this tragic predicament.

The media label this many things: apocalypse male, bye-bye brothers, the death of dudes. Just to name a few. Radical feminists call it revenge of the vaginas. And paradise.

Whatever you wanna call it, estimates are only forty million of us remain. Worldwide. That's it. Us obsoletes have been and continue to be written out of herstory. Cold hard facts one day, fake news the next. Herstory is being re-written. I think of my ramblings as an historical view from the losers, an addendum to The People's History of the United States. This madness is happening everywhere, but I will focus on here in America, in my hometown in North Central Ohio.

I'm dictating this into my BestFriendFhone, an LG BFF model 3. This is their ad campaign:

Your Best Friend

In Your Pocket

My phone is certainly my bestie.

So I'm recording what I assume will be the end of my life. Goddess knows if this will even matter, my memories digitally buried among the quadrillions of things that crowd the data universe. Even if my memories do go viral, the shelf-life never lasts long. I'm not shooting crazy dance videos or looking for "likes" or any of that and I doubt I'll have enough followers to make a dent in the online world. I just hope someone in the future will watch, listen, or—heaven forbid— read my thoughts. I love books, the antiques of the entertainment world, and hope that my ramblings can be turned into one. I plan on asking my lifelong friend, Gaia, to edit and publish it. I'm counting on you, Gaia!

Before I get into my story, let me set the scene because the world is changing so fast. Goddess knows what it will be like when you read

8

this. It's 2032. For brothers, life has been exponentially evil. For Sisters, life is off-the-charts better.

Women are now called Sisters. Always capitalized. Sister Emily, Sister Mother, Sister Doctor.

"Hello, Sister."

"Have a nice day, Sister."

I'm sick of the word.

Men are called brothers. Always lowercase, with no other name or title attached, without individuality, insignificant, endangered, nearly extinct. The words man and male, and their derivatives, woman and female, can no longer be written or spoken. Is it a coincidence the root *male* is so close to the Latin mal, meaning bad or evil? Seems we brothers were doomed from the start of civilization, or at least from the start of language.

I'm risking imprisonment just speaking these words, but it's like speeding, we still do it.

Language is the least of my concerns.

We believed robots and A.I. would take over the world. Instead, the "weaker sex" controls almost everything, almost everywhere. America is led by Sister Olsen. We call her Mother President. China is led by Madame Wong. They call her Mother Premier. Russia is led by Vladimir Putin's daughter, Sister Katerina. Militaries around the world are All-Sister.

Let's see, what else. . .

There have not been many big new inventions lately. Fancier, yes, sleeker, sure. Smarter cars and planes, TVs, computers, cell phones. Better cancer treatments, better medicines, better replacement body parts. Everything today is just improvements on

9

things we already had. Health care is completely controlled by the state and free to all. It seems ridiculous that America fought this for so long. The state has nearly eradicated several forms of cancer, the Big C, only to have it be replaced by a far deadlier virus, The Y. If you believe in conspiracies, then this is the most radical invention to date. We thought the Covid pandemic got us prepared. We were wrong.

I'll give you the gory details of The Y later on.

Privacy is now extinct, has been for a couple decades. In 2030 it became mandatory for brothers born after 1999 to be microchipped, implanted just under the surface of forearm skin, tracking their every move. Thank goddess those of us born in the last millennium were grandfathered-in and not required to be chipped. I think Sisters worried about violent resistance from us older brothers. We millennials, X-Geners, and Boomers are still tracked by our drones, ranging in size from raptors to beetles. We are each assigned one. Mine is the size of a hummingbird. I'll introduce you later.

The Internet is so a part of us, we don't even call it the Web anymore. Just *It*. We say, "What did you do on *It* last night?" The Internet has gobbled up a pronoun, just as *It* has devoured free time.

These are the hi-tech dark ages, and certainly as bloody, with war more widespread than ever. Hundreds of scattered conflicts suddenly merged into one great big one—The War of the Sexes. Brother versus Sister. I'll give you a rundown soon, trust me. Sounds like I'm putting off telling you the truly dark stuff. You're right, I am.

Hmmm, what else. . . ?

Oh yeah, the Great Climate Disaster of 2025 killed hundreds of millions across the globe. The weather was fuckin' crazy. Biblical fires, floods, and intense storms were the norm. A massive tornado hit New

10

York City, blowing out half the glass in Manhattan. Miami flooded, creating America's new Venice. Fires charred much of California's forests, nicknaming the Golden State the Black State. This is when Sisters really started to wrestle political control away from brothers.

Here's some good news: with population cut nearly in half, carbon emissions are cut in half too. I guess what's bad for brothers is good for the planet. Also, water is no longer in shortage, though water quality became a serious health issue, contaminated by corpses. Dead brothers in homes, dead brothers on the streets, dead brothers floating down rivers and lakes. The scent of death soured the air as earth's atmosphere became overripe with rotting flesh and flies, rats, and disease. Then a pair of smart entrepreneurs, The Exterminator Sisters, devised sprayer drones that located and disinfected corpses with an all-natural organic spray and just a splash of sulfuric acid to keep the bugs and worms away. Until the bodies could be discarded.

All dead brothers end up in the same place, burned in makeshift crematoriums. Funeral pyres are a symbol of the times, ashes blowing across the land, figuratively and literally. The Great Ash Bowl. For the first two years, the smell of burnt flesh clung to your hair, your nostrils, your clothes. Planet earth became one big urn. Cheery shit, right? But if you had stock in crematoriums, funeral services, or cleaning supplies, you made a killing, even as you yourself were dying. Fortunately, there aren't that many bodies to burn anymore.

Marijuana is legal on most of the planet, as are psychedelics like psilocybin and MDMA, routinely prescribed to brothers and Sisters nearing the end of life. Personally, I don't want psychedelics, the world is surreal enough. But I do take CBD and Kava tinctures that my friend Gaia mixes. They help me deal with all this madness.

11

Prescription painkillers and heroin are still problems, even with Sisters who have it so good. Overdoses take the lives of way too many of both genders. Marx got it wrong. Religion is not the opiate of the people. Turns out to be actual opiates.

Speaking of religion, that has died too. The Catholic Church was crucified on its own cross, due to the molestation scandals, and then, of course, all the dead Fathers. Sister Priests now lead churches—it took a plague for that to happen—but it is too little too late. Many Sisters and surviving brothers fled the church in droves. Protestantism fared better since Sisters had been ministers for decades but as the church drifted from Jesus and towards Mary, churches splintered and congregations fell apart. And Islam, such a stronghold for brothers, collapsed under its own weight. To be sure, Muslim Sisters still pray to Allah, but most shed the dark cloaks and traditions that had confined them for so long.

There's a new kid on the block, Spiritual Sisterhood, rising up the religious charts with a bullet. It's actually pretty cool, one of my favorite things in the new world. It's all-embracing without all the dogma. Each Get-Together is a unique place to express your faith in any way you wish: prayer, song, dance, art, or group therapy, often happening simultaneously. Other times, the Get-Togethers are like old-school revivalist meetings, where the whole room becomes one, sharing in a deeply moving way. It's about what the people bring to it, not about what the church lectures. I've been to a few Get-Togethers and I loved 'em. It's what church should have always been. Unfortunately, I don't feel welcomed any more, I watch from a bro-only section in the back.

12

I believe it was Nietzsche who said God is dead. That's certainly so now. Long live Goddess.

States don't matter anymore either. They still exist in name, but America is federalist now. One community, one nation. Goddess bless America. Sisters come together across the political aisle, united better than brothers have ever been, getting things done with co-op capitalism. Sister Leaders bitch as much as brother leaders did, but then they talk it out and don't go to war over their problems. Except when that problem is us brothers.

BTW, the Declaration of Independence has been re-written. Amendment 29: All Sisters are Created Equal.

Abortion is no longer a hotbed issue, now that brothers are out of politics, and is performed almost exclusively on brother fetuses.

And strict gun control exists. For brothers.

To me, the most surprising change is the speed of life, which had been moving exponentially fast. But these last two years, time has slowed the fuck down. Death will do that.

I know I'm being somewhat flippant about all that's happened. Screw it. They made comic books and movie musicals of the Holocaust for chrissake. Goddess—he/she/whatever the hell it is— has bestowed the blackest humor on us. Has throughout herstory. If I didn't make fun of some of it, I'd go completely mad. To laugh is one of the last true freedoms I have. And before you accuse me of being insensitive, just know that my brother, then my dad, almost all of my friends, my uncles and nephews and neighbors, all of them died horrible and ugly deaths. I am tapped-out of sensitivity. I'm running on emotional fumes. Death has left a foul taste on my soul that I'm sick and tired of.

13

So, if you can't laugh at the darkness, you might as well stop right here. I won't be offended. But if you believe it's in the ruins that we find the rhyme and the reason, and if you're curious at how the hell we got here, then by all means, continue on.

THE FACTORY

Brothers have always been machines. Emotionless machines
of labor, of war, of paternity, of sex.

- The brothers Manual to Survival

I am lucky to be alive. Roughly a hundred of us brothers remain in the city. That's it. Compared to 30,000 or so Sisters. We have "flattened the curve" worldwide as they say, our decline stabilizing to forty million or so brothers, which is nothing when you spread us out around the globe: a couple dozen here, a few hundred there. We peaked at well over four billion brothers, so forty million feels like the tiny one-percent it is.

Why am I a fortunate one? My job saved me. I get paid to yank, wank, and whack off. I stroke the one-eyed snake, choke the chicken, and grease the monkey. Sometimes I butter the corn, slap the salami, and tickle the pickle. I could go on and on, we say 'em all at "work" and work is exactly what it is. There is no pleasure in what I do, no sex allowed, hell they discourage us even looking at porn. Something about the purity of the sperm's spirit.

Except for the no-sex part—and most of us guys weren't getting laid anyway—this is a brother's dream job. We spend 15-20 minutes

15

working and the rest of the time surfing *It*, playing video games, working out, or just killing time. Tens of thousands of us spermers are scattered around the world. We don't really know how many, we have no union and no interaction with other spermers, except those who dare navigate the dark *It*.

Here at our *The Factory* franchise, we call ourselves Appleseeds. Johnny Appleseed spent years in these parts in the early 1800s planting apple trees. Statues and shopping centers were named after him, although the statues have recently been torn down, the centers renamed. In other areas of the country, spermers have different names: handymen, seeders, 'bators, and rabbits. In Nevada they're called one-armed-bandits. In Texas they're drillers. In Detroit, pistons.

It's the only job, other than giving birth, where gender is still a requirement.

Sisters now do all other "masculine" jobs. They drive trucks and tractors, lift heavy things and build skyscrapers, fight wars and win them. What they don't do are menial or domestic jobs. Robots now do many of those. And what robots can't do, surviving brothers will. We dust, clean toilets, wash windows, and do laundry.

I live in my hometown Mansfield, the capital of Richland County. The city is surrounded by corn and soybean farms, flat on the north and east, rolling on the south and west. Red barns with faded, peeling painted signs—Chew Mail Pouch and Ohio Bicentennial—lean over at impossible angles, as if being blown sideways. And it's not unusual to pass black horse-drawn buggies on the road. The largest Amish community in North America is less than an hour southeast. The city is blue-collar, rust-belt, salt-of-the-earth. In the booming post-WWII era, Mansfield called itself the appliance capital of America.

16

Westinghouse, Tappan, GM, the Steel Mill, and Mansfield Tire kept factory work thriving and the city of 50,000 humming. But it became an industrial ghost town in the 1970's. Hulking factory skeletons remained, fossils of the fossil-fuel age, empty and bloated, five-story walls lined with broken windows, crude graffiti, and the burned scars of homeless campfires. Parking lots were infested with weeds the size of cornstalks, sidewalks erupted from the roots of trees long since cut down, and roads were spotted with potholes the size of craters. It's the classic Midwest tragedy; factories moved overseas and local shops moved out of downtown to a shopping district in nearby Ontario. Main Street was barely a minor street anymore.

A renaissance has sparked here in the last few years. Medical companies sprouted, owned and staffed by Sisters. And the last of the behemoth factories, Westinghouse, has finally been torn down. Yet to us brothers, the city still feels like a ghost town, abandoned first by industry and now by dying brothers.

The city was re-named Sisterfield in 2029 in a campaign by the Sister Mayor, part of a nationwide flurry of name changes. Mansfields everywhere were renamed: in Illinois, in Louisiana, in Massachusetts. Los Angeles became Las Angeles. Williamsburg, VA became Wilmasburg. You get the picture.

Sisterfield is just off Interstate 71 and Highway 30, conveniently located near many major markets: Cleveland, Columbus, Cincinnati, Detroit, Indianapolis, and Pittsburgh. We're within a three-hour drive to the waiting wombs of millions of Sister-Mother-Wannabes. That's why we got franchise rights to The Factory, which opened in 2029, one of nearly two hundred across America. That's the actual stupid name of this sperm mill, ironic since factory jobs all but disappeared in America. I think Sperms 'R Us would be a helluva lot more fun. JK.

BTW, we aren't a sperm bank, we don't store seed here, we just produce it. I'm told as many as a thousand little baby girls have sprouted from my seed, which makes me a 21st Century Johnny Appleseed. Not that I'm all that crazy about having kids. Don't get me wrong, I like kids, I taught kids, I just never wanted the trouble of any of my own.

It's now Wednesday evening, going on midnight, and several of us Appleseeds are hanging out in the cavernous drawing room. Thumbs flicker and swipe across digital devices—this generation has the best opposable thumbs in human history. Eight of us live here, I'll introduce you in a minute, but first let me show you around the house, the most famous in town, built in 1926 on a 47-acre garden estate, Kingwood Center, now called Queenwood Center. It's a three-story stone French provincial mansion with dozens of large windows, gabled roofs, and many chimneys. The Queenwood Center Foundation could no longer afford to maintain it, so the State of Ohio took over the property and opened The Factory inside the mansion.

French-style gardens are still open to the public for strolls, though they are not properly maintained anymore. Dozens of tree species, hundreds of different plants, and thousands of weeds rise among the terraces, lawns, ponds, and woodlands, the dying scents of summer irritating my nose. The area within fifty yards of The Factory is off-limits to the public. No fence or security guards are necessary, warning signs seem to do fine. Sisters respect us, as they should. We give them our seed; they give us space. It's a win-win.

18

A sign over the front door greets you:

The Factory

We Build Life

You enter the grand foyer with its high ceiling and wide, curved staircase. You could almost be in 18ᵗʰ century France, except your classical senses are abruptly jolted by digital screens everywhere: wall screens, door screens, screens that climb up along the staircase wall, fridge screens, toilet and shower screens, even ceiling screens over some beds. We tricked-out this place on state government expense and are never more than a step or two away from digital content. Except for the dining room, it's screen-free. This seemed like a good idea at the time, but the mansion is digitally claustrophobic, surrounding us with annoying ads and content.

We usually hang out in the drawing room, it's like a hotel ballroom with French doors, high ceilings, two chandeliers and large floor-to-ceiling windows. Wisps of ancient dust float in the air. I do not feel worthy of the grandeur: the faded 18ᵗʰ century couches and tables and a 19ᵗʰ century grand piano, a Steinway, that I love to bang on poorly. The house feels old and cold and musty. All the digital screens don't change that. They just add to the chill.

We Appleseeds, all eight of us, wear masks and gloves and a few wear goggles or eye caps—I never got used to putting those on my eyeballs—and when we talk, we do so behind mask filters, with slightly buzzy and muted tones, almost like computers. The standard government-approved mask is a clear latex that wraps snugly across your chin and cheeks. They make us look and sound brobotic.

We are fed, clothed, and sheltered, rent-free. Groceries are delivered weekly and we receive monthly medical examinations over

It. We are watched very closely, nurtured, monitored, and re-evaluated for product satisfaction every six months. We're underpaid, like mothers and childcare workers have been throughout herstory, especially since, without us, Sisters would cease to exist. How do Sisters justify our low wages? They say any brother can jack off.

Our work is mundane, sterile, and strictly about production. Sisters only care about the quality and quantity of sperm. The gig is kush, don't get me wrong, but our value to them is no more than that of prized cattle. Our "work" is scheduled in half-hour blocks, although 3–5 PM every afternoon is happy hour, where no appointments are necessary—first come, first serve, pardon the pun—and it all happens up on the third floor, in two bedrooms dedicated as depositories, where we can look down on the trees and rolling lawn. The salty smell of semen is masked by pungent aerosols. Each room has a lush bed and a soft tube nicknamed Mr. Suck that you wrap gently over the tip of the penis right before ejaculation. For quality control purposes, we are filmed every time we play pocket pool. Once a daily pleasure I lusted for, orgasm is now merely the end of stage one of production. My semen slides down a tube, with the aid of soft puffs of air, sending the hundred-million little buggers swimming in a neutral fluid, as if on a water slide, into a centrifuge contraption called The Spinner. It immediately separates my sperm's X's from the Y's; the wheat from the chaff. The unwanted Y's are flushed down a disposal machine into a jacuzzi-hot tank we call sperm hell. The other half, the X's, are then separated and scanned to select for traits like hair and eye color. Evaluated by computer, under strict health standards, a few hundred thousand of my Grade A wigglies are deemed marketable and are retained. The millions of rejected X's are then flushed away like Y's.

20

My chosen sperm—swimming laps in the neutral fluid—are carefully routed into networks of thin glass tubes, dozens of them, temperature-controlled liquid environments known as fallopians. These tubes are machine-sealed and placed in liquid nitrogen tanks. They are picked up daily and delivered by refrigerated armored truck to Malabar Farm, about a half-hour away, on the way to Amish country. It's a huge farmhouse mansion built in 1939 by forgotten Pulitzer-Prize-winning author Louis Bromfield, an early conservationist who practiced sustainable, organic farming even way back then. The farmhouse once hosted the wedding of Humphrey Bogart and Lauren Bacall. (Famous actors after WWII. Google 'em.) It is now a fertility clinic they call The Womb, one of over 3,000 franchises around the country, all situated in lovely, serene settings, with gardens and nice views. Sisters believe in providing beautiful locations to both spawn sperm and fertilize eggs. The theory is it makes for happier, healthier zygotes.

Mother-Wannabes order our sperm on-line from The Factory website. Their eggs are extracted and stored at The Womb. I've never been there but from what I've been told the fallopians are warmed to the temperature of a uterus. The eggs are dropped into each of the selected tubes containing my pre-qualified sperm, suspended in their comfy liquid. If my sperm fail to do their jobs, lab techs intervene, injecting a lucky bugger directly into the egg. (I wonder, what does it mean that both acts, natural and synthetic, require penetration, a form of assault?)

EDITOR'S NOTE: Parenthesis are typically, but not always, mine.

One way or another, after fertilization occurs, Mother-Wannabes are summoned to The Womb, in well-appointed bedrooms, surrounded by the best spa amenities. While they relax to facials and deep massages, the pre-ordered, certified, and insured zygotes are implanted into their wombs. So Orwellian, so Kafkian. None of the messy ordeal of relationships or sex to contend with.

Some restrictions apply.

Most of my wigglies are rejected, obviously, but when business is booming, a good crop can produce dozens of zygotes. Unused sperm are quickly flushed away. As our The Factory slogan brags:

Guaranteed Fresh From Farm to Fetus

I can fertilize hundreds of thousands of eggs per ejaculation. You do the math. One brother, in a matter of months, could re-populate the United States. However, inbreeding, a serious future issue, would be catastrophic. Sister Scientists are working on that very problem. For now, controls are in place, so that Sisters born from one lot—mine is 793—will not grow up and breed with sperm from that same lot. Cross-pollination of eggs and sperm from different regions is mandated by law. And Sisters keep good records.

So what does a Sister who requests my sperm get? They get the genes of a 39-year-old Millennial, thin, 5'11", curly light brown hair, streaked with early gray, cursed with love handles that never wanna go away. I'd say I'm easy-going, except when I get anxious, which is more and more often these days. I like to hike and read, write and sing, play guitar and piano, not very well but I'm improving. I used to be a gamer but gave it up. As Millennials go, I'm an old-school soul. I also used to be a history teacher, so be warned I will bore you with historical tidbits. I love to travel but it's very difficult for brothers these

22

days, we're harassed on the streets. Most brothers never leave home at all.

Good news is there's no diagnosed mental illness in my family tree, very little cancer, just a little high blood pressure. I don't drink. (Used to.) Don't do drugs. (Used to, a lot.) I abide by HSD—the Healthy Sperm Diet, eating foods rich in zinc, folate, B-12, vitamins C and D. That translates to leafy vegetables, fruits, fish, red meat, nuts and beans, all to promote strong sperm. As I've said, everything we do is about production. I'm a once-a-day dude, standard production, and I usually take Thursdays off. Drew, one of the other Appleseeds, says he squeezes 2-3 times a day—

Well, speak of the stud!

THE APPLESEEDS

DREW

He scrolls on his phone, doesn't look up:

You know what I say—volume, volume, volume.

You do know I'm recording, right? I say, holding up my cell.

Thousands of satisfied young mothers!

Drew wears a scarlet-and-gray Ohio State brobot mask. He reeks of Axe body spray. He is 34, almost six years younger than me, short and stocky, a former farm boy, a dying breed around here even before the world went to hell, when corporate farming by Tyson, Archer Daniels Midland, and Farmer Sisters wiped out family farms. Drew is golden-haired, German, always clean and color-coordinated, his clothes from designer catalogues, his nails manicured, his pierced right ear cauliflowered from high school wrestling.

Real wrestling, he says, not that WWE drama-queen crap we used to watch. I qualified for state at 170, he boasts, his chest puffed.

And he claims he's hung like a curtain rod.

My opponents, Drew says, would get me in a hold and if they bumped my crotch, they'd react. That's all I needed, that moment of hesitation to flip and pin them. My junk won more matches than I did.

Drew fled his family farm when he turned 18, moved to Columbus and majored in econ at Ohio State. He tried out for the wrestling team, as a walk-on, the last wrestler cut. He worked in finance for a while and then moved back home at 31, trying to save the family farm. They lost it in foreclosure, yet here he is, a farm boy still planting his seed. He's a gamer, snowboarder, and a Purple Cow addict. (Red Bull was renamed after being bought out by Sisters.) He is materialistic, narcissistic, and always right, whether he is or not. You can Google it! he likes to say, pointing his index finger like a pistol, winking and double-clicking his mouth. He was a total womanizer back in the day when you could be such things.

I stop recording.

How's my description so far?

Spot on, he says. A-hole.

Unlike the rest of us, Drew doesn't cuss. He's a good ol' farm boy.

This is just like any other Wednesday night, hanging out in the drawing room in an olfactory stew of musk, sweat and testosterone, sharing a physical space, all eyes focused on our digital devices.

Going around the room, we have—

STEVEN

He's a former Marine—

Hey, he interrupts, once a Marine—

—always a Marine, everyone chimes in, bored.

Steven is in his early 20's, tall, lean, tatted from his shoulders down, with the boots, crewcut, and attitude of a Marine. He still dresses in camo pants, shirt, and mask, as he sits stiffly on a high-backed art deco chair, playing Call of Duty up on a wall screen. He is angry-bitter, always wanted to be a Marine, and he was about to graduate near the top of his class at Camp Lejeune in North Carolina, when he was discharged on the day of graduation. The day the military went all-Sister.

Worst fucking day of my life!

Brothers are not allowed to own guns anymore, but rumor is he owns a couple, keeping them stashed away.

No comment, he says.

He's the kind of guy that got drunk on Saturday nights and drove around town bashing in mailboxes with a baseball bat. Even more macho than Drew, he would have been a great mill worker, back when this was a steel town. After being booted by the Marines, he came home and opened his own gym.

His books were a mess, Drew pipes in, so the gym went bankrupt.

I hired you to clean them up.

I'm an accountant. Not a miracle worker.

Steven is the only brother here, besides me, who listens to classical music. Go figure. When we met I had him pegged for rap or hardcore smash-grind but instead, he's into Wagner, Shostakovich, Beethoven.

Mozart's for sissies, he says. Except the Requiem in D minor. That kicks ass.

BERNIE

He's in his late-twenties, enlightened, Buddhist, and gay, a popular combination for spiritual Sisters. The yin to Steven's yang. He wears a gold mask and practices Tai Chi, quite a sight to see, the slow-motion movements like from The Matrix, especially because he's a chubby white guy. I joined him once, it's a helluva lot harder than it looks, I couldn't keep my mind and body from wandering and stumbling over each other.

How'd you get your name, Bernie? I ask, knowing the answer, but I ask anyway for my recording.

My dad loved Bernie Sanders, ever since his famous Senate filibuster speech about corporate greed. Dad quoted lines from the speech like it was the Bible. Me, I could care less about politics. I used to tell people I was named after the stupid movie, Weekend at Bernie's. Dad hated that.

We all love Bernie, he's like a big gay teddy bear. But he's a fashion nightmare. Right now he wears bright orange sweatpants and a torn, purple tie-dye Nepalese t-shirt.

Aren't gays usually smart dressers? I ask.

My boys need comfort, not fashion. It's not like I'm going clubbing or anything. I haven't had sex since I was seventeen.

Impressive, I say.

Not really, Drew interrupts, he gets off on mindfulness.

We should live in the moment, Bernie says.

Even when I fart? Steven goads him.

You should even be mindful of your own gas, yes.

So, you're saying if I fart, be in the fart?

Be in the fart.

We all have a good laugh.

A'ight then, I say, this is a little too deep for me.

I move on.

27

ANDRÉ

Our African-American spermer, late-20's, he sways intensely in a rocking chair. He's got tight dreadlocks and *Live Long and Prosper* tattooed on his right forearm. An Enterprise logo sticker adorns his brobot mask. He loves all the Star Treks, from the original to Enterprise to the all-black spoof, Black Trek. (Once you go Deep Space Black. . .) We call him Dreadlock Spock, although he most identifies with Worf from The Next Generation. André often furrows his brow deep in thought but I think it's really to resemble Worf's volcanic forehead. He's watching an episode of the current Sister Generation on his iPad.

No way! he yells at the screen, throwing up his arms in disgust. Totally illogical, couldn't happen!

That's good, I say. Wanna say anything else to the camera?

He ignores me. I know what will get him talking: Star Trek is so corny.

He turns slowly, Spock-like, to face me.

It's about universal truths of nature. In any galaxy.

To each his own.

If you must know, my gramps turned me onto it.

The rich pharmaceutical dude?

I wanted to follow in his footsteps, curing cancer or diabetes. Instead I'm doing this.

Is your gramps dead?

Of course he's dead.

Disgusted with my pedestrian questions, he pushes himself out of the rocker.

I'm gonna go beam myself up.

He's used that work euphemism before and we're not supposed to repeat ourselves, but I know he gave me that one for my recording. It's an Appleseed tradition. Every time we mention work, we have to come up with a new euphemism for it, like "Time to fire the extinguisher" or "Gotta go massage the client." We spend more time thinking of euphemisms than we do actually working.

KIMCHI

He's our Asian Appleseed. His family name is Kim, I don't even know his first name, but we call him Kimchi—real original, I know—because he absolutely hates the national dish, a sour, pickled cabbage.

Don't all Koreans like kimchi? I ask.

What's to like? Too sour.

He was born in South Korea, came here as a boy and is now in his mid 20's. If Sisters want brainy seed, they go to him, though truth is I'm better at math than he is. And he sucks at chess. We tease him that he's actually popular for his K-Pop chops.

Anything you wanna say for my post?

Annyeonghaseyo, mutherfucker!

Kimchi laughs through his mask plastered with anime characters. I couldn't tell you the name of a single one of 'em.

Show us some Tae-Kwon-Do moves, Steven says, teasingly.

Just because I'm Korean?!

29

You don't know Tae-Kwon-Do? Steven continues. And you don't like kimchi? Are you at least Buddhist?

No, Bernie's Buddhist. I am Christian. Many Koreans Christians.

That's because we showed you the way! Steven brags.

Kimchi, I say, changing the topic, play something on the piano. I'll record it.

Oh no.

Go on, show 'em.

Oh no, I could not.

But he slides onto the stool of the 150-year-old Steinway and plays a sonic atonal thing, his own creation. I try to find a groove, I can't, but I nod along anyway.

Cool, I say, lamely.

As you can see, The Factory offers a variety of seed for Sisters to choose from. We also have a Latino, Selfie, who's not in the room right now. He never hangs out with us. His name is Uriel but we call him Selfie, not because he takes Selfies, but because he's a loner. I haven't seen him in weeks. Hopefully we'll have a sighting at some point. And we have one other brother, Cody, the newest and youngest Appleseed. I don't know where he is right now.

Don't forget Killer, Drew says.

KILLER

Drew rubs the belly of our house dog, a goofy black labradoodle, a scruffy goat-sized mop. Drew found Killer on the streets last year, one of thousands of abandoned pets searching the city for their dead masters. Killer jumps up on an antique couch, happy as a puppy. We don't mind the boundless energy, even when he knocks over an old ceramic vase, or spills a Coke on a laptop, sticking the keys.

Who's a good boy? Drew says, rubbing Killer's belly. The dog lays back on the couch, panting bad breath, kicking one hind leg like a piston.

These are my friends now. Necessity is the mother of today's friendships.

I sit at the Steinway and roll some C chords up and down the keyboard, making it look and sound like I know what I'm doing.

Let's see, where was I before I introduced you to these cases of arrested development? Well, um, boy babies are rare. A few are allowed to be born from uninfected Sister Mothers, bred and groomed for the sole purpose of becoming our replacements, the next generation of Appleseeds. Raised in sterile nurseries by Clean Sisters, they will provide the future sperm of America.

I already know who's replacing me. He just walked in.

CODY

He is texting, his brobot mask painted like Spiderman, with fuzzy white slippers, and a ratty t-shirt with a bright blue slogan:

Corporations Suck

Individuals Rock

We bob heads in greeting. He's only been here a month, just 19, the minimum age in Ohio for spermers. He stands six-four, without an ounce of fat, as trim and sturdy as a straw, with dreamy blue eyes that pop out from his pale skin and unruly curly brown hair that goes weeks without meeting a comb or brush. He licks red *Flaming Hot*

31

Cheetos dust off his fingertips. He hasn't worked a day in his life and, like most of us Appleseeds, he's a gamer, always playing something on the screens around the house. Watch the way he flops down on one of the high-backed couches, both clumsy and graceful, like a giraffe. He's a nice kid, jokes around, doesn't have to be asked to lend a hand. Although he says "like" way too often:

Let's, like, go get some, like, food or something.

He's the son I never had. I can't say anything bad about him, except that he's here to take my place. We don't talk about that. I should resent him, but I like him, I truly do. Cody is his nickname. I don't know his real name.

It's Kevin, he says matter-of-factly.

We call him Cody because he writes computer code. Well, he *dreams* of creating code, mostly he just plays. He doesn't say so, but I think he dreams of developing a computer program to wipe out Sisters. He sure shoots enough of 'em in his games. Right now, he's uploading *The Hunt* video game on a PlayStation. It's pretty cool, life-sized Sisters chase and shoot brothers around our wall-to-wall screens. It's tilted for the Sister Hunter to win, but Cody is skilled enough to give them a good battle.

You keep playing the same crap that's going on outside these walls, Drew says, maybe you should go play the real thing for a change.

You go out there and, like, play the real thing.

And risk damaging this? Drew says, sweeping his hand alongside his body as if a game show model.

Cody smirks underneath his mask. He's extremely cute, most Sisters think so, and he's here to fill my niche, the more-creative, less-testosterone-driven type.

How do you ever sell enough sperm? I tease him.

Sisters, like, love me.

His thumbs—his nails painted black and blue—flutter over his controller.

He's our top producer, you can look it up, Drew says, pointing his hand like a pistol, winking, and clicking.

Bullshit, I say, knowing it's probably true, since Drew does The Factory accounting.

JONATHAN

Evening, ladies, he says, entering with his usual greeting.

I almost forgot about our father-brother, Jonathan. He watches over us like a college R.A. As long as we fill our quota of sperm, he leaves us alone, just happy to have a job that gives him purpose and keeps him alive. Aren't we all? He's in his 50's, an average guy with an average gut, a lingering cloud of Old Spice wafting around him, and just a tweak of an edge. He is impotent, from testicular cancer. All The Factories have a father-brother, an older dude, usually a cancer victim unable to produce sperm. Impotence is a job requirement. Sisters fear father-brothers contaminating the supply with their own sperm, even though there is no real justification for that. But where there is desire, there is always fear, so we are closely monitored, from the moment we grease the beast until we close Mr. Suck, vacuum-sealing the product. Jonathan is our quality control, monitoring us on

33

cameras. When I started here a little over two years ago, he told me that at any given time one or two of the babies in the Sisterfield General Hospital maternity ward are probably mine.

I should get a kickback from the hospital, I joked. I remember him looking at me like I was spiritually clueless.

How ya doin'? Jonathan now asks, somewhat sincerely, since I'm the oldest Appleseed, about to turn 40, about to be kicked to the curb.

S.O.S. (Same Ol' Sperm) I say, lying.

Excellent, he says, moving off to the kitchen.

So here we are, Appleseeds, brothers in our 20's and 30's. Drew and I are Millennials, two of the last such brothers alive in this city. The other Appleseeds are all Gen Z'ers. We live here, safe inside this mansion, sheltered, not oblivious to the horrors of the world, but less affected by them. You might say we're brothers in a bubble.

All around us, explosions fill the drawing room wall screens like indoor fireworks. Cody's thumbs fly over his controller, positioning his superhero avatar over a wounded, dying Sister Soldier. He raises some kind of cool-looking, ultra-powerful weapon to finish her off.

Gotcha bitch!

She grabs his avatar by the balls—video games have only evolved so far—and flings him off her. His superhero bangs into a wall and crumples to the floor. She reaches behind her fashionably-fitting suit of armor and pulls out an even cooler-looking weapon, shooting a blinding flame, burning him into a charred crisp.

Damn! Cody yells. Every, like, freakin' time!

He cocks his arm back, ready to fling his controller at the wall screen, but thinks better of it. Drew plops down on the opposite end of the couch.

34

Saddle up, brother, I'm coming after you. But we're going holo this time.

He taps his phone and a hot hologram, a life-sized Amazon Sister, appears to walk through the front door.

Well hellooo, Sister, he drools.

Cody taps on his phone until his new avatar comes to life, an eight-foot-high, longhaired survivalist with his almost-exact-replica face. And a buff body the size of an armoire. Cody smiles under his mask.

It, like, looks just like me.

The two holograms bow to each other.

Namasté, they say and then bow to their human controllers.

Cody and Drew bow back.

Namasté.

Cody's thumbs fly across his controller. His longhaired hologram darts across the room, hurries into the foyer and up the wide, curved staircase. Drew's Amazonian hologram gives him a few-seconds head start before she cocks her nuclear-looking weapon and follows him up the staircase. The chase is on. Cody and Drew follow behind, directing their movements, the holograms darting in and out of the high doorways, shooting around corners, dodging behind desks, back downstairs, into the dining room, the kitchen.

Don't worry, I'm not gonna get deep into the gamer stuff. I used to play. I was a Madden Football addict in elementary, a Guitar Hero junkie in middle school—I'm much better on that than I am on a real guitar—and in high school I became a Fortnite fanatic. I sat zombie-eyed in front of a screen, any screen, forgetting to eat, wash, or brush my teeth. I don't know how many times I fell asleep, controller in hand, only to wake up hours later and hit play and start all over again.

But I saw what video games did to my pops, William. He got laid off in the Great Recession of 2008, when I was in my teens. I watched his self-esteem fade away, humiliated by the low-skilled jobs that employers would offer him. Always a boisterous jokester, he tried telemarketing, but couldn't close a deal. All talk, no walk. And since he wasn't working, we hung out more, which was a blast, playing epic video game battles that lasted until mom pulled the plug.

Dad accepted one lame job after another, complaining he was too old to go back to college and mom stuck with him for a few years—for better or worse, right?—but eventually divorced him. Then, a couple years ago, dad got sick with The Y and—sorry, I'm getting choked up—he was a good dad, he just lost his way. I feared I might end up just like him so I quit gaming. I don't think I've played more than ten times since. Instead, for my thirtieth birthday I picked up a guitar, no Guitar Hero bullshit, a real steel-string Martin. Now, being a musician looks good on my donor profile.

But I digress.

Here at The Factory we follow the laws of supply and demand and are paid bonuses for reaching quotas. The Sisters have it all down to a science. You need X number of brothers to produce Y amount of sperm to supply Z number of Sisters. My seed, labeled Lot 793, has created maybe a thousand little girls. Unfortunately, I'll never know. We are given no information about our offspring, so I force myself to think of them more as products I've sold. And that's not too difficult to do. As I've said, I never wanted children. I remember growing up, my dad said, more than once:

There are so many things I could've done, if I didn't have you kids.

I pause the recording, take a moment, take a breath, try to forget. Then I hit record:

We have a short shelf life. They retire relics like me when we turn forty, replacing us with new spermers like Cody. They say you go live out the rest of your life on a beautiful spread. So far, we've had only one Appleseed retire from The Factory, Denny Rogers, a fun guy, he loved to laugh. He left The Factory a few months ago and supposedly lives in Myrtle Beach. Of course, none of us believe this, not for a minute. We are allowed no contact with him. It reminds me of those lies told to children about their missing dogs running around happily on an upstate farm. No proof exists that Denny is still alive. Oh sure, *It* shows us pictures and videos of supposedly happy retired spermers— never any of Denny—and I believe these videos are staged.

I keep noodling on the piano, trying to remember the little riff on *Something I Can Never Have* by Nine Inch Nails. I've lost Steven and Kimchi as audience members, they've headed upstairs.

Hah-hah, sucker!

Drew's Amazonian hologram toasts Cody's avatar running down the upstairs hallway, disintegrating him into pixel ashes that sprinkle down the staircase.

I switch it up, pounding a few simple chords to Monty Python's *Sperm Song*. (YouTube 'em, 70's British, you'll either love 'em or hate 'em.) It's our theme, our chain gang song, we goof on it regularly, translate it into Spanish or Korean or Klingon. We might sing it reggae, country, or punk. Now, we do it Gospel-style:

Every sperm is sacred

Every sperm is great

If a sperm gets wasted

God gets quite irate.

We layer the backup voices and it would be rather impressive if it weren't so corny, so blatantly wrong. We sing it again, modifying it as we often do. Bernie takes the lead:

Half our sperm is sacred

Half our sperm is cool

All the rest gets wasted

The Goddess's golden rule.

Grins all around. Cody yawns and jumps out of his seat.

I'm gonna go hack the mainframe.

So, I bet you're wondering about sex. I would be. Heterosexual sex is frowned upon, lesbian sex is the national norm. According to the latest Fox/CNN poll (they merged after Sisters took over) 70% of Sisters say they would not return to heterosexual sex, at least not exclusively, even if readily available. Many Sisters dis sex altogether, preferring conversation or their devices.

There is still a brother prostitute trade—bro-hoes—and the all-Sister government is their pimp, unofficially sanctioning them. Government may be a lot of things—corrupt, incompetent, evil—but it's not stupid. Bro-hoes are registered and regulated and can only have sex with the handful of Sisters who are not carriers of The Y.

Sisters have resorted to elaborate dildos of all shapes and sizes and Stud Bots with smooth, creamy, realistic flesh, that are oh so close to real sex. But still not quite.

38

You might ask how we eight Appleseeds, like slaves, can propagate more and more Sisters, when my fellow brothers are endangered, suffering, underground, dying. I've asked myself that repeatedly. But do I dare decline the privilege of continuing my bloodline in thousands of lives? Do I object, and if so, in what meaningful way that won't just be suicide? Or do I do what all brothers throughout the howl of herstory have done?

Survive.

But I'm not aging so well, tiring quicker than ever, and I suffer from an enlarged prostate. In my job, it's about count and if you have a high, healthy sperm count you are valuable. But sperm quantity and quality begin to decline at my age. Forty is the new obsolete.

I believe I mentioned my 40th birthday is in three weeks.

Did I also mention I'm freaking out?

THE SHACK

I didn't just get this Appleseed gig. I had a connection, one Sister, the reason that I wake up at 5 AM this morning, Thursday, September 30th, and every Thursday morning. The old stone mansion feels like a cooler. I wriggle my legs into my shorts, my feet into my running shoes, and my shoulders into my touristy t-shirt:

SISTERFIELD

THE HEART OF

NORTH CENTRAL OHIO

Wearing it looks good if I get stopped by a Sister Cop.

I run every Tuesday and Thursday mornings, like clockwork. Tuesdays just to let Big Sister see me, to establish a bi-weekly routine. But Thursdays, ahh, they are the real reason I run. I pop a multi-vitamin and two Ibuprofen—my vitamin I—and top it off with a Viagra, which is contraband. I fit on the brother's "official" street wear: sanitizer gloves and the clear latex mask that fits snuggly, pinching my cheeks, a filter in front of my mouth. I am a brobot. BTW, I don't know if I told you, but Sisters don't have to wear masks or gloves. They are already carriers and immune and many are not all that concerned about spreading it to us.

I gaze into a retinal scanner mounted beside the front door. It approves my eye, the lock clicks open and I am logged out of The Factory. Darkness welcomes me, no sign of dawn yet, just the light of a few old lampposts and beyond that, forest black. I breathe in the end-of-summer air, the musky-sweet scent of forest decay. I twist my torso, stretch my legs, and pretend I can touch my toes. I skip down onto the brick portico and through a Midwestern version of a French garden. The once-fine-trimmed hedges are now misshapen and patchy. I pass beds of shriveled roses, flattened Hosta, and trellises of brittle leaves. A few determined irises and lilies still poke through the dry and dying bushes. Back in the heyday, leaves shone like emeralds, blooms burst with palettes of color, strolls inspired. To feel its beauty today, you need to look up. The trees are still magnificent with their glorious crowns: the sycamore and elm, beech and oak, lilac and maple. Even a couple redwoods, strangers in a strange land. The awesomeness towers around me, strong survivors faring much better than the shriveled plants and shrubs underneath them. I soak in the forest bathing, telling myself I must be strong like a tree, even though I feel more like a weed.

I get goose bumps, even after two years of these insanely early-morning Thursday runs, elated, running down a long, narrow strip of lawn lined by conifers. I turn, like I usually do, and jog back toward the two-story mansion, just for the rush of it, running in place for a few seconds, with no one around, pretending I am lord of the manor. I do live in an amazing mansion, even if the circumstances suck.

If you look hard, you can see perched up on the slanted roof the small silhouettes of three Shadow drones that follow us older brothers: Drew, Jonathan, and myself. My Shadow is on shut-down

41

this morning, so I get to run solo as I cut through a row of firs and down a serpentine path that crosses a rolling lawn, loving the lingering smell of yesterday's mowed grass. Tiny golden-green firefly torches glow on and off as if unaware it's long past their bedtime but very aware their lives are almost over.

I turn left onto Trimble Avenue, onto cracked and crumbling sidewalk, the street barren this morning except for one pair of taillights in the distance. Mornings are quiet these days, with no more rushing to get to a job. Such a brother way to live: rush to wake up, rush to get to your job, rush through lunch, rush to the gym, rush home, rush through dinner. Get up in the morning and rush again. One silver lining for Sisters *and* brothers is things move at a more relaxed pace. Traffic is so much lighter these days, there's barely a rush at all.

I'm breathing heavy, sweating already, running uphill, staying inside the bro-only lane, a dedicated pedestrian lane for brothers, separated by red dashed lines. We brothers walk or run on one side of the street only. There are bro-only sections in restaurants and theaters, and driverless broCars. All this segregation is meant to protect us from deadly physical contact. In reality, it's just another form of bro-control.

I stop at a traffic light, even though there is not a soul around. I obey my lane, except for an occasional rebellious step or two outside the red dashed line, immediately getting back in place, just in case a Sister is watching. Normally, outside The Factory, I am watched, followed by my own personal drone, my Shadow, the one up on The Factory roof. Because I'm not chipped, I have an assigned drone to track me. If bad weather doesn't permit electronic surveillance, the drone will alert a nearby Sister Tracker to monitor me via cameras mounted on roofs, trees, and power poles. 2032 feels so 1984.

Everything you do can be watched online if anyone really wants to bother, but so much digital content is out there, footage has to be exceptional to be noticed. A brother jogging twice a week does not generally warrant a Sister's attention. And every Thursday I have a four-hour window of privacy from 5-9 AM. That's when my drone powers down for routine maintenance and software-updating. A Sister Tracker shift change happens at the same time, so no one gets assigned to me. I can move freely until my drone goes back on-line at precisely 9 AM. For four hours every Thursday I am free as I can be.

Sister Leaders turn a blind eye to these power-down periods, when those two-percent of Sisters who are not carriers can have not-so-secret sex with brothers. While not completely banned, unauthorized sex with a brother can get a Sister sanctioned. If anybody bothered to report it.

My drone is off-line at the same time my tracker shift change happens because I have a contact in high power. She sees to it that my drone maintenance and tracker schedules stay synced, never changing.

Have I mentioned I'm sleeping with the mayor?

She is why I run every Tuesday and Thursday mornings like clockwork, rain, snow or shine. On Tuesdays I run for appearances and to help keep me in shape for my Thursday hook-ups. I start off both mornings in the same way, running south, uphill on Trimble, but on Tuesdays I turn left on Park Avenue, past some Victorian mansions surrounding city parks. On Thursdays, like today, I keep going south on Trimble, past the Metronome Music store and suburban homes and pretty quickly I find myself in gated horse-country estates. I turn off Trimble and race up a winding road to a shoulder-high stoned wall with tarnished gates. A brass plaque reads:

You are entering Sensitive Estates

I push open the bro-only pedestrian gate and run on a paved road that circles around a Gloria Steinem statue rising up from a fountain. Her marble face is framed by wire-rim glasses and long, flowing hair, striking an intense speaking pose, her arm outstretched, pointing us the way to the future. Gloria is one of many Sister Statues that sprouted up all over the city the last few years. Most brother statues and phallic obelisks have been torn down, except for Lincoln and Martin Luther King, Jr. Sisters tend to leave their statues alone. The others are smashed and dumped into the landfill. Sisters have been known to take late-night target practice at the concrete and marble heads of Washington, Jefferson, and both Roosevelts.

Sister monuments rose quickly, often overnight, under cover of dark. Brothers sabotaged many during construction, but they couldn't stop the concrete and marble tide: Joan of Arc, Susan B. Anthony, Rosa Parks, Mother Theresa, Kamala Harris, and Greta Thunberg, everywhere you look. Right now I run past a Ruth Bader Ginsburg statue, graffitied from head-to-toe with *Stop The Slaughter* spray-painted red and *Free The Vaccine* dripping purple.

I enter Harriet Tubman Park, a nice swath of oaks and pines. I can imagine slaves hiding behind these trees—the Underground Railroad had several stations near here—as I dart up a steep hillside, on a root-and-rut-infested trail. The crescent moon is snooping between the crowns, barely illuminating my way. I navigate the forest like my own home, feeling almost normal here among the shadows of

44

trees, the sounds of animals, the faint scent of dying blooms. This is the one thing I look forward to every week, seeing Mayor Miriam, my only physical relationship of any kind. I can be with Miriam only because she is not a carrier. I think she's been secretly vaccinated. Even though they claim no vaccine exists.

While I pretend to be a runner, Miriam actually is one, she loves it, jogs five mornings a week, her solitary time to think, without aides or reporters hounding her. She lives near here, behind a gate, very alert of being followed or watched by paparazzi drones. She comes downhill—on the mornings she does come—through a patch of forest at the opposite end of the estates. Every now and then she does not show up. I am allowed no cell or digital contact with her, so I usually learn the following Thursday the reason for her absence:

- I couldn't come because of (choose a mayoral event).
- The paparazzi have been hounding me.
- I was exhausted.

I walk the last thirty yards, my warm-down, on dirt paths that meander through a quarter-acre of neglected gardens. I tread carefully on mossy steppingstones in the shapes of rabbits, turtles, and lady bugs. I pass the main house, a Mediterranean mansion that's been abandoned for the two years I've been coming here. I walk around the dark greenhouse; there's nothing green about it. Rusted frame, cloudy glass, stacks of empty pots.

I reach my destination, the boxy guesthouse, and step up onto the small porch. I type a code into a keypad. The lock clicks. I push the door open. The place once belonged to a bank executive but now it's a hook-up spot—we call it our Love Shack—a nudge-nudge, wink-wink, say-no-more place where powerful Sisters who aren't carriers can pretend times are simpler, when all you wanted was a good lay. The mayor let it slip that a judge and Council Sister also use the Shack for liaisons. There are no cameras here. Or there are many, hidden in every nook and cranny. Either is possible.

The uphill run here always kicks my butt so I pour myself a glass from the fancy, curled faucet. I suck the water down and glance at a sign above the sink:

brothers used to control Sisters

but

Sisters have always controlled life

Signs like these are everywhere. Sisters love their affirmations.

Mayor Miriam is prompt for public events and speeches, but always late meeting me. I sit at the kitchen table, catch my breath, keeping my gloves and mask on. I stare at a glass vase of calla lilies, the yellow phallic pistils protrude from the white vagina-ish petals. It reeks of Georgia O'Keefe. I open the fridge that's always stocked with organic food, grab an apple, bite into it, the crispness heavenly. I fish my phone out of my pocket and video the interior for my "book" starting with the chick kitchen with white cupboards, an island with industrial burners, and a beautiful Amish oak dining table ruined when some Sister painted it white. In the main room there's a gigantic TV screen on one wall and a bay window with lots of fluffy pillows— Sisters love their pillows—where I sit and play guitar for Miriam. There is no guitar here right now, hasn't been for months, it was removed to be re-strung. She probably got tired of hearing me play, we only have three hours together every week and making music of a different kind is far more vital.

My favorite feature is a river-stone fireplace that's always clean and stocked with a ready-to-light tepee of kindling and small logs. Above it is a painting of a peacock and next to the hearth three medium logs are stacked in a wood carrier, never more, never less, just enough wood to burn for the three hours we're here. Someone prepares this place for us every Thursday morning. It's not cold in here but that doesn't matter, I grab a box of long matches from the mantle and strike one, introducing it to the kindling. Flames spread up the tepee, crackling and popping. We seldom bother with the bedroom, either doing it here on the brown, eight-foot-long leather couch or on the floor in front of the fireplace, on a rust and turquoise rug, a plush mash-up of Southwestern motifs and Sister symbols, those circles with crosses on top.

Let's take this to the bedroom, I sometimes say.

Let's just keep it right here, Miriam replies.

She never gets much of an argument, right here is good enough for me. And I think it gives her the sensation of being a naughty high school girl, doing it on the floor. Sisters miss their nasty pasts too.

Back in the kitchen, I remove a test kit from a cabinet and place it on the table, like I always do, next to the vase of calla lilies. I set my cell alarm for 8:30 and place it face down on the kitchen table. When Miriam comes she will do the same, we are like gangsters relinquishing our weapons before a sit-down. We unplug for three hours. I feel tingly from my chest down to my loins. I don't want to get my hopes up, like I said sometimes she doesn't show, so I flop on the sofa and surf through some YouTubes on the wall screen: rapper Sista Soul, Queen Electronica, Algorithm & Blues. I switch to SCN, Sister Comedy Network, and their awful remake of Seinfeld. Growing

47

up, barely in junior high, I had a major crush on Elaine, what boy didn't? Brothers hate the new reboot. Instead of three brothers there are three Sisters, Jenny, Georgia, and Kristal, and only one brother, Alan. I'm not attracted to any of the Sisters, but if I had to pick one it'd be goofy Kristal, with the same kinky black hair as Kramer.

BTW, some things you don't see on TV anymore: beauty pageants, cheerleaders, housewives, bleach blondes selling beer, and brother characters—except bumbling or corrupt ones.

I stop channel-surfing on a news recap of Mother President's speech last night. Five weeks before the election, she's on TV a lot, running for her 2nd term. Behind her, supporters wave signs:

MOTHER FUTURE

2032

MOTHER OLSEN

She brags about how bombings and attacks decreased in the last year of her presidency and how the deaths of brothers stabilized. Of course they have, I snap at the TV, you've wiped us out! I reign in my rage, flashing a small JK smile, never know who might be watching.

I guess I should explain:

THE CHANGE

Sisters took control, creepingly slow at first. Their hidden power spread over millennium and we had no idea how deep it reached. In Utah, there is a single clonal colony of quaking aspen, nicknamed the Trembling Giant, 80,000 years old, a massive grove of trees spread out over 100 acres. Only when the trees fall do you see the immense network of roots. Sisterhood is like those roots, the depth and strength of support realized only when the brothers' grip on society toppled.

Throughout herstory, brothers hunted and were adventurous, independent, quiet, loners. But we became lazy. Today, we hunt in video games from the comfort of our couches. Like my father, we lost our essence. We lost our way. Sisters, in contrast, feed off friendships and connections and this suits them better in the new social-media world. They have maintained their essence.

This cultural transformation is commonly referred to as "The Change". As in any movement, there were stages, and herstorians disagree on the causes. Some say it dates back to pre-herstory, when brothers usurped the fertility goddesses, converting control to judgmental gods in a power trip like the world had never seen. Sisters have been biding their time ever since. Some herstorians trace The Change back to the Seneca Falls Conference of 1848 and the

49

decades-long suffrage movement. After the right to vote, Sisters felt empowered and never looked back. Yet, it was a slow rise. As recently as the 1960s, Sisters were still property in America, needing husbands to co-sign on credit card apps or apartment leases.

Most herstorians agree that the Pill liberated Sisters, giving them control over their own bodies. We brothers should have seen the handwriting on the wall. In vitro fertilization followed and suddenly sex changed. Always a symbol of power for us and an evolutionary ploy for them to attract us, it now became unnecessary. It sounds crazy today, I know, but sex was how we usually made babies, even just a few years ago.

Sister Scholars often cite the shift in education. Since the late twentieth century, more American Sisters have earned college degrees than brothers, dominating careers like pharmacists, doctors, and lawyers. Sisters evolved for the job market, while brothers faced a devastating loss of hope and bemoaned the past, even wearing Make America Great Again caps in the later 2010's, trying to revive a past that never really existed.

Millennial herstorians point to the #MeToo movement of 2017, when Sisters stood up to employers and co-workers who had sexually harassed them. At the same time, brother-controlled state governments pushed to re-criminalize abortion, angering Sisters who enjoyed control over their own bodies and weren't about to give it up, leading to further protests and division between the sexes. The Change was happening all over the world and the momentum became impossible for brothers to stop. One thing was clear: Sisters lusted for power, primed and ready to take over, voting for themselves in droves.

50

They wore bold-colored t-shirts with just this sign:

=

Followed by t-shirts like this:

>

As with technology, society changed exponentially. I could bore you with all kinds of statistics and details, but the bottom line was this: everything was going Sisters' way. Jobs, laws, power. Everything. Then they got greedy and realized they don't need us anymore. But people don't give up power voluntarily. Brothers struck back, trotting out stale images in the media: Sister Candidates who abandoned their roles as mothers and wives; who engaged in sexual misdeeds; who had abortions. "Never-Sister" brothers organized. Bumper stickers adorned pick-up trucks:

Any Brother

Is Better

Than a Sister

It was too little too late. By 2026, Sisters held roughly 40% of elected political posts in the U.S. and about 30% worldwide. Sisters plastered their own bumper stickers on their SUVs and chanted at rallies:

We Want It All

In 2028, Samantha Olsen became the first elected U.S. Sister president. A safe choice, a salt-of-the-earth mother of three, a former pig farmer from Nebraska, then mayor, state senator, and governor. She took the title Mother President and became a balm to soothe the country following all the divisiveness. What followed was anything but soothing.

These political shock waves shook the earth, shifted the gender power dynamics, and re-shaped culture as it collapsed and then rose like a Phoenix into something new, something sliced in half. But the real change wouldn't come via the ballot box.

MIRIAM

A little over two years ago, when roughly two billion brothers still roamed the planet, I ran into my old friend Gaia walking with the mayor. Gaia and I were best friends growing up, I adored her, but with The Change she'd gotten all behind Sister Power. It was new and addicting, I got it, but then The Y came and it was not safe to hang out. She's a carrier. We hadn't spoken, just texted a few times, I hadn't seen her since this all started. I reached to hug her, a reflex—

Don't! Gaia yelled.

Shit, I said, I knew better, of course, but the surprise of seeing her threw me off my game. I backed away, sharply, both of us standing there, trying to process this new dynamic in our friendship. Frankly, she looked shocked to see me.

I heard you were dead.

Just hiding out.

Gaia is a green-eyed lady with curly auburn hair, a freckled new-age feminist with a post-retro-Deadhead vibe, her clothes always flowing off her body. She wears spiritual well. She was my one that got away. Well, not exactly, we never dated, I never hooked her and lost her. I wanted to be her boyfriend from day one but she always kept it to just friends. After high school, we drifted apart like clumps of kelp in a stormy sea, occasionally finding each other again.

I tried to call you, a few months ago, she said.

I changed my number. I texted you three or four times.

My phone must have blocked you. Why didn't you stop by the store?

That hotbed of Sisterhood? No thanks.

Gaia owns 'Round & Ground, a downtown bookstore/coffeehouse/tincture shop. In the back rooms, she counsels Sisters how to move on without brothers and guides brothers in how to die. She makes her own salves and tinctures, many crafted to ease Sisters through this emotional transition. She makes a few for us brothers too. They help my recent anxiety.

Gaia introduced us:

Sister Mayor Miriam, this is my dear old friend, Bryan.

I smiled through my mask. They make an odd couple, I thought to myself, the pale, new-agey Gaia and the brown-skinned, business-suited Miriam, half-Native-American, half-Indian. Indian-Indian, as people joke. Her perfume smelled professional, not too sharp, not too sweet.

I've heard a lot about you, the mayor said.

Not as much as I've heard about you, I said.

Gaia gave me a stern look with those gorgeous soft eyes, the color of copper domes turned green.

Not from Gaia, I said, I mean from the news.

Gaia campaigned for the mayor in the last election, even held town halls in her bookstore. I was not a fan. The mayor hadn't done much to help brothers. I don't really know what she could've done, I mean, money, medicines, none of it really alters our doomed reality. Only a vaccine could do that.

Gaia and I caught up on our lives and then she input my number into her cell and promised to call me.

It was nice to meet you, Bryan, Sister Mayor said. She leaned closer, almost as if to whisper, even though still a good six feet away. She noticed my unease and did not advance any further.

It's okay, she said, I'm not a carrier.

I looked to Gaia for confirmation. She gave me a nodding shrug.

What can I help you with? the mayor said.

Seriously? A vaccine would be nice.

She smile-frowned.

You know how many times I've been asked that?

You've got Mother President's ear, right?

Everyone knew our mayor and the president were friends, meeting at an Ohio fundraiser years back. Mother President had once been a mayor herself and made a campaign appearance for Miriam.

I'm sorry, mayor, Gaia apologized, giving me her spiritual stink eye. We need to be going.

If a vaccine is created, Sister Mayor said, I promise I'll put you at the top of the list. Anything for a friend of Gaia's.

They exchanged warm, sisterly glances. I didn't believe her, figured she promised that to all the brothers who asked.

It's good to see you, Bryan, Gaia said.

Good? I thought. It was great seeing her. Always is.

Be well, Bryan.

I'll try.

As they walked away, I overheard the mayor:

55

He's cute.

Yeah, I guess so. In a pathetic way. (Gaia may be spiritual but she is always busting my balls.) He's a musician, Gaia says.

Is he any good?

Well, he doesn't clear a room when he plays. But he definitely thins it out.

A week later, Gaia texted me. She gave me the address of this mansion, along with the security code to get inside the guesthouse, our Love Shack. She told me to show up very early on a Thursday morning. I did as I was told and I've been showing up every Thursday morning since. And that is how I eventually got my gig as an Appleseed, by sleeping with Miriam. Even in an apocalypse, it's not what you know, it's who you know.

I think I hear Miriam humming, sounds like Love On Top by Beyonce, one of her favorites. She has a few standbys: anything by Beyonce, also Weird Sisters. A go-to is the Friends Theme. Miriam can't sing, I tried to get her to, but the one time she did I learned my lesson. She couldn't find the right key, even in her pocket, although she can hum the hell out of a song. My theory: humming is just messing around; singing requires committing. And she can't commit, at least not to me.

The kitchen door opens. I pull down my mask and reach behind a framed photo of Mother President on the mantel, grab a box of green Tic Tacs, pop a couple. I listen to Miriam's routine in the kitchen: the clunk of her on the table, the quick rip of the test box, the pop of a sealed wrapper. She claims to be one of the two-percent of Sisters who are not carriers. But every time we meet she takes this home test as a precaution, in case she somehow got infected the week before.

56

I hear her humming shoot an octave higher—hmmmm-HMM! I picture her pricking the flesh of a fingertip, drawing a drop of blood and adding it to a vial with buffer. The flick of a switch is followed by a whirling, like a tiny fan, on the electric centrifuge next to the toaster. Then another flick of the switch and the whirling stops. This is our initial foreplay, a two-minute verbal blackout that feels much longer, separated by a doorway. We don't talk during the ritual, there's no point getting too worked up in case the result is positive, which I trust she'd tell me. And trust is pretty much extinct for brothers.

Miriam appears in the doorway, a subtle smile on her face.

We're good to go.

I rise and tear off my mask and gloves. I'd like to say she falls into my arms, but we bump knees and my lips reach to kiss her lips, hers reach for my cheek. Even though we meet like this every week, it always feels slightly awkward, like teenagers.

I've missed you.

Missed you too.

Slowly, we embrace, our heads finding each other's shoulder. Miriam always starts a little stiff, taking a few minutes to warm up. She speaks to thousands without a thought, but for an audience of me, she's shy. Our lips slowly find each other's, her stress pouring out, until suddenly she backs off like an over-stimulated cat.

Did you set your alarm? she asks.

Of course.

She stands in front of the blazing fire, removing her FitSis from her wrist. The Sisters Union is threatening to strike, she says, removing her yellow top. And the sanitation department keeps violating codes, she adds, as I casually pull off my t-shirt. And

57

ohmygoddess, the homeless brothers are stirring up problems at the shelter.

I gently massage her shoulders and neck, her skin the color of an old buckeye. When she is happy, her face shimmers; when stressed, it's muddy. Not that I ever tell her that. This morning, she shines with sweat. She's five-and-a-half feet, with straight black shoulder-length hair and light brown eyes like burrowed acorns. I love how they slowly notice me, scanning my shoulders and chest, down to the tip of my curly pubic hair already turning gray and peeking out from my running shorts. I've got no six-pack, no guns for biceps, but my skin is smooth for almost forty and I'm trim, except for my love handles. Miriam likes them, she says, pinching 'em when I piss her off.

We stand in front of the fire, swaying, as she vents about work. I don't pay much attention, I could care less about politics. I trace my fingers down her arm, across her stomach, following that with kisses at different stops along her flesh. When it feels like her report is winding down, I rise and kiss her lips softly. Time is always an issue but I make sure we start slow, kissing delicately, only lips at first, like brushes, followed by a light flickering of tongue before we go deep and slow and suck on each other's souls. The whole time our hands trace each other, smoothly, like we were made of sand.

I unsnap her peach running bra without a hitch, always the same style snap. I toss the bra aside. Her breasts are not large but firm and friendly and the color of ginger root. I fondle them, giving equal attention to both. Then I get down on my knees and pull down her Lululemon floral running pants, to her ankles, which she lifts one at a time. I toss them aside and trace my tongue up her thigh. I bite her panties, playfully, like a matador with his rose. She smiles and moans.

We sink onto the plush rust and turquoise rug. Our limbs wedge into our nooks and crannies, our bodies melting into "The beast with two backs" as Shakespeare wrote. We press flesh, glowing, cool to the touch, soon warming from the heat of the crackling and flickering fire.

Lick me.

She always asks for that, cunnilingus, the original tongue-and-groove. I oblige. All that warming up is worth it, she goes crazy.

I want you inside me.

Again, I oblige.

She rolls on top of me, a Sister in her full glory, mounting me, moving freely, not trapped underneath my sweaty body, her hair bouncing off her shoulders as she slowly twirls her head and arches her back. Her middle fingers encircle her nipples, her nails always perfectly manicured and painted, today a sky blue, an unusual shade for a mayor. I love how she gyrates in one direction for a while then switches it up the other way. I know the horrible things Sisters have done to us, but there is nothing more beautiful than a Sister riding on top of you. Her hips gyrate, her eyelids flutter, her pupils roll back up into her head. I could watch her for hours, but we have less than three, so I grab her by the hips and flip her onto her back. Her blue fingernails dig into my buttocks. She moans and begs and—

Okay, that's not exactly how it goes. Sometimes it's hot, sometimes it's cold, sometimes I make her orgasm, sometimes I don't. I can't ever take it personally, she's not easy to please and I'm not a horse. I often climax early the first time, that's why I pop Viagra when I leave The Factory, to help me with round two. Miriam is very forgiving of round one. Our sex is usually gentle and loving and just

59

the icing. She wants the cake, an intimate relationship with a brother, since she deals with Sisters all day long.

When I do explode it is nothing like when I cum at work, I feel that sweet chill of teenage ecstasy, as if we're rebelling in our parents' basement, cheating time and death. I smell her bottom note of citrusy sweat mixed with a top note of yesterday's perfume. We work our way into a slow groove, like Ashanti or Alicia Keys, but neither one of us can keep that sexual crawl going for too long. I give her everything I've got, for her and for me. If I can keep pleasing her, maybe I can keep working as an Appleseed way beyond my 40th birthday.

Stop, she says, as her body stiffens and shudders and her fingers and toes flutter. I stop moving but stay inside, cocooned in her warmth, cuddling in the silence between gentle kisses, the only time I can truly forget all the shit that's happened these last several years.

There's some chatter, she says, about undergrounders plotting an attack.

(And the shit comes right back.)

Where?

I thought you might know.

Just because I'm a brother?

I'm just asking.

I'm not an undergrounder.

I know that. Simmer down, Bryan.

I try to smother this fog of reality, burying my head in her breasts, and she twirls my curls with her fingertips. It's way more sensuous than anything we did earlier.

This is what I miss most, I say.

Don't lie. You miss sex the most.

60

We have discussed this before yet she always challenges me.

Yeah I miss that, of course, but it's also the kissing, the spooning, all of it. You're my only human touch.

I interlace my fingers with hers.

I started recording my life, I tell her, pulling out my cell. So when I go there's something left behind.

You're posting them?

Yes.

You can't post on *It*. They'll arrest you.

Cody showed me how to post on the dark *It*.

Don't you dare record me, she says, grabbing a blanket from the back of the couch, wrapping it around herself like a serape as she scampers off to the bathroom.

No video, I promise, nobody has to see you. I'll transcribe your words. Anonymously.

There is a brief trickle and then the ruffle of toilet paper.

Who'll read it?

Nobody, I'm sure.

You promise no video?

I'm just turning on the voice memo, okay?

There is a long pause.

Okay. But I get delete rights.

A'ight.

I hold the mic toward the open bathroom door.

For the record, state your name and occupation.

Stop it!

Just kidding.

I clear my throat and speak into my phone:

61

I'm here with a dear friend, she wishes to remain anonymous. I want to ask her a few questions. First, be honest Miss Anonymous, do Sisters miss us at all?

Silence fills the space, long and deep. I'm about to tap stop—

Yes, we miss you, her voice drifts out of the bathroom. I love brothers. You'll always be in our DNA. Thousands of years of loving and hating you, cursing and nurturing you. There's a saying: Older Sisters remember the girls they left behind. I still remember my boy-crazy, romantic thirteen-year-old-self with pink braces.

Is that good or bad?

Neither. Just different. The ground rules today are not the same. It's not what I grew up with.

Tell me about yourself.

No.

You talk about yourself all day.

That's different.

All right, then I'll tell your story——

Her hand reaches though the doorway and snatches the phone. She turns it off and steps out in a white cotton bathrobe.

I know you want me to tell how I'm American Indian-Indian, and how my father, Poli Anand, may he rest in blessed peace, came over here from Delhi. How he faced great racism, but was a savior to many, giving medical help and only taking what people could pay. And my mother, Greta Big Teeth, they called her, she was Shawnee but had been adopted by a German-American farm family. They met at the Richland County Fair, fell in love, got married, and dad never looked back, never once went home. I grew up knowing very little about my heritage on either side.

Weren't you curious? I ask.

I was too driven.

She disappears into the bathroom with my phone.

Tell me more about your mom, I say.

She died from cancer when I was seven. Dad claimed it was the farm pesticides she inhaled as a child, running in her forest of cornstalks. Dad raised me alone.

Silence seeps from the bathroom like steam.

Your dad died from The Y, right?

I'd rather not talk about that, if you don't mind.

Let me describe Miriam a little more for you. Her chin is too square, too masculine. Of course I'll never tell her that. She's 38, looks older, webs of crow's feet around her eyes, gray roots in her raven hair. When she smiles big, an inch too much gum shows at the top of her teeth, which I would miss if not there. She is always busy, always professional, intimidating because she gets things done. She claims she misses simpler times but this new world energizes her. She is bright, complicated, driven, and can do whatever she sets her mind to. There seem to be many of those Sisters these days.

She owned her own company, Mirror Meds, a leader in the healthcare industry and a driving force in the city's renaissance. She won a city CouncilSister seat, then four years ago was elected mayor. She's a trusted advisor to Mother President Olsen. Like I said, they met at a fundraiser and hit it off. Two solid Midwest Sisters who see each other a couple times a year, whenever their schedules fit.

Miriam hasn't done a helluva lot to help us brothers. Politically, I get it, we are such a minority that we have no skin in the game. I'm not gonna harp on her record but there is one thing she did that I hate:

63

renaming our city. Brothers marched outside her office and protested to no avail. I told her she was being petty and vindictive. She told me to go fuck myself. In a polite, professional tone, of course.

She tells me I remind her of her younger brother, Dev, he died from The Y the day after his 32nd birthday. Normally, an incestuous comparison like that would creep me out but nothing much creeps a brother out these days.

She had a son, her only child, lost him early to The Y, almost three years ago. His death haunts her. Though she herself is completely immune, not even a carrier, she could not save her son. She told me about him only once, and I'll be honest, I don't even remember his name.

She comes back to bed, spoons with me, I wriggle into the contour of her back. I want to move in with her and marry her and even father her children. But I'm allowed to do none of these. Don't get me wrong, I'm lucky to be with Miriam, I know that, but I'm not allowed to see her outside of the Shack, can't text her, can't email her. If I bump into her in public, which I don't, I must refer to her as Sister Mayor. We never get to eat in restaurants and I've never met her family, none of her friends, except for Gaia, and I knew her first.

Let's start meeting twice a week, I say.

Can't, you know how busy I am, my schedule is crazy. You're lucky to get me once a week.

You sure know how to stroke a guy's ego.

What we have here is perfect, I don't have time for anything more. Let's just enjoy this for what it is.

She wraps my arm around her. She can relax with me. One time we danced around the Love Shack, the mayor shaking her booty.

Another time she painted my toenails a bright pink, blowing on them to dry the polish. It was one of the sexiest things I've ever felt.

She totally controls this relationship, no surprise in these times. It's a fucked-up relationship, anyway you look at it, but a fucked-up relationship can be better than no relationship at all, am I right, Sisters? Miriam can seem cold but she's got a good heart, it's just so wrapped up in the business of being mayor that it's hard for people to see her soft side. Opponents say she's a driven narcissist with very high political ambitions. I wouldn't call that description a lie. Just too stark. Trust me, she's a romantic. Luckily, I get to see her soft side for three hours every Thursday morning.

And that's all I get.

Miriam is snoring, so I squirm out of bed, grab my phone, and head to the bathroom. I tap the record button. Now is as good a time as any to fill you in on—

THE Y

Here's the herstory teacher in me: brothers became victims to the law of obsolescence—everything that exists is already becoming obsolete. It's pure economics. If a tool is not necessary in production, simply eliminate the tool; or as Sisters joke, eliminate the fool. And then came the worst virus the world has ever seen. Officially named YES (Y-chromosome Extermination Syndrome) it went through many names: Female Bomb, F-Bomb, and the one that stuck—The Y. Like HIV, it is a lentivirus. Unlike HIV, The Y discriminates, targeting the Y chromosome. It attacks you simply because you are male. Don't matter if you're straight, gay, young, old, healthy or sick. The virus quickly mutates the Y chromosome, causing cell breakdown, severe joint pain, inflammation, hemorrhages, and organ shut downs. Victims become bedbound within weeks of infection and die within two months. Many go mad. There are no known cures. It's extremely difficult to avoid infection since it's passed on by all bodily fluids: blood, sweat, tears, spit, semen, vaginal secretion. Sex kills, kisses kill, sneezes kill. The only thing that doesn't kill these days is a look.

"Biology is destiny," was never truer than it is today.

Native-American brothers are immune, thanks to a gene mutation rendering the virus harmless. They call it The White Man's Disease, retribution for 500 years of brutal history. That explains why Miriam, half-Native-American, is not even a carrier.

Since they don't have the Y chromosome, no Sister has ever gotten sick from the virus, according to the SEW (Sisters Embracing the World) which replaced the United Nations in 2030. SEW is the voice of Sisterhood, a group of 30 Sisters from around the world, making decisions for the entire planet.

Sisters infect us. So brothers avoid proximity with pretty much everyone except other just-tested brothers. You won't see us on the streets without our masks and gloves. Some wear goggles or eye caps, transparent lenses that fit over our eyeballs. They're a pain to get in or out and I hate putting things in my eyes, so I don't wear them. I do sometimes wear wrap-around sunglasses.

Fortunately, time can be a savior. The virus doesn't live long outside the body, usually no more than thirty seconds, although that's long enough. Signs and commercials everywhere preach:

2-10

2 Minutes To Touch　　　Keep 10 Feet Apart

So, Sisters already gained near-political-parity when suddenly this new viral bulldozer wiped us out, one in which Sisters are carriers but immune. And one that just happened to strike in the first year of Mother President's reign. Coincidence? Yes, says the SEW. I don't think so, say brothers. We don't believe anything we read or hear anymore, hell I don't even believe my own eyes. Truth is just as endangered as brothers are. But there is no smoking gun implicating Sisters and even if there was what could brothers do? To whom would we appeal? Sister Judges? Give me a break. Brothers who criticize the government usually disappear or quickly shut the fuck up. Free speech today is only free when it's positive. But at the risk of being silenced, here is:

THE SEVENTH CONSPIRACY THEORY

Conspiracy Theory #1 – The virus was originally designed by white supremacists to eradicate blacks and Jews, but it backfired, killing the brother scientists that created it and then almost all brothers.

Conspiracy Theory #2 – Sisters created the virus to reduce but not eliminate brother sapiens. Then things got out of control.

Conspiracy Theory #3 – Sisters created it to do exactly what it's doing, eliminate all but a few brothers.

Conspiracy Theory #4 – This one claims radical feminists worked on a male plague as far back as the 80's. AIDS was a failed first attempt.

Conspiracy Theory #5 - Brother doctors worked on a vaccine but all have died or disappeared.

Conspiracy Theory #6 – A vaccine exists but is kept under lock and key.

Conspiracy Theory #7 – It links all six theories into one: The Seventh Conspiracy.

Many conspiracists believe SEW allowed our population to decrease to the one-percent it is now, and will soon make the vaccine available to stabilize our numbers, so Sisters can continue to use us as spermers, bro-hoes, and house boys. If this is true, some Sisters say they waited too long. Radical feminists say they haven't yet waited long enough. One way or another, the government probably created/ dispersed/did not stop The Y. This makes the moon landing and "Who shot JFK?" conspiracies look like parlor games. To all you Sisters out there, the way I see it, what you did is indefensible, but it's over, it's done, we can't change it. But you can save those of us still alive. And if you don't try, then you really are some cold, hard bitches.

The first outbreaks of The Y occurred in the early winter of 2029, mysteriously and simultaneously, in five small, remote towns in Crete, Nigeria, China, the Australian Outback, and New Mexico. The United Nations Conference in Berlin, April 2029, declared this public health enemy #1. World leaders—over half still brothers—promised quick medical action, while a private sub-conference of Sisters debated behind closed doors. This group would soon become the SEW.

Because victims could go days or weeks without symptoms, The Y spread before brothers knew what hit them. Airports and harbors were closed too late. What had been five local epidemics became an epic pandemic. Death spread like fog. Some brothers fled cities and went off the grid—we call them O.T.G.s—dying alone in woods or deserts like wild animals. Most hid in abandoned Sister-less apartments and houses, already infected, not knowing it yet, soon dying alone in dreary homes or apartments that no Sister wanted. Many committed suicide.

The speed of death was astonishingly quick, much too fast to stop. In the first three months, close to a billion of us died. Three billion within six months. The use of masks and gloves and social distancing flattened the curve—we learned that from Covid-19—but this killed far too quickly and within a year almost four billion brothers were dead. Now, over three years after the outbreak, well more than four billion of us are gone. Numbers are impossible to verify, but what took millenniums of generations to grow took only a fraction of one generation to wipe out. In my lifetime so many things have become obsolete: telephone booths, traveler's checks, newspapers, CDs, DVDs, mixtapes, drive-in movies, long conversations. I guess it was only a matter of time for brothers to join the list.

The Y wiped out world leaders, and those few not yet dead went into exile, too scared to run dying governments. Sisters took over the military, took over Wall Street, took over cities and countries, took over space, took over everything. They relished these new opportunities, replacing Rosie the Riveter, with posters of Linda the Lawyer and Deneen The Doctor. They cribbed the WWII slogan "We Can Do It" with:

We Did It

Only, unlike WWII, the brothers aren't coming back.

The Y may have been designed and created, it may have been encouraged, or it may have been Sisters simply getting out of the way. In any case, who could blame them, after what brothers have done while ruling this planet. Eating the apple to cause original and eternal sin. Destroying fertility goddesses. The Crusades, conquests, mass slavery, mustard gas and trench warfare, wholesale destruction of cities and humans in two world wars. The Holocaust, genocides, lynchings, the atom bomb, the hydrogen bomb, and who knows what other fucking bombs. And of all these evil creations, how many were perpetrated by Sisters? You might argue the first one, the eating of the apple, but that was Adam's fault. Eve didn't force him to eat it, he just blamed her for it.

To be sure, Sisters mourned, oh how they mourned their fathers and brothers and husbands and sons. Intense universal grieving slowed everything down. Life dragged on like a church service, dreary as one long, on-going requiem. The joke became, "I'm going to a party." "Oh yeah? Whose funeral?" You left one service early to get to another. Flags flew constantly at half-mast, people dressed in black every day, veils hung from Sisters' faces. Mothers wept for their husbands and sons. Little girls cried for their lost daddies. Death became so commonplace that we grew desensitized to it. Over time, Sisters emerged from the mental wreckage, picking up the pieces of their lives, rearranging them, and discovering very appealing new lives. And the rest, as they say, is herstory.

Some of the last Sisters to arise, not surprisingly, occurred in Arab countries. Saudi Arabian sheiks isolated themselves in their palaces and held onto power longer than most brothers. But all the money in the world can't protect you from underlings or harems seeking revenge. And nowhere else in the world do Sisters now enjoy the taste of freedom like in the Middle East, throwing off their hijabs to drive and dance and drink in the streets.

To be fair, there were many Sisters on our side, brother-lovers, chanting "We Want Men!" at rallies and posting their support all over social media. They tried bringing us back into society, but were

71

ridiculed and persecuted and, well, you don't see many brother-lovers anymore.

After the initial wave of hundreds of millions of deaths, federal laws mandated cremation. Now, all men are cremated equally. Ledgers are kept. Dead brothers are number-coded based on state, city, and neighborhood, reminiscent of the Nazi bookkeeping during the Holocaust. Numbers dehumanize our humanity. Numbers numb.

Our memories are being deleted, Sisters aren't recording our courageous moments and brave deeds, we are being written out of herstory. Another reason why I hope my words will somehow survive.

***

How have I avoided The Y? By doing the wrong thing at the right time. I was teaching history at my alma mater, Madison Comprehensive High School. In my ninth year, I wrote the college application essays for two nice students who deserved better than life had given them. Both came from horrible homes: his was physically abusive, hers drug-infested. The girl felt guilty and turned me in. I was put on administrative leave. The union pretended to protect me, but I knew I was gonna lose my job. I had just fucked my career.

I needed to get away. I went on a one-week brothers' holistic retreat, outside Millersburg, in the heart of Amish Country. My friend Gaia had harped on me about meditating since childhood. I never took to it, tried in high school, wanted to connect with Gaia on that level, but it just wasn't for me. Can't quiet my mind long enough. But I figured, what the hell, I needed some serious reflection, so I found myself at the retreat. Meditation and yoga were only part of it, there was organic gardening, cooking, music, and poetry, and it gave me a chance to escape the local media—news and social—that attacked me. My reputation was toxic in a world where I was already being marginalized. A retreat sounded like just the ticket. It went well, at first, I didn't meditate much and did no yoga, but I began to forgive myself and explore within; doing some good work as they say. Then, only three days into the retreat, news broke that The Y—up to this point something scary happening somewhere else—was in Ohio. We didn't hear anything that first week, we were on cellular blackout, but a brother snuck in a cell phone and shared news updates. The Y had been here already for months, first in New Mexico, then across Texas and the Southwest, and when it hit New York, fuhgeddaboudit. When we first heard, the virus was already a pandemic, sweeping across most of the country. It hit Ohio particularly hard. The retreat suddenly became less organic and more survivalist, which is the original organic. While others meditated, I packed my bags. But where was I to go that was more secluded and safer than here?

We quarantined ourselves, nineteen of us, including staff. They closed the gates to all outsiders. We stocked up those first few days, making constant trips to local markets, emptying the shelves of bottled water, masks, gloves, canned goods, rice, pasta, flour, sanitary wipes. And toilet paper, thanks to the memory of Covid-19's great TP shortage in 2020. Food wasn't so difficult, we had already been growing and canning our own fruits and vegetables, storing them in a massive cellar. The retreat had been vegetarian, almost vegan—milk and cheese from our own cows were allowed—but when we heard what was going on everywhere out there, many of us morphed back into omnivores. We hunted deer, turkey and quail and no one stressed over eating meat. For other supplies, deliveries would be left for us at the end of the driveway. We didn't yet know the virus's life expectancy outside the body, so we let the supplies set for days and then disinfected them. If we did get sick from things like colds, doctors examined us on *It*. Hospitalization meant never coming back.

I cleaned dishes. I didn't mind my hands soaking in sanitized liquid two hours a day. I was also in charge of entertainment. The center had a piano and after spending the first few days glued to screens—the "no devices" rule was out the window—the other retreaters actually hung out and listened to me banging the keys. One guy, Uriah, had a flute, so we often jammed. It was, all in all, an idyllic place to be when the world was falling to pieces.

My one-week stay became five. I ran up massive credit card bills to pay for it, figured bills won't even matter anymore, who cares what I owe if my lenders are dead. We spent hours debating if this virus would be the death of debt and crossed our fingers. Naturally, the economy crashed. Unemployment wasn't the issue; workers had been cut by more than half. Instead, assets became worthless. There was so much property out there now—empty homes, abandoned cars, unsold appliances—and it became a help-yourself world. And after five weeks the retreat stopped charging us. It was no longer a business, it was a brotherhood.

In the first two months, I lost two uncles, three cousins, and four neighbors, but I couldn't attend any funerals. To leave here meant never returning. No outsiders, no exceptions. No funeral was worth my own life.

Then my brother Tommy got The Y. I couldn't visit him, I was stuck here, but when I learned he was days from death, I decided to go say goodbye. I called home. Mom begged me not to come.

I am losing one son, she told me, I can't lose you too.

I stayed put.

Three months passed. The dead were piling up everywhere, the numbers staggering, many millions, so many the counts couldn't keep up. Chaos ensued, rioting and looting, but not for long, survivors had more important things to do than smash glass and steal jewelry and TVs. We worried more about stealing time.

Sisters took back to the streets when it was obvious none of 'em were afflicted, while brothers kept hiding inside. It was isolation that kept us survivors alive. And at the retreat the menial work proved therapeutic, a feeling of accomplishment in a failing society. The weekly massages didn't hurt, either. We found a community groove that could keep us safe, we could wait it out until a vaccine came. Unfortunately, because we're humans, The Y wormed its way into the retreat. A Sister Staffer had snuck out, got infected, brought it back. One by one we succumbed. It was a great group of guys that are now, as far as I know, all dead. I was one of the first to flee, thankfully, and I didn't know if I was infected or not. I headed back to Mansfield—it had not yet been re-named—even though it was hard-hit and early January, cold and snowy.

With a paranoid awareness of everything around me, I came back to my hometown. My apartment building was off-limits, swarming with dying tenants, so I moved in to my parents' never-finished cement-block basement. I went on *It* and researched "How To Survive The Y," ordering boxes of masks and gloves and wipes. Mom stayed upstairs, I lived downstairs, and we talked on the phone. Mom was a carrier and severely depressed and she could not come downstairs to see me. Then one day, she gave me the news:

Your father is sick.

She and pops had been divorced for ten years but remained friends and traveling companions. She took him back in. It was so bizarre to be home like this, with Tommy gone and pops dying upstairs in his brown La-Z-Boy recliner and me forced to live downstairs. We didn't know enough about the disease yet, we knew it was airborne, but we didn't know how close we could or couldn't get. So we chatted on SisFace, separated by the basement ceiling. I would stand next to the utility sink and washer/dryer, directly underneath his chair, so we could be as close as possible. I usually kept the app open 24-7, to check in on him, just in case. I did stand outside the living room window a couple times and waved to him, but when he was conscious he was dopey on morphine drops. It became too hard to be there in person, you know what I mean, I'd much rather do it over a screen.

My pops, William Bowman, was a gentle ham, he loved to sing and had a hard time getting out of his own way. He'd screw up a joke more times than not, giving away the punch line or, worse, forgetting it. Didn't matter, he'd laugh anyway and his joy was so infectious you'd laugh too.

Mom was a musician, studying piano as a child, learning to sight-read. I would come home early from school and hear her play Elton John, surprising her, and she would stop immediately. She had no interest in sharing music with anyone. Pops, on the other hand, would stop people on the street and sing to them. Beatles and Broadway tunes, and—when he became a grandpa, thanks to my Sister Sis—he'd belt out "I'm My Own Grandpa."

His last few weeks, over my phone, my iPad, my laptop, he'd tell me stories, how he never made much money, investing in a few harebrained schemes, working office jobs, retail sales, telemarketing. He was fired from most for talking more than selling. He told me that in high school he tried selling drugs, but he hung out so much with his buyers that they ended up smoking most of his product. But he did manage somehow to sell himself to my mom. And despite his financial failures, I respected pops for all the things he didn't do. He didn't abuse us in any way. He didn't smoke, drink, or curse. Except at traffic: "Learn how to drive, you fuckin' moron," was a favorite.

The last two weeks of his life, I paced in our basement, watching him—on my laptop—sleeping in his La-Z-Boy. I was amped with a weird energy, as if coked-up, like I could do anything, with the focus to do nothing. I would talk with Mom and Sis several times a day on SisFace or mom would stand at the top of the basement stairs and call down to me. No one ventured downstairs. I had a fridge, toilet, shower and utility sink. Groceries and supplies were left in the garage at the top of the stairs but I would not go near them for days. I did the laundry that came tumbling down a chute, again waiting days before touching it, and when I did, I suited up pseudo-hazmat. I washed and dried and folded and left the clean clothes at the top of the basement stairs. Mom would collect them and check up on me: You warm enough down there? or, How's the laundry going?

On one of his last days, pops wouldn't take his morphine drops. Mom grew frustrated and went grocery shopping. I remember playing our way-out-of-tune player piano, circa 1900, my great-grandmother's, unused now, even by my mother who could play but chose instead the electronic keyboard in the dining room. As kids, Tommy and I used to pump the pedals and pretend our hands were flying up and down the keyboards. We tried to out-fake the other. All the neighborhood teens loved hanging out in our basement, pumping the player piano, shooting pool on our old Brunswick table, getting drunk on the sly. It was a suburban speakeasy. So, this one day, mom was at the store, and I was pumping the pedals and pretending to bang The Sound of Music on the yellowed keys when I heard the most painstakingly slow step, a long pause, and another step, long pause, step. I stood up from the piano and backed away from the open doorway. The old brother walking down those stairs, hanging onto the railing, looked nothing like my father, not the one I remembered, not even the one I'd been watching on my screens. In person, he was a sketch of a man, ravaged by The Y, gaunt, blotchy. I even thought, for a moment, maybe he was still upstairs and he had passed and I was speaking to his ghost, but I looked over at my laptop and saw on the screen that his La-Z-Boy was empty.

Pops? What are you doing?

I fumbled my mask on and pressed myself against the far basement wall, with the old pool table a barrier between us. We were a good twenty feet apart, but we didn't yet know how far the virus might infect when airborne.

You shouldn't be down here, I said.

I heard you playing, he coughed. It's a really bad day, son, I hurt all over.

Then why aren't you taking your drops?

Because I can't talk when I'm on that stuff.

We stood on opposite ends of the basement. He leaned against the cement block wall, scared and exhausted, catching his breath.

I was thinking the other day, he said, remember when we laid out on grandma's old farm and watched the stars?

78

A light smile touched his ghastly face.

We'd count shooting stars, he said. You always won.

You always let me, I chuckled, then sniffled. This sucks, pops.

I know but what can you do?

Silence lingered between us, something I notice more as I get older. For my part, I didn't know what else to say. Small talk just didn't cut it.

Is there anything I can do?

I wish you could give me a hug, kiddo.

I wish I could too.

We took in the presence of each other across this cool basement space and didn't speak for the longest time.

There is one thing you could do, he said, finally.

Anything.

Rack 'em up.

Pops, you can't play in your condition.

I'm not gonna play a game. Just one break.

He grabbed a cue stick and dammit if I didn't rack up the faded balls. I backed away from the table as far as I could. He chalked his stick and bent over to shoot. He stumbled. I found myself moving toward him, to break his fall.

Pops!

But I stopped myself, scared that helping my father could kill me. I could only watch. Thank goddess he caught himself, clutching the bumper. He pushed himself up and bent again at the waist, one arm on the bumper, trying to steady the cue in the circle he made between his thumb and index finger. The cue-stick quivered.

Blasted thing life is, he said, the aches get worse as we go. Then at the end, Mother Nature piles on the pain like a fireworks finale.

He pulled the cue stick back, smacked at the cue ball, barely nicked it. The ball wobbled a few inches away. I felt so sad for him, once one of the best players in Sisterfield.

He lined up his shot again.

It's okay to let go, pops, I said.

Yeah, I know, he replied, easier said than done.

He pulled back the cue stick, took a breath and shot and this time it connected squarely but with only enough power to roll the cue ball across the faded felt until it clanked against the triangle of balls, nudging a few an inch or two. He laughed and shook his head and, using the cue stick as a cane, he turned around and shuffle-stepped back toward the door.

Maybe I should call mom?

He waved me off with a weak flap of his hand and he turned around at the base of the stairs.

Stay safe, son, stay safe.

He struggled back upstairs, one slow step at a time. I wanted to help him, but of course I couldn't, all I could do was listen to him coughing after every other step.

That was the last time I saw my father in person. A few days later, he was sleeping in his La-Z-Boy, his breathing heavy, and I heard a rattling moan and rushed over to the laptop and there was a brief flash of pain on dad's face. He scrunched up his nose and forehead, and then his body seemed to rise a millimeter or two off the recliner, I swear to goddess, before he sunk down. His crinkled face softened and he looked comfortable, more peaceful than doped-up sleep, as content as I've ever seen him.

Mom?!

Funerals were already frowned upon, backed-up for weeks, and it took two days before a cremation crew had an opening to come to our house. Dad lay there in his La-Z-Boy as if still sleeping, with mom sitting by his side for half-hour stretches, very orderly. She touched his hand many times during that 48 hours, traced little circles on it. I kept the live feed on, watching my father in the room above my head. This wake gave me a creepy peace, if you know what I mean. I felt his presence just as I did when I watched him alive, there's no difference from the other side of the screen. Mom said the stench was awful the last few hours before the Sister Cremators came. They triple-wrapped him in organic, pearl-white, environmentally-friendly plastic—they made sure to tell mom that—and they hauled him away like an old coffee table, laying him as respectfully as you can into a van, on top of many other dead brothers, all going straight to the crematorium. We held a Goodbye Service. We used to call it a Celebration of Life but there's not much to celebrate these days. Mom and my sis Emily attended, along with a few other Sister relatives. I watched from the basement, via video stream. Due to the risks, pop's few living brother relatives and friends could not attend, except one, old Marty, the last of his pool buddies. Marty didn't bother to wear a mask. He looked ready to follow dad to the great beyond.

I couldn't continue to live at home, where dad and my bro-bro had died, so after the funeral I found a free place just off Fourth Street in one of Sisterfield's slums, nicknamed brother town. It was near Central Park, which was designed by Frederick Law Olmsted, who designed New York's Central Park and seemed to have run out of names. Sisters didn't want to live here, brothers didn't either, but since Sisters weren't around, it was a safe 'hood, and convenient to corner markets, which I would need if I were to survive.

It was a decrepit, abandoned two-story vinyl-sided house, a drug den for years, long before all this had happened. We bought meth there in high school. Yellow safety tape was strung in an X across the front porch and the second story porch sagged in two places, like wooden buttocks supported by a thong column, waiting to collapse. I entered through the back door off a narrow alley, swept discarded condoms and needles off the floor and ratty furniture. I didn't bother going upstairs, nothing good could come from that, just more rubbers and syringes, and I really didn't plan on staying there long. It was late spring, so I didn't have to worry too much about cold. I had some blankets, toiletries, a few clothes. Not much else. I chose this house because no one had bothered to shut off the water yet and I could still shower and I knew no Sisters or brothers would bother me here, not with all the better homes available. The problem is, if a brother squats in a nice abandoned home, it's never long before they get kicked out by Sisters. Sisters move up. Brothers move down.

I played musical houses for a few weeks, finding a double-wide trailer with the utilities still on and stocked with lots of alcohol. This was when I met Miriam.

***

She now stands, radiant-brown, in the bathroom doorway.

Give me that, Miriam says, grabbing my phone. What have you been saying about me?

Nothing. It's all about me.

82

She taps the screen: You may not believe me, she records, but the absence of brothers creates a hole in our soul. We just can't admit that, it's not politically correct. She pauses, her thoughts sinking deeper. It's strange, she continues while staring at me, a week goes by, I get used to no brothers. Then, after our time together, I remember how much I miss you guys. It's like I feel all out of balance. Everything gets flipped upside down.

She stops recording, looks at herself in the mirror, checks her teeth, showing those gums. She hums the Friends Theme while pulling on her running pants. If she was a Friend, I think, she'd be Monica. As you can guess, I've fallen hard for her. It's weird, Gaia is more my type, and I know what I have with Miriam is just what it is, weekly sex in a desperate grasp for normalcy. It's the worst thing an obsolete can do, fall in love with a Sister. Heterosexual love is all but forbidden. Sisters marry Sisters. A few brothers still marry each other, since gay marriage is the only sanctioned union these days. As Miriam said, everything has flipped upside down.

I'll never forget, right around the one-year anniversary of our very first hook-up, I told Miriam I loved her. Her lips crept into a cringing smile. Not exactly the response you wanna see. She gave me a hug. But she didn't volley back those three little words. She never has.

Every day, Miriam pops a regimen of seven pills to maintain and boost her immunity, promising she will notify me if she ever becomes a carrier. I think that's all a ruse. I believe she's been vaccinated. What follows is a conversation we've had more than once:

So, about that vaccine—

She throws my phone like a bullet across the room, directly at my chest. I'm lucky I'm able to snatch it out of the air.

Damn, where'd you learn to throw like that?

I was a shortstop. High school and college softball.

(BTW, few team sports still exist although softball and volleyball are as popular as ever. Football is no longer America's favorite pastime. Social media is.)

I pocket my phone.

I just want the truth, Miriam.

Truth isn't going to bring anyone back, she says, joining me on the rug, now fully-clothed in her running gear. She turns her back on me. There is no vaccine, she adds, so stop asking me about it.

Two ring tones go off at almost the exact same time, the rhythm of her seaside ditty a half-second before my piano riff. I turn mine off, she does the same. I stoke the dying fire, stirring the last glowing embers away from the front of the fireplace, into a heap of ashes. I pull the metal screens across the front.

We step outside, in a state of back-to-the-real-world melancholy. I close the door, she enters the security code, we do our stretches. Mine are simple and stiff, hers mind-blowingly complex and limber. I give her a quick kiss then pull on my mask and gloves. I always dread the goodbyes. I'm not sure she does.

Have a great week, she says.

You too.

We run in different directions, away from the Love Shack. I race through the woods, underneath the kaleidoscope of tree crowns. Leaves are in their first stages of falling, it looks like a good year for color, with patchworks of brown and orange and gold loosely quilting the ground. A single flaming red maple leaf catches my eye and settles on the forest floor. I listen to frogs croak, crickets crick, and mockingbirds mock. The morning is already humid and I burst with perspiration, as I emerge from the forest, running under cumulus clouds, gray and white mountains that follow one behind the other like a line of evacuees. I pass the statues of Ruth Bader Ginsberg—now graffiti-free—and Gloria Steinem and I run out through the gate and back onto Trimble Road, keeping to my bro-only lane, my shoes slapping the pavement, sprinting downhill, my adrenaline pumping. A carload of Sisters drives by, pretending not to look, the whole time gawking at me. I slip through the gate to Queenwood Center and run across the rolling lawn. Up near the house, I come upon Drew walking Killer, his labradoodle.

Did you have a good bang?

Always. You have a good time ejecting your thumb drive?

Always.

I gaze up at his raptor-sized drone hovering overhead, so much bigger than my hummingbird-sized one, on shutdown still for the next five minutes.

C'mon, admit it, he says, catching my eye, you've got drone envy.

I ignore the comment, watching Killer take a dump at Drew's feet. Drew doesn't bother to clean it up.

Did you watch her take the test?

No.

Dude, you need to see her test.

She wouldn't lie.

Yeah, right. You're "in love".

He adds air quotes and I don't care to talk anymore. I know Drew is right, I just don't wanna hear it spoken. I jump up onto the portico and stare at the security screen beside the front door. 8:59 AM. The

85

retinal scanner authenticates me, the lock clicks, the massive door opens, just beating the 9 AM power-up of my drone on the rooftop.

I go to my room, plop down in bed. I do not jam the joystick today, never work on Thursdays, my one day off. I pull out my phone, send a text to Gaia, and stare at the ceiling.

THE WAR OF THE SEXES

I didn't record much over the last few days, didn't wanna lose my post-Miriam buzz. Until I crashed in my usual post-post—Miriam funk. I texted Gaia again, asked to see her, still no reply. She's too busy to compose a few words?

It's now six AM Tuesday, my other running day, I'm getting excited about seeing Miriam in forty-eight hours. I fit on my brobot mask, jog down the curved staircase, and leap down the last three steps, into the front entryway, the landing hurts. I groan and hobble to the door. I stare into the retinal scanner, the door opens, the house logs me out.

Outside, it is dark, no moon, only a gray blanket of clouds and many towering trees suddenly illuminated by flashes of heat lightning. For a brief moment the entire sky flickers white like from a faulty fluorescent workshop light. The crowns of elm, beech, and sycamore are black silhouettes against the flash of white.

Wow.

It's already humid, in the mid 70's before the sun's even up, on one of the last warm days we'll have this year, what we used to call Indian summer. I've recently heard Sisters call it brother summer. Whatever, it's a pale imitation of summer, it doesn't last as long or shine as bright, but is even more welcomed, just as life today is a pale imitation of what used to be, yet is cherished all the more. I chew on that thought as I leave Queenwood Center, jogging onto Trimble's broken sidewalks, not straying from the bro-only lane. I pass under one of the city's last billboards—Sisters have cleaned up the billboard blight—with stark white letters glowing on a dark background:

JESUS IS COMING

Scrawled underneath it is red paint:

HE'S TOO LATE

Unlike Thursdays, today I am followed by my drone, the hummingbird, hovering above me, spying on me, also protecting me from the twisted Sister Kissers. They sneak up on you, pull down your mask, smooch you on the lips, then run off laughing, a sick fad to infect brothers. I've seen it happen, like witnessing a murder that will take two months to complete. But my drone has the new SisterEye facial recognition, top-of-the-line, so few Sisters will take that chance. Infecting a brother is just a misdemeanor, but infecting an Appleseed is a felony.

My drone soon bores with tagging along and drifts toward a stunning African-American Sister cruising in a convertible down Park Avenue—it looks nothing like New York City's—while I turn left on it and jog through the city's small parks, enjoying the warm morning and the flashes of heat lightning. I pass a strip mall of boarded-up small businesses. I cross the street to a Starbucks—some things haven't changed—and walk up to the bro-only window. I order two shots of espresso and a bottled water. The Drive-Thru Sister places my order in the pick-up window box. I wait the requisite two minutes, jogging in

88

place, and before I know it the box dings. I remove my drinks, down the espresso, chase it with the water, and run home.

You can always tell when older brothers are nearby, by their drones in the sky. Mine hovers with three others over the intersection at Trimble, a drone get-together fifty-feet over the heads of brothers waving Ad-Trons—poster-sized programmable electronic signs—at morning commuters:

SISTERS
WEAR MASKS & GLOVES
IT'S JUST RIGHT

EQUALITY
FOR ALL

I approach the half-a-dozen brother protestors, young and old, black, white, and brown, keeping my ten-foot distance, exchanging looks of solidarity. Then I see him: my longtime friend, Miguel Aguirre. I recognize his brown face, that long, squat Mayan nose, those intense eyes above the BLM logo on his brobot mask. He directs this little protest, holding up his own Ad-Tron, programmed with bright yellow letters:

RELEASE
THE
VACCINE

Miguel Aguirre, I say, I thought you were dead.

I was certain you were, he replies without looking at me.

Miguel's family came here from Central America—Guatemala, Honduras, or Nicaragua, I forget where. He and Gaia and I have been friends ever since elementary school. We were the Golden Trio;

89

Harry, Ron, & Hermione. We read all the Harry Potter books, at the same time, often in the same place, digesting, regurgitating, arguing, and re-reading them. We had the glasses, the robes, the broomstick, the Quidditch cards, the board game, we had them all. It was more Gaia's thing, we were just along for the ride. My favorite Potter book was The Prisoner of Azkaban, I loved the Dementors and Sirius Black, they took the series to a darker place. Miguel and I always fought over who got to be Harry. He usually won. He once Sharpied a black lightning bolt scar on his forehead, just like Harry. It's much more timely, Miguel said, to have Harry be Latino, don't you think? Gaia agreed. So, I was usually relegated to being Ron, the sidekick. Don't get me wrong, I like Ron, but no one dreamed of being him, every boy wanted to be Harry, right? It's all so silly now, but those books were the Krazy Glue that bonded us. Then once smart phones came, forget it, we moved on to other worlds.

Miguel and I fantasized about Gaia. She played us for a couple years, led us both on, before she chose him. I wasn't exotic enough. She never actually said that, didn't have to, I'm 5-9, and white like Elmer's Glue—although she's almost as white as I am—while Miguel is tall and dark and was shaving way back in sixth grade, years before I ever held a razor. When he spoke Spanish with his silky Latin accent, Gaia melted. Most girls did. I envied him, even hated him, but stayed friends because of Gaia. After a while he grew on me, like a patch of burnt skin, a disfigurement that disrupts your sense of who you are, yet becomes an essential part of you.

Gaia and Miguel were a hot-and-heavy teen couple. We all assumed they'd get married and I would be the best man. Then in tenth grade, she dumped his ass and started skipping school. Rumor was he beat her up. I asked both what happened, many times, and they denied the abuse but refused to explain the breakup. The secret lingered over The Golden Trio like a foul cologne, though we managed to remain casual friends. This is how geeky we were, when we turned 18, for spring break we took a road trip to Orlando to the newly-opened Harry Potter Theme Park. But the trip felt forced, like a three-day getaway to save a marriage, all three of us knew it, and when we got back, we went our separate ways, the last time we have ever been together. Gaia and I went off to different colleges while Miguel stayed home and worked at Gorman Rupp, one of the last of the obsolete factories. He quickly rose to union management and led a two-month strike that nearly bankrupted the business. He's always been an activist. In school, after his breakup with Gaia, Miguel fought for better lunches, for Spanish as a required second language, for Cesar Chavez Day as a school holiday. I used to tease him about it:

Who died and made you Che?

We're all Che, brother, we're all Che.

Our friendship faded like an old t-shirt kept in the bottom of a drawer, not worn anymore but not discarded and we managed to hang out once or twice every year, reminiscing, always stuck back in high school, never moving forward. Meanwhile, Gaia and I stayed friends, always platonic, and she remained the moon of my life, affecting my inner tides, drifting in-and-out of my life. To my knowledge, she and Miguel have not seen each other for a long time.

He looks worse since I last saw him: thinner, edgier, more tightly wound, which is hard for me to imagine. He came out of the womb wound-up.

Where you been? I ask.

91

In Cleveland, down in Cincinnati. Fighting the good fight, my friend. I hear you're an Appleseed. He snarls as he says it.

I ignore him, we play catch-up and talk about brothers still alive we think the other might know. We come up with no one.

Have you seen Gaia? I ask.

Be careful with her, BB.

(BB—Brayan Bowman—was his childhood nickname for me.)

She's our friend.

No she's not.

Whatever happened with you two, let it go.

I know I am in denial of the obvious, that Gaia is a Sister and therefore *is* the enemy, but I refuse to see her that way, don't think I ever can. I change the subject, describing the recording of my oral herstory—

Whoa-whoa-whoa. *History*, dammit. Fuck that herstory crap.

I pull out my phone, smiling.

Would you like to explain The War?

You're the history teacher, he says.

It'd be good to get another perspective.

I set my cell timer to two minutes, place it down on a curb.

What do you want me to say?

Just explain how it all happened.

You mean how it's happening.

Exactly.

I back away from him and the phone.

Okay, he says, but no video. Just my voice.

Fine. Voice only, whatever.

We wait, while the brother protestors flash their ever-changing Ad-Trons. Sisters drive by, some look, some don't, no one honks. The piano riff tickles on my cell, signaling the wait is over. Miguel picks up my phone, taps the screen, holds it up to the filter in his mask:

Qué tal? This is Miguel Aguirre. I was born in Choloma, Honduras.

Ah, that's it, Honduras, I say, I couldn't remember.

He looks at me like I'm an idiot.

Maricon.

I flip him off.

When I was seven, he resumes, I left home with momma and my older sister, Citlaly. We walked all the way across Mexico, man, we crawled through a tunnel under the Arizona border fence. Papa was already in this country, working at a car wash. My luck, it was not L.A. or New York, but O-fucking-hi-O. I'm a taco drenched in mayo. I met this fool here in, what, seventh grade?

Sixth grade.

I think it was seventh.

Whatever.

BB was always the sensitive one. I was the hellion. Remember launching loogies from the balcony at your church onto those Sister Churchgoers walking down the aisle to take communion. They're feeling all high and mighty, and clueless about our spittle dripping down their fancy hairdos.

I remember someone snitched, I butt in, and the pastor scolded us in front of everyone.

You cowered in the pew like a puta.

Enough about us, I say, get back on track.

93

Miguel clears his throat.

The first thing to know about The War is it's still going on. Not as intense as a few years ago, it's more a limited-strike guerilla war now. We brothers are well-armed, but we're too small in number, man, too spread out. We're not allowed to even gather. Unauthorized meetings of three or more brothers are illegal.

So how are you holding this protest?

We got a permit. Sisters issue them every now and then. Makes it easier to keep an eye on us.

He points up at our drones, my hummingbird, his raptor, and two others hovering.

Did you explain what SEW is?

Yes. Sisters Embracing the World.

Their army is massive, over five hundred million soldiers worldwide.

So who started the fighting?

Oh, brothers definitely, no one disputes that. We were pissed off.

Miguel really gets into his spiel now, his hands gesturing, his elbows flailing.

We were losing control of everything. We fought each other for the leftover crumbs. Brothers vs. brothers, for whatever power the Sisters hadn't already snatched away. We turned on each other, like dogs tossed a single bone. But we learned, like smart dogs do, and we united against the oppressor, man. All local wars merged into one big one, *The* War, brothers versus Sisters. It was white supremacists who woke us up, believe it or not, uniting us in the first wave of resistance. Remember, back in the day, they hated blacks and Jews

94

and immigrants. Not anymore, now their anger is stoked by Sisters. All colors and religions joined the resistance.

Penises unite! I joke.

He shakes his head.

We rose up against Sisters all over the world. Clashes killed dozens, hundreds, thousands at a time, can you imagine? SEW tried to stamp out the resistance, but when their police and military responded one place, we took the fight somewhere else. Our fervor was brotherism. Even the most passive of brothers rebelled. This puta—he stares at me—needs to join up.

I'm a lover not a fighter, I say, twirling my hand at him, the universal "continue" symbol.

Yeah, yeah. So we armed ourselves and formed modern-day militias. We did what we all instinctively know how to do; we fought back. And we had a few Sister diehards on our side, Sister Rednecks mostly.

He taps my phone screen.

Good so far?

Great.

I should have been the history teacher, he says. Hey, let me have a sip of your water.

I look at him like he'd just asked to kill me.

I'm clean, he says, I assume you must be too, Mr. Appleseed.

I toss the bottle to him. He twists off the lid and waterfalls the liquid. He belches loudly and tries to toss my bottle back.

Keep it, I say, backing away. I'm good.

Where was I?

He searches his memory and latches onto something. He taps record:

Standoffs and battles went on but we refused to stand down. Sisters passed new laws making it illegal for brothers to own guns. They nationalized all weapons manufacturers. They confiscated guns from dead brothers, right off their still-warm bodies. Saw it with my own two eyes, one Sister grabbed a revolver off one dying brother and pumped a couple bullets into him from his own weapon. Man, they control every military, they out-arm us, out-soldier us, out-survive us. They have released their inner animals.

They're beasts not bitches.

Amen, BB, amen.

He furrows his brow.

Did you tell them about the SisPistol?

I think I may have mentioned it, I'm not sure.

It's a small but badass .38 caliber. Designed by Sisters, for Sisters, it's the most popular gun in the world.

He imitates a smoky Sister's voice from an infomercial: "Small because you've already got enough in your purse. Powerful because you've already got enough on your mind."

He laughs and continues his rant: Sisters are divided on the Second Amendment. Sister Doves, they want to do away with all guns. But Sister Hawks want every Sister to own one. They just passed a law this year requiring mandatory military training when Sisters turn 18.

He sips.

Officially, the war is over in America, ended four months ago, with the treaty of San Francisco. Brothers who surrendered peacefully

96

were rewarded with fix-it-uppers, doublewides, the dregs Sisters didn't want. And if they swore allegiance to Sisters, they got an upgrade.

He looks straight at me with his penetrating eyes.

A few brothers still get to live in opulence.

I shoot him my best "What the fuck?" look.

Adaptation versus survival of the fittest, he continues, this is the choice most brothers deal with today. Either accept it or die fighting. You'll probably die anyway, so might as well fight the power.

Some of us prefer to adapt and survive, I say, no matter how horrific the new world order.

True. Some brothers have lost their huevos. They are Sister-Lovers, like BB here.

I'm not a Sister-Lover, I say. Give me back my phone.

They take what morsels the Sisters will throw their way.

I got lucky, I say, you'd do it too if you were offered.

Wrong, brother, so wrong. I would never cavort with the enemy. And I certainly wouldn't re-populate them.

He mic-drops my phone into a little patch of grass along the sidewalk, never bothering to set the timer.

Asshole, I say.

He laughs.

I need to get back to work.

He fits his BLM mask back over his face and rejoins the protestors, flashing a multi-colored message on his Ad-Tron:

Brothers

Lives

Matter

I wait the two minutes for my phone to be safe to touch. I'm rumbling with emotions but decide not to say anything, unity is the one power we still have left. I bend and twist and stretch, my left leg quivers. I decide I've waited long enough, I pick up my phone, run fast and furious, winded and exhausted, until I'm running on fumes.

GAIA

Instead of heading back to The Factory I run south on Trimble, mad at Miguel but I gotta let it go, as I've done for thirty years, jealous of him since we were kids, struggling still with my mix of anger and admiration. He got the charm gene, the nerve gene, and the girl. Now he's out there fighting the noble cause. Always showing me up. And seeing Miguel makes me miss Gaia, I've called her, texted her, she's avoiding me. It happens sometimes in our relationship, but I need to see her now, to remove the bad taste from Miguel.

I pass elaborate two-story homes, some abandoned with stenciled FF (Food Free) spray-painted forest green on the front doors. Sister Cleaners have removed all food from these vacant homes to prevent critter infestation. The FF also means all alcohol and valuables are gone too, booty for thieves and cleaners. I eye these, knowing I will need a new home, knowing I may soon be homeless—

Halt!

The nasally voice booms over a speaker. I obey, looking immediately down at my feet. Yup, I'm in my bro-only lane. I gaze around, spot a cop car parked in a vacant church lot. The driver's door swings open. A Sister Officer climbs out and swaggers toward me in her burgundy uniform, sporting a crew cut and no makeup. If it weren't for the subtle curve of breasts underneath her badge, I'd swear she was a brother cop.

What did I do, Sister Officer?

ID.

My lagging drone suddenly catches up with me and hovers, curiously, as I pull out my phone, tap the face, hold it out in front of me. Sister Officer taps her screen and my digital ID airdrops to her police phone. Instant background check.

Oh, you're one of those, she snickers, stepping closer, breaking the 2-10 safety zone, stopping maybe six feet away, looking me directly in the eye. Think you're something special, don't ya.

I populate the world with Sisters, so, yeah, I do, is what I want to say, but I just avert my eyes.

No, Sister Officer.

Any jerk can jack-off.

Not just any man—

Watch your mouth.

I meant *brother*.

I could haul you in for that.

Sorry, Sister Officer.

Where you headed?

Just exercising.

I can feel her eyes all over me, checking me out.

I saw you talking to those brother agitators, she says.

I used to go to school with one of 'em. Hadn't seen him since all the madness started.

The what?

The Change. Sister Officer.

That's better, she says, stepping back. You can go.

May I ask why you stopped me?

You were outside your lane.

I know I wasn't, she's lying, I was being very careful, but to argue would be pointless, it would just give her a reason to charge me with something more serious.

I'll be more careful, Sister Officer.

You do that.

She turns on a heel and heads back to her cruiser. You'd think Sister Officers would be cooler than brother cops, more empathetic and all that, but I think the opposite could be true. The power trip goes with the job, I guess.

I resume running. My drone drifts around, bored again, while I pass long white fences undulating up and down over rolling hills. I reach stables and spot Gaia's yellow pick-up truck, a Ford Spirit Guide, parked near horse stalls. Gaia comes here often to ride before work. Through the fencing, I watch her lift a saddle onto her reddish-brown Morgan.

Thought I'd find you here, I say.

Morning, Bryan.

I texted you. And called the bookstore. You avoiding me?

No, she says, adjusting tack. I just have to be in the right space to talk with a brother.

Oh, so now I'm just a brother?

I didn't say that.

Gaia Alt is a free spirit, a bohemian in Goddess's country, with high cheekbones and high shoulder blades, lightly-freckled like constellations in a bright, moonlit sky. Growing up, she had long,

101

flowing, light brown hair, often braided down to her waist. But in her 30's, she suddenly cut it off into a pageboy cut. Today, her Egyptian-like bangs are dyed royal purple, hanging underneath her tan cowgirl hat. One thing hasn't changed—her soft green eyes. I could gaze at them forever.

We met in fourth grade at Eastview Elementary. I sat behind her, thanks to the alphabet; Alt and Bowman. One day, the teacher, Mr. Drinkwater, turned the TV on and we watched the twin towers fall. I remember teachers crying and telling me I would always remember this day, 9/11, and they were right, but not for the same reason. Gaia and I began talking about what happened—the crumbling towers on TV just felt like a video game to us, and we didn't fully understand it—and from that day on, we became inseparable, sharing lunches, homework, and gossip. Tragedy brought us together; tragedy has since torn us apart.

I sat behind her and sang Green-Eyed Lady, one of pops' favorites—mom had flecks of green in her eyes—until Gaia would turn around and flash them at me. She was an earthly beauty, radiating pure energy to my awestruck eyes.

We're just friends, she'd say, pushing me away whenever I tried to kiss her. I'm sorry, she'd add, I've always liked you too much to mess it up.

I always wanted her too much not to try.

Then Miguel moved to town. He and I spent the rest of middle school seeing who could pop better wheelies or climb higher trees or rock out more on *Guitar Hero*. Until Gaia learned to shred and beat us both. But she preferred the world of Harry Potter, so Miguel and I learned to love it too, the Golden Trio in our own little magical world.

Gaia, like Miguel, was not really from here either. Her mom, Crystal, was a New-Age hippie chick, she drove a VW bus and had been a waitress, slinging Mexican food to tourists at the boardwalk in Santa Cruz, California, a surf mecca. She had a fling with an Ohio tourist, Chris, a customer at the taqueria. Chris and Crystal, phonetically meant to be, right? He was only 25, she was 38. He had come to California to "make it" either by surfing (he'd never surfed in Ohio) or acting (he'd barely acted in Ohio). He ended up just hanging out. And getting Crystal pregnant. She had no family, she had bounced around foster homes, orphaned as a baby, and Chris decided to do the right thing, marrying her and moving them back home to Mansfield, where he had family support. She named her baby Gaia, which means earth, because her baby was now her world. Chris freaked out upon being a father and fled back to California. Crystal stayed in Ohio, preferring to raise Gaia in the Midwest rather than on the California coast.

I liked the authenticity of the people, she once told me, even if it is about as far from being hip as an ankle.

Crystal stood out, everyone's only California gal pal, unlike in Santa Cruz, where you could shake a surfboard and dozens of hippie chicks would tumble out. When Gaia was little, Crystal face-painted the *Om* symbol on her tender cheek and Gaia didn't wash it off for a week. We called her Om Girl. To this day, Gaia always flashes an Om—tattoo, earrings, pendant—somewhere on her body. Right now it's on a buckle on her cowgirl hat which tops-off her outfit: jeans, floral cowboy boots, turquoise jewelry, and a loose jade-colored top that flows like a waterfall. Her nouveau cowgirl look, one of many looks she displays. Tattoos of a snake and the tree of knowledge swirl

103

around her forearms and wrists. Me, I don't have tattoos or piercings or wear jewelry. Gaia loves reading poetry: Mary Oliver and Sister Muse are favorites. She makes up new gerunds, adding "ing" to words, like "You're nervousing me," that feel like they should be words. She donates time at Sister retirement homes and is, in many ways, a total package. Except she's now a lesbian. And a carrier.

I watch those green eyes flash in the scarlet morning sunlight. She handles her horse, Magic, doing groundwork in a dance of beauty, obedience and affection. She fits her cowgirl hat onto a post, and dons a black helmet over her purple hair. She grabs the saddle horn with her left hand—her purple nails are perpetually chipped—and places her left foot in a stirrup. Like a gymnast, she swings her right leg up and over, mounting Magic. With a flick of the reins, she turns her horse, riding counter-clockwise around the pen, first a slow warm-up walk, then a trot, and finally a canter. She bounces up and down in the saddle, dust clouds swirling as she rides past, strands of her royal-colored hair poking out from underneath her helmet. I video her.

Just so you know, I yell, I'm recording this.

She straightens up in the saddle.

Brothers are supposed to ask first, she says, riding away from me, making another loop, looking regal on her auburn horse. I can't take my eyes off her. I remember the first and only time she took me horseback riding, in high school:

Relax, she told me, the horse will feel your fear.

I tried, but I felt so out of control, no gas pedal, no brake, the reins doing nothing to alleviate that. The horse realized how clueless I was, taking off like a wild mustang. All I could do was hold on for dear life, my arm clamped around its neck, one foot in a stirrup, the other dangling uselessly to the side. I'd never been so scared. Gaia said I screamed. Thank goddess the horse eventually tired and Gaia caught up with us. Embarrassed as all get-up, I begged her not to tell anyone, especially Miguel. She never did.

I now notice my drone has returned, hovering, checking out Gaia as she passes, bouncing up and down in the saddle. Watching her, the minutes pass like seconds. I'm disappointed when she climbs down off her mount and ties Magic to a post. She pats his long reddish forehead, just above the white misshapen star that looks like a dripping paintbrush stroke. Gaia offers a small apple in her palm. The horse chomps with his massive teeth.

You know you can't post your recordings on *It*.

I'm posting on the dark *It*.

Why?

I wanna be remembered.

That's rich, Bryan, you've got a thousand offspring out there.

They won't know me from Adam.

Do they need to? Your spirit is in them.

I want them to know who I was.

Sounds like you're egoing.

I wanna turn my recordings into a book.

Ah, I see. You want my help.

You have connections.

I can't sell it at my store.

I know that.

Besides, I don't like memoirs.

Gaia removes the saddle and wipes sweat off Magic's back.

I turn forty in a little over a week.

Welcome to the club.

Shit, I think to myself, I forgot her birthday. So much going on right now. The summer insect chatter suddenly sounds louder and a horse neighs from another stable, as if gossiping about my blunder.

Gaia lovingly brushes Magic's shiny coat with long, self-absorbed strokes, and her black mane as if a child's long hair. The mane looks so silky, but I've been around horses enough to know that the hair is almost always coarse.

So what are your plans? she asks. I don't see you on the run.

I don't either.

Just the suggestion triggers my left leg, quaking up and down, the toes tapping the fence post, the energy twisting up into a knot in my gut. I stop recording.

When did that start?

A few weeks ago.

She looks me up and down.

It's your breathing.

What about it?

It's too shallow.

What's that got to do with my leg?

Everything. She breathes deeply, demonstrating, exhaling slowly. Breathing keeps you grounded.

I follow her lead, feeling silly, like I do every time she points out my deficiencies. But I have to admit, my left leg now twitches less.

There's nothing more important than your breath, she says, it's the first thing you do when you're born and the last thing you do when you die.

Seeing as how that day is coming soon—

106

Oh stop it. You're not going to die, you're just being put out to pasture.

I need to change the subject, the twitch in my left leg is amping up again.

I saw Miguel a few minutes ago.

Her brushing of Magic grows more vigorous.

Oh really? How is Harry?

Intense as always.

They say he's an Undergrounder, did you know that?

Hardly, he was protesting in plain sight.

A great blue heron lifts off from a field and soars overheard with grace and power, its neck stretched long. Our eyes follow the smooth flight, a straight line against the now-cloudless blue sky. It's one of those moments when you feel greatly connected to the universe. I don't know how many more beautiful birds I will witness, how many more things I will share with Gaia.

Goddess ignored the blueprints when she created us, she says.

How so?

Nature's balanced, right? Light and dark. Good and evil.

Brother and Sister. So?

Think about it. When it comes to humans—and most mammals—Sisters supply everything: the egg, the womb, the birthing hips, placenta, breasts, milk. Love. All you brothers do is supply the sperm.

We give love, I argue. We feed them.

From *our* milk.

You think Goddess intended us to become obsolete?

Maybe. But if so, why create you at all?

She must've wanted us.

107

Maybe she grew tired of you.

I think you all have.

Yeah, you're lucky you've survived this long.

Tell me something I don't already know.

She smiles with those captivating green eyes.

I admire how you can still be friends with me after all that's happened.

Friends forever.

Translation—you still want to sleep with me.

That'd be a death sentence.

You still fantasize about it.

That ship sailed a long time ago.

Has it?

I don't reply. Who am I kidding? Not her, as she knocks dirt off the brushes.

Do you know what a relief it is not to have to work to attract you guys?

You never had to work at it.

You know what I mean.

You still have to attract other Sisters.

Not the same thing at all. We understand each other. We connect.

Sounds simplistic to me.

That's just it. Things are way simpler without brothers.

She explains why in great detail but I can't help feel that it is rote, more propaganda than heartfelt truth.

Are you saying you don't wanna hang with me anymore?

Not at all, I like hanging with you. You've always had a little Sister inside you.

She returns the brushes to her tack caddy. Her phone pings. She reads a text.

Oh geez, I didn't realize it was so late. I have to get back to the store. Come by. I made a new tincture, Kava Karma, it's infused with two CBDs. She looks down at my leg that hasn't stopped shaking. Looks like you could use it.

She turns her Morgan toward the stall, sidestepping piles of manure, walking stride-for-stride, almost as if she were an appendage of her horse. I should offer to feed Magic or muck the stall, but it feels like it's time to go. I leap down off the fence.

I'll stop by soon.

Be well.

She mucks, dumping it into a rusted bucket while I jog towards home, rejuvenated by a visit with an old friend. Before I know it, I pass the Sister Officer sitting in her cruiser. We nod. I come upon the brother protestors marching and holding up their *Ad-Trons* at the intersection. Miguel and I make eye contact. He looks beyond me, glaring in the direction I came—from Gaia's stable.

I go into a funk. I need to do something, I can't just wait for my death sentence. I text for a broCar and wait outside the Queenwood Center gates, sweating like it was late July. This "brother summer" is lingering and I take that as an omen, that I should not let go either. I watch a black homeless brother sitting on a broken bus bench that's never used anymore, sorting through a ratty backpack. I've seen him hanging around here once or twice. He wears a faded black t-shirt with stark letters:

I SKIPPED THE CLASS
WHERE THEY
EXPLAINED EVERYTHING

His hair is wind-swept, his skin leathery, the veins in his hands twisted like gnarled trees. He wears bright blue Crocs over thick socks. He has no belongings that I can see, except that backpack. He hunches over like a stalk of wheat in a slight breeze, not broken, not feeble yet, but he's getting there.

My ride pulls up, a driverless silver broCar, a bro-only sign on the back door. I climb in and buckle up. The homeless brother watches me, his eyes glazed. A large, tight grin slices his walnut-shelled face. I suddenly feel very creepy.

That could soon be me.

SISTER MOTHER

The broCar drops me off outside The Sisters of Mercy, a sprawling single-story nursing home. My little drone hovers outside as I enter the bro-only side door and bypass the lobby lined with Elderly Sisters, some waiting to die, some just waiting, forgotten, their husbands and sons all gone. I never see other brothers here, resident or visitor. I walk past paintings lining the walls, charming landscapes of forests and canyons and beaches, constant reminders of how beautiful life should be, but probably never was, and definitely isn't any more for these old souls. I hear TVs talking over each other—GMA, Fox/CNN News, soap operas, nature channels—punctuated by the groaning and moaning and snoring of old age. I walk past one room where two Gamer Sisters, one large and loud, the other small and feeble, laugh and battle it out on Final Fantasy on a classic PS4. The controller drops from Feeble Sister's hands into her lap.

Oh fudge, she says softly, I give up.

Oh no you don't, Loud Sister says, wedging the controller back into Feeble Sister's hands. Keep playing! You're doing great!

I turn right, down another hall, turn left, and I'm here. Room 15. I hear the wailing sax of Bob Seger's Turn The Page. Mom loves her Classic Rock. I push in the half-opened door, the sharp scents of hospital bleach and stargazer lilies scorching my nose, even through my mask. Baskets of mums and tiny roses hang from curtain rods and are crammed on cabinets, crowding out medicines, ointments and nail polish bottles on the nightstand. My mother Ellen lies in bed, asleep, seventy-three, creamy white, with bright red lipstick and meticulously-painted red nails. She looks sharp, even if her mind isn't. When I was growing up, she was a quiet saint, hard-working, always there for us physically but never emotionally. Buck up, she'd tell us if we even considered shedding a tear over a sprained ankle. Half-Irish, half-German—there's a Celtic cross on the wall, a large beer stein as a vase—she functioned like a machine all her life, doing what was expected of her as a working wife and mother. She grew up in the era of burning bras, but she still handwashed hers and hung them to dry. I've never heard a story of her breaking a law, a rule, or even a heart.

Pops, on the other hand, would enter a room happy and joking, demanding to be the center of attention. In a group with him around, mom wouldn't say anything. Pops *would* say anything, something he shouldn't have said, something racist or sexist, never meaning to be offensive, simply not realizing he was. Mom would correct him, he would ignore her.

Mom's memory is not well at all. Docs say it's not Alzheimer's—old-timer's as she calls it—instead it's DDS, Death Doldrums Syndrome, a newly added diagnosis to DSM-VI, the psychiatrists' bible. The condition is defined as an apathetic outlook on life due specifically to the numbness caused by constant death. It's a very specific depression categorized by amnesia. Mom does not remember anything recent, not The Change, not The War, not The Y. I think she just doesn't wanna remember the loss of every man she's ever known. I am the only brother left in her life and she remembers me only in the past.

I stand in the doorway and watch her sleep, a large print book, always a mystery of some sort, opened up on top of a Rock 'N' Roll Hall of Fame blanket spread across her lap. I don't know why she bothers, she never gets closer to solving it. She just re-reads the same two pages, not realizing she's already read them, not really caring that she has. Our conversation never strays far from small talk. I'm jealous, in a way, of how she can't remember all the horrible things that have happened.

I put up with her soft, repetitive questions:

Where do you live?

What is it you do again?

Why are you wearing that silly mask? Covid's over.

(Click and repeat.)

All her life, she served my father and supported his schemes and dreams. They divorced years ago, but remained friends. She got infected before anybody knew about the virus. She went to a movie with my brother, they shared a tub of popcorn. Two weeks later, Tommy was diagnosed with The Y. He doesn't know if he got it from her, but he called to tell her he had it, only got her voicemail. He texted her but she never checks her texts. She was eating with pops at Olive Garden and after dinner kissed him goodbye, lightly on the lips. Soon, he was diagnosed too. When Tommy died, mom lost hope. When pops died, she lost even the desire for hope.

She talks about the Challenger explosion and 9-11, fondly, like they were just yesterday, how Americans pulled together in a time of

113

crisis and treated each other more humanely, if only for a short while. She is nostalgic for a less-tragic hard time.

Dust In The Wind by Kansas now plays. I wanna record mom, but she's soft-spoken, so I turn off her JBL speaker. I take a deep breath, hold it in, and move closer, breaking the 2-10 protocol, placing my phone on her rollaway bedside table, pointing the mic toward her. A Sister Caregiver enters at the exact moment I tap record.

What are you doing?!

I step back toward the doorway, sheepishly. Sister Caregiver fiddles with a machine monitoring mom's vitals. A good minute passes before mom's eyes open and she looks over at me.

Oh, hello. Um——

Bryan.

Yes, I know. Come sit next to me.

I can't, mom.

Sister Caregiver shoots me a nasty look.

I mean *Sister Mother.*

I just can't get used to calling mom anything but mom, but my correction appeases Sister Caregiver and she goes about her business. Mom squints her eyes at me.

Why do you wear that silly thing?

I've got a cold.

So wear a scarf.

I don't wanna get you sick.

You've never gotten me sick a day in your life.

I pull a few fading petals off a chrysanthemum in a basket near the door.

So where is it you're working now? mom asks, struggling to find info in her shrinking databank. It's so sad to see the woman who taught me how to walk and cook pasta and use a computer and be faithful to one person, to see her fading away so rapidly.

Are you bartending?

No. I used to.

Working at that office?

Used to.

What was it?

Sales.

I had been a budtender at a dispensary in the first couple years after legalization. I told her I worked in sales, which, technically, I did.

What are you doing now? A flash of excitement crosses her face. Are you still teaching?

Here I usually give in and say yes, my gift to her. She likes remembering me as a teacher and doesn't recall my being put on administrative leave. But because I'm recording this on my cell, I tell the truth.

I provide sperm.

Sister Caregiver's eyebrows rise.

You what? mom says.

I make sperm.

Mom twists her face into a scrunchie.

Does that bother you? I say.

Sperm?

No. What I do.

Oh, I don't know, the world these days, I don't know.

A few months ago, I had described to her the scientific details of my job: the impersonal Mr. Suck, the journey of my sperm through the machinery, the fertilization process, the works. She was quite disturbed for a few moments, then forgot.

Come closer, she now says, you're too far away.

I can't, mom.

Sister Caregiver shoots me a needle-sharp eye.

Oh get a grip, I say, can we have some privacy?

She leaves the room in a huff, probably to report me. Mom flicks her TV remote and turns on The Sister Hour talk show.

I saw Gaia today.

Who?

Gaia. From school.

Oh yes, yes, how is she?

Same ol' Gaia.

I never liked her that much.

That was one of mom's many "secrets." She never explained why, as usual, probably saw how tortured I was by love. She gazes somewhere between the TV and the book in her lap. I step forward, snatch my cell from the bedside stand, and step back into the doorway. I'm sure the mic picks up my sniffles.

I have to go.

Where are you going?

Home.

You are home.

No, mom, this is *your* home.

She looks up at the TV and down at the book in her lap and seems to be trying to remember which one she was doing. She looks over at me.

What is it you do again? Are you teaching?

Yes, mom.

I raise my gloved hand to my masked mouth and blow her a kiss goodbye.

I love you, mom.

I know you do, she says. I do too.

She lowers her eyes, down at the never-to-be-solved mystery in her lap. I turn to leave, wondering which one of us will die first, knowing most odds are on me. Mom's as strong as an ox and could live for many years to come.

I step out of her room. At one end of the hall, Sister Caregiver talks to Security Sisters. I head the other direction, toward the bro-only exit. Security doesn't follow me, probably doesn't consider me enough of a threat, just a nuisance who's leaving anyway.

Minutes later, I stare out the back window of another broCar, still thinking of mom. I'm dropped off at the entrance to Queenwood Center, my hummingbird drone levitating behind me. Across the street, I see the black homeless brother again, sitting on that same broken bus bench. He looks to be in his 50's, wearing a plush golden sweater, the sleeves rolled up to the elbows, shimmering in the heat. Brothers can score some great clothes these days from all the abandoned closets. I notice his filthy gray feet, still encased in muddy blue Crocs.

He catches my stare with his bloodshot eyes, mumbles something, digging into his backpack, his fingernails cracked and soiled. He removes a length of loose dental floss. He lowers his brobot mask and wriggles the floss between his teeth, solid and straight, if horribly yellowed. He reminds me of somebody.

I nowha u r, he mumbles, flossing.

What am I? I ask, fluent in mumble.

He pulls the strand of floss through his teeth.

You're lost.

Aren't we all?

Not like you. You're on the wrong side.

I'm still alive.

For how much longer?

Now that's the rub.

I can see your aura, dude. It oozes fear.

That's it. The Dude. He reminds me of Jeff Bridges in The Big Lebowski, one of pops' favorite films, we watched it all the time. Except this guy is The Black Dude. He chuckles to himself, bunching the floss into a small ball, stuffing it into a pocket. My drone is bored and drifts off.

If you're so smart, I say, why are you living out here?

He zips up his pack.

I go inside when the weather's bad. But Big Sister is a bitch, man. She sees everything. They find me, kick me out, I hate all the in-and-out. 'sides, the streets are safe enough for now. Sisters don't bother you, not like brothers used to. 'cept for a few feminazis.

And Sister Kissers.

Yeah, always watch out for those.

He leans back on the bench and fits his gloves on and looks up at the half-bare crowns of trees.

118

I feel freer out here, he says, closing his eyes, his skin warmed by the sun. And freedom is about all we got left.

***

In the evening I stroll the grounds of Queenwood Center, keeping my distance from Sister Visitors. The forest sounds soothe me: the birds' chirping goodnight, the crickets' chirring hello. I sit on a stone bench and admire the sparkle of fireflies blinking around the barks of the trees. Above the treetops, puffy pink clouds float in violet twilight.

Psst!

I look around, see no one.

Up here!

I look up at what first looks like a large firefly, but is just the glow of a cell phone, way up in a massive American sycamore.

Bernie? What the fuck?

I know, wild, huh?

He sits like chubby Buddha in the lotus position on the ledge of a half-built treehouse. My little drone rises to check him out.

Come on up.

He shines his cell flashlight down the trunk, illuminating foot-long planks nailed as steps into the mottled trunk.

When did you do that?

Last couple days.

I hesitate. It's getting dark and that's a long climb, he's at least forty feet up.

I'll take a raincheck, I say.

Anytime.

How's the view?

Divine.

Sitting at the base of this tree, with Bernie the Buddha up in it, I think how this is a moment ripe to peel away the small talk:

Bernie, what do you think happens to us when we die?

You must not dwell on that, he says, his voice floating down over me like a leaf. The future is an illusion. So is the past. The present is all we've got. Don't worry, on a karmic calculator, I think you're on the plus side.

Unlike most platitudes I see and hear, this one actually makes me feel a bit better.

This will pass, he says. Every sickness has its cure in nature.

So you're believe there's a vaccine?

You misunderstood me. We're the sickness. All of this is the cure.

I don't even wanna think about that, I yawn. Think I'll head in.

Of course. Have a nice sunset.

I look up. From what little I can see through the trees, the sky's spectacular, a purplish-blue with pink puffs of cotton candy bleeding orange.

You have a nice sunset too, Bernie.

Back inside The Factory, I play my Martin steel string in the drawing room. Everyone else is holed-up in their bedrooms. Jonathan, our father-brother, walks a beeline from one end of the long room toward me.

You haven't put in any work today, he says, his form of hello. You sick?

Not in the mood.

Not in the mood to make money?

His thumbs type on his cell screen.

Seriously? You're gonna write me up?

120

I don't think you're in a position to be taking time off.

That's exactly the position I'll be in soon.

He types. Stops.

Should I hit send?

Fine, I say. I'll go finger the fretboard.

Good. Numbers, Bryan, numbers.

He busies himself, tidying up the room, picking up empty chip bags and pop bottles, the detritus of twenty-and-thirtysomethings. I slouch upstairs, disappear into the bathroom, and get down to work. It's uninspiring. But I provide my usual quality product.

DINNER AT THE FACTORY

Once a week we dine together, a weekly Appleseed ritual, for a sense of normalcy in this abnormal time. Before we can sit down at the table, we have to test negative. After we do, it's a chance to sit, mask-less, around the eight-chaired antique dining table, underneath a lacey-looking chandelier, surrounded by faded French floral wallpaper and light gray curtains bordering four eight-foot-high windows. A ghetto Versailles, still much too elegant for us. We tear three pizzas apart and rip into bags of chips, washing it down with pop. Drew sits in Abercrombie attire, Steven in camo, Cody in slippers and a beanie, Kimchi in an old torn BTS shirt. André's tight dreads dangle like a curtain around his plate. Bernie munches on sprouts in a saffron robe. Selfie is locked away in his room as usual, father-brother Jonathan is nowhere to be seen, and Killer sits in the corner, licking himself.

This room is digital-free, a house rule. No screens on the walls, no devices on the table, in here we force ourselves to communicate the old-fashioned way—we talk. I make an exception tonight, telling them ahead of time I'm recording us but I keep my phone out of sight, under the table, on the one empty chair.

EDITOR'S NOTE: For ease of use I present the dialogue in theatrical format. Not that anybody goes to plays anymore.

STEVEN (THE EX-MARINE): This pizza sucks.

DREW (THE MACHO DANDY): They always give us the old dough.

KIMCHI: Thin crust is better. Nobody listen.

We complain yet fight for extra slices, seven pairs of grabby hands.

CODY (THE NEXT ME): You ever, like, think things will

       get back to normal?

ME: You're not even old enough to know what normal is.

KIMCHI: Normal will return. After disaster, always return.

BERNIE (THE BUDDHIST): We must accept this as the new normal.

ANDRÉ (DREADLOCK SPOCK): That's some Pollyanna bullshit.

KIMCHI: What is Pollyanna?

ANDRÉ: Not what. Who. It's from an old children's book. She was a

       young girl who put a positive spin on everything.

STEVEN: How the hell you know that?

ANDRÉ: Because I read, jarhead.

Drew cranks up some Sista Rap and our dessert turns into a verbal game, typically at Sisters' expense. We keep our voices low, letting the music drown us out.

DREW: I got one: Sisters are awesome and anxious.

STEVEN: Okay, I got ya. They're beautiful and bitchy.

CODY: Cuddly and cruel.

ME: Deep and dark.

BERNIE: Enlightened and enigmatic.

ANDRÉ: Fabulous and fucked-up.

KIMCHI: Gorgeous and gossipy.

DREW: Hot and hoes.

We get stuck on "i" and the game fizzles out. We're not real deep in this house.

DREW: You know what I hate? I can't stomach the blasé way
        Sisters have accepted everything.

BERNIE: They can be praying mantises.

DREW: Where's the love?

STEVEN: Where's the obedience?

ANDRÉ: Where's the vaccine?

ALL: Fuck yeah, where's the vaccine?!

ME: (shaking my head) We live like we're stuck in second gear.

Kimchi and Cody, the younger ones, look confused.

DREW: Neither of you have driven, have you?

KIMCHI: Why would we?

Drew, Steven and I share disbelieving stares.

ANDRÉ: (teasingly) What do you Millennials miss most
        from back in the day?

STEVEN: NASCAR.

ME: Music festivals.

DREW: Football.

DREW, STEVEN & ME: Cheerleaders.

CODY: You need to put all that into, like, a brothers
        museum.

DREW: You newbies don't know how good we had it. Hell,
        we didn't know. It was a Garden of Eden.

STEVEN: At least we thought it was.

DREW: We had privacy.

STEVEN: We could travel wherever we wanted.

ME: Privacy, travel, hmm, those ring a distant bell.

CODY: I don't have the patience for, like, nostalgia.

DREW: That's cause you don't have anything to be
      nostalgic about.

ME: I love the past. I just can't imagine the future.

STEVEN: Don't you pansies get all weepy on me. We are
      still men. We're survivors. Act like it.

Our bitch-fests usually end with a toast. We raise our glasses of pop.
We rarely drink alcohol, it's bad for production.

ANDRÉ: (softly) Screw Sisters.

We clink glasses.

ALL: I wish we could!

Drew gives me a knowing look. I glance away, down at the leftover
pizza crusts on my plate. He's the only one who knows about my
weekly hookups.

CODY: You guys think this is all a part of, like, evolution?

ANDRÉ: It's evolving a hole inside of me.

STEVEN: In your case an asshole.

ANDRÉ: Empty, man, just empty.

DREW: Listen to you all marinate in your own stupidity.

ME: Our world has been robbed of hope.

BERNIE: I still have hope.

KIMCHI: Hope is four-letter word.

CODY: (kicks his chair away from table) You guys are,
      like, bumming me out. I'ma go put some, like,
      cream in my coffee.

He heads up to the third floor.

We reconvene in the drawing room, lounging on the overstuffed furniture, the screens bursting with battles and explosions and people doing silly dances and animals doing funny things, all with no sound, except for the tapping of fingertips on devices. Everyone's got AirPods or SisBuds in their ears. I've got a book, an actual, real book in my hands: *A Fucked-Up New World*.

Father-brother Jonathan comes down the stairs, enters the dining room then re-emerges.

Clean up your mess, guys, I'm not your mother.

Thank god for that, Drew says.

I mean it.

No one budges. Jonathan will clean it up, he always does.

If you'll excuse me, Steven says, it's time to polish the chrome.

He disappears upstairs.

Drew roughhouses with Killer, working the big labradoodle into a frenzy, throwing a tennis ball down the long, wide hallway. Killer fetches it, slipping and sliding.

I head up to my room. Usually I make my daily deposit before bed, to help me sleep, but on Wednesdays I deposit in the morning. I see Miriam in a little less than seven hours and don't wanna waste my ammo. I lay in bed, thinking about how I've been lucky, insulated from so much of the darkness out there. Sisters don't hurt us, brothers don't bother us.

You busy? Cody says, appearing in my doorway.

Just contemplating life.

Sweet. You, like, mind?

He grabs my guitar, curls his gloved fingers around the fretboard. The strings sound muted.

126

You're gonna have to take those off.

Oh yeah, duh.

Cody removes his gloves.

Do you remember a C chord? I ask.

Naw. I, like, forgot. Show me.

I demonstrate with my gloved left hand how to finger a basic C chord. He struggles to form it, the strings buzz, normal for a beginner. I reposition his ring finger.

Guys never wanna use our ring fingers, I joke.

Cody doesn't get it. He strums a couple times, then arpeggios and looks up at me for approval.

It's getting less buzzy, I say.

I leave him space to fiddle, while I look around my large, old room, taking quick inventory of my meager possessions: my guitar in Cody's hands, my digital devices, a few toiletries, my clothes, some books. Can't take much with me, can't go home, can't blend in anywhere, can't imagine going underground.

Ow! Cody says, sucking on a fingertip.

Don't worry, you'll develop calluses.

Show me later?

Anytime.

I lie in bed, can't sleep, my thoughts swirl, excited to see Miriam, sure, but I realize this might be our next-to-last time. I turn 40 in a couple weeks. The bedsheet shivers on top of my twitching left foot. It sucks fearing the thing you most look forward to. I get up and wander down the wide staircase, heading toward the kitchen for something sweet. I hear a heavy clank-clank coming from the library at the end of the hallway. I check it out, the walls lined with shelves holding a thousand dusty books. Few, if any, have even been opened, at least not in this millennium. I imagine my own words bound in a book up on a shelf. Someday.

The typical armchairs and tables with reading lamps are gone, replaced by weight machines, two treadmills and a stationary bike. Steven is alone in here, in his camo outfit, pumping iron, bench-pressing three hundred pounds. The room smells like musty books and sweat.

Since when do you come in here? Steven grunts between reps.

Can't sleep. I feel like I'm waiting on death row.

Would you rather—grunt—death came by surprise?

I think I would, yeah.

Steven lets the weights clang down hard. I flinch.

Not me, Steven says, I wanna know the exact moment I die.

Why?

He sits up, mops his sweat with a towel, and lowers his voice:

So I can flip off the fucken' Sisterhood before I go.

He rises from the bench, drapes the towel over his shoulders, swigs from a Purple Cow energy drink and heads toward the hallway.

You need to get prepared, he says, all of you pussies need to get prepared.

HOOK-UP #2

It's Oct. 7, a Thursday, always the easiest day to get out of bed. I pop my vitamins and Viagra and I'm out the door. I do my stretches—nothing snaps, always a good sign—and I run my usual Thursday morning route, without my drone trailing me, all alone except for the tentacles of breath seeping out from the filter of my brobot mask, the first time I've seen my breath in months. Wind bites my cheeks, cracks my skin. The weather has turned, a drop of nearly forty degrees since yesterday. Even Mother Nature seems against me.

I didn't dress properly, just in a thin t-shirt and shorts, feeling as naked and insignificant as a leaf, but if I go back for warmer clothes I'll be late, and if I'm not there, Miriam might take off. Something is up ahead, crumpled alongside the bro-only lane, I know what it is instantly, a brother, draped off the edge of the pavement, one arm dangling down into a ditch, the other bent up, touching his face. As I get closer, I notice the light coating of frost on skin and clothing. I don't stop. Sister Sweepers will come along soon enough and heave the chilled brother into the back of a truck. If they are delayed, a disinfector drone will spray the corpse until the Sweepers can remove him. I give him a wide berth, stepping outside my lane, nodding, acknowledging his presence. Other than that, I give him the same attention as I do a dead bird or squirrel. Sounds harsh, I know. That's just the way it is.

I arrive at the Love Shack first, as always, no worries, thinking about what Drew said, about how I can't keep trusting Miriam, and I do need to hammer her harder about the vaccine. I've asked many times, never pressed, gotta be careful, she's in control.

I leave my cell on the kitchen table and go light the fireplace kindling. The flames crawl and rise, crack and snap, and lick their wicked tongues at me, smelling of cedar and pine. Humming approaches, don't know the name of the tune, I only know it's Taylor Swift. Miriam hums her just to bug me. The kitchen door opens, followed by the sounds of foreplay: a box tearing, wrapper ripping, plastic snapping, a soft grunt. Her humming resumes, a little softer.

Before I know it, Miriam stands in the doorway, smiling. Negative as always. I rise off the sofa and she comes to me and slowly removes my mask. She launches into her day's itinerary:

What a day I've got planned, a 7:30 this, a 10:00 that, two things at noon.

She talks and unbuttons and I listen and unzip until I can't listen anymore.

Miriam, is all your testing just a charade?

Her schedule recital grinds to a halt.

Well hello to you too.

You've been vaccinated, haven't you.

I press my left foot hard to the floor to keep it from trembling.

Where is this coming from? she asks.

I just want the truth.

I've told you the truth. I'm not a carrier.

130

That's so rare.

I have Native-American blood, you know that.

Just admit it.

Do we really have to do this? I get so tired of your conspiracies.

Vaccinate me and I'll stop.

You need to just simmer down, Bryan.

I promise I'll never ask another favor.

Even if it did exist, I couldn't risk my career giving it to you.

And your career is more important than my life.

Her eyes flash me a "You said it, I didn't" look.

I wish you trusted me.

All I do is trust you, I've trusted you too much.

She peels off my left glove.

I wanna keep trusting you, I add, more than anything.

Then do it, she implores, peeling off my right glove.

It's hard. I'm freaking out.

I can see that.

She pulls me closer, sinking down onto the long sofa. We lock lips and just like that I submit because I am, after all, a guy. I feel myself detach, watching her gyrate and arch her back and toss her hair around, sweat dripping from her glowing bod, a little bitter scent, like lightly burnt popcorn. I think of all the things I love about her. She's a lethal cocktail: intelligent, loves to laugh, fun in bed. She lets go when she's here, releases all that mayoral stress. For me, being with her is three hours of life the way it used to be. Or as I fantasize it used to be. But it's always the same dynamic, giving her what she wants, always trying to please, like a fucking housewife. I roll Miriam off me and onto her back, but this time I waste no time, thrusting as hard and as fast

131

as I can, groaning and grimacing. Normally I would explode in an instant at this pace, but no matter how hard I try, I can't climax. After a while we both tire of the gymnastics, it's just rote now, our passion in timeout, so I fake orgasm, pretending to do what I get paid to do every day, just so we can stop. Not climaxing is happening more frequently these days and I collapse. We fold into a cuddle, stare at the ceiling, catch our breaths. She gazes at me extra deeply, as if getting a good last look.

That was rougher than usual. Care to talk about it?

I don't have to say it, we both know why. Two weeks from forty, two weeks closer to being shut down, turned off, obsolete. My powerful lover can't protect me much longer.

Don't make me beg, Miriam.

Oh for goddess sake, Bryan.

She pushes me off and sits up in bed, first angry, then fighting back tears.

Jason died from it. Don't you think if there was a vaccine, I would've saved my own son? She rises off the sofa and walks across the room, naked. Normally, I would enjoy watching her nicely-curved cheeks, even with those little cottage-cheese patches of cellulite wobbling underneath, which I find oddly sexy. But now I feel nothing in my loins, I'm awash in doubt and disappointment.

So how will this work? Does it actually happen on my birthday?

We wouldn't be that insensitive, she says, pulling on her running pants. Sometime after that.

How soon after?

I'll let you know.

Promise?

132

I promise. Start thinking about where you want to retire.

If that's true, put me in touch with Denny Rogers.

Who's that?

He was the first Appleseed to leave. They retired him last year.

I can't do that.

Because he's dead?

No, because I don't know where he is. We're not allowed contact.

Why, are we pariahs?

A black market could follow retirees, she says, looking in a mirror, running her hands through her pillow hair. Believe me, Sisters are grateful for your service, she adds. I'll see you next week.

We say goodbye, an hour early, without even a kiss.

Halfway home, I give up running, walking back to The Factory, far too tired and sad. And now late. I spy Cody performing jumps on his skateboard and Drew walking Killer along a row of trees. Killer stops to poop, Drew stops to pee. He zips up and engages Cody in a way-too-intense conversation so early in the morning. I approach, they stop talking, and we get looks from some strolling Sister Visitors, the kind of looks Amish get from diners when they walk into a Denny's.

Killer sniffs and digs into a flower bed, on the scent of a critter.

Leave it, Drew commands.

Killer keeps digging.

Kill her!

The dog stops. I stiffen and glare at Drew.

What?

You said, "Kill her."

No I didn't.

Say it.

133

Kill-her.

Am I wrong, Cody? I ask.

It does kinda, like, sound like it.

Two peacocks strut past, they've lived here forever, the male puffing up his blue, green, and gold plumage. Three Teenage Sisters race over to snap photos, they must be playing hooky, freezing in t-shirts and shorts, refusing to let go of the last remnants of summer, paying no attention to us, not even as an oddity. They gather around a cell phone in a blonde's hand.

Are you crazy? That's ugly.

You're the crazy one.

You're both crazy cunts.

Fuck you.

Fuck both of you.

They giggle.

In case you didn't know, the C-word has been appropriated by Sisters, just as the N-word was by blacks and the B and F-words by pretty much everyone. The C-word has become so common that SisPunks, one of the first to push the word into the mainstream, have already abandoned it.

The blonde holds up her cell phone for a series of selfies. They flash their youthful smiles, for likes on social media, then critique the photos, swiping back and forth.

Does this one meet your fucking approval?

I don't think so.

If I have to pose for one more photo—

That one! It's fuckin' perfect.

The blonde's thumbs flutter over the screen, sending it goddess-knows-where.

Done.

They laugh and link arms and walk away, best of friends. Meanwhile, Killer tries to jump into a pond to chase after ducks. Drew yanks back on his leash. Not far away, two adorable Toddler Sisters play in grass. One chases a butterfly and falls flat on her tiny ass, looking like she might cry.

Do you wonder if every little girl you see is one of yours?

I assume most are, Drew says, not joking.

He loops Killer's leash to a fence post and then, out of nowhere, lunges at me, pulling me down into the grass.

What are you doing?!

Relax, I'm clean. I tested this morning.

I try to break free, but it's useless, so I put up a fight, also useless. Drew is playing with me like I'm a fish on the line. He loves horseplay. Cody laughs at us, grinding a rail on his board, as we draw an audience of Curious Sisters, mostly young. Wrestling is something they don't see anymore.

Drew spins me into a hold. This is a front chin lock, he says.

You can let go now. My voice is hoarse from the pressure.

He jerks my arm—

OW!

—twisting it over my head.

And this is an arm wrench.

STOP!

He flips me around and props me against his back, facing behind him. He spreads my arms out. And this is the crucifix, he says, falling backward onto me.

Oomph! I spit out grass as he spins around and wraps my head in the crook of his arm.

And this is—

—a half-nelson, I wheeze the words out. It's the one hold I know. He flips me like a pancake onto my back and pins me to the ground.

Uncle! I squeal.

He doesn't relent. I try one last time to squirm loose.

Say "I'm not gonna die."

I'm not gonna die.

Say it like you mean it.

I'm not gonna die!

Damn straight!!

He pounds the ground and releases me, laughing. I cough and massage my raw throat.

Asshole.

He feints like he's gonna wrap me up again, I flinch, he laughs.

You better come up with a plan soon, Drew says, unlooping Killer's leash from the fence post. You'll never make it out in the real world on your own.

I'm hearing that a lot lately, I say.

C'mon, Kill-her. Time for me to go pop the cork!

He, Cody, and the labradoodle amble off toward the house. I follow, limping, my every limb sore. My hummingbird drone spots me, awoken from its roost on the roof, just in time to see me approach the front door. I wave at it quickly before I enter The Factory.

'ROUND & GROUND

Thanks to Drew I'm too sore to do anything the next few days but make deposits and gather my survival supplies. I stack sweaters, sweatshirts, long underwear, digital devices, chargers, Power Bars, rolls of cash, a single Swiss Army knife. In the unlikely event that Miriam is correct, that I can pick a place to retire, I think about where I'd like to go. We Buckeyes love Florida. The Carolinas are nice too. Never been to California, always wanted to go, seems too scary to try now. Definitely somewhere warm, I don't wanna have to survive on cold-ass streets like these.

It's Saturday, Oct. 9. A broCar drops me off downtown at the corner of Main and Fourth, just off the Square, near the old-fashioned hand-carved carousel. A century ago there was a carousel factory here. My drone circles around the glorified merry-go-round full of Little Sisters and Sister Mothers riding the horses and unicorns, tigers and giraffes. My stomach turns every time I see the animals spin. Once in middle school, I came here with Gaia on a hot summer day. I bought us ice creams, she ordered strawberry, so I did too.

Let's ride! she squealed. She handed a couple dollars to the brother carousel operator and straddled a unicorn.

I can't, I said. I don't do circles.

You don't do circles? She laughed. What is that—you don't do circles?

I lowered my embarrassed eyes. She patted a tiger's back beside her unicorn.

If you ride next to me, maybe I'll give you that kiss you've always wanted.

She gripped the shiny brass bar that rose from between her bare, tanned legs. Her shorts were three-quarters of the way up her thighs. She leaned back on the unicorn in her green tank top, her Om earrings dangling.

You coming or not?

I couldn't move, couldn't even speak.

Suit yourself.

Gaia tilted her head back and closed her eyes. The brother operator, bored as hell, hooked the yellow chain across the front of the line, separating me from my beloved.

Wait!

I pressed two dollars into the operator's palm. With a yawn, he opened the chain and allowed me to pass. I climbed up on the tiger beside her. Gaia's face glowed. She reached over and took my hand and I gritted my teeth and smiled, filled with horror and joy as the operator pressed buttons and pulled levers. Calliope music swirled and so did we, creeping slowly, counter-clockwise, and I closed my eyes, sitting there next to Gaia. I remember thinking I can do this, squinting, unable to believe what I saw, our hands squeezed together, our fingers interlocked. The happiness on her face trumped the ugly knot in my gut. We swirled faster, my stomach churned rougher, and after three or four circles we were at full speed. I felt an elevator of vomit rise in my throat. I scrunched my eyes, hunched my shoulders, tightened my stomach, and fought like hell to keep that ice cream down. I opened one eye to see if Gaia even noticed. She was elated by the world revolving around us and for a split second, I was too, my fantasy spinning out of control and I couldn't hold it in any longer. I erupted, a strawberry lava flowing over our locked hands.

She yanked her fingers out of mine.

Gross!

I heard the laughter of other riders, children and adults, revolving 'round and 'round, on this long, spinning nightmare. I heaved again. I wanted to climb off and crawl down through a sidewalk grate and die and when the ride finally, mercifully came to an end, I stumbled off the carousel, bumped into a trash can, struggled to find my way back to equilibrium. I leaned against a wall with every step, somehow found the bathroom next to the gift shop, locked the door, and slumped on the floor. I pressed my back against the wall, next to the toilet now spinning alongside me. The tangy odor of urine filled my nose. My head and stomach swirled in opposite directions, pinkish puke dribbling down my chin.

I heard a light tap-tap-tap and Gaia's voice:

You okay in there?

I erupted again. I flushed, heaved, flushed, and after what seemed like an eternity, I rose and looked in the mirror. I didn't think it was possible, but I looked even paler than normal, my milky pallor now like sun-bleached bone. I washed my hands, rinsed out my mouth, wet-down my stained shirt, and sucked in deep breaths. I slowly pulled the bathroom door open and saw Gaia at the check-out counter with a unicorn keychain in her hand. I had planned to buy her

139

a token of our date, but now I wanted nothing to remind me of this day, only wanted to turn back the clock and refuse to ride.

The ride operator snarled at me, hosing the last of my stomach's contents off the carousel and surrounding pavement. A line of pissed-off riders waited. Gaia frowned at my chalky face.

You sure you're all right?

I nodded, weakly. She grabbed my head between her tiny hands.

A promise is a promise, she said.

She closed her eyes and planted the quickest kiss of all time on my lips. She let go and wiped her lips and hurried to a drinking fountain to rinse them off. The look of disgust on her face still haunts me. Gaia never brought it up again, not any of it, not the vomit, not the kiss, never told a soul. No wonder I liked her so much. Her legend solidified in my mind.

We never kissed again.

***

The riders twirl 'round and 'round, and I feel a deepening queasiness, a stomach-acid flashback. I turn away. Cattycorner from the carousel is Gaia's store, 'Round & Ground. Three Sister Customers sit at outdoor tables, focused on their devices. My drone hovers lower, as if trying to read what's on their screens. I peer at book titles in the large storefront window:

Is Your Soul An Innie or an Outtie?

A Sister Without A brother
Is Like
A Computer Without A Sausage

Carousel trinkets and postcards crowd the check-out counter. Behind it stands an apothecary cabinet, with drawers labeled calendula, echinacea, ginger, and sage, the scents tickling my nostrils. Bookshelves are devoted to Sisters' studies, spirituality, and biographies of famous Sisters. I see Gaia, her hair now a cobalt blue, so bright it's hard to look at anything else. The hue reminds me of the famous stained-glass windows at Chartres Cathedral in France. My ex-wife and I visited there on our honeymoon, a tour of old churches and castle ruins, the tour lasting almost as long as our marriage.

I wait outside the open door, listening to Gaia explain a book to a Sister Customer:

In Norse mythology, the Norns are a trio of Sisters who rule the past, present, and future destiny of gods and Sisters. They create and control fate, weaving tapestries of destiny at the center of the cosmos.

Sounds like gibberish of the goddesses to me, but her passion sucks me in. I think of my own Norns: mom, ruler of my past; Miriam, ruler of my present; and Gaia herself, ruler of my legacy, if she'll agree to edit my ramblings. Gaia rings up the sale. She sees me, grabs a small amber bottle from a counter display case, and comes outside, wearing a flowing gold top with a fashionable hole the size of a pancake, exposing her Om tattoo around her belly button. Oh to be that Om.

She sets the tincture bottle down on a table.

Kava Karma. Just a drop or two. I think you'll like it.

I hope so.

You still anxiousing?

A little bit, I lie.

Since the virus might linger on the bottle from her fingertips—2-10—I let it set.

I like your hair, I say.

Really? I think it clashes with my eyes.

It does. I sing: *Green-eyed lady, lovely lady*. Remember?

Of course. She smiles.

On a table, next to a half-empty coffee cup, I notice a book, Life Without brothers. I leaf through it.

In another generation or two, what do you think Sisters will be like without brothers?

Pretty successful. Pretty lonely too. We're gonna miss you guys.

Sister Customers look up from their digital devices, some doubt it, some believe it, but all eyes have an opinion.

There is a hole in each Sister, Gaia declares, like it or not.

The Sister Customers don't argue that and return to their devices. I think about how Miriam said the same thing and I think about the black hole I would feel if things were reversed, if all Sisters I knew were dead. That would suck, but would I get over it, I wonder, and adapt like they have? I've waited long enough, so I open the tincture bottle, unscrew the dropper and squeeze out the dark honey-colored liquid, holding the dropper under my tongue, like a toothpick.

Let me know what you think, she says. Good or bad.

I 'ill. I 'omise.

A brown brother walks by, south on Main, in the bro-only lane. He gives a quick look at us. Followed by a long second look at Gaia.

Did you see that?

I'm 'ure he men' 'nohin', I mumble, the dropper dangling from my lips. I remove it.

142

Oh, he meant something. I can't let that go.

It's not worth it——

Hey!

The brother walks on.

I said, "Hey, bro!"

The brown brother stops, stiffly, reluctantly.

Show a little respect to a Sister next time.

He turns, looks at her, then down at the sidewalk.

We don't just expect it, she says, we demand it.

Yes sir.

Yes what??

Yes. Sister.

All right then. Go on your way.

He gives me a look of contempt by association and then resumes walking. She winks at me, then snaps back at him.

Hey!

He stops. Turns.

I like your shoes.

They are nice, I agree, two-toned brown loafers. Gaia then waves to the brother to move along, which he does. She smiles at me.

Power never gets old, does it.

***

I feel a little tingly from Gaia's tincture, as a broCar drops me off at the Queenwood Center gate. My drone hovers above me then gets bored and flies over to the intersection of Trimble and Park Avenue, watching a steady flow of Sisters in fancy, self-driving cars: Lexus, Mercedes, and Nemesis. I see the black homeless brother sprawled out on the rolling lawn between the road and the forest. He looks

143

rather content gazing up at the tops of trees. He sees me and his unmasked nostrils flicker, as if a predator smelling prey. He pulls up his latex mask.

You're becoming a regular here, I say.

It's close to Betty's Burgers. They got the best fries.

You wanna come in and look around?

Hell no, I see all I need to see from here.

He gets me thinking: You mind if I record you? I'm doing an oral history of my life.

What do I know about your life?

Tell me about yours.

No, not today, man, not today. Tomorrow. If I'm around.

I'm pretty sure he'll be around, I think to myself.

Ok, I say, maybe tomorrow.

I wonder what could be so different from today to tomorrow but then I think how fragile his existence is, how fragile any brother's existence is, and I don't push it.

You need anything?

He looks at me as if I just asked him a complicated mathematical question. He gazes up at the trees and incoming gray storm clouds.

Well, have a good day, I say, heading down the winding path, toward the small patch of forest—

Shoes.

I stop.

Good shoes.

I look down at his feet in those filthy blue Crocs.

Clothes, coats, empty houses, you can find all of those, he says, but decent shoes, they're gold.

144

A'ight. What kind? Jordans? Mahomes?

Uggs.

Uggs?

Yeah, Uggs. You're old enough to remember Uggs, ain't ya?

Oh yeah, I remember Uggs.

Those muthers are comfortable.

Okay, I'll see what I can do.

Weather-treated.

Got it.

I walk on, wondering if we brothers have become as shoe-obsessed as Sisters. Brothers don't have much, but at least our feet should feel comfortable, right?

Size eleven! he calls out so the whole block can hear.

I find an online store, Shoeby's that still stocks Uggs. From my bedroom, I order a pair, pay extra for weather treatment and the next day there is a box of tan Uggs waiting on our doorstep.

YOU CAN'T GO HOME

I ride a broCar down nostalgia lane, through the suburban 'hood I grew up in. I marvel at the towering trees, swear they've doubled in size since I was a kid. There are few fences, yards just blend together, great for ball-playing kids. We turn onto Fleming Falls Road and stop at the brick single-story ranch house. I haven't been back here in the two-and-a-half years since dad died, couldn't muster the strength. The house felt like a funeral home. I let myself in with my old key and stroll down the hallway gallery tracing our family evolution: baby pictures, Easter outfits, my Sis's wedding photos. Then the pictures stop, as if our timeline froze. Soon after her wedding, my parents divorced.

I straighten my fourth-grade picture. I had white-blonde hair then, a tow-head surrounded by my raven-haired family. They all wore glasses, I didn't. They were conservative, I was liberal. The hair, the glasses, the politics—I always believed I was adopted. My older brother Tommy had photo albums neatly arranged and captioned in a shrine to the first-born. I never saw my baby photos. Kindergarten seemed to be when I came into photographic existence.

Your baby pictures are in a box in a closet, mom would say.

146

In high school, I blabbed to all my friends that I was adopted and they blabbed to their parents who blabbed to mine. Only then did mom bring out my box of baby photos—infant nudes, first bath, first crawl—and she made me look at every embarrassing one. I felt overwhelmed. After that day, it took another ten years for her to put them into an album.

I now stand in the doorway of the bedroom I shared with Tommy, the room he died in. There are our twin beds. I grew up with a Teenage Mutant Ninja Turtles blanket and graduated to a Harry Potter comforter. Tommy had a Cleveland Indians quilt and later a NASCAR. All since donated to Goodwill. Today our beds are covered with matching bright pink floral bedspreads. Yuck. My bedroom morphed into a guest room, for guests that no longer come. The bookshelves have been overrun by mom's tchotchkes, Amish fiction, and every Barbara Kingsolver novel. Photos of my brother and I remain: on our Little League teams, at Cedar Point Amusement Park, our high school graduations, and a small picture of my wedding. Proof that I had grown up here, a part of the history of this house, the museum of my life, the only one that will ever exist.

I grab the one photo from the wall above Tommy's old bed, one of the last photos ever taken of him. He doesn't look sick, just lost. Growing up, he was never lost, he always knew what he was doing. He was a good brother, did what older brothers are supposed to do, he had my back several times. And I wasn't there for him when he died. To see a picture of him like this, over his old bed, makes me wonder what my last picture will look like.

Bryan?

I poke my head out the bedroom doorway. My Sister Sis, Emily, five years younger, stands at the other end of the hallway, her brunette hair speckled with gray, dressed business-casual with a glittery, fake Gucci mask for my benefit.

How do I look?

She models a profile pose that soon collapses under the weight of her own giggles.

I hate these things, she says, tugging on her fancy mask.

You and me both.

Emily is as sweet as they come, an old-fashioned Sister, like my mom, not thrilled with the world today, she'd rather have things back the way they were. She still cooks meat and potatoes, listens to country, refuses to become a lesbian, refuses to accept that this is God—not Goddess's—will.

I'm breaking with the Sisterhood over this one, she often says.

Her husband died soon after our dad. She now maintains our old home, can't bring herself to sell it, even though she lives an hour away. I'm grateful that she doesn't sell, since the Museum of Bryan is here. When it closes, my artifacts will be dispersed to her attic or, more likely, the trash.

I listen to her first-world problems: a leaky hot water heater, the gardener ripping her off, problems at work. I shake my head at what sounds super trivial to me.

What are you complaining about, you're a Sister.

Life's not so easy, let me tell you.

Trade you.

She holds up a GE clock radio from the 70's, the kind where numbers turn over on a wheel.

Remember this?

How could I not? I say, recalling how we always woke up to WMAN—now WGAL—the local talk radio station, a mix of conservative talk radio during the day and classic rock at night.

Why don't you get rid of that thing?

In case you haven't noticed, I don't get rid of anything.

You're such a sentimental bitch.

A smile creases her fake Gucci mask. A long pause creases the moment.

I went to see mom, I say.

She's getting worse.

How did everything get so fucked up?

Listen to you with the f-bomb. You never used to curse.

I didn't have much to curse about.

We stand there, quietly, siblings who've become near strangers to each other.

So, what's up, Bryan, why did you want to meet? I hope you're not thinking about hiding out here when you *retire*, she says, this is the first place they'll look.

Don't worry, I'm not. I just wanted to see you. And get one last look around the museum.

We laugh that comfortable yet edgy familial laugh that only siblings share. She follows me around the house like a security guard. We trade stories about things in every room. I lift up dad's La-Z-Boy to reveal cigarette burns in the faded shag carpet.

Tommy's big high school party, she says.

Mom and pops were pissed when they came home from Myrtle Beach. Thank you for not snitching.

149

You kidding? Tommy would've kicked both of our butts.

We enter the dining room. I smile at the brass ceiling light fixture from the 70's—mom and pops never remodeled—and I make a face at the enormous glass globes.

Get rid of that ugly thing, I say.

Oh, I could never sell that.

It's got a crack put there by over-exuberant Tommy. One day, I beat him at Super Mario—he hated to lose—and he leapt up, angrily, banging his head on the fixture, slumping onto the dining table. Pops drove him to the hospital. He had a concussion and didn't remember my winning at all. Or so he said.

Down in the basement, where I had lived briefly when my world started dying, I run my gloved fingers over the antique pool table and player piano. I pluck out a simple version of the intro to Bohemian Rhapsody on the chipped and yellowed piano keys, remembering how pops taught me the one song he ever learned to play. We'd bob our heads up and down during the solo, just like Wayne's World. (Google it.) Dad was like that, he'd learn how to do one thing in any activity. He cooked one great meal, shrimp scampi, excelled at one game, Scrabble, and played one great hole in every round of golf—a birdie, even an occasional eagle—and then bogey the rest. I stop playing Bohemian Rhapsody, not because playing the song is too emotional but because the keys are out of tune. My ears can't stomach it.

I try to make peace with my time here, both as a child and adult, but it's difficult with my little Sister following me. She never trusted me. Growing up, she was sweet, yes, but she was also my original drone.

So how you doing with the forty thing?

My left leg trembles like a quaking aspen. Gaia gave me a tincture, I say. I hope it helps.

How is Gaia? Still into her crystals?

Same ol' Gaia, I say, a little too fondly.

God, Bryan, are you still hung up on her?

No.

Uh-huh. So, really, why are you here? You hoping for some great revelation?

I guess I just need a little family time.

Family, right. You and Tommy were so mean to me.

I'm sorry. I wish I could take it all back. I wish I could hug you.

Me too. I hate how there's nothing I can do.

I know you do.

She looks at a text on her phone.

I really have to get back home. A Sister's coming out to fix the hot water heater.

Okay, go ahead. I'll just stick around a bit.

I'd rather you didn't, she says, holding out her hand, palm up.

Seriously?

I didn't know you still had a key.

You shouldn't need to lock the door, since Sisters are so *honest*.

She keeps her hand held out.

You'll be less tempted to hide out here if you have to break in.

I toss my key. She tries snatching it out of the air, but has to pick it up off the floor. I call for a ride and wait in the driveway as Emily closes the front door.

What are you doing for your birthday?

Hanging with the Appleseeds.

151

Nice. You need any money?

No.

Why don't you get out of Sisterfield?

I think about it, I say. But go where? I'm still a brother, wherever I go.

A black Honda SUV broCar pulls up. Might as well be a Hearse. I open the back door.

Hey bro.

I look back at my Sis.

I love you.

Love you too.

And that's it for our goodbye. No warm hug, no kiss on the cheek, not even a handshake. I refuse to look back at my boyhood home as the driverless black SUV carries me away, turning onto Beal Road, heading back toward Sisterfield.

SISTER BETH

It's Tuesday morning, I run to Starbucks, return home, throw a Frisbee with André out on the rolling lawn. We test first, but still wear special grabber gloves with disinfectant on the grips, so we're not potentially passing the virus back and forth. André's good, he catches anything I throw at him, off his foot, between his legs, behind his back. My dad was good at Frisbee too, it was big when he was in college.

I drop an easy one.

Where's your head? André says, shaking his.

On everything but this, I say.

Early in the evening I ride out to Charles Mill Lake, one of my favorite places. Large cigar-shaped clouds float by, giving the sky a Magritte look. Should be a colorful sunset. My drone buzzes overhead. I give a little wave to the hummingbird, always wonder who I'm waving to, probably nobody watching or paying attention at all, just the illusion that a Sister is.

I come here to clear my mind. I think best alongside rivers and lakes, although Charles Mill is a shadow of its former self, shrinking toward pond-hood. Once-deep coves are now cattail lagoons and narrow marshes and trees grow where water had flowed. A remnant of what it used to be. Like a brother. The surface is amazingly still, a reflection of itself dying. I try skipping a rock. Plop. I still suck at that, although I do create a ripple, a circular crack that undulates across the mirror. Nice thing about this time of year, the leafy colors burst out of their hibernation of green. Reflections of oak, elm, birch and maples shimmer their Crayola colors on the last of the ripple's wake. Anxious leaves fall and lightly touch down, floating on the water like brown, gold, and red canoes. Jesus Christ bugs—water striders—skate back and forth across the surface. I feel so connected with this place, as my eyes drift along the calm shore. Until I suddenly realize I am not alone. A fisherbrother stands with his back to me, holding a simple rod and reel. I haven't seen anyone fishing here in years.

Catch anything?

Yeah. A tan and a buzz.

I laugh, noticing the pint of Captain Morgan at his feet. I plan to ask what his story is, how he has stayed alive, but he turns to face me and I see the sunken eyes, the gauntness in his cheeks. I recognize that look anywhere.

Oh, geez, I'm sorry.

He focuses again on his line. I step back. This shouldn't bother me so much anymore, it's just daily life, but this is my go-to, my getaway, is there no sacred space anymore? I have to tell myself to snap the fuck out of it, the brother is dying, what have I got to complain about?

You need anything? I ask.

Yeah, he says, reeling his line in. A time machine.

Life sucks, doesn't it.

Life doesn't suck, he says. Death sucks.

He twists his torso, pulls his rod back, whips it forward, casting the line out, smoothly, beautifully, like he's done this thousands of times. And as if this cast could be one of his last.

Have a nice sunset, I wish him, leaving him alone to enjoy it. I stroll along the banks of the lake, and the sky suddenly disappoints, the sun hides behind a massive cloudbank well before it ever reaches the horizon. Like a round of golf, as Twain said, the walk's been spoiled. I can't shake the image of the fisherbrother and my funk only grows worse. I pull out my cell and order a broCar.

***

Tuesday evening is Bible Study at St. Peter's Cathedral, downtown, just off the square. Built in the mid-1800s, St. Pete's twin bell towers are topped by copper-green domes. This is not my childhood church, I attended a boring brick Lutheran church. Protestant churches are practical, the IKEAs of churches. Anyway, I come here because I know I can catch Sister Beth. I climb the steep steps that should come equipped with trekking poles. When I reach the top I look out at the sun emerging from behind the cloudbank horizon, awed by the vibrant orange spreading like paint poured from the clouds. It's gonna be a good sunset after all and, everyone knows the best color is after the sun vanishes, you gotta stick around for the after-show.

Around the country, many churches, temples, and mosques are boarded-up. They had acted as sanctuaries for the suffering and dying, but as we began to understood how contagious The Y was, these sanctuaries became taboo to brothers. Dying believers suddenly had no place to go to kneel and pray and beg for mercy.

155

And as things grew worse, brothers desecrated the holy buildings, tagging them with red spray paint, like the one here:

THE BLOOD OF CHRIST

ALL OVER AGAIN

Brothers blew up churches and temples and mosques. St. Pete's has not escaped the wrath. You'll see when we go inside in a minute. And there's one thing that's at most holy sites, I'm looking for it now, there's gotta be at least one here, on one of these four columns towering alongside the front doors. Not on that one, nope, not there either, let me check another. Here we go, scratched into the marble:

F Y G

You can guess what that stands for.

My drone lands on the church roof, hanging around like a tiny gargoyle, as I open one of the three wooden church doors. Paintings of saints loom high overhead on the ceiling, none looking any too happy, darkened by smoke. Chunks of marble are missing from these interior columns. Saints' broken, decapitated heads lay at their sandaled and concrete feet, assaulted by angry dying brothers armed with sledgehammers. On the wall behind the altar is the imprint of a six-foot-long silhouette of a missing crucifix, the wall lighter than the candle-smoke-stained grayness surrounding it. The wooden lectern tilts at a Leaning-Tower-Of-Pisa angle. For whatever reason, the Sister Elders deemed it best to leave the church in this dilapidated state. Probably pure economics, since the church has few parishioners left, no tithes to fix anything and no pressing need to do so. Most Younger Sisters have left their former churches and joined the Spiritual Sisterhood.

I don't bother with the font of holy water. Raised Lutheran—I'm now agnostic—we don't dip our fingers in water. Except to baptize. Besides, the holy water smells rancid, even from ten-feet away. I head to the roped-off bro-only section in the back, the pews as dusty as barn benches. Against the wall at the end of my row is the pieta, Mother Mary holding her dead son in her arms. How appropriate.

I slide to the middle of the pew, away from the aisle. I am the lone brother here. There are three older Devout Sisters, relics from the Bible Study class. I feel bad for the church, dying just like we brothers are. Then an old, doughy Sister enters and approaches the marble font, and from the look on her face, she doesn't want to touch the water either. Flies buzz around her as she taps the water with two fingers. She forms the sign of the cross from forehead to abdomen and across her flabby chest, finishing with a slap of her cheek and the flick of a smashed bug from her fingertips.

Swirls of intense colors, rubies and sapphires and indigos, stream down from the sunset onto the pews below. Looking up to my right, on the wall thirty feet above me, stained-glass windows ablaze with images of Sisters Mary—both of them, the virgin and the whore—and Theresa and Joan and Ruth Bader Ginsberg and Mother President. These vibrant windows shine brand-new, emporeringly bright.

I gaze at the opposite wall, to my left, up at the old, original stained-glass images. Century-old grime clings to the glass, the colors pale in comparison to the new windows. These are mostly brothers: Jesus of course, John, Moses, Abraham, David, archangels Gabriel and Michael. These windows are some of the last un-tampered images of brothers that publicly exist in Sisterfield. And though most biblical brothers are reduced to bit parts in the Sisters Bible—first

157

published by Spiritual Readers in 2030—they remain here, frozen in time within the colored glass. As I've said, I'm not religious, but this is one of the few places I can still go and relive the glory of my gender.

I pull out my tincture bottle, squeeze a few drops under my tongue. Scaffolding reaches from the ground up to the stained-glass brothers. Two Sister Workers stand on a board at the top, their angelic voices echoing down as they remove a glass pane of headless John the Baptist from its window frame. Looks like I won't even have these brothers to look up to much longer.

BTW, you still see paintings and statues of Jesus around the city, but not nearly so many. He too is being phased out. Could there be a church without Christ, what would that even look like? All about Mary, the virgin mother? (A birth without sex back then was a miracle; today it's the norm.) If Jesus is no longer considered the Son of Goddess— or if his role diminishes in importance—I still think he'll be revered for his sensitive relationships with Sisters. They loved him. Whatever else you think he might be—God, prophet, or just a brother—Jesus most certainly was Sister-friendly.

Behind the altar, a door opens and Sister Beth enters the sanctuary, wrapped in a purple frock below her head of silver curls. She's in her 60's, a Hodgkin's lymphoma survivor, her heart so weakened that doctors told her it would give out before she turned 21. She wanted to see the country before she died, so she drove big rigs coast to coast. For twenty years. At age forty, she quit, went to college and became a nurse who healed not so much by her medical knowledge but through her caring soul. Then, when the Catholic Church collapsed, nuns were promoted to the priesthood. The call went out to Sisters to attend the seminary. She signed up the very first day, becoming one of thousands of new Sister Priests rushed through to replace all the dead brothers.

I come today to talk to her, not because she is a priest, but because her words soothe me. She speaks in a calm Mr. Rogers' way and she always makes time to laugh and cry with me and feel my confusion and pain. She is an amazing soul, and for me to ever become a good one, I need to learn from one of the greats. She slides awkwardly, almost stumbling across a pew three rows away. Even though she's a priest, we can't be too close.

Good evening, Bryan.

She sips from a metal chalice in her hand. I pull my mask down. Seems only respectful.

Evening, Sister. How was Bible Study?

More like Bible Naptime, she says, winking at the three Devout Sisters mumbling the rosary. So, how are you today?

Fine.

She nods. How is your Sister Mother doing?

The same.

That's better than worse. Tell her I'll stop by soon, she says.

I will.

Are you coping any better?

With mom?

With making peace with death.

Not really.

I squirm in the hard, dusty pew, fingering the little amber bottle in my pocket. I tell her how I've read and re-read Revelation lately, like many brothers who are still alive. Clichéd, I know, and like I've said, I'm not religious, but it's as if I'm looking for a spiritual loophole. I

159

remove a Bible from the pew, turn to the back, flip through some pages. I feel my anxiety amping up, but I push forward.

Revelation, I read, chapter nine, verse six. "Men will seek death and will not find it; they will long to die, and death will fly from them." I close the good book with a great thump. Guess the Bible got that wrong, I harrumph.

Perhaps, she says, but it got the plague right.

We chit-chat a little more about scripture and things. I don't have much to share, other than the Book of Revelation. I could fake a little Daniel, more doom and gloom, but scripture is not why I'm here.

Turning forty sucks.

She nods.

Did you know, she says, that forty is a magical biblical number? Forty days and forty nights of flood. The Israelites wandered the desert for forty years before Moses led them to the Promised Land. Guess how long he was on Mt. Sinai.

Forty days and nights.

Bingo, she says. She sips.

Didn't Jesus fast for forty days and nights, too?

Yes, he did. And the Book of Exodus has forty chapters. In fact, the number forty is mentioned 146 times in the Bible, more than any other number greater than ten.

Sounds like biblical writers were just lazy and forty was their default—

Oops!

Something flat and very colorful plunges from the sky. John The Baptist flashes at us. A second later he shatters in glass splashing across the cathedral floor, jagged flickers of crimson, indigo and gold.

Sorry, Sister Beth, one of the angels calls down.

That's Sister Butterfingers, Sister Beth whispers, winking at me. This is when I could use a handy brother.

I smirk. Silence settles around us.

Why do you think all this happened? I ask.

You mean what role did Goddess play?

I'm not blaming her, I say, I just wonder why she didn't stop it. She never does, does she? Stop tragedy, I mean.

Sister Beth shifts and listens.

I think we're responsible for all of this, I add. We had to be dominant and distant, when all you Sisters really wanted was connection. But we couldn't give it. Not like you wanted. Still, Goddess could've intervened, could've given us a sign, could've told us to be smarter and you all to be cooler.

I believe She gave you plenty of signs. Look, I won't pretend to tell you what to believe, she says, and I won't even tell you that you should believe. After what's happened these last few years, no one should act on faith alone. You have to want to believe. You need to feel it. Once you do that, it'll make all this so much easier.

There's another flash of light followed by the smashing of more glass. Shards bounce off the cream-colored stone like sharp raindrops. A few slide under my pew. We gaze up at the second hole where there used to be biblical brothers.

Jeezzus Christ! Sister Beth spits out, then composes herself. Sorry Sisters, she says, trucker talk never fully leaves you.

She registers my surprised look.

Don't be so judgmental, Bryan, this is hard on all of us.

We look up at the Sister Workers on the scaffolding.

161

Could we be a little more careful, pleashh? she says.

Sorry, Sister Beth, says one of the meek heavenly voices.

Yes, sorry, Sister, says the other.

Their voices drift down over us, their last bit of angelic gossip before going into a time-out on the scaffolding. The church becomes so quiet even the silence echoes. I lean over the front of my pew, look into Sister Beth's tilted chalice. Expecting red, I am surprised to see clear, bubbly liquid. I doubt that's mineral water.

You're drunk, I whisper.

No, I'm not.

She lowers her chalice behind her pew. She bends forward and whispers:

I'm just a little buzzed.

I laugh.

Champagne?

Vodka fizz.

(Sisters love their vodka.)

The wine here sucks, she chuckles. Look, Bryan, I don't have anything figured out either. I always loved it, all of it, the solemn beauty and ritual, the candles, the chanting. I dreamed of being a priest since I was an acolyte. I marched and protested for our right to wear the cloth. Then came The Y and we won the fight by default. I am finally what I wanted to be. And look, she says, sweeping her arm around the empty cathedral. No one comes.

She sips from the chalice and looks up at the stained glass windows, muted now, the sun having sunk, the last patches of color disappearing on the pews below.

Was the fight worth it? I ask.

162

Was any of this really worth it? Catholicism is doomed, don't you think? Humankind, I believe, is ultimately doomed. Maybe the Final Judgement is finally here. I don't think Sisters will save the planet. We'll end up messing it up somehow too, just like you guys did.

She leans forward.

If you tell anyone I said any of that, I'll deny it.

She drains the last of her chalice.

You're not making this any easier, I say.

Oh, eazzy is what you want?

She mumbles something soothing to herself in Latin.

Be honest with me, Sister Beth.

Of course.

I know it's your job, but do *you* still really believe in a higher being?

She stews in that person-of-the-cloth contemplative mode.

Most days, I do, she says, standing. Well, I must be going. More last rites to perform. Seems that's all I ever do. Would you like to pray?

Sure. Figure it can't hurt.

Ahh, one of the main reasons people still turn to Goddess.

She bows her head slowly and I wait for the inevitable words, but then she lifts her face and focuses on mine.

I know you seek answers, it's okay to question and explore, that makes us human. You're confused and scared and angry.

I'm looking for guidance.

Prayer guides us.

Will it make me feel less scared-shitless?

163

Depends. Is it your knowledge of fear that scares you? Or your fear of knowledge?

Both.

She smiles, nodding.

We can always try to prepare, she says, but we never really get there, do we? Prepared, I mean. You should live these days happily. You should be honored to do what you do. Remember Ruth from the Bible?

Not really.

She was the great grandmother of David. In the Book of Ruth, chapter three, verse nine, it says, "I am your handmaid Ruth. Spread your robe over your handmaid."

I'm not sure how that relates.

You are the handmaid. With a gender twist. Let Goddess spread her Sisterly love over you, for you were chosen to keep the human race going.

Correction. Keep Sisters going.

You were chosen to keep the *human race* going. Feel honored.

Like a sacrificial virgin.

Doesn't change the fact you were chosen.

How did you get to be so wise?

I drove trucks for twenty years. Gave me a lot of time to think.

I want to say more but the words don't take shape. I slide out of the pew.

Good luck, Bryan. Your journey is difficult. But it is a journey that you must take to its conclusion. Whatever that may be.

I walk down the aisle, maybe a little more buoyant than when I entered.

Bryan?

I don't have to look back, I know what she is doing. I can feel her blessing me with her hand.

Let the goddess give you comfort.

She can do whatever she wants, I say, but then I do turn around, walking backwards toward the doors: Hey, I thought you were going to pray for me.

I have been, this entire time.

I open the middle church door, illuminated by twilight. I look back inside the sanctuary for Sister Beth but I only see dark. I hear her say to herself:

It's what I do.

I climb down the steep cathedral steps, look up at my drone waiting on a ledge, suddenly flying into action, hovering over me as I make the trek down those steep steps to the street.

BOOM

A dark cloudbank hovers over the city like earth's own drone. Leaves tremble in the trees and tumble on the grass. I'm in full gray sweats, more bundled than I've been since April, my little hummingbird hovering a little closer than normal to me, probably because of the shoebox under my arm. It's late morning and I approach the homeless black dude waiting for me on a bus bench. He's fidgety in his purple Crocs, a dusting of dandruff clinging to his shoulders.

Those my Uggs?

We walk apart—2-10 ingrained in us like washing your hands before you eat—and I study his dark, beaten face, his broad brow and crooked nose.

By the way, my name's Bryan.

Justin. Justin Tyme.

You serious?

It's T-y-m-e. My old man had a sense of humor.

Your mom was okay with that?

She died giving birth to me.

Oh shit, I'm sorry.

With brothers dying everywhere, you almost forget that Sisters still die too. I think of my own mom, my thoughts a mash-up of past and present, pain and more pain, as we cross Fourth Street to Betty's Burgers, an old Bob's Big Boy, the goofy boy statue redesigned as a butch Betty.

You're buying, right? he says.

Whatever you want.

We walk up to a bro-only window and order over a speaker mic. Mine takes just a few seconds, a #2 with sweet tea. His order takes longer: the #3 and #4 meals, extra this, none of that, sweet tea and a chocolate shake. I wave my cell at a scanner and we wait at the bro-only pick-up window.

You think if we met before all this, he says, you'd even give me the time of day?

I try to think up a lie but can't. Probably not, I say.

Now at least that's some truth. I 'preciate that.

A Fast-Food Sister inserts our bagged meals into a window box with a digital clock that counts down—120, 119, 118.

So, what's it like, getting paid to spread the mayo?

It's a job.

A hand job, he snorts behind his brobot mask.

I describe the different sterile steps that are involved in my work. He listens intently.

You're right, he says, it's just a job.

The timer beeps. I open the box lid, reach in, pull out our three bags of burgers and one of fries. He grabs our sweet teas and his shake. We sit at a picnic table, alone, not unusual in the bro-only section. I set down the box of Uggs, start my phone timer, scoop up my food—I have to wait to grab my drink, we may have contaminated each other's stuff—and go sit at a different table. I can see it's hard for him to keep from attacking his food. Or tearing open his gift.

Remember when we didn't have to go thru all this bullshit?

Those were the days, I say, looking up at the storm brewing in the distance.

Long enough? he asks.

A watched pot never boils, my grandma used to say.

A just-bought app never downloads, he adds.

My cell timer chimes. Justin pulls down his mask, tears open his bag, stuffs fries into his mouth. He has perfectly straight, yellowed teeth. They can't be real, must be dentures, right? How could a homeless brother have such orderly teeth? He rips the top off the shoebox, kicks off his purple Crocs, and pulls out the new tan Uggs. He beams, fitting them on his feet, stretching his legs out, wriggling his toes inside. He walks around the pavement like a little boy, shoving more fries into his face. We chat while chewing and I double-check that it's okay to record him and he says yeah, why not, and I pull out my phone and place it on the table, aiming the mic his way.

Do you think a vaccine exists?

Hell yeah I think it exists, he says. But the damn government, brother, Sister, don't matter, you can't believe anything it says.

He mumbles something which I'm gonna guess is offensive. He proceeds to tell his life story, punctuated by chewing, with twists and turns like every life, long story short, everyone he knew died from The Y. Then he got it. I find myself moving further away.

I wanted to die, he says, I was throwing up things I never even ate. I had chills for days, my whole body felt like it was in a vice. I welcomed death.

168

He shudders, recalling the pain.

I quit my job, gave away all my things to my two brother friends who were still alive. He shakes his head at the stupidity of it all and continues: two false positives, man. I just had a really bad flu.

That sucks, I say.

Beats the alternative.

So why are you homeless, with all the abandoned homes out there?

Those are traps. You can check in anytime you like, as the song says, but you can never leave.

Hotel California, I say, realizing I was wrong when I thought of him as the Dude from The Big Lebowski. The Dude hated the Eagles. So did pops.

Justin gulps his sweet tea and lowers his voice.

I don't deal with the enemy, he says, it'll mess you up. Look at you.

I'm not gonna apologize for surviving.

More like aiding and abetting.

Without brothers like me, the human race is doomed.

If we perish, they should go down too.

If we keep the human race alive, we can come back.

You're a fool. We're never coming back.

I prefer to have hope.

Hope is a joke.

Let's drop it, I say.

No, no, no you don't. I want to know—how do you sleep with yourself?

I'm giving life. What are you doing?

Not living in a mansion is what I'm doing.

So where do you sleep?

I already told you. I squat. Never two nights in a row anywhere.

He continues his life story, devouring his burgers, his mumbled memories about living on streets once controlled by brothers but now controlled by Sisters, and how he had a German Shepherd, Tick-Tock, his one true companion. A Sister stole his dog and he now sleeps like a cat, any little noise stirs him and he's usually out of a building before a Sister can even enter and—

BOOM!

Our table shudders. Justin and I shoot looks at each other.

Holy shit!

What the fuck?!

Sweet tea sloshes in our cups. My bones tingle. A dark plume of smoke rises from the east, over the treetops, coming from downtown, less than two miles away.

I gotta go!

I snatch my phone and run downtown, calling Gaia, first on her cell, it goes to voicemail, then at her store, same thing. I text her: UOK? I wanna call Miriam too but I'm not allowed to ever call her, not on her cell, not at home, not at her office, my phone is blocked on all of them. I try to order a broCar, get no responses. Even driverless broCars don't wanna take a brother into a war zone. I run down Fourth Street, on adrenaline, following the rising smoke, struggling to stay in the bro-only lane, now is not the time to get stopped by a Sister Cop. I keep up a pretty good clip, getting lots of looks, but I'm headed toward the blast not away from it and no one tries to stop me. Alarms pierce the air. Ambulances, fire trucks and cop cars roar past.

170

A Channel 56 news van speeds by. It feels like a minute—but was probably more like ten—before I see the chaos unfold a block ahead of me, at the corner of 4th and Main. Cop cars form a perimeter around the scene. Bricks and plaster legs of horses and zebras are strewn across the pavement and dangling in trees and awnings. The front half of a unicorn lies smashed through the windshield of a black sedan. An elephant leg is wedged one-story up between an art gallery and the Coney Island Diner. The long neck of a giraffe is on fire on a sidewalk. And where there once was a carousel—symbol of Sisterfield's glory past—there is now a smoking crater, scattered flames rising from its depths.

My eyes only now focus on the human wreckage spread out on the streets and sidewalks. Adult Sisters, teens, little girls crumpled on the ground, not moving, or carried away on stretchers, moaning, among the confusion and frantic action of paramedics and citizens, all trying to help. Nearby, a Teen Sister in a scarlet Ohio State sweatshirt leans back on her elbows, blood seeping out from a tear in the big red O. She looks down at her bloodied vowel, in calm shock.

Sister Beth is already here, kneeling over a Dead Sister who's missing an arm and half her face, giving her last rites, closing the one eye. Nearby, a Little Sister's head lies on its side next to a curb, her blonde curls speckled with blood, her face frozen in an expression of carousel-riding joy. I almost step on a girl's severed arm, the fingernails painted sparkly-pink. I feel time pause, as if life gives me a good look at the horror. I have the dreadful sense this changes everything and I close my eyes to see if I can rewind time. I pull out my Kava Karma and squeeze drops of the tincture under my tongue. I open my eyes. All at once time unfreezes and fast-forwards: Sister

171

Emergency Responders rush past, carrying bodies on stretchers; Sister Firefighters hose down burning debris; Sister Cops hurry back and forth tending to the Wounded Sisters still lying on the ground; bystanders sit, shaken but alive, so traumatized they can't move. Sister Deputies tell crowds to back off, placing black-and-yellow Stay-Back boxes in a perimeter, temporary invisible fencing that shocks you if you try to enter the crime scene. Sister Detectives question witnesses. I wanna roll up my sleeves and help tend to the wounded, but I cannot risk it, I cannot get contaminated by blood or guts or sweat or spittle.

I look away and tighten my mask and I see, cattycorner from the blast site, Gaia pacing, talking frantically on her phone outside her shattered storefront window. Her store itself appears otherwise unaffected. She kicks the smoking head of a tiger away from her sidewalk tables. She catches my eye from across the street, glares at me with disgust, and turns her back, disappearing into her store.

It looks like The War has finally come to my hometown.

***

Seventeen Sisters die in the carousel bombing: five adults, three teens, and nine girls. Oct. 13, 2032 becomes the bloodiest day in Richland County's history, bloodier than the Copus Massacre which killed a dozen residents and Native Americans in the war of 1812. The days following the blast are filled with checkpoints and bunkers, candlelight vigils and social media threats. Flowers and signs pop up:

We'll Never Forget Our Sisters

We Love You

172

R.I.P. Sis

Here are the victims:

Sheila Huntzinger, the youngest, age four, and her mother, Monica, 27.

Samantha Tingley, age six, and her mom, Charlene, 32.

Janice Shuster, age seven, she loved ballet.

Lily Spade, age eight and her aunt, Carolyn, 41.

Cinthia Hernandez, age eight, a computer whiz.

Lorena David, nine, and her sister Tabitha, 12.

Jodi Harrod, 11.

Tamara Gomez, 11. She loved horses.

Identical twins Rachel & Ramona Sponseller, 13.

Erika Snow, 16. She wanted to be a doctor.

Liz Kemper, 21, and her girlfriend, Taylor Wills, 23.

Miraculously, two riders survive the blast but lose limbs, eyes and other organs. The ride operator, Phoebe Owens, somehow survives, paralyzed from the waist down.

I can't stop thinking about all those dead Little Sisters, their body parts strewn up and down Main Street. I hope to hell Miguel wasn't involved, but I suspect he was.

Mayor Miriam immediately issues a curfew of brothers from 10 pm to 7 am. So much for my early morning runs.

Wealthy Sisters pay for all the funerals, which disrupt everything for a week following the blast. Armed Sisters post watch as Sister Beth delivers the eulogy for some, Mayor Miriam for others. President Olsen phones the families personally to offer condolences. The somber events all go off beautifully and peacefully.

173

Sisters are enraged like I've never seen them before. Downtown becomes a war zone. Windows are boarded-up, Sister Soldiers stand guard in bunkers lined with sand bags that perimeter the square, Sister Snipers post up in hi-rises, making target practice of suspected undergrounders. The crack of gunfire and screams of brothers shatters the normal calm. Sisters patrol the streets in riot gear, strapped with ammunition belts like macho jewelry around their chests. Brothers who try to assemble or mourn are arrested and strip-searched. We avoid the streets altogether, becoming more ghostlike.

Skirmishes and suspicious accidents take the lives of at least eleven local brothers. I say "at least" because details about brothers—unlike the deaths of Sisters—are sketchy. We seldom make the news. I know of one incident: four brothers are accused of trying to steal a car and are chased by Security Sisters to the old Blockhouse in Central Park. They break inside, barricading themselves. The Sisters insist they surrender. A two-day stand-off ensues. On the second night, the historic building goes up in flames and a deadly shootout follows. The official spin—that the brothers set the fire to frame Sisters—is as suspicious as it is typical. A YouTube video clearly shows someone in dark clothing, moving like a Sister, sneaking up to the fort at night and planting something along a back wall. How could she sneak up like that, the fort was surrounded by police, unless police were complicit? Fire then breaks out minutes afterwards and the shooting begins.

I hear of another brother found assassinated inside a broCar on Ashland Road. Normally, broCars are programmed to deliver wounded brothers to the bro-hospital, but the car's computerized dash was shot up as well. There are rumors of two bro-hoes found

174

strangled by purse straps and pockmarked by the kicks of stiletto heels. Another rumor claims a Sister General somewhere in Ohio severs penises from brothers' corpses, preserving them in formaldehyde in glass ornaments that she plans to hang from a Christmas tree during the holidays. All just rumors, but isn't most news these days?

Meanwhile, brothers receive no fancy funerals or calls from the president, no memorials, no flowers. Their names do not show up on any official lists. I offer them here in the hope that they are not forgotten:

EDITOR'S NOTE: Bryan meticulously listed details of the brothers' lives and deaths. I had to make concessions to the publisher. One dealbreaker required that I not list the fallen brothers' names. Sisters fear the murdered will be martyred. So I deleted Bryan's list.

The city takes on a medieval aura. Three brothers—one white, one black, one Latino—hang from lampposts in the West Park District, I'm not shitting you. Official word is they were traitors, spies for Sisters, and that undergrounders hung them there. I don't wanna believe that, but anything is possible. Mayor Miriam orders the corpses pulled down and cremated and their deaths investigated by Sister Detectives. All talk of the incident is wiped off of *It*.

Sister Mayor issues a proclamation re-opening temporary holding cells at the city's castle-like prison, The Ohio State Reformatory, closed for over 40 years and now a museum. It's where the movie Shawshank Redemption was filmed and is the city's biggest tourist site. Most of it was torn down, but the big stoned walls of the administration building still stand, along with two long-walled cellblocks. Imposing from the outside, it is even worse inside. The cellblocks are cold, damp, and toxic and one now houses the brothers arrested for involvement in the carousel bombing. Or simply suspicion. Mayor Miriam is making a statement by re-opening this barbaric and iconic hellhole. While keeping the museum open at the same time.

Fringe Sister supremacy groups rise up. The biggest, Sister Nation, vows to wipe out all brothers except for Appleseeds like myself. They say once Sisters discover how to create sperm in a lab—one day I'm sure they will—they'll do away with us too. Sister Mayor condemns these groups and some brother haters are arrested, but their scare tactics work. I believe Sister Nation hung those three brothers from the lampposts.

In the midst of all this, Miriam goes on live TV, speaking without a teleprompter, calling for peace and a truce between the genders:

I talk to you today not as mayor but as your fellow Sister. I knew several of the innocent victims of the horrible carousel bombing.

She wipes away tears that look authentic but feel too perfectly timed:

Sisters, I am as offended and as full of grief as you are. But these retaliations, they are not who we are. As the great brother Gandhi said, "An eye for an eye makes everyone blind."

I cringe and swipe her clichéd speech off my phone.

YOU'RE LUCKY
YOU'RE AN APPLESEED

Sisters give us evil eyes, their typical indifference now ratcheted to vile hatred. Sister Cops harass us more than normal. My digital ID has saved my ass, thank Goddess, plus an *A* I scrawled on my mask—for Appleseed, my Scarlet Letter—to give cops a heads-up.

Just today I walked the gardens, breathing in the cool autumn air, listening to the chirpy melodies of songbirds. A Sister shouted at me:

You're lucky you're an Appleseed!

I turned to look and a loogie nailed my mask, over the bridge of my large nose. I stopped breathing and ripped off my mask. A pod of Sisters laughed heartily as I wiped my face with my shirt. Shit, this is not good, I panicked, sprinting to The Factory. I stared at the retinal scanner, my eye wide with terror. I leapt up the staircase, tore off my clothes, showered under scalding water, scrubbing and scrubbing, knowing that wouldn't save me, not if I breathed in the virus.

I'm dictating this now, hiding out in my room, my door locked, waiting the recommended six hours after exposure—the virus wastes no time in replicating itself—before I can test. Six excruciating hours. I'm staring at my cell, my walls, my books, berating myself for not wearing a Face-The-Future shield, it could've protected me from this

177

nightmare. I have two—one is polarized—but I've gotten lazy. They're ugly and bulky. hardly any brothers wear them. Vanity over safety?

My heart is knocking against my chest, like it wants to break free through my rib cage. I suck on tincture, that usually helps, but not now. I insert my Sisbuds in my ears, listen to a soft jazz playlist, hope that will mellow me out. Doesn't work, too much mental wiggle room in the music. I avoid the Sisters playlist, that would just piss me off, so I try Oldies. I'm up, I'm down, I snap and sing along to My Girl, it lifts me a little but the buzz doesn't last long, the song's too short. I try some Marley, too happy, I need something grittier. Rage Against The Machine. I listened to them in high school, and then Eminem, he's always pissed-off, I can feed off that. I grind my teeth, singing along. Nope, that pisses me off more. I try Shostakovich's Symphony #5 in D minor—Steven turned me onto it—and the intense waves of passion, alternating between pastoral and military, steer me outside of myself. I surrender to the orchestral vortex of tension, escaping my own mind, finally. Okay, this might be working, and as soon as I think that, I am back in my own head.

My heart won't stop pounding—one-two, one-two—syncing to the double-strokes of bows on strings that so matches my frantic mood, taking me to the Gulags during The Purges. I realize things could be worse, I could be a brother in a Siberian prison. I feel some heaviness lifted by the universal suffering, that herstorically, brothers have been strong, through billions of struggles, and this relaxes me. This and the Kava Karma. The music's swelling and the climactic death march is prolonged. I hit replay and listen to the whole symphony again, worn-out like a zombie by the barrage of strings and horns. After two rounds, I can't listen any more, I have to recharge, so I scan endless

178

YouTubes of people doing the dumbest things, exactly the mind-numbing activity I now need.

My cell chimes. Finally. Time to test. I grab a kit from a stack in my closet, prick my finger, scoop up a drop of blood, insert it into the vial, add two drops of solution. I hurry down the hall to the walk-in-linen closet, now empty except for our whirly-girly, a toaster-sized centrifuge, the same model we use at the Love Shack. I place the vial inside, flip a switch, and the shaking starts. The viral blitzkrieg reveals itself within hours which is excellent for testing purposes. Not so good for survival.

I wait thirty aggravating seconds, remove the vial, hold it up to the light—a red double line means I'm doomed—and my entire body is shaking. I look away for a second, then re-focus. A clear single line. Negative. Yes! A chill of relief ripples through me. Wow, that was intense. I must've wiped the spit away in time, or maybe the Sister spit blanks. Could be a false-negative, to be safe I'll avoid the others tonight, and confirm with a test tomorrow morning. I'm so grateful I get down on my knees and clasp my hands together. I don't know what to pray, so I say:

Thank you, goddess.

***

I test negative again the next morning, Thursday, but with the curfew in place I don't go out on my morning run. I miss a hook-up with Miriam. It's not unusual for the mayor not to show, but in two years this is the only time I can remember not going. I'm jonesing. Yeah, I know sex is only a balm but that balm gets me through the week. Its absence fuels my anxiety which flares into depression. The end feels closer and I wonder if I'll ever go out again. I jump on the treadmill in the library, something I never do, running fast, for a half-hour, craving my morning routine. Craving Miriam.

Over the next week the tension simmers, another new normal develops. A few Sister statues are bombed, so Sister Guards post-up 24/7 to protect them. But no Sisters are hurt in these attacks, no fighting occurs, with so few of us alive to fight. I hear at least ten of us are now locked up at the old reformatory.

I squeeze tincture under my tongue. Fuck, I'm already running low.

***

It's Monday morning, October 18th. I turn forty in four days. I "resin my bow" for one of the last times, watching my product slide down the tube, destined for wombs unknown. I shower away the remnants. I stuff a backpack with essentials to take on the run. Steven stops by my room.

The secret to hiding, he says, is to think like a squirrel. Stash shit all over the city. Don't use storage lockers, Sisters won't rent to you and even if they do, they'll track you. Bury your shit. You run out of something you dig up a pack. Keep a stash of cash in each one, no credit cards, you don't wanna be leaving a digital footprint.

I'm already all over that, I've been pulling money out of ATMs on a regular basis and hiding it here in my room.

Later on, all of us—except Selfie—gather in the drawing room, our faces buried in our devices. Mine's in a book, The Decline of Brothers. I realize, on the run, I won't have room for books, everything I read will be digital. I smell the stale paper and ink, the faint scent of binding glue, while a WSFD TV Anchor Sister is babbling something—the volume is off—on screens all over the walls. Miriam is scheduled to give a TV speech any minute now. How weird this feels, my lover going on TV to talk about the crisis and I have no idea what she's gonna say. And I still pretend that what we have is intimacy?

Miriam approaches the podium in a creamy pantsuit and flashy gold necklace. I never pay much attention to what she wears to the Shack, her running outfits are never for more than a few minutes. Now she looks business-hot. Serious CouncilSisters and young Sister Staffers stand behind her. The camera zooms in on Miriam's muddy brown face hovering over us from every screen in the house. I bump the volume.

Good evening, Sisterfield. This is the worst time in our city's long history. We are better than what we've shown these last nine days. I believe in our city. I believe in our Sisters *and* brothers. I have consulted with CouncilSisters and my staff and after careful deliberation, I have decided to lift the curfew, effective tomorrow morning at sunrise.

The others exchange baffled looks around the room—that's it? But I wonder, hmmm, it's three days before our next rendezvous, four days before my birthday, is her lifting the curfew a coincidence? Maybe a birthday present to me? Dare I think she misses me too?

It is time for our city to heal, Miriam continues. I call on all of Sisterfield to respect the life and rights of brothers. We must remember the compassion and empathy we all share as Sisters.

Yes, let's Make Sisters Great Again, I joke, getting a couple brotherly snorts.

The war is over, she adds, brothers, you can come out of hiding. I will grant amnesty to any undergrounders that surrender to authorities.

181

Okay, I think, that's something. Miguel is probably on that list.

It's time to move forward, she continues. Goddess bless Sisterfield. Good night.

André taps pause. Miriam's intense brown face freezes on screens all over the house.

Curfew, big deal, André says. Where is the BBR, Sister Mayor? Where are our basic rights?

The BBR is a proposed list of 10 amendments to the Constitution, like the original Bill of Rights. Both Houses of Congress debated it last year. The House narrowly passed it. Changes were made in Senate committees. Here is our version:

THE BROTHERS BILL OF RIGHTS

Brothers have the right to:
1) Life
2) Liberty
3) Respect
4) Privacy
5) Dignified death
6) Use masculine terms like man and male
7) Marry and have sexual relations with clean Sisters
8) Be treated *almost* equal to Sisters
9) Unmonitored usage of It
10) The Vaccine

In #8, "almost" was added to soften the language for hardcore Sisters and, in a later version, #10 was rejected and replaced by Love. I list the original BBR because that's the one most brothers

182

support. Even with amendments to the amendments, it's no surprise the BBR was rejected 71-29 by the Senate.

Everyone mumbles, complaining about the speech. I plop down at the Steinway and tease a plodding cathartic solo out of all 88 keys. I look up at Miriam's speech-giving face, her mouth frozen open, so many of them on the walls surrounding us, like she was going to eat us from every direction. Suddenly, all the screens change to Shawshank Redemption, already in progress, an innocent-man-goes-to-prison saga filling the walls around us. Most of it was filmed here in Sisterfield, at the reformatory.

Oooh, this scene I love! Kimchi titters.

The rest of us gaze up at the walls, even André, who usually has a hard time looking away from his Star Trek Black Generation. It's the scene in Shawshank when the inmates are tarring the roof, under a blistering sun, and Andy scores some contraband—icy cold beers. The inmates take a break, sit back, and enjoy. That simple brother-bonding moment allows the inmates to feel free again, briefly, and gives them hope, at least twelve ounces of it.

Killer growls. No one pays him much attention, we're too into the film. We relate as prisoners of a sort. Forty years after its release, it's still a great film.

Killer gets up off the floor at Drew's feet, stands rigid and growls again, louder now. He stares toward the wall of tall windows, all closed-off with curtains. His growling intensifies. I stop playing and turn around on my piano stool. Steven and Drew go over to the windows, peek outside, then sweep all the curtains open, revealing a crowd of Sisters assembled in the dark, on our rolling back lawn, chanting something and holding torches, I kid you not, like the Dark

Ages or Victorian Frankenstein or Charlottesville. I pull out my Kava Karma and squeeze out the very last drops. Steven cranks open one of the many window panes so we can hear what the crowd of Sisters is chanting:

We support you!

You are important to us!

Hell yeah you need us, André says, you don't wanna have to get your sperm from Chicago.

That's the next-closest Factory, eight hours away. Regardless of their motive, we're all feeling good hearing Sisters say that, like how Sisters used to make us feel. But the more we look at the crowd, the more we realize that while most are chanting support, some are not. The torches illuminate plenty of angry faces.

Why don't you text your girlfriend, Drew says to me, and tell her to call the dogs off.

You know I can't do that, I say.

A lot of good your effing connection does us.

He is absolutely right, Miriam cannot come to my rescue, she will not even come to my house, and I have to laugh at how meaningless my life really is and then I realize how my expression must appear to some in the crowd outside my window. I turn my face away from the Sisters. The last thing I want to do is piss one off—

SMASH!

A rock breaks through a window, glass sprinkling behind me, the rock tumbling across the floor. I run for cover behind a high-backed chair, look out on a light scuffle in the crowd of Sisters outside.

A chick fight! Steven crows.

Even with severe shortages of brothers, Sisters don't fight over us anymore. Just doesn't happen. (Never did.) Anger is brewing out there and several Sisters rush the building, smashing other windows. Drew and Steven race to the kitchen. The rest of us hide behind the overstuffed furniture. Sinister-looking Sister faces fill the spaces of broken glass. I get ready to bolt upstairs but Drew and Steven come back in with drawers of knives and kitchen utensils, emptying them out—clank-clink-clunk—on top of the grand piano.

C'mon, cunts! Steven yells, amped, armed with a butcher knife in each hand. We all grab blades and utensils. I clutch meat scissors. We tighten our masks and wait for the onslaught.

This is not the way! one Sister Dove pleads, standing between the crowd of torches and our windows. We are not like brothers!

A Sister Invader smashes her way through a broken window pane, crawling into the drawing room. Murderers! she screams, struggling to her feet. She and Steven face off, a couch between them. He waves his blades back and forth.

We had nothing to do with the bombing!

We're just spermers! André adds, wielding a knife and rolling pin.

You're all *brothers*! Sister Invader spits out the word like we're vermin.

Then bring it on, Sister, Steven says, bring it on!

She looks around the room, at all of us armed Appleseeds, crouched behind our antique furniture, except for Steven, standing exposed, in his element. Sister Invader is weaponless and thinks twice about what she's doing. She probably just came here to scream at us, never intended to break in, getting swept up in the collective emotion. A wrong move here could create pure hell, so we give her

185

the space to make the next move. I worry that Steven may not wait much longer.

Sisters, please disperse now, a bullhorn barks outside, or you will be arrested.

Flashing blue lights set up a perimeter around our house. I've never been so happy to see cops—Sister or brother—and some in the crowd applaud, some sneer, before turning around, the tide of torches drifting away. Sister Invader has no option really but to return through the smashed window in which she came, where Sister Cops handcuff her. Inside, we slump onto the furniture, still clutching our weapons, but it's over, thank goddess, nobody got hurt. Kimchi and Bernie grab brooms and sweep up the broken glass. Steven still wields his butcher knives, intense frustration on his face, like a guy who's just had foreplay but no orgasm.

A Sister Detective takes pictures of the broken windows and questions us. She's cool and Drew flirts with her from a safe distance. She flirts back, says she'll keep a couple Sisters posted around the grounds the next day or two, just in case.

You need to control your Sisters, ma'am, Steven says, still looking for that release of rage simmering inside him. Drew wanders over to calm him, to get between them if he has to. The rest of us thank Sister Detective but make it obvious it's time for her to go.

You boys be careful out there, she says, looking at all of us in our masks, like she's gotta tell us that. Just because curfew's over, she adds, don't mean hunting season is.

We spend the evening boarding up the broken windows with plywood sheets from storage. When you have a hundred large windows around the house, you learn how to deal with broken ones.

This is, like, crazy, Cody says, nailing plywood over a window, I didn't sign up for this.

An hour later, lying in bed, it bugs me how I couldn't ask Miriam for help, can't ever call her, can't see her outside of our hook-ups. What am I waiting for? We're so over. Hell, I'm probably over. I go back and forth about whether or not to even go meet her this Thursday, the day before my birthday.

The next two days, I try reaching Gaia. She doesn't answer my texts or calls. I try her at the bookstore. No answer there either. Since curfew is over, I visit the store—the large front window, broken in the bombing, has been repaired—but I'm told she's not in. I go to the horse stable, under ominous clouds, the threat of rain lingering as it has for days, but she's not there either. I ask around. No one wants to help me. I feel more and more obsolete.

There's one place I haven't tried.

***

As I suspected, Gaia's yellow Spirit Guide truck is parked in front of Shooters. It used to be a Hooters but now it's a shooting range. Many Sisters have taken a real liking to guns. All are required to learn how to handle firearms, even pacifists. Mother President once demonstrated her own skills, shredding a brother-like silhouette target on the White House south lawn, streaming it live. Sisters must also learn CPR and basic medical care. In other words, train 'em how to shoot and then how to stop the bleeding.

My drone hovers over the parking lot off Lexington Avenue, as I tighten my gloves and brobot mask and enter the lobby. A wiry Sister Attendant looks up from cleaning a disassembled rifle.

Hey, you're not allowed in here.

Duh, I say, walking right on past, hoping she doesn't notice my trembling left leg. I'm getting bolder or stupider, I'm not sure which.

I'm calling the cops!

She whips out her cell. I ignore her and enter the range, searching. Several Sisters stand in booths, legs straddled, shooting at targets. It's hard to identify Gaia, everyone has noise-cancelling headphones over their baseball caps or hoodies.

Gaia?! I shout.

Sister Attendant follows me, tapping her cell screen:

I've just dialed!

Gaia?!!

I spot a few unruly strands of cobalt-blue hair poking out from underneath a hoodie, near the end. I hurry over. On a table next to her are two handguns. She is re-loading a third, a SisPistol.

Gaia!!

She yanks off her noise-cancelling headphones.

What are you doing here?

I motion toward the Sister Attendant following me with her cell phone.

It's okay, Becca, Gaia yells, he's with me.

Sister Attendant backs up toward the lobby, but gives me the universal "I'm watching you" signal, her index and middle fingers pointing at her eyes, then her index finger at me. I start to give her one finger back. But I reel it in.

You're ignoring me again, I say to Gaia.

She clamps her headphones back on her head. Her loose-fitting blue-and-purple tie-dye top ripples when she shoots three shots, all within millimeters of the paper bulls-eye, piercing the chest of a target

188

silhouette. Still, she looks disappointed. She has the soul of a New Ager but the eye of a sniper.

I didn't have anything to do with the bombing! I yell.

I know *you* didn't!

All around me, sporadic rounds burst. I plug my ears with the tips of my index fingers.

Can I shoot one?!

She points to a pistol.

That's a police-issue Glock 9mm Luger.

Is it loaded?

What do you think?

I probably shouldn't, but I reach into her booth, lift it gingerly, then step away. She tells me how to check the magazine—I do, it's fully loaded—and how to release the safety.

You know how to shoot?

Of course I do, I say, I used to shoot at cans on my uncle's farm.

But it's been over twenty years, so naturally I'm nervous as I step into the next booth, fit headphones over my ears, take a deep breath, hold the pistol in my right hand, and clamp my left hand over my right wrist. I close my left eye, tense up, and aim at the target in the chest of the silhouette.

They got any targets that don't look like brothers?

Gaia doesn't hear me. I re-aim, never sure of myself, whether shooting guns, shooting pool, or shooting the shit. I squeeze the trigger. The kickback sends my hands into my forehead, punching myself. I rub my brow and squint at the target. My bullet barely nicked the edge of the paper, nowhere near the silhouette. I aim and

189

squeeze three more shots, spraying holes, only one actually tears into the target, nicking the silhouette's upper left shoulder.

You really suck! she yells.

Good, I think, at least she's interested enough to notice.

She pops another shot. This one misses a bit more than the others. I smile, happy that maybe I have affected her. She takes a few seconds to aim, squeeze and fire off another shot that rips through the bulls-eye.

You think Miguel was involved in the bombing? I ask.

I know it. I can feel it.

She fires. This time the bullet splits her two best shots inside the bulls-eye. She doesn't celebrate, she expects great shots like this. She re-loads.

I think it's best we don't hang anymore, she says.

I know this is best for her and I'll be going away soon, still, I am stunned.

Gaia, don't do this.

She moves her stare from her target to me.

I'm not doing this. I'm not doing any of this.

She pops another couple of rounds. Dead-on. I can take a fucking hint.

A'ight, I say, I'll go.

I set the Glock down on the table in my booth.

By the way, I'm out of Kava Karma, I say.

She re-loads her weapon without even looking at me. I head toward the lobby, walking past her.

You were my best friend, Gaia.

This is not the first time I've called her that, but it's been years. I imagine a whispered, "You were mine too," but all I hear is the next barrage of bullets echoing around me, thick, like a violent aural fog.

THE PARTY

Three days before my 40th birthday and I feel like I'm running away from home, stuffing another backpack with a warm change of clothes, two pairs of socks, gloves, beanie, toiletries, water, Power Bars, a charger, and two rolls of cash. What I don't have is tincture, I've run out, my leg is twitching. I see Miriam in two days, probably for the last time. That thought stirs equal doses of lust and fear.

Calling all spermheads! Steven shouts, strutting down the hallway. Drawing room in ten minutes!

He stands in my doorway in camo sweats.

How many of those you packed so far?

This is my second.

I'd do at least ten. Follow me, we've got work to do.

We gather in the drawing room, the broken windows boarded-up with plywood. Less light streams in now, giving the huge room a darker, man-cave feel, if you ignore the two chandeliers above us.

Pony up, Steven says, pointing to a stack of test kits next to the whirly-girly on the grand piano. We all go through the motions, drawing blood, inserting vials into the centrifuge, waiting for the results. We do this so often, we've got track marks on our souls.

Yesterday taught us a lesson, Steven says, we need to get ready.
He lifts an old heavy chair over his head, carrying it out of the way.
The centrifuge dings. He checks every vial.

Clean as shit, ladies.

We remove our masks.

Steven directs us to clear the antique sofas, chairs, and tables,
making space in the middle of the room. We roll out mats, layering
them into three cushioned rings. He leads us in calisthenics, barking
instructions:

Feel the burn, bitches!

What a sorry group of mamas' boys.

Drop and give me twenty, pussy willow!

Who, like, died and made him a dick? Cody whispers.

Steven struts over, getting in Cody's face.

You wanna lead us, thumb-twat?!

Cody shrivels, shaking his head.

You sissy shits love to pretend you're warriors and bad-asses on
your little screens, Steven mocks, flickering his thumbs. Don't worry, I
won't work your thumbs, he adds, those are already in good shape.

André turns around.

I'm outta here—

Steven grabs André's thumb, twisting his arm behind his back,
underneath his dreadlocks.

Thumbs ain't gonna cut it in real combat.

You know that hurts, right? André says.

Steven releases him. André shakes his sore arm as Steven
circles around, scanning us with his eagle eyes. He taps his phone.
Oboes, then clarinets, seep over speakers, as we exercise, eerily

193

quiet at first. Soon, a crescendo fills the room: beastly drums, stomping strings, horns and winds screeching like raptors.

What the hell is this? André says.

Stravinsky's Rite of Spring, Steven replies. Make you uncomfortable?

Hell yeah, several of us say.

Good, it should. People rioted in the theater when they first heard it. The streets are rough, he says, looking straight at me. You can't properly train if you're in a happy place.

For the next three hours, Steven gives us crash trainings in self-defense and hand-to-hand combat. Drew shows us wrestling holds. We pair-up and bow and lunge and block and flip each other onto the mats.

Drew manhandles Cody, pinning him quickly.

That wasn't, like, what you showed us, Cody complains.

I'm ad-libbing, Drew says.

Cody tries a move but Drew flips and pins him.

Next to them, André and Kimchi square-off, an even match, maneuvering around each other. André's dreadlocks flapping in their faces.

I'm partnered with Bernie. He may be a chubby pacifist, but he drops me on my back. Once—

Oomph!

Twice—

Ow!

Three times.

Sonofabitch! That's enough!

I rise and catch my breath, sneaking my foot behind his heel, trying to take him down. I grunt. He doesn't budge.

Steven brings out different blades, from pocket knives to machetes and we're all much more excited now. It isn't long before blood drips from Kimchi's finger onto a mat.

What the hell, ladies, Steven says, stopping everything. You're supposed to draw your opponent's blood, not your own.

Kimchi excuses himself, hurrying off to the bathroom. Soon, a sofa is stabbed by Cody. Steven shakes his head.

I'd say that's enough for today.

We all take long showers and crash very early. The next afternoon, we limp downstairs and drag ourselves into the drawing room to do it again, bitching and moaning, but Steven's right, we need to know this shit. We test, do our calisthenics, review some self-defense. Then he brings out the big boys, a revolver and a black, semi-automatic rifle. We stare in awe.

You don't actually see these, he says, fondling the rifle. Anybody know what this baby is?

AR-15! everyone but me calls out.

He demonstrates how to load a clip, how to hold it and aim, how to squeeze the trigger.

Now you try.

He tosses the AR-15 to me. I flinch but manage to catch it.

Don't worry, it's not loaded.

I don't believe anybody should own one of these, but I have to admit something almost spiritual happens when I wrap my hands around the cold metal, the primal feeling of power. I raise it up to my head, bumping my chin—

Ow!

After the assault weapon show-and-tell, we follow Drew to the library/gym where he leads us in push-ups, planks, bench presses, crunches, and treadmill runs. The room steams with sweat.

Later that afternoon, we all collapse, exhausted, in the drawing room, our bodies slumped and sprawled, arms and legs dangling on the uncomfortable antique furniture, mouths groaning and snoring like weary travelers, too exhausted to even look at our devices. What we need now are our beds, those firm, king-sized mattresses—only the best to rest our testes—however, we are too tired to trudge upstairs.

I never knew I had, like, so many muscles, Cody complains.

I have too much poop to fight, Kimchi says.

We wanna laugh but laughing hurts.

Two days till your birthday, Drew says. Right?

I nod, weakly.

You're seeing your hook-up buddy tomorrow?

I'm supposed to, yeah.

Well, brothers, he speaks to all, we better throw him a party right now. Friday may be too late.

I shake my head. I'm like Kimchi, I say, I have too much poop.

You'll get a second wind, Drew says with the swagger of a cocky salesman, trying to rally the others who glare at him with all the enthusiasm of death row inmates.

Let's go old school, Steven says.

We seldom drink. Alcohol hurts sperm production and we have to wait 48 hours and pass two breathalyzers before we can resume production. Jonathan won't be happy, Big Sister dings him if we go a day without masturbating. He'll have to file sick reports on all of us.

I don't want anyone complaining, Drew says, adopting a girly voice: It'll hurt my sperm. Jonathan will get mad. His real voice returns: Eff that. What are they going to do, fire us?

The others exchange "Well, yeah," looks.

We're getting drunk for Bryan's birthday, Drew demands, and that's that! So if you haven't made your daily deposit, do so now.

We look at each other and realize everyone did their business this morning, knowing we'd be too tired to do so after another workout today. So the party moves to the game room, it's got billiards, pinball, darts. And lots of screens that Drew turns off. We shuffle in and plop down in chairs. He grabs a cue stick and starts poking us, like cattle, to get us up and moving. Cody grabs a cue. The two of them fence— click-clack-clack-click—around the two pool tables, their dueling cues evolving from Three Musketeers' swords to Star Wars light sabers.

André bumps some reggaeton, I couldn't tell you who, but it's loud enough to drown-out our conversation to listening Sisters' ears.

Steven pulls out a liquor cart filled mostly with bottles of vodka: Absolute, Grey Goose, Sista Vodka.

No Sister Juice, I say.

Drew removes a bottle of Boys Will Be Boys Bourbon, one of the last liquors still brewed by us, in Tennessee. He pours shots for all.

Now we're talking, Steven says, passing the small glasses around, raising his own.

To Bryan! We're gonna miss your ass.

To Bryan!

We tip our shots and tilt our heads back. I feel the brown liquid slide down slowly, burning the sides of my throat like thighs on a

197

playground slide on a hot August afternoon. I shiver. Steven refills all our glasses.

I can't believe it, I say. Forty! How did this happen?

It's just a number, Cody smirks. A big, like, fucking number.

We drain our shots. Bernie and I climb up and sit on a table, talking about the old times when we got drunk and checked out girls—or guys—and seldom got them. We compare that to now and how we don't drink or get high anymore but how we still check out Sisters—or brothers—even if we can't be with them. We talk about stupid stuff that seems funny because we're drinking. We don't smoke trees at this party, weed is great, we love it, most brothers do it to numb the pain. But Jonathan administers weekly urine tests—standing behind us, which I hate because I have stage fright—and if you test positive for pot, coke, heroin or meth, you are kicked out. The harder drugs I can see, but pot? Sisters say THC affects sperm count and it's all about production. Sisters will allow a little booze now and then because it doesn't stay long in our systems.

I tap the red record button on my phone.

EDITOR'S NOTE: Once again, because so many are talking, I've listed their drunk talk as theatrical dialogue:

STEVEN: I just wanna go fuckin' crazy!

DREW: Hell yeah!

They both bang on whatever is nearby.

CODY: You guys are so, like, last century.

KIMCHI: Pre-herstory.

ANDRÉ:(smiling) Pre-seven-eleven.

198

ME: It's *nine*-eleven.

ANDRÉ: Seven-eleven, nine-eleven, who cares? It's ancient
    history.

BERNIE: Not to change the subject—well, actually, yes,
    to change the subject—why is it, gentlemen,
    that we never talk about all those babies out
    there that are ours?

CODY: What's to talk about? We'll, like, never know them.

BERNIE: That's what I mean. We should share how that
    feels. We never talk about the important stuff.

STEVEN: No Debbie Downers. This is a party.

DREW: Yeah. Another time, dude.

We bop our heads, our bodies, our whole beings to the music.

CODY: Do you guys think, like, all future superheroes
    will be Sisters?

KIMCHI: SuperSisters.

STEVEN: That's just wrong.

ANDRÉ: We are the villains.

STEVEN: You guys are so out of touch with your inner macho,
    it's pathetic.

ANDRÉ: We're tilting at windmills.

CODY: What the fuck?

ANDRÉ: It's from Don Quixote.

CODY: Again, like, what the fuck?

STEVEN: (raising his glass) A toast. Our future is dependent
    on us brothers sticking together. United we stand.
    Divided we fall.

ANDRÉ: Yeah! Screw Sisters!

199

KIMCHI: Sisters suck!

Bernie lowers his hand, face-down, the universal keep-it-down sign.

BERNIE: Careful, guys.

Our banter becomes a moment in this bleak, bleak world where I feel a little happy, drinking with my buds. I remember reading somewhere how reminiscing is the first sign you've peaked. I have to laugh. We've all peaked and I can't imagine any brothers ever reminiscing about these current days. We drink more shots and grunt like animals and the music changes to rap, Lil Wayne, I think, and we eventually get around to talking about the elephant in the room—me.

CODY: What are you gonna, like, do, Bryan?

ME: I'm told I get to pick where I retire.

ANDRÉ: Retire. Yeah, right.

DREW & STEVEN: Florida!

KIMCHI: (singing) I wish they all could be California Girls.

ME: I'll probably live on the streets. If I'm lucky.

CODY: How will you, like, know when to run?

STEVEN: I've been trying to tell him he needs a plan.

ME: And then what? I don't even know what the future is.

    I've never been good at looking ahead.

    Looking back, I'm all over that.

We nod a collective nod, drink a collective shot.

ANDRÉ: What if they come after you tonight?

ME: I got a couple backpacks ready to go. Anybody hear
    or see anything, text me.

Heads nod, followed by mumbles.

STEVEN: Whatever you do, go out strong, brother.

    Death with dignity.

200

CODY: I say run. As far away as you, like, can.

ANDRÉ: Take your own life before they take it for you.

BERNIE: Don't listen to them, Bryan. Do whatever feels
    right. Honor your feelings to the end.

ME: What's it matter how I go out? Nobody's gonna
    be around to care.

CODY: We'll care. (reaches behind a chair, pulls out
    a plastic bag) Happy birthday.

I tear it open, a little kid on Christmas Day, revealing a backpack
plastered with superhero patches: Batman, Black Panther, Iron Man,
Superman. But no Wonder Woman, Black Widow, or Sister Snake.

ME: Thanks, Cody.

CODY: I wish you weren't, like, leaving.

ME: Me too.

Then the strangest thing happens. He hugs me. Brothers never do
that anymore, not even bro hugs, even after we've tested negative.
We're out of the habit. I feel awkwardly moved and don't know what to
say, so I pick up my guitar and strum our anthem. We sing it with
inebriated glee:

ALL: Every sperm is sacred
    Every sperm is great
    If a sperm gets wasted
    God gets quite irate.

Kimchi steps forward, singing and dancing like a K-Pop star.

KIMCHI: Every sperm inspected
    Every sperm every day
    If boy sperm detected
    Goddess say throw away!

201

We flash thumbs-ups to Kimchi for his sweet ad-lib. I keep strumming, my delicate tinkling of the bottom strings sounds almost like rain. We sit quietly now, too buzzed to do much else, reflecting like buddies hanging out one last time with a friend before he goes off to war. Bernie hands me a gift, wrapped in tissue paper.

I remembered too. Good luck.

I fold open the tissue, revealing a vintage gray True Religion hoodie with a Buddha playing guitar across the front.

I found it on eBay, Bernie says, placing his palms together, bowing.

Namasté.

I get up to follow suit. Namasshtey. I almost tip over. I'm fucked-up, I say, I gotta go to bed. I lean on different pieces of furniture, staggering across the room.

Wait! Drew stops me, feigns like he's gonna take me down. Instead, he grabs me in a gorilla bro hug. I am stunned by my second hug in minutes. My world is spinning, in more ways than one.

Now eff off, he says, moving across the room to drink with Steven.

I make my way to the staircase, clinging to the banister, climbing up the daunting steps. Cody approaches me, carrying my Martin.

You, like, taking this with you?

Wasn't planning on it. Gotta travel light.

I watch him ogling the pretty rosewood.

You can have it, I say.

Fer real?

Yeah. Just promissssme you'll take good care of it.

I will.

Remember the chords I ssshowed you?

I hug the banister as he struggles to finger a C chord. The strings buzz. But a huge smile spreads on his face.

That's good, I lie, pulling myself up the stairs.

I'm gonna, like, miss you, Cody says.

I don't tell him how I've been longing for the Sisters in my life to say that, anything like that. Instead, it's a brother. My replacement.

Me too.

I pull myself the rest of the way up the stairs.

THE LAST HOOK-UP

I have just enough brain cells functioning to scoop up some B-12 and Vitamin I to minimize the hangover I know is coming. I grab a blue Gatorade from the little fridge in my room. I'll need those electrolytes. I plop face-down on my firm mattress, wanting to pass out, longing for soft and feathery. My ears are ringing and soon I'm spinning, mental gravity pushing on me like I'm in a twirling, tumbling plane. I rise onto my hands and knees, my head down, hangdog style. Nope, ain't working either, so I turn over, prop up on my elbows, and lean back, bracing myself against the high-backed, ornate headboard. I press against it in vain hopes that this is the ticket to stop the world spinning. Knobs dig into my spine, the old carved wood imprinting the flesh on the back of my arms. How could I be so stupid? I haven't been this drunk since college. Fuck! Tomorrow is such a big day. I know that's why I got drunk, why I let myself go, I'm such an idiot.

Damn it room. Stop!

At least it's early, nine-something, I can get a lot of sleep in before I see Miriam. Fuck, now the room is dropping like a broken elevator. It's like I got a black-hole gut and I'm about to get sucked down into it. My head is throbbing. What the hell should I do? Should I even hook-up with Miriam—in, what, seven hours?—knowing I could be taken away and retired right then and there? Will she even bother to show? Why should she? She promised she'd let me know when the shit went down and they wouldn't just take me away, but can I believe her? What if this is it? My head is fucking killing me. Why did I drink? I'm a fucking idiot. I hyperventilate, trying anything to make the spinning stop. Damn, that makes it go faster, at the speed of our planet, and it's a wonder we're not all getting sick all the time, that barfing is not as common as breathing. I pop some Tums and chew 'em down real quick and grab hold of the headboard, and hang on tight.

One good thing about getting drunk is I do eventually pass out. I typically don't sleep much before seeing Miriam, too excited, but tonight my sleep is deep. I have a thousand dreams but can't remember one of 'em. All I know is my cell chimes way too soon, like a fire alarm. My head vibrates like a katzenjammer jackhammer. I feel like a cracked egg, my eyes throb and freak out at light, my gut gurgles, my lower esophagus rumbles, like the lava monster could surface at any moment. I belch as loud as I've ever belched since high school. I nearly throw up the Gatorade, thank Goddess I don't, nothing grosser than blue chunks, don't think I could handle looking at that. I gotta get out of bed, but I can't, I'm plastered to it. What a way to go out, I have such mixed feelings about seeing Miriam. I wanna make epic love to her, go out with the greatest bang ever, but then I think, shit, will I even be able to get it up? Hangover hard-ons are nearly impossible, if I remember college correctly. I don't wanna go, I could be walking into my final trap, and I fear Miriam now like I've never feared a Sister before. I breathe deep, three times, everybody's always telling me to breathe.

205

I force myself to get up and move, at the speed of snooze, taking a good ten minutes just to get into my running clothes and shoes, pulling them on like I've never worn such things before. What should I do if Miriam doesn't show? What am I potentially getting into? Maybe I was right to get drunk, maybe I should just stay here. But I open my closet and grab one of my two packed backpacks, a basic black one, the first survival kit I prepped. I hoist it weakly over my shoulders and I already feel like resting. Out into the long, wide hallway I go, it stretches in front of me like a foggy eternity, but somehow I navigate it and reach the top of the wide staircase which now feels like a mountain. I cling to the banister, working my way down, step by stupid step, managing not to fall. I reach the parlor, stand before the front door and stare into the retinal scanner, wondering if it will recognize my bloodshot eye. It does. I slouch out onto the front steps, the cold air slapping my face, the door closing behind me. I could be logged-out forever, you never know. I slowly stretch and breath in the carroty-crisp October air, tighten my mask and gloves, and slump down the three brick steps, landing on the stiff brown grass. I jog, my backpack jostling off my shoulders, my brain jiggling in my skull. Looking back at the mansion, I feel like the lord of the manor, for perhaps my last time. So be it. I turn away, wondering if my mechanical hummingbird might start following me now, maybe the normal power-down schedule has changed, now that my end is near, but my drone remains up on the roof, recharging, recalibrating, re-whatever-it's-doing up there. I scan the skies. No drones in sight.

I walk through the forest, looking up at the silhouettes of trees against the inky sky, all of them succumbing to autumn's yanking, their leaves tumbling and falling, in curls that carpet the dark thinning lawn. I pass under one of the few working lampposts and spot splashes of fiery red and soft yellow within the arc of light. When I reenter shadow it all turns shades of gray. I reach the street, turn left, jog in the bro-only lane, a hungover object set in motion, my anxious momentum carrying me to where I know I probably shouldn't go. Do I go because I'm a guy? Or simply because I'm human? If the roles were reversed, would a Sister do this to get one final fuck?

Headlights approach, I think it's a van, uh-oh, that can't be good, I imagine it pulling up beside me, the doors swinging open and a couple Sisters shoving me inside. I stiffen, ready to sprint, and the van drives really close on my right. I lean to the left. If it pulls over, I'll take off, back into the patch of forest surrounding The Factory, I could lose them in the trees.

No worries, it drives by, a white Femme Floral delivery van. I laugh and breathe and look back to make sure it's not doing a U-turn. The red taillights turn left on Fourth and soon vanish. I really need to stop to catch my breath, but I can't lose my focus, need to stay inside the bro-only lane—a bitch when you're hungover—but something triggers my foggy radar and I look around and see a Sister Silhouette running on Park Avenue. Don't usually see Sisters running this early. We are both on pace to reach the intersection of Trimble and Park Avenue at the same time. Coincidence? I slow down a little, she slows down a little. I speed up, she speeds up. She's got an angle on me and I'm forced to stay in this goddess-damned bro-only lane. I look around for others but she is alone. Here it comes, she's now under streetlights, and I recognize that fanatic look in her eyes—a Sister Kisser. If she can, she'll grab my mask with one hand and plant her smooch of death on my lips, or at least settle for a cheek. I let her get

within a couple steps of me, then I feint like I'm turning east on Park
Avenue, draw her over that way, then I dart back onto Trimble, and
she swings around and lunges, missing me, twirling awkwardly, but
not breaking stride, continuing in the direction she was heading,
running east on Park Avenue. I leave those killer lips in my wake. My
backpack slides off my shoulders, I catch it with the back of my arms,
hunched forward, panting now, my head pounding, my heart pumping,
the backpack bouncing against my shoulder blades. I am fully awake
now, racing up the hillside streets, past the Sensitive Estates gate and
the fountain statues of Gloria and RBG.

I don't remember ever being so tired reaching the Love Shack,
except maybe my first run. I reach the grounds and slow to a fast
walk, heading straight for the greenhouse about twenty yards behind
the Love Shack. I've scoped it out the last couple months, it's never
used anymore. I try the door, still unlocked. I enter and sweep my cell
flashlight around the cluttered space. Shovels and rakes and hoes
hang, casting long, eerie shadows in the moonlight. Stacks of empty
pots on tables look like castle spires. Shriveled plants droop over the
edges. The place reeks of dried peat moss but it's a good spot to spy
on everything, so I hide behind a stack of pots and wait for Miriam to
show up, late as usual. I know she probably monitors me from her
phone, probably sees me hiding here, but I commit to this anyway and
wait. I shiver from damp, chilling sweat, breathing hard and quick and
my left leg kicks into gear, trembling like it does—my leg has a mind
of its own—and I dig into my backpack, grab a bottled water, take a
sip and end up chugging the whole thing. I rub my arms to keep
warm. Figures, my luck, I go on the run just as autumn deepens. I
couldn't have been born in July, could I. Had to be a Libra.

I weigh my options. If this is it, I can't go home, neither to The Factory nor where I grew up. I could house-hop, but Justin, that homeless guy, says it's getting much harder to do. Maybe I can hang out with him, he could show me the ropes, I'm sure things have changed since I was homeless, briefly, at the beginning of all this. I check my cell, I'm a little late myself this morning, but Miriam is definitely late, twenty minutes now. I watch the forest trail that she usually comes running down, see no sign of life. This is not good. Looks like it's time to go and it really hits me now, how unprepared I am. I have been so paralyzed by fear, all I do is think and not do, I should've packed more backpacks last night and hidden them all over the city. I should be long gone. It's just, Miriam promised me she'd let me know when my time comes. I trust her. *Trusted* her. Fool.

My leg quivers, my headache ratchets. I pop some more vitamin I, gotta stop that, bad for the kidneys, but today my head outranks all other body parts. Okay, now Miriam's getting really late, even for her. She's not coming, of course not, who am I kidding, it's been less than two weeks since the carousel bombing, she'll probably never come again. I should hightail it outta here—

The kitchen door opens and a Mysterious Sister emerges, bundled, her face wrapped in a scarf. She is too short and stocky to be Miriam. WTF? She locks the door, taps in the alarm code, and moves off into the dark, opening a sedan that I hadn't noticed parked in shadows on the other side of the main house. The Mysterious Sister drives off. Now what do I do? I've never seen anyone else here before. Why did I not notice anything going on inside the Shack this whole time? I know why, I'm too stuck inside my head. What the hell was she doing in there? Do I dare risk going in? Was the Sister hiding

209

out to kill me, but she tired of waiting? Did she set a trap? My left leg is tapping the floor like a woodpecker and I close my eyes and focus on my breathing, like everyone tells me to do, and I wait a few minutes more before curiosity gets the better of me. I clutch my backpack, exit the greenhouse, tiptoe up to the Shack. I type in the alarm code. Click. I step inside. Nothing looks disturbed, except for the kitchen table, where a shiny silver wrapped box sets, about the size of a paperback novel, tied with red ribbon. Leaning against it is a blank envelope. I grab a kitchen knife and carefully slice open the envelope, still fearing a possible booby trap, possibly anthrax. Using only two fingernails, I tug out a card, a beautiful autumn landscape photo of the Mohican covered bridge, a local landmark, forty minutes from here. I read the note:

> Happy Birthday! Sorry I can't see you today.
> It's not because I don't want to. And I know
> you had nothing to do with what's happened.
> See you next week? I hope you like the gift.
>
> Love, Me

Love? She has never told me she loves me. Not spoken, not written, not telepathically, nothing. I search the living room, the bathroom, the closets. I am indeed alone. I pour a glass of water, chug it, sit down at the table, trying to make some sense of it all. Is it the vaccine? Don't get your hopes up, moron. But I can't help thinking this elegantly-wrapped gift holds my destiny, a future I'm scared to unwrap. I could just leave, run, hide, begin my new life. That would be the smartest thing to do. Yeah, right, do I even know myself? I can't leave a gift unopened. I must know. But do I wanna know? Oh just fucking open it already! I unfurl the perfectly-curled red ribbon—still

210

wary of a trap—and carefully unfold the glossy silver paper. I lift the box cover, peel back white tissue paper. Inside is a document, a small handwritten certificate with a gold border. I lift it from the box.

SIX-WEEK EXTENSION

This document entitles the bearer to:

Six more weeks of work at The Factory

Effective 10/21/2032

Expires 12/2/2032

Be productive

Mayor Miriam Stewart

It is embossed with the official Sisterfield mayoral seal. I reread it, can't quite process it with my achy head. I sit back in the kitchen chair. Six more weeks? I laugh, first a little trickle of chuckles, then a gush. I feel so insanely relieved. I've got a new lease on life, even if short-term, and I reread the certificate one more time, just to be certain. I fire-off good-news texts to Gaia and my sis. I fold the certificate, wedging it into my phone case. I lock up and enter the security code and hide my backpack inside the stack of pots in the greenhouse and run back the way I came. The morning feels ten degrees warmer, the first soft light of dawn peeking out like a lavender rip in the black blanket of night. My head doesn't hurt any more, imagine that. It seems like it's only moments until I'm running through Queenwood Center. The forest sprouts alive with waking butterflies and dragonflies fluttering and floating as if enjoying their last days before the real cold arrives.

Back inside The Factory, I want to show everybody my certificate, but no one's awake yet, they won't be up for hours. I leap up the

staircase, flop on my bed, brimming with excitement, until Mr.
Hangover comes roaring back and I do what my body begs me to do:
I crash.

NIRVANA

The other Appleseeds stop by my room after they wake, checking to see if what they've heard is true, that I'm back, snoring in bed. Later, at breakfast, we drink tart elderberry juice and I proudly display my certificate and the others congratulate me, hopeful that our expiration dates are not so etched in stone. They ask how I know the mayor. A friend of a friend, I say. The others soon drift off into their digital worlds. Except Cody.

Here's your axe, he says, handing over my steel-string.

You'll get it back in six weeks, I say.

That afternoon, a broCar drops me off, with my backpack and guitar in hand, at Charles Mill Lake. I walk a trail that meanders along the muddy coastline. Crickets and frogs burst with the renewed joy that I now feel. Here, like everywhere, the trees are half bare. Gold and brown leaves float on the water curled like gondolas. I stuff the backpack into a dark green garbage bag, twist-tie it, then wrap another bag around it, double-twist-tie that, and I stuff the whole thing down into the middle of a clump of tree stumps, well away from the water. I pile wet masses of twigs and leaves on top of that and smoosh it all down with a heavy, watermelon-sized rock. Then I hike a little further to my favorite spot, a log at the edge of the water. I tune my guitar, tame all six strings. I strum one of my own songs, start to sing. A startled frog plops into the water.

                    It's good to be alive
                    Go ahead and cry
                    That's what it's all about
                    Free the passion and the pain
                    Locked up inside
                    Oh it's good to be alive

You're not that good a singer are you.

The raspy brother's voice startles me. I recognize it and notice boot tracks a couple inches deep in mud near the edge of the lake. My eyes follow them to rubber boots, maybe ten yards away, just off the trail, pointing toward the sky, water licking at the heels. Blue jeans stretch out on the bank, nestled in a bed of leaves and twigs, perpendicular to the water. Fisherbrother. The guy I saw the last time I was here. His fishing hat and vest droop on his skeletal frame that's as thin as the fishing pole beside him. I see no line leading into the lapping water.

Remember me? I ask.

Fisherbrother weakly tilts his head. Mosquitoes feast on his welt-covered face. He winces.

No.

He lays his head back down on the pillow of twigs and leaves.

Maybe we should get you to a hospice.

I don't need no damn hospice.

You'll be more comfortable.

I don't want comfortable, he coughs. I want to feel this.

214

Sounds crazy but I respect that, coming here to die. Elephants do that, they have a hallowed ground they walk to when it's time. Don't think I could do it, not like this. I'd rather die drugged in bed under a warm blanket with a good book.

I change the subject: My pops once told me about a beast people saw around here, back in the 60's, when he was a boy. They called it Orange Eyes. It was ten-feet tall with glowing eyes and the most-foul stench. Did you ever hear about it?

No reply. I can't tell if he's even breathing.

Okay, I'll leave you be, I say, packing up my guitar.

His head lolls to the side.

Know any Nirvana?

Nirvana?

Yeah.

I can fake it, I say, pulling the guitar back out to play.

I was in high school when Kurt killed himself.

I was barely born, I say, nailing the simple riff to The Man Who Sold The World, the one Nirvana song I know. I sing and he listens politely, his left boot swaying slightly in rhythm. I forget the last verse, but his boot keeps swaying even after I mercifully end the song.

Kurt's turning over in his grave, fisherbrother chuckles. And y'know that's a David Bowie song.

Yeah, but it's on Nirvana Unplugged, I say, packing up my Martin.

No, no, keep playing.

I don't know any other Nirvana.

Play something else.

I strum another of my own songs—Are You There?—one that questions the existence of Goddess and yet begs for it. I put my heart and soul into that one. Fisherbrother doesn't react.

Any other songs I might know?

Playing covers is like playing with someone else's kids, I joke. Fun, but you still prefer playing with your own. But I oblige him, wailing on Bob Dylan's Knockin' On Heaven's Door, one of my dad's favorites. Fisherbrother's left boot sways to the melody and when I come to the line "Bury my guns in the ground," I substitute "Bury my fishing pole in the ground." I think I see a corner of a smile on his bumpy face, just for a moment, as his head lifts up and he looks out at the muddy water, the sunlight shimmering like tarnished gold. I end with some "Ooh-oo—oo—ooohs." It feels right to stop there.

Can I get you anything?

He doesn't answer, lying stiff, quiet, his left boot still swaying slowly back and forth. I text for a broCar and walk back to the road. Just my luck, I come here to celebrate and, once again, get bummed out by Fisherbrother. He is one brave dude, though, inspiring, taking his dignity with him. There are a billion strong stories like his.

And another billion brothers who don't go so nobly. I wonder which one I'll ultimately be.

Who am I kidding?

I know.

FUCK, I'M FORTY!

My birthday comes and goes without fanfare. To celebrate and drink again would incur another hangover, not to mention the wrath of Jonathan. No surprise that Miriam doesn't call to wish me Happy Birthday, that's against our protocol. What saddens me is that Gaia did not call or text. Emily, my Sis, did text:

> Happy birthday, big brother. Forty, wow. Well, call me when you can. Hope you're still alive. Oh gosh, that's rude. Call me. Love you.

Mom texted too, she never texts anymore. Emily sent it for her:

> Happy Birthday. All my love, mom.

I spend the day in a weird space, that's for sure, too worthless to do much but walk the gardens and strum my Martin. I show Cody how to play a G chord. I don't even do my usual lube job, we all must wait at least 48 hours after imbibing, which makes for a tense vibe in The Factory. I catch up on my posts, haven't uploaded anything in days, so I push everything out at once on the dark *It* website Cody set up for me. I don't know anything about that stuff, I just post, don't know if anyone's even visiting it, don't look at comments. Anything negative would paralyze me.

Suddenly, I see a flash of something you usually don't see around here, heading down the hall.

Selfie?

Thinking I might be suffering from alcohol deliriums, I poke my head out into the hallway just as the bathroom door closes. The light goes on through the crack underneath it. Huh. A Selfie sighting on my birthday, that's special. According to Jonathan, Selfie only comes out to self-lubricate in the early morning hours, when we're asleep or ensconced in our rooms on our devices. He never answers when we knock on his locked door. I've said maybe ten words to him in the year he's been here. Maybe this sighting is an omen.

Later, Steven stops by my room and tosses me a backpack made of camo canvas that nearly knocks me over. I open it up and find six fold-up—

Trowels?

Not just trowels, Steven says, Survival Buddies. Seven-in-one-tools. He demonstrates, opening one, whipping it around, flashing its different possibilities. You got your pliers in the handle, he says, plus a knife and a screwdriver. The end of the handle is a hammer, there's a bad-ass little saw on the edge of the trowel blade—see, right here—and a hidden compartment to hide your cyanide tablets.

My what?

Pills not included.

He folds up the trowel—click-click—with the efficiency of a Marine closing his rifle after a cleaning.

You're nuts.

Keep one with each pack, he says, and one in your pocket at all times. It fits pretty snugly around your ankle too.

218

Thanks, I think.

Oh, you'll thank me.

André texts me to stop by his room, so I do. His walls and shelves are lined with Star Trek paraphernalia. A Worf coffee mug sets on his desk. André points to his bed, to a light gray backpack with the Star Trek Enterprise patch sewn on.

That's for you. Six more weeks, eh?

Yeah. Now I have an expiration date.

Better than expired. It's a blessing, Bryan, now you can better prepare yourself. You weren't ready before.

Maybe Miriam knew I wasn't ready, I reflect, maybe she's protecting me. I head back to my room, stuff my new backpacks with the usual survival supplies, adding a Survival Buddy trowel to each one. I wrap up the Star Trek pack in two garbage bags, sneaking it outside with the trash, rolling the garbage bin to the maintenance building. My drone follows me, but bores quickly and hovers over some attractive Sister Visitors. I grab the pack out of the garbage and hurry into the forest, walking almost to the end of the grounds. I find the biggest elm tree around, measure six feet from the tree, due east. I get on my knees and pull a trowel out of my back pocket, unfold it, and dig into the soft soil. It takes a while, the trowel blade not much wider than a wallet, but it does the trick. I bury the pack, covering it with dirt and forest fluff. When I head back toward the house, my drone finds me. I gaze up at it, see strips of sunset colors—cloud grays tinged with deep reds—between the limbs of half-bare trees. I see Bernie up in his treehouse, sitting lotus-style, wearing a traditional Buddhist saffron-colored robe and his brobot mask.

How's the view?

219

He doesn't answer, staring off in a sunset trance. I climb halfway up the wooden steps nailed into the trunk.

Bernie, you all right?

You know how I was named after Bernie Sanders?

Yeah.

But how I told people I was named after Bernie's Weekend?

Uh-huh.

What happened to Bernie in that movie?

He died at the very beginning. Oh. Oh no.

Bernie stares off into the sunset that now looks like raw, rancid meat.

Tested positive this morning.

Wow, I'm sorry.

I must accept what is inevitable. Thick Nhat Hanh said, "Peace is every step of the journey. Not something you strive to attain." This is just my next step.

We silently watch the bloodstains in the sky spread and deepen.

Do you know how you got it?

He shrugs. He knows.

You're so young, this sucks, why is this happening?

There is no meaning, what would it be? Giving meaning to things is just a human need, like scratching your back, something we do to feel better. Life has the meaning you decide to give it.

Aren't you pissed-off?

Leaving this world with bitterness is not healthy for my next stage. He gazes down at me. It is tragic and tragedy requires forgiveness.

Forgiveness? What does that even mean when there's so much to forgive?

It is your last great act on earth, he says.

I chew on his words as two cop cars park near The Factory and a Quartet of Sister Cops climb out, pointing at us up in the tree.

Oh shit, Bernie, you gotta go.

I called them, he says, watching the Sister Cops approach.

How can you be so chill?

What am I going to do? Wherever I go, I'm still a dying brother. This is my fate.

The Sister Cops surround the tree trunk.

Let's go, Bernie, one says.

I climb down first, noticing near the bottom, carved in the tree: Bernie 2032. I reach the ground and move aside as he calmly climbs down and softly touches the ground.

Stay strong, like a tree, he says. Trees can bend in the wind. We brothers didn't bend enough.

And with that he offers his arms in surrender. The Sister Cops escort him to a cruiser.

Have a nice sunset, he says, back over his shoulder.

You too, Bernie. You too.

A Sister Cop cups his head and folds him like a prisoner into the backseat.

Sisters, I beg, looking sheepishly down to the ground, can you please tell me where you're taking him?

No can do.

And off he goes in the cruiser, the last I see of him is the dark hair on the back of his head.

He's the first of us Appleseeds to get the Y. We quarantine for three days and test daily for the next week—thank Goddess we're all negative—and we spray and wipe down every surface at the Factory, which is pointless because the virus lasts less than two minutes outside the body, but father-brother Jonathan is anal and paranoid and right now that's okay.

Where did they take Bernie? I ask Jonathan.

I don't know.

What happens next for him?

Don't know.

Nice talking to you, as always.

I think back to when Bernie joined The Factory, from Bucyrus. Jonathan introduced him as our new gay Appleseed.

Well, I guess you could say I'm gay, Bernie explained, but lot of good it does me. Who am I going to sleep with? One of you guys? I must say the field of choices is uninspiring. And I don't even like sex. Everyone's too hung up on the destination. Not the journey itself.

I feel my eyes moisten at the memory. I contact the bro-only clinic, Bernie isn't there, I call the bro-only retirement home in Lexington, not there either. It's as if he disappeared. I can't stop thinking of his advice to me about my last great act on earth.

But is that last great act forgiveness?

***

The night is nippy on the nipples as they used to say. I'm bundled in a parka, a Browns beanie, and my latex mask. It's after closing, Gaia's store is empty. I tap on the glass. She looks up from behind the counter, surprised to see me. Her hair is streaked stark red, as if dipped in blood, a symbol of the recent violence, though red hair and green eyes might just mean she's gearing up for the holidays, it's hard to say with her. She unlocks the door—I notice her Om nose piercing—and she returns to her espresso machine. Cinnamon incense greets me, making me hungry.

You're still around, she says. Hey, happy belated birthday. She places two amber bottles on the counter. Sorry I didn't text.

No worries, I forgot yours too.

I guess we're even, she says, knowing full well we're nowhere near even.

Y'know, I kinda miss the blue hair.

Clashed too much with my eyes.

Like red doesn't?

Clashing doesn't count during Christmas.

I browse the bookshelves and think back to the one time I played guitar here. I ended the gig with Nine Inch Nail's Something I Can Never Have—remember I played it at The Factory?—a simple, haunting riff that bores into your skull. I put some serious angst into my performance, an obvious statement about her that Gaia didn't appreciate. She never asked me to play here again.

My friend Bernie got the Y.

I'm sorry, Brayan.

Silence. Nothing much more to say, not after so many times hearing "I'm sorry." I drift over to the Russian Literature section, it only takes up half a shelf since there are so few known Russian Sister authors: Svetlana Alexievich's War's Unwomanly Face, and Sofia Petrovna by Lydia Chukovskaya & Aline Werth, along with a few others. Gaia says a glut of new young Russian Sisters' books are coming, to add to the already overflowing shelves of new American Sisters' books. I browse the shelves. Russia has always fascinated me. The fall of the Romanovs, The Revolution, Rasputin, the Gulags,

223

all still so relevant today. At first the novels intimidated me, the characters' names longer than some sentences I write, but when I read Turgenev's Fathers and Sons, a slim read, it spoke to me. Then I devoured Dostoyevsky's The Brothers Karamazov and Crime & Punishment, saving Tolstoy for later. Russian authors were masters at chronicling the human condition during the most difficult, depressing times, crafting stunning prose out of pure human misery.

Miriam got me a six-week extension for my birthday.

That's wonderful.

Yeah, it is, I say lukewarmly.

What's wrong?

It feels like an expiration date.

I hear you. It'd be tough to wrap my brain around that.

I linger on the few Russian brothers' classics: Chekhov's Three Sisters, Tolstoy's Anna Karenina, Dostoyevsky's Crime And Punishment. The Brothers Karamazov always seems to be missing. I pick up the hefty Anna.

I wonder what the great Russian writers would have made of all this.

Not much, Gaia answers, being brothers they'd all be dead.

I hope I can leave something behind like this.

You are, you're leaving thousands of little girls.

Thousands that will never know me.

I don't think you get how spiritually awesome it is. A sliver of your energy, of *you*, is going to be all over the Midwest. What better legacy to leave.

I guess.

I flip through Anna Karenina.

I remember in college lit, the Sisters thought Anna's death was so romantic. What bullshit. It sure wasn't romantic for the railroad worker cleaning up her mangled and bloody body from the train tracks.

The train, Gaia explains, was just a symbol for modern society. It killed her.

Just like us brothers.

I become aware of my left leg shaking, again. I flatten my heel to the hardwood floor to stop it, but in dealing with my shaking leg, I fumble the book onto the floor—THUMP—and Gaia jumps back, bumping a stack of coffee cups that clatter on the counter. She holds her hand to her chest.

Oh shit, I'm sorry, Gaia.

Ever since the bombing. I've been insomniacing like crazy.

I had nothing to do with that, I say, picking up Anna Karenina, returning her to the shelf. I wander over to the counter, grab the tincture bottles, pocket one, look at the label on the other: Mellow Me Out.

You should take a few drops yourself, I say, squeezing drops under my tongue.

Oh, I do, trust me.

There's the most awkward of silences. She shuts down her computer.

You still posting your ramblings?

Yeah. I have a few more to upload.

If I publish it I'd be risking my career, she says, her words drifting across the store, lightly brushing all the book spines lined up on the shelves, absorbing into the words of others, the millions of pages of consonants, vowels, and punctuations. When you buy a book from

225

Gaia, you are buying a bit of her too, her thoughts, her breath, her energy.

She turns out the lights, opens the door.

Be well, she says.

EDITOR'S NOTE: I'd already been reading his posts and watching his videos on the dark It, editing them into book form. I just hadn't figured out if I could safely publish them and I didn't want to get Bryan's hopes up.

WE FINALLY MEET AGAIN

I don't record or post anything for a few days, don't have the bandwidth. Instead I walk the dying gardens of Queenwood Center, finding a patch of mums thriving in burgundies, oranges, and golds. I inhale the perfumes of the forest and forest bathe, absorbing the pheromones of elms, willows, curly oaks and sycamores, so tall, so strong, yet they too shall fall, eventually, and I take some comfort in that. I climb up Bernie's tree, clinging to the boards nailed to the trunk, it's scary, hoisting myself up into his treehouse, a roofed, three-walled room. The west wall is missing on purpose, so he could watch his beloved sunsets from the treetops.

Smokey, boiling clouds coming straight for us. So far it's been a mild fall, but a storm has stirred for days. Thunder grumbles, getting so close it's biblical, and I don't have an umbrella or a poncho, but that's okay, I don't want one. I try to sit lotus-style, but I'm not limber like Bernie—for a chubby guy he's quite a pretzel—and I give up, dangling my legs over the edge. Thin lines of rain begin falling not far off and lightning cracks the charcoal sky. A clap or two follows. I smell sulfur in the air, and I await, my thoughts and emotions so many, so brief they don't even have a half-life. Then the rains hit, the first downpour we've seen in weeks, sudden and massive, pelting me,

227

dumping all the brother-angels' pent-up tears. I pull off my mask and raise my arms to the heavens, like Andy in Shawshank, a "Yes" to the universe. Rivulets stream down my arms and cheeks and I feel baptized in cool water. Before long, the sky eases up and I shake my head like a dog, spraying droplets. I sense connection with something bigger and then the rain pounds again, as if that something bigger can't make up its mind.

Thursday morning arrives, October 28th, the coldest morning yet. I bring out the winter gloves and wriggle into my thickest sweatpants. I pull on my guitar-playing-Buddha hoodie in honor of Bernie and pop on a Browns beanie, feeling nostalgic, longing for football and the World Series but both are gone. I don't really miss them that much, not specifically, I'm more in a perpetual state of missing everything, consumed and wistful for so many things until it numbs me and I eventually stop missing anything. Does that even make sense?

I Sharpie a thick *A* on my latex brobot mask—the old *A* wore off in the rain—then logout, step outside, do my usual stretches. Definitely quicker about it now, less chill in this chilled air. My breath feathers around me, caught in the waning moonlight, while pearls of frost sparkle on the tips of spider webs stretched between branches.

I run with more vigor through the grounds, energized, stoked that my lover has granted me more time, hopeful that maybe this portends good things to come. A brother can still hope, can't he?

Approaching headlights glow in the distance. My left leg trembles. I crouch down into a deep ditch, paranoid perhaps but what guarantee do I have—now that I'm forty—that I'm not a marked brother? The certificate folded up in my wallet? How much weight does a piece of paper carry these days? I lay low and wait, my breath rising from the ground like morning steam. Shit. I hold my breath and wait until the crawling headlights pass overhead, wait until the taillights vanish, wait to exhale. I jump up, brush myself off and jog on.

I get to the Shack my usual few minutes early, go into the greenhouse, check on my backpack. I hide behind the stack of large, cold pots, rub my hands together and brace myself for anything. My leg trembles. I suck on tincture.

Someone's coming from the other direction, could be Miriam, could be a cop or her security guard, so I brace behind the stack of pots and think about what Steven showed us, how to defend myself, how to strike, how to escape, how to hide. The Sister emerges from the soft forest shadows into the quarter-moonlight, wearing thick cold-weather clothing. I hear her humming Fly by Nicki Minaj and Rihanna, a Miriam favorite. She types in the code, hums and enters the kitchen, nonchalantly. I see no one else inside or out, all's good so far. I watch Miriam search the shack and swipe her cell screen a few times. I rise, bumping into the stack of pots. Quickly, I duck back down. Miriam peers out the kitchen window. I curse myself for being so careless and now I'll look ridiculous hiding out in the greenhouse. When she turns away from the window, I tiptoe out, close the door softly, and pretend to just now run up to the Shack. For the first time that I can remember, I enter after her. She's seated at the kitchen table, jabbing the tip of her ring finger.

You're early, I try to say casually, knowing I sound as suspicious as I feel.

I've missed you.

I watch her go through her testing routine—usually I'm in the other room—however, I notice right away she's different. She often exudes

229

a don't-bother-me-I'm-busy mayoral vibe, but this is not that, this is a subtle alteration in her behavior. A little less busy, a little more spacey. I wonder if the Sister Soldiers are coming, if she has already turned me in, given me up. She caps the vial, inserts it into the centrifuge, then looks at me, neither of us saying a word. What am I doing here? I should bolt, go hide, go underground. But one part of me in particular still wishes to stay.

Miriam pulls the vial out of the whirly-girly, holding it up to the light. We gaze at the detection strip inside the glass. Negative as always. She gets up from the kitchen table, strides over, reaches behind my head and pulls my hood down.

Take this silly thing off.

She unloops my mask and kisses me in the passionate way that usually takes her minutes to work up to. It's odd, not having that awkward first few minutes. She doesn't vent—I almost don't know what to do without that—and we reach a deep state of tongue, very quickly, intense but not as intimate. Have we both begun pulling back? Maybe I'm overreacting, maybe our hook-up is out-of-whack. She did enter the Shack first. And we haven't been together for three weeks. I can't help think: should I make love or should I go? She did grant me an extension. But I'm paranoid. You can't really call it paranoia when almost all the other paranoiacs you know are dead.

She eases up on my lips.

Did you get your present?

I did.

The less-than-thrilled look on my face hurts her.

You could say, "Thanks, Miriam."

Yeah, I know. Thank you. It's awesome.

But?

Whaddya think?

You were expecting a vaccine, she says, her whole body slumping. She turns away, enters the living room, opens the fireplace screen and lights a long match, touching flame to the tepee of kindling and logs. It's the first time I can remember her ever lighting the fire.

To be honest, Miriam, it's the most depressing gift I've ever received.

That's so nice to hear.

Six more weeks to live? And it's only five now.

It's five more weeks of *work*. You'll keep living in retirement.

You say that.

It's true.

She blows on the young flames.

I know it's not a lot, but c'mon, *five more weeks*.

What about a year?

I can't. There are rules.

You're the mayor.

I'm only the mayor. This goes much higher than me, Bryan.

We sit on the Native Sisters rug and watch the fire slither up the tepee of wood.

They took Bernie away, I tell her.

I heard. I'm so sorry.

Can you tell me where he is?

It wouldn't be proper.

See? Denny, Bernie, we just disappear.

I know the same thing is going to happen to me soon and a cold feeling stirs inside me. I don't even see it coming, a storm like the one that drenched me the other day, only this one is internal. I'm mad at Miriam as she wraps her arms around me. I tremble, muscle by muscle. She simply holds me, comforts me like no one ever before, not even my own mother, as if she needs this too, for different reasons. I feel the warmth of her armor surround me. I have never ever felt so wrapped, so blanketed, so cocooned by flesh.

I'm here for you, she tells me.

Even acting as a mother, she's efficient as hell. This is one of the few times I pour my heart out to her, telling her what I want and need, much of the stuff I've been spewing to you. It feels fucking great to be as vulnerable as I can, rambling about others I have lost: my pops, my big bro, an uncle I adored, a neighbor I loathed, my favorite teacher, my new-born nephew, the list goes on and on and she's heard much of this before, in dribs and drabs, but she lets me rattle away and of course she has just as large a list, probably larger as mayor. But I, not her, have the common denominator with all of them—brotherhood.

Miriam mushes my head into her chest and strokes my hair and I feel so much like a son right now—yet another incestuous comparison—which should creep me out, but as I've said before, very little creeps us out these days.

So much death, she says, stroking my hair, you without a chance to grieve any of them properly. You go right ahead and let it out.

It takes a moment, but I do, I grieve, man do I grieve, like I've never grieved before, as if all I needed was someone's permission. She hugs me, I weep, she shifts her body, I weep a little more, she eases her hold, I weep even harder, using her sweatshirt like a Kleenex, soaking it in my pain. A long time passes before the tears stop. I feel depleted.

232

Mind if I change the subject?

Please do, I say, blowing my nose.

I'm worried. Your numbers are way down.

Then why did you grant me an extension?

I'm trying to help you.

You mean before you give me up.

She unwraps her arms from around me.

That's not fair.

Seriously? You wanna talk about fair?

I'm being real with you, Bryan. Keep your production up.
Otherwise, the extension gets pulled. I can't help you if you quit
producing.

I feel faint. I've just cried my heart out to my mother, my lover, my
sponsor, all wrapped up into one, and now she has crapped on me
like a boss. She gets up and meticulously places another log on the
fire. An orange glow encircles her backside silhouette.

Have you met with Miguel recently?

What's recently?

I sincerely hope you're not involved in any of this, she says
sternly, unbuttoning her blouse, slowly. I keep my clothes on.

Are you kidding me? she says, it's been three weeks.

Are you really helping me?

Of course I am.

Why don't I feel like it?

She fondles my crotch through my sweatpants.

Feel that?

I must admit, I do. Maybe I'm overthinking, overstressing,
overreacting. It doesn't take long for the blood to rush on in, never too

233

sad for a stiff one. It doesn't take long for my hoodie and sweats to come off, and we make love, which doesn't take long, but is exactly what we should be doing. She knows what I need, although only once, a sure indicator that things are indeed different. She is extra quiet after sex. I worry her silence has sealed my fate and there is nothing I can do to unseal it.

What are you thinking? I say, a question she usually asks.

I wonder what we could've been in another time.

We still can be.

I didn't want any of this. I hope you know that. I love men.

I lean back, surprised to hear her say the banned word.

Men, men, men, men, men, men, men, she says. She sighs. I would gladly give up everything I have to get my son back.

I know.

I place my hand lightly on hers.

Tell me about him.

She gathers her memories.

His name was Jason. My beautiful boy. He had big round brown eyes. A smile from here to Shelby. Always a gap in his teeth, sometimes two or three, from tripping and falling and breaking a tooth. He loved animals. He loved his father.

Here she gives a pause for the ages.

How old was he?

Seven. Just turned seven. She wipes away a long, continuous tear. I couldn't save him.

It's not your fault, I say, it's nobody's fucking fault. That's what everybody keeps telling me.

I wrap all my limbs around her and we spoon, like strands of DNA, like John and Yoko on that album cover, like all couples should cuddle.

Jason loved skateboarding, she says, twenty-four-seven. Even when he wasn't riding, he'd walk around in his helmet and gigantic goofy elbow and knee pads. He looked like a bug.

She sobs quietly into my neck. I kiss her tears dry, my turn to comfort. Tonight has become the most tender night we've ever shared, all the challenge and chaos and panic and pain. I cry again, right along with her, another first. I sense she has more she wants to tell me. Maybe she loves me? Maybe she wants to save me? Maybe.

She sits up, wipes her face clean, pretends to smile.

What are *you* thinking?

I want to bring up the vaccine again, but to complain now would mar the intimacy. Nothing, I say, as I shut back down, like brothers have always done. Our quiet says more than enough as we caress and trace each other's bodies, a very tender moment inside a very awful time. I figure, what the hell, I get on my hands and knees and straddle her and look as deep into her eyes as I can.

I really need the vaccine.

Bryan?! She tries to shove me off but I don't budge.

Don't you think if there was one I would've used it to save my son?

Yes, I do. If there had been one at the time.

She looks away. That got her.

I'm scared, Miriam, I'm really scared. I thought I might be taken away last week. And then Bernie and—

You're not gonna be scooped up and taken away. I promise.

235

Ever?

I told you, I will let you know when the time comes.

I don't know what else to say. Or do. Exhausted, I lay back down beside her and close my eyes, our bodies intertwined like octopi, and the next thing I remember is waking up and feeling a huge weight lifted off me. I reach for her and she is not there.

Miriam?

I get up, naked, and check the bathroom.

Miriam?

I find a note on the kitchen table. We never text—for obvious security reasons—and I don't wanna look at it. Of course, I cannot not look at it:

> I have an early meeting with the city manager. I loved
> our morning, loved feeling so vulnerable with you.
> Please, try to enjoy your gift. See you next week.

I reread the note, pretty much memorizing it as I pull on my underwear and socks. And so it continues to be. She has the power over our relationship, the power over my last weeks, the power over everything. That is hard for a brother to get used to. Death and war happen, always have, but the subservience and loss of power, those are hard for a brother's ego to take.

I crumble up the note and toss it into the glowing embers. It whooshes into a flame that quickly dies.

TELL ME MORE

I'm running under ice cream clouds, euphoric, I just had sex, Miriam loves me in her own way, and I feel like nothing can stop me—

A Sister in a knit bunny hat jumps out at me. I leap sideways, startled, stumbling outside the bro-only lane. Shit, another Sister Kisser, only steps away. I struggle to regain my groove and get back into my lane, sprinting ahead of her.

Slow down, BB.

Her voice is disguised as a chick's, but I recognize my nickname.

Miguel?!

I ease up on my throttle, look back over my shoulder, see him off to the side, ten-to-fifteen feet behind me, running outside the red lines since it would look odd for a Sister to run in a bro-only lane. I check him out. It's not unusual to see a brother trying to blend in, but it is startling to see macho Miguel as a Sister. Mascara streaks the pink scarf he wears instead of a mask, and his honeydew breasts bounce way too much under his black Pink hoodie. Figures Miguel would overstuff himself. He keeps his face down, hidden from any eyes in the sky.

Don't worry, I tell him, my drone's not following me.

I turn right, cross the lawn, and enter the Queenwood Center gate. He follows me, running further and further behind, until we are in a patch of forest, frosted white. I dart down a muddy path underneath the almost-bare crowns of trees, lead him to a steep creek bed, down an embankment, sidestepping roots and rocks. All's good until we slip and slide, one after the other, into muck, plopping in up to our ankles.

Asshole!

We lean on opposite sides of a wide hickory tree that rises from the creekbank, our heads just above trail level.

I fire questions at him in-between my own gulps of air: How could you? The carousel? All those children?

For once he is silent. I knew it.

I need a place to hang, he says, out of breath.

Who's after you?

All of them. Maybe no one. I just need a few hours.

You don't need my permission. This is still open to the public.

I've never needed your permission. I need your support. With a stick, he scrapes mud from his shoes: Gotta tell ya, I'm not crazy about my Brooks.

I gaze at my childhood friend with his bouncy-house breasts and silly bunny hat, flicking mud with a stick, true worry in his eyes. Years of jealousy swell inside me. What the hell am I doing, risking my life being seen with the bastard. On the other hand, he's fighting for our rights and is the only living brother from my past, and by the past I mean anything more than two years ago. I can't turn my back on him.

A scratching sound startles us both. Miguel spins around, one hand gripping something inside his hoodie pocket. A squirrel scrambles down the trunk within arms' reach; even a forest rodent

238

doesn't notice us brothers anymore. Miguel sneers and rambles on about the struggle and being on the run, talking rapidly like he's on coke, more nervous than I've ever seen him.

Wait.

I pull out my cell phone, start the timer at 2:00, place it down on a tree stump.

Tell me more about The War.

Here?

You can't go in the house. No one will hear you out here, the gardens don't open for another two hours.

Okay, sure, whatever. Miguel digs mud out of the tread on one sole. Just so you know, he confesses, I was against the bombing. I didn't participate in it.

But you knew.

You're hating on me after all they've done to us?

You killed kids.

Bugs buzz around us and a brittle leaf falls onto a creek rock, hanging on for dear life, just out of reach of the gurgling water. Miguel tosses the stick, rearranges his floppy breasts.

I see why they can be so bitchy, having to deal with these things.

My phone alarm chimes. He grabs it, taps the voice memo icon.

I don't know what the old man here has already told you—

Hey, *you're* forty-one.

Yeah, but I don't *act* old. He looks up through the skeletal limbs of trees, trying to remember where he left off: We were brought up that you don't fight ladies, right? So it all started mano y mano, brothers fighting brothers, for territory and squatting rights. Brothers were dropping by the millions. The Y spread like syphilis among the troops

239

and Mother President kicked all brothers out of the military. Those not already dead or dying were dishonorably discharged, court-martialed, stripped of medals and honors. So we panicked and did some stupid shit against each other, all over the world. Until we realized it was insane to be fighting each other. No more Bloods versus Crips, black versus white, rich versus poor. We bonded in brotherhood, against the real enemy, pledging loyalty to each other, to fight Sisters and the system, for pure survival, like ancient times, except we aren't fighting saber-toothed tigers. We're fighting she-devils.

He taps the screen.

How's that so far?

Great. Now explain how The War actually started.

Got it.

Tap.

So, the thousands of little wars merged into one, brother versus Sister, and all hell broke loose. One night, in the Johannesburg Riots, over one-thousand Sisters were hacked-up by machetes. South African brothers had had enough of the new shit. The following night, nearly as many brothers were shot and bludgeoned to death by retaliating Sisters who had also had enough of the same shit. Then there was the Watts Massacre. Fed-up Sisters rounded up their deadbeat baby daddies, twenty-nine of them, lined them up against a wall outside a Walmart. Assassinated, point-blank. You know what one of them told the baby daddies before they pulled the triggers? All you gonna die anyway, she said, might as well get it over with rather than livin' off our asses. Then there were the Mexican Wars. Senoras had taken over the presidency and half the legislature, so of course

240

they got involved in the cartels and things evolved from there. Mucho vida loco. Poisoned tortillas, missing mothers, decapitated brothers. Later that year, I think, was The Louisville Slaughter at Costco. One-hundred-and-three Sisters held hostage by three dozen armed brothers. The Kentucky National Guard was called out. At that time the Guard was about fifty-fifty brothers and Sisters. Most of them did their job, they protected the Sister Hostages, however, a few brother guards switched sides. The standoff lasted almost a week, all played out on *It*. Then someone fired shots inside—it's unclear who—and SWAT Sisters stormed the warehouse. In the end all the Sister Hostages were killed, a couple SWAT Sisters too. Twenty-seven brothers died. The National Guardsbrothers that defected were executed on the spot.

Battles flared all over the world. Aboriginal brothers rose up in Australia, Kurd brothers attacked in Syria and Iraq. ISIS and the Taliban kept doing what they'd always been doing. Russian brothers went ballistic on babushkas. Gender fighting spread to every corner of the world. Conspiracy theories fueled the fire, about how Sisters invented The Y.

Miguel stops, surveying the forest as if expecting a Sister to suddenly appear from behind a tree.

I already talked about the Seventh Conspiracy, I say.

Seventh? Man, there are at least fourteen now. Most historians— he tilts his eyes at me, changing his voice into a pompous prick—most *historians* like BB here agree that the conspiracy was the last straw, the final draw, the spark that erupted earth into one big war zone.

Miguel drops the exaggerated teacher's voice but continues the lecture: Guerrilla warfare and terrorism were everywhere. Cities, big

241

and small, became battlefields, a different sex on each side. Entire cities burned to the ground. Fortunately, we've been mostly spared here in Sisterfield.

Until the carousel.

He ignores me.

We were armed but not like they were. And we weren't organized in ideology. You get what I'm saying? Some brothers fought to regain control of it all. Others for equal rights. Radicals wanted to kill as many Sisters as they could get their hands on. We fought for everything, which meant we weren't fighting for anything. Close to half-a-billion brothers have died fighting. Mind-numbing, right, until you remember that The Y killed as many as four billion.

It was like World War One and the Spanish Flu all over again, I add.

Yeah, homie historian. Just way worse. We kept running out of brothers. The Sisters had an endless supply of Soldiers, waiting us out.

Something they'd gotten good at for millennia, I say.

Are you gonna keep interrupting me?

I'll stop.

Now get this, some Apologist Sisters have the cojones to say we should thank them. For returning us to our primitive hunter state. Can you imagine? He shakes his head, but the motion morphs into a nod. The bitch is, I do definitely feel more like a man. No more trying to please them, no more wishy-washy-where-do-I-fit-in bullshit.

He glares at me.

BB here—he's a Sister Lover—he works against his own gender.

I'm not a Sister Lover.

You're working with the enemy.

A'ight, I say, it's time to wrap it up.

He waves me off.

The war "officially" ended six months ago, with the Peace Treaty of Hong Kong. SEW guaranteed abandoned homes and free food for any soldiers who surrendered. Many brave warriors agreed, usually those already diagnosed with the virus.

He leans against the thick hickory in his furry bunny hat. My ears are freezing here in the frosted forest and I am suddenly very jealous of that hat.

Have you talked about how assisted-brother-suicides are legal?

I shake my head.

Or how they're mandatory for the stricken in some places?

No.

What the hell do you talk about?

Never mind that. Talk about the undergrounders.

Sisters call them la ratas. The rats. An underground railroad—the BURs—sprouted up all over the world, shuttling most-wanted brothers to safer areas, to rebel camps in jungles and deserts and abandoned buildings.

Where is your camp? I ask.

I don't have a camp.

Okay, your safe house, whatever the hell you call it.

He laughs.

Like I know.

So what do the undergrounders do?

I'm *told* they assemble weaponry and hack Sisters' websites and mount counteroffensives. They want the vaccine, like we all do. Then

243

they plan to form their own civilizations with Sister Breeders who will help re-create a new, stronger brotherhood. Pero, many undergrounders want to eventually overthrow the Sisterhood.

That's delusional.

Dream high, he says, and settle for something less.

Like the carousel?

His mouth doesn't speak but his body language does.

It freaked Gaia out, I say.

That's for the best, she's the enemy.

His words settle between us like a new layer in the forest detritus. One of us has turned his back on our childhood, I'm just not sure which one that is.

Did you know, he continues, that a nuclear warhead annihilated a rebel colony near the Texas border? Ordered by our compassionate Mother President.

I never heard that.

There's a lot you don't hear about. One more thing, he says, holding his fist up in defiance, even though he's not videoing himself: Vaccine primero. Peace segunda. He taps the stop icon and drops my phone onto the tree stump.

How was that, teach?

Great.

Join us, he says, before it's too late.

Stop recruiting me.

Stop running away.

I give him a "drop it" look I've given him since middle school.

Suit yourself. But I still need a place to stay.

There are a gazillion empty buildings.

Getting risky. I've lost most of my contacts these last few weeks.

My left leg twitches upon hearing that. He eyes it suspiciously. I pull out my amber bottle and squeeze a few drops of tincture under my tongue. He eyes that even more suspiciously.

What the fuck has happened to you? You're Sister-whipped.

I ignore that, busy replacing the dropper in the bottle.

Just a few hours, I offer grudgingly, thinking, how can I say no. Even though I do hate him. I lead him to a small maintenance barn with broken-down mowers and rusty lawn tools.

It'll do. You got anything to eat?

I'll bring you something.

I step outside, leaving the door cracked open.

¡Y algún cervezas!

***

I'm getting home late from my morning run. My drone is operational, perched on one of the roof gables, its tiny camera focusing on my face. I jog up to the front door, give a little wave, pretending to be out of breath, like I've just run for hours. I stare at the retinal scanner, the door opens and welcomes me back inside. I hurry to the kitchen, grab a couple bananas, some granola, a poppyseed muffin, and a growler of a local brew, Phoenix Ale, stuffing it all inside a garbage bag—

What'cha doin'?

I turn around. Cody is staring at me

Just taking out some trash.

I doubt he believes me as I head out the front door, my drone following me but like always getting bored and soon drifting toward some Sisters feeding ducks at the pond. I dip inside the maintenance shed and unwrap breakfast. Miguel goes right for the growler, chugging a third of it, before contemplating the food.

What, no bacon and eggs?

He wolfs down the banana and muffin. Suddenly, the shed doorway darkens. Cody, Drew, and Steven enter.

Damn it, Cody.

Who's this? Steven asks as Miguel casually wraps the scarf around his neck to hide his Adam's apple.

My cousin, Michelle, I lie.

What's she doing in here?

I step outside, look up for Drew's raptor-sized drone.

Don't worry, my bird's over with yours, checking-out some Sisters.

So who are you, really? Steven asks.

I introduce them: Drew, Steven, Cody, this is a childhood friend of mine, Miguel.

He unwraps his scarf to reveal his Adam's apple in all its angled glory.

What was Bryan like as a, like, kid? Cody asks.

His nickname was BB. I used to kick his ass up and down the playground. Our friend Gaia did too.

She did not, I protest.

You know she did. That time you tickled her underarms when she was on the monkey bars. She fell and you laughed. She dragged you down in the sand and pinned you, wailing on you, lefts and rights.

He mimics me covering up my face and crying.

What can I say, I'm not a fighter.

Miguel pulls on the growler. I can tell the others sense something important about him, something more than just being my friend. I don't

246

know if they realize he's an undergrounder, but they start asking pointed questions.

Is there a vaccine? Drew asks.

Do Sisters shit on us? Miguel replies.

Are they, Cody asks, like, working on artificial sperm?

Do Sisters shit on us?

I hear they're even working on artificial wombs, Steven says.

Sisters even shit on themselves.

If we're lucky, Drew chimes in.

He and Miguel exchange air fist bumps.

I like this you, Miguel says, pulling on his growler. We could use some brothers like you. I've been trying to recruit BB here to the cause.

I've been working on his survival skills, Steven says.

How's he doing?

He's a work in progress.

Miguel shakes his head.

Do you ever get, like, tired of fighting? Cody wonders.

Some days, yeah, Miguel says, but if we don't resist, then what? Besides, amigos, we're hardwired to fight. So—he gulps and burps—what about you guys? You all like what you're doing?

Beats the alternative, Drew says.

Miguel laughs, raises his beer and toasts: To survival.

To survival, we answer back.

We hear the annoying buzzing of a drone outside.

The nag is back, Drew says. Grab a tool, guys, look busy.

He grabs a hammer, Steven grabs a socket set, Cody grabs a screwdriver. Steven salutes Miguel. Miguel salutes back. The Three

247

Amigos leave the shed, carrying their decoy tools back toward The Factory.

I should be getting back too, I say.

I won't be too much longer. Just waiting on a text.

He wipes his mouth and uses a knife as a mirror, applying a touch of lipstick.

You thinking of a sex change?

I know I look hot, he says, but let's not get carried away.

He adjusts his bouncy, lopsided breasts.

You need a boob job, I say, you look ridiculous.

You kidding? With these babies, nobody's looking at my face.

I don't know why but I suddenly feel the need to blurt out:

I'm seeing someone.

Oh really? Cody?

What? No! A Sister.

That's suicide, brother.

She's immune and clean. She tests every time.

Double-dipping with the enemy. I hate you even more now. Who is she?

I can't tell you.

You're a real piece of work. If I hadn't grown up with you, I'd kill you right here, right now, with my own two hands.

No need to. My time's almost up.

It's never too late.

Yeah it is.

You are so Sister-whipped. Be a man.

By killing little girls like you?

Collateral damage.

That's messed up.

You're the one that's messed up, supplying sperm to the enemy. He tilts the growler, drains the last drops.

Gaia could have been killed in that blast, I say.

Gaia is no angel.

She's our friend.

What do you think goes on in her store? You think that's all books and coffee and tinctures? She holds anti-brother meetings there. She wouldn't give you the time of day if we hadn't been childhood friends.

Oh, direct hit. I think back to my conversation with Justin, the homeless man who came up with the same conclusion about my new relationship with him.

Tell me, I redirect, when did killing innocent people become ok?

About the same time it become okay to die because you're a guy.

We don't know for sure they developed The Y.

Wake up, BB. Coincidences are fairy tales.

So are conspiracies.

He glares at me with penetrating eyes.

There are two groups of brothers. Fighters and pussies.

Martin Luther King wouldn't—

Martin Luther King can suck my dick.

Okay, we're done here, I say, turning my back on him, stepping toward the door. I really wish he were not my long-time friend, it'd be so much easier to turn him in. I bet there's a hefty reward.

It must be nice, he says, having Sisters protect your ass. You won't have that when you leave these gates.

Tell me something I don't know.

Ping. He grabs his cell, checks a text message.

Perfect timing, he says.

Give me your number.

Can't do that, bro. It's always changing. Here.

He tries to hand me a Cellina, a cheap, reloadable cell phone. I back away from it.

I told you I'm clean, dude, he says. He places the phone down on top of a mower. The password, he says, is the number of floors at Hogwarts, Harry's Quidditch number, and the number of players on a Quidditch team.

It's been twenty years since we've talked about Harry but Miguel knows I won't forget it. 7—7—7.

There's only one app on the phone, he explains. Click on it. It'll text me your location. Only once, that's it, then throw it away. Not into the trash, in a lake or incinerator. Destroy the thing. Got it?

Okay enough.

Thanks for the hang, he says, wrapping the scarf three times around his neck, hiding his fruit of all evil.

I grab the phone, peek outside the shed, look up, see my hummingbird circling the gardens, looking for me.

Wait a few minutes before you leave, I explain, walking away.

Hey BB?

I look back.

It's not too late. Soon, it will be.

EUCHRE

Halloween comes and goes. We don't hand out candy at The Factory door, for health reasons, but we leave Kit-Kats, Reese's, and M&Ms in a basket in an empty bird bath about fifty feet from the front of the house, a self-serve honor system. Little Sisters stop by, dressed as Wonder Womans, Ruth Bader Ginsburgs—very few princesses anymore—and a few costumed as goofy brothers. Inside The Factory, we watch slasher movies, rooting for Freddy Krueger and any brother that's slicing-and-dicing Sisters. Cody is dressed up as Iron Man. Steven dons his full, crisp Marine uniform. The rest of us don't bother, I mean, hell, we wear masks every day.

It's now Tuesday morning, I finish my run, shower, and hang out on an overstuffed armchair in the drawing room. Four of us are spread out, playing our weekly card game, Euchre, a simplified Pinochle, very popular in Ohio. Cody and I team-up against Drew and Steven. The creatives versus the studs. Steven sits in front of a window, tapping his tablet, shuffling digital cards. He taps again, dealing out five, in groups of twos and threes, airdropped to our phones and tablets. We arrange our hands. I'm at the piano, touching my iPad, dragging and rearranging my cards, my ten of hearts over to my ace of hearts, and my jack of diamonds next to my king of diamonds. I also have a

251

queen of clubs. Not a great hand, but I can help screw our opponents with what is called a Euchre, the name of the game.

The king of spades is face up on the kitty pile on our screens.

Pass, I say.

Pass, Drew agrees.

Cody passes too.

Spades is trump, ladies! Steven taps his tablet and drags the queen of spades from the kitty into his hand. He discards onto the kitty, which now swipes off our screens.

I sit to Steven's left. I lead with the ace of hearts.

Everyone's got a heart, I say.

My ace appears on the "table", a shared window on all our devices. Everyone has to follow suit and lay a heart if they have it, clicking and dragging a card to the "table". Drew, pacing the room with his phone, tosses a queen of hearts. Cody, sprawled on a couch, gets rid of a nine. Steven trumps me with the ten of spades, swiping the trick into his pile. He then drags the jack of spades, the right bower, unbeatable. We follow suit, throwing our worst trump. He sweeps up all our digital spades. Cards fly in quickly, faster than a beginner can keep up with. Steven thinks he has them all but on the last trick, Cody slaps the ace of clubs on Drew's king.

Gotcha bitch!

Cody sweeps up that trick. We exchange an air hi-five, even though Drew and Steven still win the hand, earning a point. They now have seven, we have three, according to the scorecard flashing on our devices. Ten points wins the game. And it's now my turn to deal. I swipe on my tablet, left, right, back and forth, shuffling the digital deck.

252

I'd like you guys to record something for my posts, I say, setting the timer on my LG BFF 3, placing it on a coffee table.

And say what? Steven asks.

Whatever you want.

Can we text or email? Cody says.

If you prefer.

We play another hand. Cody and I lose again. My timer chimes.

Drew snatches up my cell, spending the next fifteen minutes giving his life story, I won't bore you with the tales of wrestling and his tax prep days and how before this gig he sold Teslas to Sisters.

That's what got me here, he brags, I sold myself. It's easy when you've got a great product.

He motions to his crotch. Three pairs of eyes roll.

You are the epitome of arrested development, I say.

What's the point of evolving if we're becoming extinct?

A'ight, I think I've got enough from you, I say.

Your loss, Drew says and he sets my cell timer to 2:00, tapping it and placing it down on the table. We play another hand. Cody and I win this one. My timer chimes.

Anyone else? I ask.

There don't appear to be any takers.

I reach for my cell, but Steven marches over, grabs it.

My name is Steven Guthrie. I'm twenty-four. Born and raised in Shelby—Go Whippets!—and all I ever wanted to be was a Marine. I do one hundred pushups a day, have since I was five.

You did one hundred pushups a day at age five? I say.

Yes sir. Took me a couple weeks to build up to it.

Every day since?

253

Every day. Well, I did have my appendix removed, so I didn't do any that day. Or the next.

Insane.

My dad was a Marine, my uncle was too. Camp Lejeune was awesome, best time of my life.

Did you deploy?

(I already told you some of this, but it's good to hear it from his own mouth.)

No I did not. Day before graduation, I got my orders, I was going to Iran in two weeks. I couldn't wait. Then two Sister Generals came to camp. Shut it down. Said they were going in a different military direction. They let the Sisters graduate but kicked us brothers out entirely. They FUCKED me.

Nothing scarier, I think to myself, than a vengeful Marine. Unless it's a vengeful wannabe-Marine.

Cody shuffles and deals, while Steven spews the rest of his life story, centered around his family's military record and his desire to protect. This guy's a classic soldier, exactly what we need to defeat old-school enemies. But Sisters? That's a whole other game, has been throughout herstory. I tune Steven out and think about life, wish it was a card game, one in which we could pass if we didn't like the hand we were dealt. Of course, if someone else calls the suit, we have to play the cards we're dealt, and right now Sisters are calling the suit. We're forced to play our crappy hands.

Then I wonder how much battery life I have left on my phone.

And in my life.

***

It's election night. On our many big screens is a very happy Miriam celebrating at a Columbus victory party for Mother President, cheering and speaking on behalf of her good friend. Miriam looks stunning, an assortment of purples, pearls, and panache. The election is a foregone conclusion, a landslide, Mother President re-elected with a whopping 77% of the vote, easily beating her opponent Sister Lelani Wheaton, a dove who campaigned on reconciling with brothers, promising to restore their place in society. Lelani didn't stand a chance.

Four more years of this madness, André says, turning away from the many screens. I'm going upstairs, he adds, to aggregate the data from my own poll.

I head up to my room too, to plan my next steps.

The next night, Wednesday, November 3, I can't sleep, as usual, I toss and turn and snack and ramble into my cell, deleting most of it. I think about what Bernie once said, about how we don't talk much about all our offspring out there. I miss Bernie so bad. I think about kids, about never having them, never wanting them, ever since dad told us, growing up, "I could've done so many things if I just hadn't had you kids." He never explained the many things he'd rather be doing, but his words stuck. Now, I wanna find one of my daughters, introduce myself, ask her what she likes, you know? Maybe I'll bring it up with Miriam tomorrow.

Thursday morning starts off normal. I shrug on my sweatpants and guitar-playing-Buddha hoodie, tighten my gloves and brobot mask. Outside, my warmup stretches are short and sweet 'cause I'm shivering. I run, the bite of the wind in my eyes, hundreds of leaves tumbling around me, like fallen brothers. I get to the Love Shack first,

255

set my cell timer, leave it on the kitchen table, light the bundle of wood in the fireplace, stoke the flames. I stare into the blaze, hypnotized, I see so many things: a tree of glowing fire, waltzing flames, fiery waterfalls, beasts, demons, the many faces of goddess. I see a monster, a ghost. I see Bernie in the ash and embers.

I see myself.

Miriam comes in, her usual ten minutes late, humming, can't tell what it is. She takes her test. Negative, of course. Our sex is mechanical, rote, not satisfying for either of us. The tenderness and intimacy of our last encounter are gone. We are both somewhere else, lying in bed, naked, back-to-back. I pull out my bottle of tincture.

What's wrong? she asks, reaching behind her back, tracing a fingertip along my shaft.

Nothing.

You mad that Mother President won?

Of course. But that's not it.

Then what is it? I don't have time for games.

You don't have time? Oh, that's rich.

I mean today.

She sits up, so I sit up too, face-to-face with her.

I have to drive to Pittsburgh, she explains, Mother President will be there—

Let's get married.

I don't know why I blurted that out, I think to myself, I never intended to say anything like that.

You know we can't.

We never do anything but have sex—

Miriam presses her finger to my lips.

256

That's right. But these last four weeks, let's have the best sex we've ever had.

Try as I might, I can't argue against that. I may be scared and bitter, but I'm not stupid. We make love again, a connect-the-dots passion, no true sensuousness, and afterwards we cuddle, stiffly. We don't talk. I don't bring up seeing one of my offspring, I don't know why, I don't even bring up the vaccine, my go-to topic. It's not long before Miriam is snoring. I sneak out before she wakes up.

THE TRUTH

Steven teaches us more survival techniques, like how to locate and identify edible plants—not real valuable in winter under a foot of snow—but we learn about chickweed, dandelion, milk thistle, and cattails. That last one surprises me. As kids we used to soak cattails in gas and whip them around as torches and flaming swords. Who knew you could actually eat your weapon? That concept might make war obsolete. Steven reminds us we can dig-up these edibles with our handy fold-up trowels. Drew jokes: The weapon recommended by four out of five gardeners. Steven demonstrates how to fashion weapons out of everyday items, like a pen hidden in your cupped hand in a clinch, jammed up someone's nostril with the shove of a palm. His lessons are intense. Afterwards I go straight to my room to nap.

Later on, I'm hanging with Kimchi and André in the drawing room, listening to some weird-ass modern shit, I don't even know what it is, way too much bass, too little melody, when our ears are tweaked by the soft and seldom-heard slide-slide-slide of slippers down the staircase, evidence of the rarest of endangered species.

Selfie's in the house! André exclaims.

Sure enough, Selfie shuffles across the foyer floor, virtual reality goggles propped on top of his head. He's got stringy brown hair, always unwashed and greasy, brown skin, an empty cereal bowl in one hand and something bag-like scrunched up in the other. He bypasses us, heading straight for the kitchen. We hear cereal pour into a bowl, followed by the closing thwup of the refrigerator door, he must have run out of milk and cereal in his room. Jonathan claims Selfie was once an influencer, he had millions of online followers, geeky brothers mostly, all pretty much dead, so basically, he is friendless.

He slinks toward us, his cereal bowl filled to the brim with organic cinnamon Kashi. We call out in unison:

Selfie!

He grins in reply, walking directly toward me, dropping the scrunched-up bag onto my lap.

Happy belated, he says.

He slide-slides in his slippers, across the marble foyer as I unfold the plastic bag and pull out a classic blue Jansport backpack.

Thanks, Selfie.

Come hang with us, dude, André says.

Selfie dismisses us with a wave and step-slides up the wide staircase, not spilling a single drop.

***

Cody shows me some new changes to the dark *It* and how to navigate it. You can go down a rabbit hole so deep with that stuff that the hole circles back around on itself, swallowing you up from both directions of reality. I pay attention because it's important to him, but TBH, it's too deep for me. I like my technology superficial and user-friendly. But I periodically check *It* for brothers' obits, seldom see anyone I know, not like at the peak when I knew two or three brothers every day. Today, I recognize the photo of the fisherbrother I met at

259

Charles Mill Lake. His name was Larry Jones and he died four days ago. Survived by his wife and estranged daughter, he had two sons, both deceased. He was a contractor, building the homes of many prominent Sisters. Unlike most brothers, he is getting an actual memorial at Wappner Funeral Home. Right now.

I dress in black and attend, the only name to sign the guestbook thus far. The Funeral Director Sister smiles behind her mask—a rare time you'll see a Sister masked-up—as I enter the viewing room. A carved wooden urn—looks like mahogany—sets on a table draped in purple velvet. There's a picture of Larry, holding up a foot-long trout, looking happy, back when he was healthy. I don't know why, but I feel honored that I got to meet him.

I sit alone in one of a dozen wooden folding chairs in the back of three rows. The funeral director obviously over-estimated. I'm surprised to feel a tear crawl down my cheek, probably shed for *my* future funeral. Like Larry, I will be just as forgotten. And he actually was somebody in the community, a successful businessman, an Elks Lodge member—you can add lodges to the list of obsolete things— and benefactor of The Renaissance Performing Arts Center. What will my obit say? That I once sold weed, taught history, and jacked-off for a living?

I bow my head, pretend to pray, wonder what's a respectful length of time to stay. Then an Old Sister enters, I assume it's his wife, in a short black dress, stoic in skyscraper heels. She seems surprised by my presence, and I catch a whiff of powdery perfume as she passes. She touches the urn and bends over. I strain to hear her whisper:

Thank you.

That is all. Thank you for what? I wonder. For being a good husband? For providing her fancy clothes? For finally dying? She turns and walks out without looking back. I consider following her, but I don't, choosing to give her the peace of space. I wait the obligatory two minutes and then walk up to the urn.

Hopefully you're in nirvana, I say, knowing that could soon be me, stuffed inside an urn or a plastic bag, nothing more, few people left with memories of me, how pointless it all is. To end up like this. Ashes to ashes, dust to dust, come in with a fuck and go out fucked. I turn on my heel and as I walk out I shudder, which morphs into a full-on quaking episode of my left leg.

***

I venture off on my Thursday morning run. The dark coldness frosts my soul, my mind swirling with emotions. I look over my shoulder every few steps, always hearing them, the Sisters coming to take me away. I've imagined every scenario: swept into a van, chased through forests, lured to a quiet spot and disposed of with a single kiss. I feel alone, even more than normal. Not another soul on these slippery streets, the bro-only pavement coated with a thin membrane of ice glistening under streetlights. My steps are slow and shortened, my hands wrapped in ski gloves and splayed out, ready to catch my fall as I slip and slide and somehow manage to keep on my feet all the way to the Sensitive Estates. I head straight to the greenhouse, check on my backpack still hidden in a big terra cotta pot.

Inside the Shack I perform my usual routine, setting my timer for three hours, leaving my cell on the kitchen table, lighting the bundle of wood in the fireplace. The guitar is back, in the corner, yay, a nylon-string Yamaha classical. It hasn't been here since Miriam sent it to get

261

re-strung months ago. I welcome the familiar wood into my arms, sit on the couch, strum a little Sista Sasha. It sounds in perfect tune, for the occasion, just as the fireplace is, but even music can't get me totally out of my head. Everything is coming on stronger: my thoughts, my senses, I must be in a pre-flight hyper-aware mode. The blaze in the fireplace feels especially warm and bright this morning, the heat hellish, the colors surreal, the beastly images spectacular. The answer to everything could be inside those flames, I think, focusing on the flickering as I organize what I want to say to Miriam. She comes in, her usual ten minutes late. I strum on the couch, listening to her on the other side of the kitchen doorway, pricking her finger, scooping the blood, testing it, waiting for the results.

Play me something pretty, she says.

I fingerpick and sing The Beatles' Here Comes The Sun, one of my go-to songs.

That's nice, she says, and I have to agree, it did sound pretty fucking great. *Now* I start sounding good. She holds up the vial in the doorway. Still negative. She reads my face.

What is it, what's wrong?

The usual existential shit, I say, setting the guitar down.

You're not going to die.

If you give me the vaccine.

There. Is. No. Vaccine.

C'mon, Miriam.

You know, not everything's a conspiracy. Sometimes things just happen.

It's too convenient.

Conspiracies are what's convenient. Reality is much sloppier.

262

Can you get it for me?

It doesn't exist.

Can you get it for me?

No.

Why do you make me beg? Don't I mean anything to you?

She turns her back. I'm a persistent sonofabitch, I can tell I've dented the mayoral armor. I take a stab in the dark, give her another way out:

Is it because it hasn't been FDA-approved yet?

You're impossible. Even if it were, you know I just can't—

Yes you can.

No I can't.

I'll get down and grovel. I'll beg like a dog in heat. I will suck your pussy until I pass out.

Stop.

You're friends with Mother President and don't tell me she doesn't know.

Enough! I want to make love.

She flicks on soft jazz with the touch of a remote, the tinkling of piano keys. She turns it up louder than soft jazz should ever be listened to, if ever at all. She leans over, looks deep in my eyes, stiffens, waits, then whispers:

From what I hear, it works best on the young. In older adults, it's only about seventy percent effective.

I can feel my eyes widen. Seventy percent is way better than zero, I say. But what I'm thinking is this: How evil, create a disease, then a vaccine that works best on the young. Eliminate the older generations. No one to remember the way things used to be. Suddenly, my entire body ripples with goosebumps.

How do I get it?

You can't.

I have to.

You can't. I can't. I wish you'd appreciate that.

I do.

The fire snaps, sparks flying like fireworks.

Please, I whisper. I'm sure your son Jason wouldn't want any other brothers to die.

Tears crowd her eyes.

There's nothing I can do. There's just not a lot of political support for older brothers.

Jesus fuckin' Christ—I curse in a whisper—what am I doing here?

I didn't mean you.

You're a real piece of work, you know that?

What am I supposed to do? she whispers, shaking off her sadness like dust off an overcoat. I can't say anything, I'll be re-assigned.

Reassigned? You're the mayor, you're elected.

She gives me a "Get real," look.

Why are you keeping it from us?

Why do you think?

She turns down a soprano sax solo and grips my arm.

I want you inside of me.

Fuck making love. This is my life.

There is no vaccine, she says, louder than the soft jazz, for anyone that might be listening.

I'm outta here.

Don't go, she says, outlined by the glow of flames.

I head into the kitchen.

You're only alive because of me. Your sperm count has been low for weeks. It isn't even used anymore. It's thrown out with the trash.

That doesn't help, Miriam, why are you telling me that?

She appears in the kitchen doorway.

Why do you think I gave you an extension?

You felt guilty.

The look on her face suggests how wrong I am. She turns away. I grab my cell off the table.

Go on, go, she says.

Then what is it?

I wait. Only silence. I open the door and stand on the threshold to the cold forest darkness, while inside, the golden fire glow shimmers around Miriam. I wait for her to say something, but what is there to say? What would really matter anymore? I step outside.

See you next week? she calls out to me. I'll be here.

I don't know if I will, I think, as I disappear into the dark.

***

What do I do with what Miriam just told me? I have to tell Miguel and the other guys here and I haven't felt this charged since I was young and indestructibly naïve. Halfway through my run home, I pull out the cheap phone Miguel gave me, type in the wizardry password: 777. The phone unlocks, the home screen glows blue with a single **B** app icon. How simple, in such a complicated time. My fingertip hovers over the **B**. So much potential in my hand. Do I really wanna do that? I realize I have nothing, no solid information on the vaccine, we already

265

knew it existed anyway. Miriam will play Peter and deny it, she'll deny me, she's a politician, it's a job requirement. And what if she's just testing me? The more I think about it, the more I don't wanna play my hand too quick. If I play this wrong, I could mess it up for all of us. I have to think, I can't just wing it, the key to survival is not to panic, even *I* know that. I turn off the phone, stuff it in my pocket.

Once home, I hibernate in my room, stuffing the last of my backpacks, trembling. I pick up my guitar, strum lazily and loosely. I'm not feeling the guitar, so I wander down to Cody's room, a museum of early computers: Old Ataris, Commodores, IBMs, practically every older Apple ever made, even the bulky see-through Macs, arranged on shelves in chronological order, a family tree of personal computers.

Music can't help me anymore, I say. Here.

I set my guitar down on his bed. Cody smiles, his anxious fingers curling into imaginary chord shapes. I used to be like that. At least I know my instrument will be loved when I go.

Cody tells me how he once devised an app—Find The Food—that pinpoints nearby available food surpluses. Great idea. But no one's buying the app, no need to, food is plentiful enough, there are surpluses of so many things. Resources aren't the problem these days. Consumers are.

After a silent two minutes, he lifts the guitar, cradles the wood in his lap, curls his left fingers into an awkward B7 that's only going to be a train-wreck of a chord. I show him a better way to finger it. I wanna spill the beans about the vaccine, but I can't say a word, what if it's not true? In some ways, I feel even more trapped than ever. How can life keep getting shittier?

Cody plucks a pretty arpeggio. I am stunned.

266

Beautiful B7, I tell him.

He beams and I leave him alone with his new love—my old flame.

The other Appleseeds check in on me from time-to-time, recording some thoughts, texting me others, but for the most part they see what I'm going through and give me space. That's one thing about guys—we know when to leave each other alone.

Except for Drew.

You know what you need? he says, tossing a football up and down, you need some exercise.

I don't think so.

I won't take no for an answer.

So I grab a test kit—we test so often I've got track marks on my fingertips—and I'm negative. I head out to the rolling hills of the back lawn, joining Drew, Steven, and Cody flinging a football back and forth. Even though we've all tested negative, we still wear masks and use gripper gloves with disinfectant palms. This is not my father's football.

I want to tell the others what Miriam told me but I can't. Not yet anyway. So I hold it inside, after all I am a guy.

We play a game of two-hand-touch. No one wants to hurt the boys, if you know what I mean. Drew, oozing testosterone, a macho-fashionista in his matching crimson and gray beanie, sweats, and sneakers with the Buckeye logo, races toward me. I backstep, covering him like a cornerback. His head feints one way, I lean, he jukes the other, looks back at Steven flinging a perfect spiral—Steven could've been a college QB—and the ball floats to rest in Drew's gigantic hands. He reaches the tree-line end zone and does a silly touchdown dance. He holds the ball out to me, taunting me, and I take the bait, reaching for it. He pulls it back and throws a bullet to Steven.

You're a jerk, I say.

Next, I run a deep route, turning on my forty-year-old burners, zipping past Cody, going out long. Steven throws another perfect rainbow that I run underneath, the ball dropping out of the sky and landing sweetly into my outstretched hands. I love rare moments like this, the past wandering in on the present, the smell and feel of worn leather, so righteous in my gloved fingers. I cradle the football, tucking it into the crook of my arm, faking out a hopelessly lost Cody, he's just a body to get in our way as we run routes around him. Cody can kick my butt on Madden but he can't anticipate even the most telegraphed moves. I cruise toward the end-zone tree-line and do my own little high-step dance. Until I'm tackled from behind.

Hey! It's touch!

What are you crying about? Drew laughs, I touched ya!

I swipe turf off my mask and forehead.

We attract a crowd of Sisters outside the black iron fence along Park Avenue. Feels like the old days, trying to impress the girls, and I wonder if it feels that way to them, too, if any of them miss cheering us. Or are they merely laughing now? Further along the fence, I spot Justin, the homeless brother, his hands gripping two iron railings. He looks genuinely interested in the action, as if he'd placed a bet.

I'm walking back to huddle with Steven, when I see out of the corner of my eye, Drew flinging a laser that thumps my chest.

What the hell, Drew?!

268

He cocks his finger into a pistol, winks, and clicks. How can one gender evolve so beautifully, I wonder, and the other fail so miserably?

After our game, I warm-down with a walk to 7-Eleven, splurging on a pint of Häagen-Dazs Butter Pecan, letting the chilly smoothness coat my mouth and the cold, creamy lump slide down my throat. It's turning out to be an okay day. I savor every luscious spoonful, walking past a parked red V sedan with a Little Sister Girl sitting in the backseat. I lock eyes with her. She scrunches her face at me.

What are you looking at?

That stops me in my tracks.

And why are you still alive?

My heart stops—correction—my spirit freezes. I can expect Adult Sisters to say that, they remember the harassment and sexist bullshit we put them through, they've earned the right to be mean. Teenagers, sure, they've been cruel throughout herstory. But a little girl? This was taught to her. Recently. I wanna curse her mother, curse Sisterhood, curse Mother Nature, but instead I scoop another spoonful of cold crack into my mouth and walk away.

***

I've had little desire to post lately. Today is Veterans Day and not a single car passes me as I run bundled under layers of running clothes, a ski mask fitted over my face mask. My cell reads 21 degrees. Only halfway through autumn and it already feels like January. Just my luck, winter coming early, a very bad omen. I reach the Love Shack, hide in the greenhouse, wait for Miriam to show up late. I wanna trust that she will still show up, will still warn me when they come for me, but how can I trust her after she lied about the

269

vaccine? I have three weeks left, I can keep living like this, mulling over my future, or I can go on the run now, join the underground, or maybe flee down south where living on the streets would be warmer. I've looked online and found bro-only villages but they come with bad reviews that boil down to this: very controlled, very creepy and very Sister-less. I don't know about other brothers, but I don't wanna live the rest of my life with just a group of guys. Hell, I'm doing that now.

Here comes Miriam, her running stride very efficient, no wasted movement. She slows down and walks the last fifty feet across the driveway, bundled in her cuffed beanie, fleece gloves, running tights, and a light, yellow jacket. She enters the code, the door clicks open, she walks inside. After a minute, she steps outside, pulls out her cell, glances at it.

You can come out of the greenhouse, Bryan.

She points to what looks like a small beetle hanging on the wall near the door and she holds up her cell. I rise slowly and sure enough I can see myself live on her phone.

Has that always been there? I say, coming out of hiding.

Yes, but I just activated it. Never really needed to keep an eye on you before, you're usually dependable as a clock.

I follow her inside like a sheepish dog. I light the fire, while she tests negative and gives me her mayoral agenda for today.

I get down to business: Anymore thought on getting me that vaccine?

Bryan, let it go.

How can I?

Are we going to make love or not? I have to give a speech at the cemetery in a few hours. I could use the time to prep.

270

Will you honor the brother Vets too?

Of course. Most of them *are* brothers. But I have to focus on Sisters, you know that. Now, are we just going to talk or should I take my clothes off?

I have a request.

Forget it, she stomps toward the kitchen doorway.

It's not the vaccine.

She stops, pivots, faces me. I appeal to her motherhood:

I wanna meet one of my offspring.

I can't arrange that.

You know, for a mayor, you can't do much.

Bryan—

Just one.

You're getting to be way more trouble than you're worth.

It's the least you could do, since you can't give me the vaccine.

She stares at me.

What? I ask.

Take my clothes off or I'm out of here.

Despite all of this, or because of it, I am horny. I give into the lust, but this time, I'm completely in charge, ripping her clothes off. With only three weeks left before I expire, I'm going out with the biggest of big bangs, an attempt to create a whole new universe.

***

Later, I'm at Sisterfield Cemetery to listen to Miriam's Veterans' Day speech. I never go to her public events, it's too hard to pretend in her presence, but I wanna visit my father, so I walk around the many monuments, stones on top of each other, most graves unkempt, the gravestones and markers toppled, broken, or faded, many impossible

271

to read. Wilted flowers and plastic arrangements give the cemetery a ghetto look. Few Sisters come to this section anymore, to weed or plant flowers. Gaia calls our bodies "The vehicles for our great energy," and if so, this cemetery is a junkyard.

They cremate all brothers now, it's the law, ashes take up less space, and the cobwebbed dark marble mausoleum is full of urns. I walk along the walls, my fingers tracing the cold marble drawers. Since the mausoleum is full, most brothers' ashes are stored in an old, brick Mansfield Tire office building downtown, an annex of ashes.

But my father is here. I wipe grime off his plaque, leaning over, pressing my forehead to the cold metal.

William Bowman

1961 – 2030

Love you, pops. I s'pose I'll see you soon.

After a few minutes, I go outside and sit on a waist-high wall that borders the much newer all-Sister section. Two masked brothers stand at the wall, one wearing an Iraqi Freedom Vet cap. We nod, subtly. I look out over the all-Sister side, closer to Route 13, where marble gravestones sparkle, not crowded like the brothers' older section. The grounds are wide-open, mowed and manicured by the loving hands of Sister gardeners, fresh flowers adorning every grave.

Sister Vets and active Sister Soldiers sit in rows of folding chairs. Miriam speaks, dressed in solemn black and gray, luminescent pearls around her neck sparkling like the tombstones. Her bodyguard—I call her Sister Bulldog—stands small but butch at the mayor's side while Miriam thanks Sister Soldiers for their service to our country.

It is you, she says, who today carry on the legacy of protecting this great land.

Her subtext, of course, is they are protecting it from brothers. She gives a respectable speech, says all the right things, preaches to the choir. Afterwards, she shakes the hand of every Sister Soldier. I want to shout at her, "Do you believe brother Vets should get the vaccine for their dedicated service?" But of course, I don't say a thing. I climb down off the wall and walk away, past the old tombstones, some belonging to brothers I once knew.

CHURCH & STATE

From a dusty pew in the bro-only section of St. Pete's, I gaze up at the stained-glass windows. Matthew, Mark, Luke, and John have all been replaced by stained-glass Sisters. Only Jesus and Moses remain. At the altar, Sister Beth passes out communion wafers to Five Elderly Sisters.

The body of Christ given for you.

The Sisters swallow Jesus' flesh. Sister Beth holds up a chalice of wine.

The blood of Christ shed for you.

They drink his blood. I feel put-off by the sacred, cannibalistic ceremony, especially while brothers are being sacrificed in the streets. I squeeze a few drops of tincture under my tongue. Sister Beth gives her benediction and final prayer. The Elderly Sisters make their signs of the cross then amble down the aisle, taking their scattered places in the pews. Sister Beth leads the final hymn, a somnambulistic version of Rock of Ages. I don't even pretend to mouth or mumble along like good Christians usually do.

Go in peace, Sister Beth says.

The Elderly Sisters make their way down the aisle, flashing warm smiles and cold stares. Sister Beth approaches me.

I'm glad to see you again, Bryan.

She sits, two pews ahead, holding her chalice.

Vodka fizz?

I could turn water into one for you if you'd like.

No thanks, I'm good.

I thought your time was up?

I got an extension.

Praise Goddess.

Not really, I'm even more freaked out. I have an expiration date.

She pulls out a pill case, tilts it toward me, an offering of tiny communion wafers imprinted with what look to be images of Christ.

Is that what I think it is?

Holy acid.

A psychedelic sacrament?

The church is evolving, Bryan.

Are you tripping now?

I peaked a couple hours ago. I'm reintegrating.

A trip is the last thing I need.

It's just a micro-dose. Might help you connect with Ms. Almighty.

No thanks.

As you wish.

She snaps the pill case. She lifts a Bible from the back of her pew, flipping through it quickly. The Book of Hebrews, she says, the only book of the Bible thought to actually be written by a Sister. Chapter thirteen, verse six: The Lord is my helper. I will not be afraid. What can mere mortals do to me?

She closes the good book with a compassionate look.

Do not let fear dictate how you enter the next stage. Let Goddess give you comfort.

See, that's the problem. Why should She need to give me comfort? She could've stopped this. Why has She forsaken us?

Freewill brought us to this point.

Okay, but She's omniscient, right?

Sister Beth nods, knowing exactly where I'm going with this.

She knew this was going to happen.

She allows it because it's what we chose.

I didn't.

We can get into this if you want, but somehow I don't think you came here to debate theology.

I came here for a favor.

I'm listening.

Can the church give me shelter?

Sister Beth sips from her chalice.

I wish we could, Bryan.

I look around at the vast emptiness.

What, you have no room at the inn?

How can I help you when the church is in despair?

You won't even know I'm here.

We have an agreement with the city.

You have an agreement not to help brothers?

Not in so many words. But there are plenty of abandoned homes around the city.

I'd feel safer here.

Really?

That's fucked up, I think to myself, a priest questioning the safety of her own sanctuary.

What I can do for you is pray, she offers.

Lot of good that's done us these last few years.

She ignores my whining and bows her head. I don't really want to, but I join her. Dear heavenly Mother, she begins, help this struggling brother to find the peace he desires, blah, blah, blah.

I don't record her prayer, probably should have, I don't remember much of it, but damn, somehow I do feel slightly lighter. Have I been missing out all my life? Or is prayer merely a placebo?

Amen.

She pulls a phone from her frock. I'm texting you a phone number for a lawyer who fights for brothers' rights. Maybe she can help you.

She then makes the habitual sign of a cross.

Go with peace.

I'll go anyway I can, Sister Beth.

I walk out into the gray wintry gloom and call the number. When I explain my situation, the lawyer agrees to see me right away. I walk the two blocks to her office, across the street from the courthouse, and sit in the waiting room, all spit and shine, not a pen out of place. A wall TV plays a video loop of a large, dark, African-American Sister in court, fighting passionately for a brother's rights to something, it's not clear what. A brother narrates: "Regina Johnson. Champion of brothers' rights. If Regina can't help you, only Goddess can."

Not really, I tell myself, the church has already rejected me.

Sister Johnson comes out into the waiting room, masked and dressed for court in a coffee-and-cream-colored business suit. She keeps her necessary distance.

Bryan Bowman?

Yes ma'am, I say, rising, fiddling nervously with my mask.

Please, call me Regina. Come on in.

I keep my social distance, following her into her near-empty office. Just her desk, two leather chairs, a table, a coffee pot.

Won't you have a seat?

Very austere, I say. Where are all the law books?

That's so Law & Order, she says. Everything's online now.

She sits behind her wide, blonde oak Amish-built desk.

Now how can I help you?

She takes notes as I explain my situation, how I'm an Appleseed, how I just turned forty, how I'm supposed to retire. She doodles, arrows this way and that. I only intended to talk about suing for the right to live, to retire peacefully, but as I blab on I become inspired to go deeper. What I'd really like to do, I tell her, is sue the government to release the vaccine.

She stops doodling.

They have it, I say. I bet you know it.

She drops her pen.

No, I do not know that. I'm sorry, Mr. Bowman, I can't help you.

Think of the publicity.

Publicity? Sweetie, that's not publicity, that's career suicide.

The vaccine exists.

That's irrelevant here.

How can that be irrelevant?

If you were a young brother, even better, a child, you might make the case for needing a vaccine. I still couldn't help you, but you might make a good case.

278

All brothers need it.

Not you. You've lived a life of privilege.

Hardly. I've never had money.

You are a white brother, cream of the crop, and an Appleseed to boot, don't get much more privileged than that. No one will sympathize with you. Not even most brothers will be on your side.

She rises from behind her desk, the universal meeting-over move.

So that's it?

That's it. I'm sorry.

What are you scared of, Regina?

With what you just told me, you are a stick of dynamite. And, honey, knowing me, in the courtroom I might light the spark that ignites you.

That sounds great.

For you maybe. If a vaccine exists—and I'm not saying it does—if I get between it and the government, I can kiss my career goodbye.

What about justice?

Sisters will argue this *is* justice.

Is there anyone else I can call?

Regina tilts her large head.

Honey, I'm the only Sister Lawyer you brothers got. But I can't fight for you all, I got to pick my battles.

And with that, she motions toward the door. I walk out of her office, depressed. The church won't help me. The law won't help me. I just keep feeling more and more screwed.

THE REVELATION AT MOHICAN

One week before Thanksgiving, two weeks before my expiration, I'm hanging in the woods near the guesthouse, looking up through the bare limbs of trees, at the sparkling kaleidoscope of stars, blowing into my gloved hands, shivering. The wind gusts, sweeping down from The Great Lakes, old brother winter is right around the corner. I wait to see who shows, hoping cameras don't reach this deep into the trees. Moths circle the light bulb above the kitchen door, orbiting closer and closer toward their imaginary sun, until the heat singes their wings and they drop to the ground like tiny Icaruses.

Miriam arrives, bundled in warm running clothes, barely winded. I come running out of the woods as if I've just arrived too and I follow her inside. I watch her from the doorway. She tears the test kit open, pricks her finger, scoops the drop of blood, places it into the vial of solution, adds drops of buffer, and inserts the vial into the centrifuge. She flips the switch.

First things first, she says over the whiny whirl, we only have one more meeting together. Start boxing up your things.

I've already packed what I need.

Good. The Monday after next, November twenty-ninth, turn yourself in to police.

Just like that?

Unless you want them to hunt you down.

I can't just walk off into the sunset?

They will give you a new identity. To protect you.

From who?

Other brothers. You will be seen as an enemy to many.

She clicks off the whirly-girly, removes the vial, holds it up to the light. Negative, as always.

What happens after I turn myself in?

I don't know exactly.

That's reassuring.

I don't make the rules, Bryan. I just enforce them.

She pulls me close.

Shall we?

I push her away, suddenly very much not in the mood. Even a brother has limits.

You've got a lot to process, I get it.

Any change of heart on that vaccine?

Any change of heart on sex?

Neither one of us budges. She hands me a slip of paper:

Nevaeh

Mohican Bridge

Saturday @ noon

What's this? What's Nevaeh?

It's heaven spelled backwards. She's almost two years old. Her mom takes her there to play on Saturdays.

It finally dawns on me what Miriam's telling me.

She's definitely one of mine?

281

One of your very first ones. Thought you'd want to see a girl that's had time to develop a little personality. But do not talk with them. You are not to make eye contact. If they notice you, you walk away.

Okay.

She could report you. You'd be picked up immediately.

No talking, no eye contact, got it.

She drives a black Titan truck and has a big dog.

I hug Miriam.

Thank you.

It's the least I could do. Now are you in the mood?

She kisses me softly, but then heaves and almost gets sick, fighting back a lump of vomit.

Sorry. I ate breakfast. Usually don't do that before I run.

She touches my face in a motherly way and we both know it's not happening now. Next week, she says, opening the door. I watch her disappear out in the cold dark.

***

On Saturday, my drone circles above as a broCar drops me off at the one-lane covered bridge in Mohican State Park. Built from dark wood, as if from an old barn, the long bridge spans the Clear Fork branch of the Mohican River at the bottom of a wooded gorge. It's a crisp day, the trees bare and gray, the sun-dappled forest smells woody. This was a summer high school make-out spot, not that I ever had the pleasure. Gaia and I did come here once with Miguel, the Golden Trio drinking and getting high. Those two started getting all touchy-feely, so I took a hike.

I'm an hour early. My drone drifts away, probably figuring how much harm can I do out here in the middle of nowhere? I carry a backpack stuffed with two water bottles, snack bars, a pair of jeans, a sweater, socks, headlamp, the fold-up trowel, and a roll of $100s in a baggie. While I'm here I plan to kill two birds with one stone.

Frogs plop into the silty water as I hike over roots and rocks on the muddy riverbank trail. Thin trees reach across the river, straining to touch the top tips of those from the other side, creating a vaulted ceiling over the water. I turn inland. This time of year, I have the forest to myself, the floor blanketed with layers of wet leaves and twigs and mushrooms. It smells damp and dead just like winter should.

I reach Big Lyons Falls, where the flow—sometimes just a trickle—is a couple feet wide after the recent rains, tumbling over a rocky alcove, fifty feet to the ground, the tallest waterfall near Sisterfield. From there I hike a few hundred yards to Little Lyons Falls, smaller but wider, the width of a long dinner table. I scout out the small cave behind the falls, but I know I can't hide the pack here, kids check the cave out, as I used to, it'd be like leaving unburied treasure. I backtrack toward Big Lyon Falls and about halfway between the two I find the perfect place—a stump that resembles a tall coffee mug. A low branch curls to one side like the handle. The kind of place I can remember. I measure six foot-lengths away from the stump, directly east, according to my cell compass. I unfold my Survival Buddy trowel and dig through the top layer of mud and forest duff. The ground is hard and I have to saw through a root with the serrated edge of the trowel. Sweat drips down my mask. This is taking longer than I thought, I could really use a shovel. I saw and sweat and eventually I get the job done. I wrap a thick Hefty garbage bag around my pack, double-twist-tie it, and wrap that with a second bag and triple-twist-tie that, another trick Steven taught me. I squish down the bag and fill the hole with dirt. I throw some old twigs and leaves on top. I fold the trowel and hide it in a rotted-out section of the tree stump.

I hike the mile back, a sweaty chill seeping through my clothes. I walk onto the dark covered bridge and stand inside like I own it, looking downriver at a grassy area with a swing set, picnic tables, and rusted firepits. I am the only one here. I'm nervous as hell.

Uphill, to the east, a bright blue vehicle flashes through the trees, driving downhill on the winding road. I step back into the covered bridge's shadows. A Toyota drives onto it and I feel the wide boards vibrate under my feet as the car crosses, then emerges, winding its way up the other side of the gorge. My left leg trembles, a residual effect, and I imagine this is what adopting families feel like the first time they meet their new child.

I hear the sloshing of hooves on slushy pavement. Coming down the curvy road is an Amish horse-and-buggy, with only a father and his son inside. If this isn't a fucking postcard, I don't know what is. I wave as they pass me inside the bridge. They nod back and ride up the winding road on the other side. A thought comes to me: maybe I should disguise myself as Amish. Or better yet, a Sister, like Miguel did. I've actually done it before, back in high school for homecoming, a group of us senior guys pretended to be cheerleaders, we dressed up in sweaters and skirts with pom-poms, wigs, and breasts. Looked pretty good, I might add.

I hear another vehicle, this time it's loud, and through the bare trees, I see it's black and could be a Titan. I lean back into the interior shadows and watch the truck pull off the road and down into the picnic area, parking near the swing set. A German Shepherd leaps out and prances along the river. A brunette Sister Mom climbs out, tossing a

284

tennis ball in the grassy field above the river bank. The dog gives chase, gallops back and returns the ball, obediently. The Sister Mom breathes in the beauty of this place, then reaches into the truck's backseat and unbuckles a toddler, lifting her out of the car.

Nevaeh. Wow.

The little girl is adorable, a towhead like I was, dressed in a woodsy sweater, old jeans, and rubber boots. She skips around a muddy patch of grass, then plops down, the sun streaming upon her. She pokes sticks at bugs and I am stunned how magical this moment feels. Like I've said, I never wanted kids, and it's too late now, but as I see her—my seed, my spore, my little shoot, one of so many I've planted—I am blown away by the sudden desire to be more than just what I am, more than a sperm provider, to be a bona fide dad, to fully be a man. I breathe her name: Nevaeh. This is me, a young Sister, that will live on, one of many little me's, and I've never seen anything so beautiful. I suddenly crave a relationship and wonder if there is any love as miraculously tender as father-daughter love? I think of all I could teach this little girl, teach all my daughters out there, that brothers are not evil, that we are lovable, and deserve to be here, even if we have screwed-up and are now only shadows of our former selves. I am overcome by a new desire to hold little Nev—I've decided that's what I would call her—a desire to talk to her and be amazed by what her new eyes can show me. I finally see the light. This is what Sisters have been telling me my purpose is, this is truly what I'm leaving behind. My book suddenly pales in comparison. Even though they won't know anything about me, these Little Sisters will carry on my essence. This is the peace everyone keeps talking about.

285

From the shadows inside the bridge, I focus my cell down on little Nev. Click. I zoom in, click a few more, then shoot some video. I'm feeling like a stalker, so I also take pictures of the scenery. I hear the annoying buzzing of my drone above the bridge—does it somehow know?—and Sister Mom looks up. I pretend to take pictures of the river.

C'mon, sweetie, she says.

No.

Mommy forgot something at home. We have to go.

No!

Sister Mom points at me, a mix of disgust and fright on her face, as if warning her child of a coyote. Nev squints. I step out from the shadows, leaning out through an opening in the bridge so she can clearly see her father, her daddy. I wave. Nev's tiny eyes pop wide in terror. I feel shot through the heart—by my own daughter. Sister Mom pulls out her cell, taps it, holds her phone up in all four directions, looking for service, frustrated. She scoops up little Nev and buckles her into her child's seat. The dog hops into the truck bed.

I cross the bridge to the other side of the river. Sister Mom jumps behind the wheel and drives my little girl away, steering the truck back up the way they came. This is so messed up. My own flesh-and-blood fears me. I am a freak, a monster to her, to all of them, my daughters, who may never talk to a brother in their lives, may only see them on TV or in museums, may need to be told what a dad is. To them, I will not live on in any meaningful way. My DNA, sure it will continue, but memory of me will be erased. All the more reason I need Gaia to publish my words, but who will bother to read them? Who will remember? My fantasy of living on is over. This whole experience really mind-fucks me, I didn't used to care about what happened with my sperm, it was just a job, my way to survive. Now it's even worse, I am frightening to them. A monster.

All of a sudden, I don't care if I do die.

GOODBYES

I SisFace with Emily. She moves on-and-off my tablet screen, busy putting up Thanksgiving decorations of plastic autumn leaves and cornucopia. I'm dying to tell my sis about the vaccine, but I can't put her in that position.

I wanna ask you something, sis. Are you gonna have any more kids?

I doubt it. If I do, rest assured, I will not be ordering your sperm.

Goddess, I hope not.

She disappears off my screen.

How's Emma? It's been awhile since I've seen her. What is she now, eight?

She's eleven.

She never seemed to like me.

She likes you. She's just been brainwashed by society.

I want her to remember me.

Sure, I can tell her how you used to pin me down on the floor and dangle a thread of spit over my face. Or how you pretended to be a bullfighter and you talked me into charging head-down like a bull toward your cape. How at the last second, you'd lift the cape and I'd bang my head into a wall behind it.

288

More than once, I laugh.

Yeah. Fun times.

We were kids.

Don't worry, she smiles mischievously, I'll tell her about all the things her Uncle Bryan did.

That's all I ask.

I gotta go. Emma needs my help with a school project. We'll get together soon, I promise.

Tell her I said hello.

I will. You're gonna be okay, bro. You'll figure this out.

I hope. Hey, I'm gonna SisMo you some money before the government takes what's left.

You don't need to do that.

What else am I gonna do with it?

There's a long silence.

Try not to stress too much, she says, hopefully it's great, wherever you're going.

Not sure that really helps, but thanks for trying.

What are little Sisters for?

She bends over and kisses her screen.

You take care, brother.

Love you, Emily.

Love you too.

She clicks off, vanishing from my screen. I know what I need to do next.

***

A carrot nose and charcoal mouth, like Frosty The Snowman, are painted on my latex mask, as I lug a big box into mom's room at The

Sisters of Mercy, to the "Na-na-na-na," chorus of Hey Jude. The usual mix of floral and disinfectant notes greets me. The clutter of pill bottles and Kleenex boxes and tubes seems to be growing. I work as quietly and quickly as I can, stringing Christmas lights along the walls, the big multi-colored bulbs that are so impossible to find anymore. Earlier today I snuck into our old home through a bedroom window and grabbed decorations. Emily's gonna be pissed when she finds out.

I place the family nativity scene on mom's windowsill. Minus one piece. You're gonna have to find baby Jesus, I tell her. I hide the plastic infant behind a potted plant. Every year the little bugger would be missing from the nativity scene, not showing up until Christmas morning. Mom and pops loved Christmas.

I save the tree for last, just a three-foot aluminum one I picked-up at Goodwill and spray-painted emerald green. I grew up with noble eight-foot firs, jam-packed with ornaments. Now I unfold this fake one onto a counter, filling the squat tree with our old homemade sequined balls, beaded Santas and Rudolphs and Snoopys. I plug in the tree. The simple white lights give balance to the rainbow of colors— seasonal and medical—draped around the room. I turn off her classic rock and softly sing Christmas carols just like pops used to, Silver Bells and Let It Snow, mom's favorites. I watch her sleep, not wishing to disturb her. I wanna hug her, something we seldom did growing up. Back then mom sure looked pretty—brunette, bright red or pink lipstick, Cindy Lauper-inspired dresses—but she was built from tough German stock. Silent, polite smiles, no tears. I don't think we hugged until my thirties, and only when I initiated it. I'd like to hug one last time, so I close the door, take a deep breath, move closer. Her body powder smells like rain—boy that takes me back—and I hold her hand in my winter glove. Her nails are painted a candy-apple red, as pretty as ever. I show her my phone, even though she is asleep.

Here's a picture of one of your grandchildren, mom. Her name is Nevaeh. Isn't she adorable?

I turn my face away, breathe in, turn back:

I see a little of you in her. And you'll be happy to know you've got lots. More than you'd ever want.

The door opens. Sister Caregiver fills the doorway.

What are you doing?!

I let go of mom's hand. I back away from her bed.

Just saying goodbye.

You could contaminate yourself.

I'm aware.

It's improper. Highly improper.

Life is highly improper.

Okay, it's your funeral, she says, fiddling with a couple machines. She steps out into the hall, stops, looks back. The lights look nice, she says.

I step back away from mom and watch her soul struggle to wake, so quiet, so proud. Her eyelids lift.

Mom?

She stares straight ahead at the tree.

Are we going to see the lights at the fairgrounds? she asks.

That was one of our family pastimes, driving through the winter wonderland of brightly-lit displays set up every year. I don't tell her that there haven't been fairground displays in years.

I don't think I can this year, mom.

Oh. Okay.

Her eyes close. She has been so strong for so long, her heart and mind could keep on chugging along, but her spirit has weakened, ready to let go. I lean closer. I want her to know, before she goes.

There's a vaccine, mom. There's hope.

I feel the quick thrill of revealing a secret, but then, who's she gonna tell? I hear a snippet of a snore, so polite, even while asleep.

I'm going away soon, I say, for good. Don't know where.

The thought tightens my chest, and I pull out my tincture and squeeze a whole dropperful under my tongue. I turn on her classic rock—in the middle of Clapton's guitar solo on While My Guitar Gently Weeps—and I step out into the hallway, looking back at mom sleeping so delicately, so peacefully.

Maybe I'll see you soon, I whisper, tears soaking my Frosty mask.

CIRCLES

I'm low on tincture so I visit 'Round & Ground after-hours, entering
through the back door, off an uneven brick patio here since the
1800's. Patchouli tickles my nostrils. To my left is a storage room lined
with lit candles and a circle of five brothers, different ages, all
slouched on folding chairs, dark raccoon circles around their eyes,
taut skin, slumped postures, heavy with the gravity of dying. Gaia sits
in the circle's middle, an Om printed across her tie-dyed blouse. The
brothers are mask-less, no need to pretend at this stage. I move no
closer and find myself tightening my own brobot mask.

Monks chant, layered over New-Age synthesizer background
music, while Gaia runs through a visualization process. She has been
known to use animal cards, psychedelics, holotropic breathing,
whatever works. Her spiritual ceremonies used to be co-ed, for all
who sought evolution, enlightenment, peace. They're now gender-
specific. You should check out a ceremony, she always tells me, it
can ease your journey through these difficult times. That's not the
problem, I say, I don't wanna *ease* the journey. I don't wanna *take* the
journey. Besides, when it comes to spirituality, I prefer to watch.

This body is just a rental, she tells the gathered brothers, a trailer
home. Imagine, your soul moving out of that trailer and into a gigantic,

293

wide-open mansion. With hundreds of acres of rolling green hills and patches of forest. Your soul will have no bounds. Now hold that place in your mind, and feel the spiritual joy as you move about freely. Survey your grounds. Smell the blossoms. Wonderful, isn't it? No constrainting—I smile at the funky gerund—like inside this tiny body of flesh. Your soul has room to move. Let it wander around right now, in the space you create.

The dying brothers squirm in their seats, maneuvering in their mindscapes.

We don't need spiritual enlightenment, we need a vaccine, I whisper louder than I intended. At the very least, we need to get wasted.

Bryan, Gaia says, that's not cool.

A couple guys fidget in their folding chairs, trying to stay in the special places inside their heads. The circle of brothers hasn't broken, but it's being grossly bent.

I apologize for his rude interruption, Gaia continues. If you have lost your soul's garden, then return to your breathing exercises, focus on that, deep breath in. Hold it. Slow breath out, smooth and even. In. Deep. Out. Smooth. Imagine doing that, just as you are now, sitting underneath your trees, so much room to move.

Her words have great effect, guiding them back to a safe place.

Now imagine the people you have lost in your lives. Your fathers, brothers, sons, even mothers and sisters and daughters, imagine them visiting you in your safe place. Hug them. Tell them goodbye, if you never got the chance. And hello again if you already have.

She gives an excruciatingly long pause.

Now, think: Have you said what you need to say to the people in your life?

I have tried, I tell myself, heading to a table of cookies and coffee. Food has not been on my radar lately, but when sweets offer themselves I'm suddenly famished. I grab six oatmeal chocolate chip, stuff them into my jacket, then devour two peanut butter. I must look homeless, munching madly in the hallway, near the Kid Sisters section of books.

A sign on an easel outside the staff breakroom reads:

EMPOWERING
OUR MOVE
BEYOND GRIEF
TO GRATITUDE
8 PM
Let go of the past
Get in touch with
Your true Sister self

Looks like Gaia's double-booked. I peek into the breakroom, definitely don't belong in this meeting. The music is soft and spiritual, chanting breathily, over soothing strings, some light synthesizer. Seven Sister Seekers sit lotus-style, some bodies sway, some keep perfectly still, all eyes closed. I crunch on cookies as Gaia walks past, ignoring me, now taking her place in the middle of this circle.

Let yourself come back with me.

They lift their heads and eyelids.

I'd like to talk to you about someone my mom loved: Krishnamurti.

295

The Sister Seekers react, surprised.

I know he was a brother, but he was deep and pragmatic, Gaia continues, and he said, "You are in relationship with everyone and everything." How true. We'd been in relationship with brothers for millennium, often toxic for sure. Now that relationship has changed, but it's still relationship. A relationship with our past. Relationship with death. Relationship with our own power. All relationships have a beginning. They grow. And then they die.

Gaia scans the room.

The beauty is, Sisters, we still have who we were inside. We are still beautiful. Say it.

We are still beautiful.

And now we are powerful.

Now we are powerful.

We are beautiful and powerful.

We are beautiful and powerful.

It's a great time to be alive, isn't it?

The Sisters nod, vigorously, in various stages from relieved to ecstatic, the buzz energizing the room. Hell, I feel it too. Gaia gives me a subtle smile.

Be with this feeling for a moment, Sisters, she says. I'll be right back. She rises quietly, exits the circle, and joins me near the Kid Sisters section. She stops short, whispering to me through the doorway: Either group interest you?

Naw, I just came for the cookies.

She holds up two tincture bottles.

And those.

She sets the bottles down on a reading desk.

296

What else can I do for you?

Do you have any extra time for sale?

She cocks her head in a sympathetic way. Can't help you there, she says. Just don't do anything stupid.

Define stupid.

You'll know it when you do it.

There's a heightened, energetic murmuring among the circle of Sisters, a natural part of the group ebb and flow.

You never once came to a meeting.

You know meditation's not my thing.

What I don't say to her is that I didn't want to share her with so many others. Sharing her with Miguel had been hard enough.

She looks across the hall to her circle of dying brothers.

I should get back to them.

I know. Listen, Gaia, I may not see you again—I clear my throat—and I just want you to know. . . I love you.

The circle of Sisters stops murmuring. Eyes crack open, pretending not to watch.

I know, Gaia says. Me too.

My childhood friend whom I adored, returns to her circle of dying brothers. I feel the cells in my body contracting. I lift the bottles—labeled Chill bro—unscrew the top on one, lower my mask, squeeze out a few golden drops under my tongue, and dangle the dropper like a cig on my lower lip.

I head out the back door, out into the cold.

MY LAST SUPPER

It's November 24, Thanksgiving Eve, one week left on my extension. I'm supposed to turn myself in to the police on Monday. But for now, all eight of us Appleseeds gather around the large dining table, even Selfie is here, not saying anything as usual, just kinda nodding along. We have all tested, the results were negative, and father-brother Jonathan announces:

Let the holidays begin!

He wears an apron with images of local tourist sites—Queenwood Center, The Reformatory, Oak Hill Cottage—as he cooks Thanksgiving dinner a day early, on my behalf because I meet Miriam tomorrow and everyone pretty much knows I'm sleeping with her. We all sense this just might be my last night at The Factory. I wanna spill the beans about the vaccine, but what's to tell? I have no info, no more than we already believed anyway.

We sit, sans masks, pretending normalcy, though this is not our fathers' Thanksgiving, no football to watch, so little to be thankful for, so few brothers alive to give thanks. I suppose we should be grateful we're still alive, but thankfulness feels hollow, gratitude feels pointless. Gratitude for what, that we outlived 99% of our gender? That Sisters were given Goddess's grace and that we survivors were given just a crumb? There but for the grace of God, my grandma Charlotte used to say, back when God was still a guy. I never liked that line, why would God or Goddess grant grace for me but not for you? The saying feels especially hollow now.

How do you feel? André asks me.

Like it's my Last Supper.

Kimchi snaps photos on his iPhone.

C'mon, no digital, I say, you know the rules of the room.

I am official photographer.

A'ight. One minute.

We pose like studs—dicks and assholes really—flexing and posing while Kimchi clicks away.

Maybe I blow one up, hang on wall.

We need to Photoshop our faces onto da Vinci's Last Supper, André says, and cover up this awful wallpaper.

But we all know we won't do either of those things.

Cody raises his glass of water: I want to, like, make a toast.

I raise a dark beer, a Monk stout. What are they gonna do, fire me? I'm already obsolete. The others raise their glasses of non-alcoholic drinks: pops, juices, flavored waters. No one else imbibes tonight, they already got drunk once for my birthday and caught hell from Jonathan. They're not gonna do it again. This is the busy season, Appleseeds do double-duty from Thanksgiving to Christmas to satisfy Sisters who love receiving the gift of conception for the holidays. After Christmas, we usually take a few weeks off until Valentine's Day demand spikes again.

To an awesome Appleseed, Cody says, raising his juice glass. Others lift their juices, sodas and waters. I raise my dark beer. I am touched. Cody adds: You're, like, a role model for me.

We clink glasses. Steven sneers.

Didn't we already toast your ass a few weeks ago?

No more toasts, Drew agrees.

We get down to business: moist turkey, mashed heaven— potatoes and yams—sourdough dressing, thick, garlicky gravy and the most exquisite green bean casserole I've ever eaten. And I've eaten many, Sisters love their casseroles. We milk this moment, experiencing what life used to feel like, taking our time, passing bowls of food back and forth, heaping piles on our plates. We butter biscuits and rolls and whiff the smorgasbord of scents rising off our plates: the baked animal flesh, the garlics and yeasts and cranberries, and a top note of yams dripping in brown sugar.

Anyone feel like saying a prayer? Jonathan says.

We look at each other with a collective: Nope. We dig in, knives and forks clanking.

EDITOR'S NOTE: Once again, for ease, I default to theatrical dialogue style.

ME: I feel just like this turkey.

STEVE: Sisters are so gonna stuff your ass.

That leads to some sick jokes that I won't bore or gross you out with. Except for one:

SELFIE: I heard a funny joke.

We all almost fall out of our chairs in shock. Selfie tells jokes?

SELFIE: Why does a duck have feathers?

We're all still too stunned to answer.

SELFIE: To hide its butt quack!

Kimchi spits out mashed yams in a burst of laughter.

KIMCHI: So sorry.

We throw our wadded-up napkins at him, bombarding him in cotton, as he wipes up his mess.

JONATHAN: Anyone gonna watch the Macy's Parade tomorrow?

STEVEN: Hell no, all the balloons are Sisters.

DREW: No more Charlie Brown.

ANDRÉ: No Batman, no Spiderman.

KIMCHI: But Dora! I like Dora.

CODY: Yeah, and Wonder Sister and Bat Sister. They're,
        like, pretty hot.

ME: I suddenly feel so old.

DREW: You *are* old.

KIMCHI: You are no fried chicken anymore.

We laugh.

ANDRÉ: It's *spring* chicken.

STEVEN: To Bryan! You are no fried chicken anymore!

Despite the no-toast ban, we clink and tilt glasses, the liquid flowing down our throats, the glasses returning to the table.

ME: Wait, wait. One last toast.

Glasses raise lazily. Everyone's in the mood to eat not toast.

ME: To Bernie. Rest in peace. And power.

ALL: R.I.P. Bernie.

STEVEN: To all brothers.

ALL: To all brothers.

My eyes water as I chug the last of my thick beer.

After dinner I hug a few goodbyes with the guys, it's feeling more real this time. Bodies flop on the antique sofas in the drawing room. Naps rule. I check my phone, see Cody has sent me a YouTube of himself playing my guitar. I can't tell what he's trying to play, but I tell him he's improving, slowly, the chord changes not quite as clunky, the rhythm not so stop-and-go.

I head up to my room and lie in bed, expecting deep thoughts about life and death, but my mind is numb, as if my thoughts—like the guys—have decided to leave me alone. I double-wrap the superhero backpack from Cody in plastic garbage bags and carry it out to the trash bin, next to the maintenance shed. I wheel the bin down to the curb, where Sanitation Sisters will pick it up after Thanksgiving. (BTW, another silver lining for planet earth: keeping earth litter-free is much easier now without brothers.) My drone follows me but bores with my chores, as always, and drifts away to Fourth Street to watch the cars drive by. I roll the bin against the curb, pull out the bag and hurry into a patch of woods. I pull out my fold-up trowel and, by the beam of my cell flashlight, dig a hole in the moist autumn soil. I bury my pack, a couple hundred yards or so away from the other one I buried out here, one of five backpacks stashed around the county. I'm a squirrel hiding its nuts, just like Steven advised. I have to laugh at myself, this is like those schoolchildren in the 50's ducking under desks in their Cold War drills. What good are a few supplies and cash gonna do me? I cover the backpack with dirt, pat down the topsoil, fold up my trowel. I head back to the house, imprisoned inside this dead man walking, in these End of Days on this planet that will not, that cannot, protect me.

302

THANKSGIVING MORNING

I can't sleep. I will soon see Miriam for the last time, I'm sure. I wanna believe this morning will be normal, that we will make love before I send her off to cook turkey for her staff, a mayoral tradition. I post the last of my recordings on the dark *It*, rise out of bed a half-hour early, and dress in extra layers, slowly, feeling each different fabric, the varying degrees of softness in my hands and against my cheek. Even tying my shoes takes on new meaning, everything I do matters so much more when I know it is the last time—the blessing and curse of the expiration date. I make my way down our big staircase and I gaze around the dark drawing room, at the still-boarded-up windows, the fancy, faded antique furniture, the cold vibe. I sit down at the piano and plink a couple high keys. Wherever I go, I hope there is music.

At the front door, I stare into the retinal scanner, almost wishing it doesn't recognize me and refuses to let me go. But the lock clicks and I step outside, listening to the door swoosh closed behind me. On the front lawn I do my warm-up stretches, extra-stiffly this morning. I look back at The Factory, experiencing a gentle wave of gratitude for having lived in a mansion for two years. Then I jog onto the winding path, into the forest, feeling the chill in my lungs on this bitter black Ohio morning. A few more cars than usual are on the road, Sisters getting an early start on holiday travel. I hear an army of howling in the distance, coyotes, maybe abandoned dogs, probably yapping over roadkill. My head pivots back and forth, hyper-alert, surveying everything around me, anticipating that at any second I could be swept up into a van full of Sisters or attacked by a Sister Kisser. I hate feeling so paranoid but at least I'm feeling something. I'll take paranoia over feeling nothing. Now I get what the fisherbrother said.

I jog in place at the Park Avenue intersection, waiting for the light, not about to break any laws, even one as pedestrian as jaywalking. The autumn air smells cold and spoiled and I pull out my tincture bottle, squeeze a dropperful under my tongue. The light turns green, and I run, like a machine, the obsolete machine I am, keeping to the bro-only lane, unsure if I will make it to the Love Shack, where I have a backpack and hopefully Miriam waiting. Or should I just keep running, past the Sensitive Estates, a couple more miles to Lexington Avenue, where I have another backpack hidden in a patch of forest behind a Dollar Store. I carry a fold-up trowel in the front pocket of my hoodie, should I need to dig up a pack. Or slice a Sister's throat.

I hear growling and gnawing ahead. Oh Jesus. Two dogs and a coyote feast on a stiff and frosty dead brother, tearing at his body in a tug-of-war of human arms and legs. Git outta here! I yell, running at the scavengers, waving my arms like a madman. The three dogs scurry aside, pacing, knowing they only have to bide their time. I sidestep the poor soul and move on, nothing I can do for him now. I imagine the dogs returning to tear at him. Missing their masters, they can at least feast on one.

I think about my next steps. I'm supposed to turn myself in on Monday at 9 AM, three days ahead of my expiration date, I guess to test if I will voluntarily hand myself over. If I don't, I'm sure they will hunt me down. I keep looking up, waiting for my hummingbird to appear, thinking that it will break its power-down schedule and follow me, but my drone doesn't materialize. All appears normal. Stars stab the moonless night, and I recognize the only three constellations I know: The Big and Little Dippers and Orion. It's hard to fathom stars guiding humans on their journeys, long before GPS, and I yearn for a simpler time like that, before The Change and The Y and The War. Earlier peoples probably thought the same thing, dealing with The Black Death, or The Spanish Flu or World Wars One and Two. These sorry-ass thoughts ping-pong inside my skull as I jog through the gate into Sensitive Estates, past the statues of Gloria and RBG, now cleaned of graffiti. I run off-road and into the hillside forest of mostly mid-size pines and leafless oaks, the pine sap especially pungent. I head uphill, running extra fast this morning, my body focused, feeling a sense of calm come over me, maybe relief that the wait is almost over, finally, my destiny here, good or bad. I come up behind a row of shrubs and around the back of the Shack. I peek in a window. No sign of life inside. I urgently need Miriam to show, I need her trust, more than I need sex or love. Sex has always been a mask for brothers' desire for something deeper.

I enter the Shack fifteen minutes early, set a test kit on the kitchen table, ignite the bundle of wood in the fireplace, like I always do. I gaze at the guitar waiting in a corner, but I don't have time for music. I slink back outside, hoping Miriam isn't watching me on her cell from the videocam. I retrieve my backpack from the stack of pots in the greenhouse, sling it over my back and trudge uphill, kicking through nature's debris of damp twigs and slippery leaves. There's no moon

305

out tonight, so I've got the cover of darkness, thank Goddess. About fifty yards away from the Shack, I find a spot behind some trees, not a single one wide enough to hide behind but as a clump they almost do. I look down on the guesthouse from here, the silvery glow of smoke whispering out of the chimney, swirling in all directions, smelling of burnt wood. I have options here, different paths I can take, with a head start, in almost any direction, where cars can't follow, they will have to drive around the winding streets of this development, while I race downhill, and they will have to guess which way I head. I've been running here for two years, I know this forest and I have darkness on my side. And with my backpacks buried around the city and all the survival tips from Steven and Drew, I definitely feel better prepared than I did just five weeks ago.

I breathe into my cupped gloves, rub my biceps to get my blood flowing. I look at my cell: 5:35. My left leg trembles. I pull out my tincture and twist off the top, not easy with thick gloves on. I squeeze the dropper, the bitter amber liquid seeps under my tongue. I'm adrenalining, as Gaia might say, and I know I should just go, but I can't move. My toes feel numb, almost frozen together inside my running shoes. If I flee now, fleeing will forever be my life. I'm not ready for that, not quite yet.

5:39.

The wait feels so much longer because I got here earlier. I'm just waiting for the charade to end and the real game to begin. A wave of shivers rolls over me.

5:40.

Where the fuck are you, Miriam?! Please don't let me down, I wanna know that I truly meant something to you. Did I? Okay, five

306

more minutes and I'm calling it. I may not know where I'm going, but I'm not waiting here to die. I have no clue, really, where I'm going, this shit's getting real now. Gotta stay calm, gotta keep cool, gotta suck on some more tincture.

A pair of parking lights appear downhill, snaking up the street toward the mansion, no headlights on, not a good sign. It's a dark van that soon extinguishes all lights, quietly parking at the end of the driveway. I squeeze out a couple more drops and watch Three Sisters-In-Black climb out, armed with revolvers. Fuck you, Miriam. I gotta run but I don't wanna make a sound, instead I watch the dark trio move stealthily to the kitchen door.

I text Gaia: *Miriam set me up.*

Two of the Sisters-In-Black enter the guesthouse. The third searches the greenhouse.

Gaia texts back immediately, surprising me: *She must be worried you'll go underground.*

The Two Sisters-In-Black emerge from the Shack, shaking their heads. All three converse. One taps her cell, they stare at it.

You're at the Shack, right? Gaia texts.

Yes. Hiding in the woods.

Soon, the Three Sisters point up the hillside I'm hiding on. Must have seen the security cam.

Okay, stay put, she texts, *I'm coming.*

The Three Sisters-In-Black whip out long police flashlights, the bright beams fanning out around the grounds. One scans the forest around the house, the other two come uphill. That's good, the videocam must not reach this far, they don't know for sure I'm up here, otherwise all three would be coming my way. The searchlights dance back and forth, their arcs moving up the hillside below me. One light moves off to my right, further away. But the other comes closer, sweeping the forest floor, getting warmer, as kids used to say. I crouch, take a step out into the shadowless dark, one slow step at a time, tiptoeing around tree trunks, hoping the Sister's light doesn't find me. I feel like a human snail slinking around fallen limbs and this isn't so hard I tell myself. I keep my head down and stay focused and—

Snap!

Shit. I stepped on a dry branch. I freeze behind a patch of aspens that partially hide me. The arc of light sweeps nearby, bouncing all around the area and it licks the back of my shoulder, caressing the corner of my head. I hold my breath. Please don't let them see me, I beg, please don't let them see me. I hear a shuffling of wet twigs and leaves as the searchlight moves off to my left. I am again in darkness. I exhale, wishing I could just hide here but I can't, she's heading my general direction, she'll pass close to me if I don't move. I take a quiet step, then another, and another.

Not quiet enough. The beam of light swings back over and focuses on me. I'm busted. Voices bark and arcs of light bounce toward me. I hustle uphill, fast as I possibly can, the backpack jostling off my shoulders, I shrug it on tighter, clutching a strap with one hand.

Pop!

A gunshot? What the fuck?!

I hunch over, tucking my chin into my chest, and leap around some rocks and roots and over a dead trunk and stumble on the landing, but I keep on running.

Pop-pop!

308

Bullets chip away chunks of pine trunks beside me. Why the hell are they shooting at me?! I bounce off a rough trunk and use a low branch of another to pull myself up a section of hill.

Pop-Pop-Pop!

I am propelled forward, as if shoved from behind. I fear I am shot, but I feel no pain, no blood flowing, and I keep moving uphill, those morning runs have paid off. I glance back and see the arc of light has lost a little ground, the Sister-In-Black is talking on her cell phone, silhouetted by the Second Sister's spotlight coming up behind her. I hurry even faster uphill, I can see stars now in front of me, the crest of the hill, and I hear voices and look back and see the other two arcs of light returning to the van that will soon be giving chase, but the third light is still climbing after me and I kick it into high gear and propel myself off the trunks of trees. I leap over a fallen trunk, coming down in front of a mesh of broken limbs and sidestep that and bump—

OW!!

I'm jabbed in the left thigh by a broken tree branch. I spin the other way, into a tree stump and somehow I keep my balance, keep running, can't stop, but now my left thigh throbs like a sonofabitch, I'm no longer close to running, I'm speed-limping, dragging my left leg a hitch, through the last bit of trees. I reach the crest of hill, thank goddess, and the forest thins out and without even breaking my momentum, I grab a dead limb from the ground, use it as a trekking pole, a third leg, and I hobble downhill, out of the forest. I cross an expansive lawn. I can get my groove on here, I can limp with more confidence, as I widen my lead, just need to keep on my feet, if I stop, I'm dead. I imagine the Sister-In-Black still charging uphill through the forest behind me, reloading and yelling into her cell. I cross Millsboro

309

Road and I have four options: one direction takes me back toward the Sensitive Estates, a no-go; a second leads me toward more forest, don't want that, not with my lame leg; a third direction leads me back toward town, not ideal either; and the fourth leads to a tall church, then into horse country. Streetlights are few and far between here, to my advantage, and deep, dark ditches line the roads, so I crouch down into one, hobbling through the frosty grass, heading along Marion Avenue, my thigh throbbing. If I can get to that church, maybe I can hide.

I see the flashlight arc cresting the hill and running down into the clearing, the Sister-In-Black is gaining serious ground, crossing the lawn, straight toward the road. I stay low, limping, crouched down in the ditch. A pair of headlights approach. I carpet the ground. The lights sweep slowly toward me, overhead, and I close my eyes and wait for the inevitable but the sound of the engine fades as the headlights turn down Millsboro and drive off another direction. Lucked out, but I know luck won't last, the van could be here any minute. I push myself up off the cold ground. Fuck, my thigh burns.

The searchlight bounces on the field across the road, obviously unaware where I am, maybe a hundred yards away, but moving my way, the logical direction for a fugitive to run, away from the hunt, away from town. My leg shakes, every twitch shooting pain across my thigh. I know I can't stay here, so I race toward the large brick church with its massive white columns glowing in the darkness. My left leg buckles under me. Gotta get to that church, no idea what denomination, looks like maybe a Methodist. I hurry around to the back and smash a stained-glass window in the door and I reach in and unlock it and leave it ajar, and then I limp straight back into the woods behind the church, praying now that the building blocked any view of me doing this. I duck behind some bushes and watch the Sister-In-Black slink around to the back door. She spots the smashed window, the door ajar. She pushes it open and follows the barrel of her revolver inside. It's a big church and will take a few minutes to search.

Thank you.

I speed-limp off into the forest and the ebony-gray Ohio morning, finding a back trail that leads me away, down Helen Reddy Road.

HOUSE-HOPPING

Some survivalist I turn out to be, hobbling through dark backyards, leaning on a tree-branch cane, my thigh throbbing like someone's hammering it 100 beats a minute. I need ice but can't even think of going into a market. Under the cover of night, I limp toward town, and when headlights approach, I scurry like a scared dog. Since most lawns in Sisterfield are without fences, I hide between homes until the headlights pass, but these neighborhoods are too nice, all the homes look occupied. The horizon glows like a thin river of lava as I limp toward brother town, the slum neighborhood west of downtown, where I squatted for a few days when I left my boyhood basement, two-story homes with sagging porches piled with ripped furniture, broken fridges and fast-food trash. Many of these houses were abandoned years before The Y. Even drug addicts fled for better digs.

Finding an abandoned home here is a no-brainer, if you don't mind the stench of death and competition from raccoons and rats. Finding a home with the power still on, now that takes some effort. Sister Environmental Electric (SEE) hasn't caught up with all the newly deceased yet, there's often a lag of months before utilities are shut off. I search for one of those houses, in the brightening morning light, hobbling on these ghost-town streets, peeking into windows, looking for signs of electronic life—little red, green, or blue lights glowing on appliances, clocks, or chargers. I find one. The front door handle is locked, I limp around to the back door, that's locked too. I rear back and stab my tree-branch cane against a small window that shatters into pieces tumbling to the floor. I break off a few jagged chunks of glass from the frame, reach in, unlock the door. The raw stench of death and rot permeates the walls and fabrics. Newly-abandoned. I limp into the kitchen, crunching shards of glass underfoot. I open the freezer: bags of frozen veggies, a tub of freezer-burn ice cream, and ice trays. I drop my sweats. A nasty yellow-green bruise, the size of a coaster, blooms across my thigh. Although it's freezing in here, I empty ice cubes onto a kitchen towel, bundle that up and spread it across my aching bruise. I plop down on a lumpy couch—its stuffing oozes underneath me—and lay back and close my eyes. The ice burns worse than the pain.

I can't believe they shot at me. I'm so pissed at Miriam, she lied, that bitch! I check out my backpack. There is a bullet hole in the lower half. I dump everything out and find a bullet lodged in a roll of Benjamins. Money may be the root of all evil but cash just saved my ass.

The water's still on, thank goddess, which I guzzle almost until I'm sick. I raid the cupboards and snack on Pop Tarts and crackers. I close my eyes and rest.

***

Brothercleaners once volunteered to clear-out abandoned homes, to thwart the invasion of hungry critters. They drove Happy Trash garbage trucks with smiling garbage bags—big and toothy—painted on the sides. The brothercleaners removed all perishables from refrigerators and rat-infested cupboards, tossing out mushy fruit,

313

twiggy vegetables, wormy flours, moldy bread and rancid meat. Brothers could keep the salvageable food, liquor, and clothing. They just had to turn in any cash, weapons, or electronics. When finished, brothercleaners marked each house with FF (Food-Free) spray-painted in forest green on the front doors. The FF is a guidepost to squatters, announcing there's nothing here. Except shelter.
Sisters don't do housecleaning these days, the work is beneath them. House bots are wicked expensive, they break down often, and they don't do windows. (You can upgrade to ones that will, but they leave lots of streaks.) Miriam told me about a plan to create a new Department of Home Purification, to attract Sisters with hefty salaries, company cars, and benefit packages. Great idea but budget issues—still the bane of civilization—stifled her plan.

I pass out on the couch, underneath a pile of mildewy woolen blankets.

That afternoon I wake up to a driverless Subaru creeping by, a Sister in the backseat peering inside my new digs. Heeding Miguel and Justin's warnings, I grab my backpack and flee out the back. I spend my next few days hopping from vacant house to vacant house, an unwanted brother looking for unwanted homes. Living like this is manageable. If I'm lucky, a home will have alcohol, and you get used to the smell of bug-infested meat, and sometimes I find a hot shower, but the nights are getting colder and I'm tired and bored and every chilly morning I wake and curse Miriam's name. I'm tempted to call Miguel on the cheap cell he left me. I fight the urge, don't wanna use my lifeline, wanna make it on my own. If I go with Miguel, there'll be fighting and dying won't be far behind. I'm one to wait to see what's around the corner, over the hill, on the horizon. Sisters plan. Brothers improvise. Another reason we guys found ourselves in this mess.

A Happy Trash truck parks in front of my latest digs, a trailer home, so I flee again, sneaking around streets clotted with potholes and stepping over tree roots that have erupted—Mother Nature stretching—through sidewalks. I focus on homes without the forest green FF painted on the front door but also with a general absence of life. There's a certain sweet spot, a period between abandonment and household rot, and the trick is to squat before the utilities and the good stuff are gone. You risk bumping into another brother occupier, but odds of that are slimmer every day.

I can tell when a house has been pilfered without ever going inside. Small broken windows near locks, pantry and cupboard doors gaping open like wooden mouths, drawers emptied on counters. You won't find much food, liquor, or weapons inside a house like that. I have yet to find one with food, liquor, water, and electricity, the grand slam of squatting. When I do find a newly-abandoned home with food, I also find rats skittering across countertops, crawling around toilet seats, even drinking out of the bowls. I rarely encounter rodents at cleaned-out houses. Even vermin know which homes to avoid.

I pinch whatever I can, raiding closets for sweaters and jeans— never need to do laundry—and I pillage toothpaste, toothbrushes, and pills. I recognize the laxatives, learned that the hard way. I find a few opioids, learned to recognize those too, but last thing I need right now is to get addicted. I leave 'em for the next bro. I pocket Extra-Strength Tylenol or Aleve when I find 'em, swallowing a few.

I don't need ice now, my swelling is gone, but I do need electricity to charge my cell. When I discover power, I unplug everything except

315

the fridge. No point in attracting homeless eyes, no matter how small the appliance lights. My cell doesn't require much juice, I turned off my Wi-Fi and cellular settings to avoid being tracked. I don't search *It*, don't stream, text or call anyone, no use giving Sisters a map to where I am. I only use my phone as an alarm, a clock, a flashlight, and to record my ramblings.

I sneak into one house that seems perfect. Power on, food in the cupboards, even some bottles of wine and gin—one good thing is I can drink again—and I pour myself a glass of muddy cabernet. I pop a can of Pringles and make myself at home, checking out the bedrooms. A raccoon family sprawls out on a king-sized master bed, some sleeping, some cleaning their haunches, surrounded by plush pillows. They look up at me like they own the place.

All yours, I say, having had run-ins with raccoons before. I slowly back out of the bedroom, down the stairs, and out the front door.

It's day five or six—the days bleed together—and I've stepped up into a higher-class neighborhood, the Malabar district, coming across a home that appears undisturbed. I check the perimeter of the house, all doors are locked, all windows shut tight. A good-sized dining room window looks easiest, so I take the butt of my fold-up trowel—I discarded my tree-branch cane days ago—and I smash the glass. I only get one leg inside when a putrid stench overpowers me, invading my senses, the smell of decaying human flesh so sickeningly sour, it stings even when filtered through my mask. I gag and leave this one to the rodents I see scurrying across the counters and furniture.

On lean days, I survive on dumpster diving and once even killed a bushy-tailed gray squirrel, throwing maybe twenty rocks at it before I stunned it, grabbed it, and twisted its neck. I had no idea what to do with it, so I risked searching YouTube on how to skin a squirrel. I used the blade edge of my trowel—Steven was right, it's handy for so many things—and I squeamishly peeled the furry skin from the butt back over the head, chopped off the legs, split the breasts. The crack of bone wigged me out the most. I coated the pieces with olive oil and blackened seafood rub I found in a cupboard. I roasted the rodent. I'd never eaten squirrel before, though my great uncle used to hunt rabbit and forced us to eat it. Squirrel tastes stringy, kinda sweet kinda nutty, a cross between chicken and rabbit. I finished half, threw away the rest. I didn't have to do this, I can always find food somewhere, but it's good to know I can hunt if I have to.

I peek through the closed curtains of a fine brick house, see a ghostly brother inside, sitting in a recliner, covered with junk food wrappers, a couple mason jars of what looks like piss at his side. He doesn't look happy to see me. I flash him a peace sign, then move on.

I find a modest ranch house with no electricity or gas, but it does have a locked closet with wood chipped away around the lock, like someone tried to bust it but gave up and moved on. I wedge my trowel into the crack between the door and frame, try to pry the door open, that doesn't work, I'm frustrated, then I realize I can just take the pins out of the hinges, so I do, swiveling the door open, now hinged at the lock. What do I find? Linens and blankets. And you know what they say: when life gives you linens, make the bed. So I sweep dust off the master mattress and layer blanket after blanket on top. On the walls are crucifixes and framed photos of a brown family of four, a mother, father, and two sons, all smiles, very 21st century Midwestern; casual, solid, and secretly troubled. In every photo, the

317

older boy is on his cell phone. Later, out in the yard, under a tree, I find two rocks side by side, crude lettering scratched into them:

Juan Garcia   Horatio Garcia

Damn. I squeeze out my last drop of tincture, tilting the bottle up to drain any leftover. I need to call Gaia. No way do I wanna continue doing this without my juice. I don't wanna rely on alcohol.

In the kitchen, there are cupboards filled with boxed and canned foods, so I actually boil water and have a feast of spaghetti with Classico basil and oregano red sauce. I mix in a can of black beans, loading up on carbs and protein. After stuffing myself with food and drowning it with tequila, I fall like a cross into bed, beneath the crucifixes and framed photos of this once happy family. I pull the layers of blankets tightly around me. I wait for sleep to take me away. Squatting takes a lot out of a brother, yet sleep doesn't want to come tonight. I check my phone, 3:11 AM. Early Thursday morning. I'd normally be meeting Miriam in a few hours. I toss and turn and record a little, even try to whittle the wood, thinking this might warm me up and tire me out, but I can't get stiff.

Water is a problem. I drink out of faucets when I can, but most homes are dry. I fill bottles at the water dispensers outside 7-Elevens and Little Angie Markets, keeping my lidded head down, topping off bottles as quickly as possible, hoping not to be recognized. For bathing or washing, I use gallon jugs to sneak water from the occasional abandoned Jacuzzi, or fountain. What I collect often looks disgusting, but if you boil it long enough it does the trick.

Next, I find an unassuming ranch-style, very orderly and clean, nothing out-of-place. Lots of crocheted things, doilies, napkin box holders, seat covers. Photos fill the walls, of a homely couple from

318

maybe their thirties up into their eighties. Different hairdos and glasses, but the same silly smiles. Good thing about this house is there are no neighbors in earshot, but also no water or heat. I won't be staying here long.

My bruise is but a ghost of itself now and I can walk with only a slight twinge of pain and no limp. One good thing about the injury, though, it absorbed the focus of my attention, and my twitching stopped. Looks like my leg just needed a beating to come to its senses. But now that I think about that, my twitch comes back. And I am out of tincture. I am tired of feeling cold, tired of feeling scared, tired of feeling tired. I grab some crackers from the pantry and plop down on a hard green armchair. Stale crackers for dinner, no tincture, no shower. And though I have warm clothes, I am still forever cold. I am so done with this lifestyle. And then I see, on the table next to the chair, that rarity of rarities, a landline telephone. I can't use my cell to make a call, they're sure to be tracing it, and I can't use Miguel's, it's for an emergency only. If I'm lucky, the phone service hasn't been cut off here yet. I close my eyes, say a little prayer to the phone goddesses, lift the receiver. Sweet Jesus. A dial tone.

I call Gaia.

GAIA TO THE RESCUE

It's early evening, I'm starving, I find some expired Lean Cuisines and a loaf of bread in the freezer. I microwave a lasagna, toast the bread and spread a jar of applesauce like jam. I wolf down a couple bites when Gaia's yellow Ford Spirit Guide pulls into the driveway. She taps her horn, must be scared to approach the house, doesn't know who might be in here with me. Hell, I don't know who might be hiding in the truck with her. I sneak out a side door, crouch behind a line of shrubs along the driveway, peer through the branches. In the truck bed is loose straw, burlap sacks, horse tack, a blanket, cowgirl boots, and a cloth 'Round & Ground bag. I peek in the cab's rear window, see on the seats an apple, earth-tone clothes and books. Gaia sits behind the wheel in a fuzzy rust jacket, tapping the horn, two short beeps.

She gives up and shifts into reverse. I pop up outside the front passenger window. Gaia jumps in her seat and glares at me.

Bryan?! Stop it, you're nervousing me.

You got it?

Hop in the back.

Why?

I know a better place than this.

I like it here.

Does it have heat?

No.

320

Then grab your stuff.

I look into those soft green eyes.

A'ight. One sec.

I run in and grab my backpack, my toast, and the lasagna. I offer Gaia some as I open the back cab door.

No, all the way in the back.

I give her a look which she mirrors right back. So I climb into the cold truck bed that smells of horse and hay and leather. Gaia makes a sharp turn out of the driveway, I bump into a steel wall, dropping my bread on the bed floor. I hang on to one side, feeling every turn and pothole in the road. I get on my knees and look through the truck's back window.

Fuckin' Miriam! She almost had me killed!

She wouldn't do that.

Well she did!

Gaia stares into her rearview mirror: Simmer down, Bryan.

Funny, I think to myself, Miriam says the same thing. I raise my head just high enough to see Gaia texting while driving.

Who you texting?

I startle her, the phone dropping to her lap.

Work problem. Now get down!

I lay down, my back braced against the cold side wall. I can feel us speeding up, don't feel so good about this, I should jump out.

How are you holding out?! she yells from the cab. It's hard to hear ourselves over the wind and engine whine, you'd think a Spirit Guide would be a little quieter.

Fine! I yell back a lie.

You know you should turn yourself in!

321

I can't believe you'd even suggest that!

I'm just saying—

They shot at me, Gaia!

We hit a big pothole. I grunt. My leg starts twitching again, banging against the cold metal as I feel the truck slowing down to a stop—must be an intersection—then accelerating again. I stare up at the sky dipped in darkness and see the first stars and I'm pretty sure one's a planet—don't know which—and I'm trusting Gaia like sailors trusted the constellations.

I packed everything you asked for, she says. Energy bars, hand warmers, a portable charger. And the tincture. I made an extra-strong batch just for you.

You're the best.

I get on my knees, transferring the goods from her bag to my backpack.

Keep down!

I obey as a good brother should, curling up like a puppy in the truck bed. I find the brown tincture bottles, both of 'em labeled No Worries—sure hope so—and I stuff them into the pockets of my plain gray hoodie I found at the last house. Days ago I gave up wearing my Buddha-playing-guitar hoodie, it was like wearing a "Come get me" sign. I pull the hood down low over my hair, a false sense of security, since Sisters can stop every brother they see until they locate and identify me. I pull empty burlap sacks over my body, hiding, as Gaia drives towards Lexington, rollercoasting over rolling hills. I'm getting queasy, grab my little bottle, twist off the rubber top, draw up amber liquid, we hit a bump, I drop the dropper, it rolls away from me, I tear the sacks off my freezing body, frantically reach around, find the

322

dropper, blow dirt off, pull down my mask, stick the dropper in my mouth, squeeze out a couple drops, the glass clicking against my chattering teeth. But just going through the ritual calms my ass, bumping up and down on these rough rural roads. I pull the burlap sacks back over me, look through the tight mesh, at pinholes of flashing light bouncing off the darkening sky, lightning, great, a storm is on its way and I'm out here in the back of a truck, what next? Then I notice reds and blues flashing and they are sweeping closer and closer and I can feel the truck slowing down underneath me until we come to a stop.

Keep quiet, Gaia warns with a whisper.

Car doors squeak open. I curl into the fetal, under the empty sacks, pulling one over the tips of my sneakers. Car doors thud-thud. I take a deep breath and lie still. Footsteps approach, crunching the roadside gravel.

Morning, Sister, a warm voice says.

Morning Sister Officers, Gaia replies.

License and registration, please.

Yes, of course.

I imagine her holding up her cell phone, airdropping her info.

I need you to step out of the car, Sister, a stern voice orders Gaia.

The driver door groans open and I feel the truck dip and then rise with the loss of Gaia's weight. Footsteps crunch gravel toward me. Metal scrapes along the truck's side. My left leg twitches like a maniac. A burlap sack is ripped off my legs, exposing me, and I curl up even tighter.

Get out of the truck! Now!

The rear gate swings open. I sit up, hands up, and see Two Sister Cops, one buff, the other thin, both aiming revolvers at me.

Pull down your mask, Buff Cop spits out.

I pull the mask down below my chin.

Yup, it's him, she says. Put your mask back on.

I do.

Get your hands back up.

I raise them.

Behind your head.

I lace my fingers together at the back of my skull. Buff Cop fits a police-blue mask over her face, standard protocol, and she grabs my left bicep, yanking me out of the truck bed, pulling me down onto my knees. Pain revisits my thigh.

Thin Cop cuffs me, frisks me, finds my phone and the one Miguel gave me, and my tincture bottles. She keeps the phones, uncaps a bottle, sniffs it.

Let him keep that, Gaia says.

Thin Cop stuffs them back into my pocket then kicks me face-down onto the gravel, behind the truck. She empties out my backpack, then gets on her radio.

We found him. Over.

A Sister Radio Voice responds: We'll send a sterile unit, hang tight.

Rogette that.

I could piss my pants right now, lying face-down on the side of the road, my cheek buried in damp gravel, my left leg thumping like a dog's scratching hind leg. My being on the run sure didn't last long, what, a week? I curse myself for calling Gaia. What an idiot I am. I

324

squirm, my cheek scraping gravel, until I'm able to see Gaia chatting with the Sister Cops. Certainly doesn't look like she's under arrest for harboring a fugitive brother. We lock eyes, mine pleading, hers averting. What the fuck. First Miriam and now Gaia?

The Sister Cops look at me and share a laugh, I recognize that look, it's common, they don't take me seriously as any kind of threat. A look bullies used to give me growing up. But on Gaia's face I see a look of shame, telling me she didn't want to give me up, that maybe Miriam pressured her.

Do what they say, Bryan, she calls over to me, they won't hurt you.

Down the road, I see a headlight, and then an ebike cresting a small hill. A bundled Amish Sister—the Amish love their ebikes— cruises toward us in her thick dark coat and white bonnet, a scarf around her face. I wish I could hop a ride, or bike-jack it, but Sisters have already demonstrated they'll shoot me in the back if I make a run for it. Doubt the Amish are much different.

I think of everything spiritual I've ever believed: heaven-and-hell, no heaven-and-hell, a no-man's-land of purgatory, reincarnation, pure nothingness, and energy that just transforms into something else and moves on, and none of this existential bullshit matters now. All I can think is I just hope they don't torture me.

The bundled Amish Sister on the ebike pedals closer, does a little lookie-loo and stares at the road ahead of her. The Sister Cops study her briefly, she looks harmless enough, and they return to their chat with Gaia. I think about fleeing and jumping on the bike, I could grip the handlebars with my cuffed hands, just need to get them from behind my back to my front. While running away from gunfire. Yeah,

325

right. I shake against the cold asphalt and out of the corner of my eye, I see the Amish Sister discreetly pulling a snub-nosed assault rifle out from under her coat—it looks mean as hell—and she lets the weapon droop at her side, blocked from view by her torso. She must've clicked on turbo mode, because she pedals fast, turning, straight for the Sister Cops. They just now notice her change of direction and reach for their revolvers. She fires a burst of bullets over their heads, a warning which they heed, keeping their hands off their guns.

Hands in the air, Sisters!

It's a brother's voice, one I recognize, and in the face of his firepower, the surprised Sister Cops obey, holding their arms up. Gaia follows suit.

The ebike comes to a stop.

Get down on the ground!

The three Sisters follow orders, reluctantly getting down onto their knees.

On your stomachs!

I see the bloodshot eyes of Justin, the homeless brother, peering over the scarf. He climbs off his ebike, fixing his weapon on the Sister Cops and Gaia.

Spread your arms and legs.

The Sisters do, splaying out like water striders.

Get your ass up! he hisses at me.

I struggle, it's not easy, flat on my stomach and handcuffed. I roll onto my side and bend and sit up, sprouting like a weed onto my feet.

Take a deep breath and hold it, Justin says to Thin Cop, taking a big breath himself, stepping closer, gripping his weapon like an old-school gangster, rigid against his ribs, the barrel focused on Thin

326

Cop's chest. He reaches down with his gloved left hand, unharnesses the revolver from her belt, tosses the gun toward the truck, does the same with her baton and taser. He steps back several feet and exhales.

This is why we should just kill 'em all, Buff Cop hisses to her partner.

Likewise, Justin says, sucking in another deep breath, holding it, moving in closer, repeating the same sequence with Buff Cop, removing her revolver, baton, and taser, tossing them over to the truck. Justin backs away, breathing normally again.

The keys to his cuffs?

Neither Sister Cop says a word. Justin steps closer, traces the assault barrel along Buff Cop's thick neck.

Did I not make myself clear?!

Buff Cop tenses, like she might spring into action, having a hard time swallowing orders from a brother. To help convince her, Justin kicks gravel into her face. I don't know who this Justin is, but he's not the homeless brother I know.

I got 'em, Buff Cop says.

Good.

Justin backs away.

Now, pig, tell Gaia where they are.

Buff Cop doesn't reply.

Does it fuckin' look like I got all day?

Still nothing. Justin digs the end of the barrel into Buff Cop's neck.

Okay, okay, Buff Cop relents, they're in my—

Thwup-thwup-thwup.

Buff Cop's head smooshes into the gravel, three times, blood gurgling from the back of her neck.

What the fuck?! I say.

I know, Justin says with a hint of glee, I only meant to shoot once.

Thin Cop crawls toward her partner.

Leave it! Justin commands her as if she were a dog.

She was just doing her job! Gaia yells.

So am I. Now do yours. Get her keys.

Gaia doesn't move. Justin aims the barrel at her.

Stop it! I yell.

Now!

On my partner's belt, Thin Cop blurts out, in a pouch on her left-hand side.

Gaia hesitates.

Do it! Justin yells.

I am, I am!

Gaia forces herself up on her knees, bending over the convulsing cop, blood pooling underneath the cop's face.

Let me help my partner! Thin Cop pleads.

Stay where you are, Justin orders.

Gaia has a hard time searching with all that blood seeping into the gravel. She wedges her fingers into Buff Cop's belt pocket, wriggles them around, finds the keys, tugs them out, dangles them away from the dying body.

Good girl, Gaia, Justin says, now toss them over to Bryan.

She under-hands them within a few feet of me. I want Justin to pick them up and uncuff me immediately, but we both know we better wait—2--10. I hear an airplane engine whine in the distance. I wish to hell I was on it.

My ph-phone too! I shiver and sputter.

Justin motions to Gaia with the barrel of his nasty rifle. She rummages through the pockets, pulls out my LG BFF 3, holds it up. I nod.

There's another one, I say.

Gaia rolls the twitching cop onto her side, blood flowing from the mouth. She searches pockets, finds the cheap Cellina that Miguel gave me. Suddenly, the dying cop jerks and grabs her. Gaia drops my LG, it bounces off the cop's face and plops into the puddle of blood.

Grab it, Justin orders.

Gaia squints and reaches down and grabs my silver cell, now dripping red. She under-hands it over by the keys, a few feet away from my shoes, followed by the Cellina. I'm in no rush for either phone, I'll wait way more than two minutes when blood's involved.

At least put her out of her misery, please! Thin Cop begs, watching her partner choking on her own blood on the ground beside her.

Why should she suffer less than brothers?! Justin snarls. Where's the fob to your cruiser?

It's in my front right pocket, Thin Cop answers quickly, squirming to give easy access. Gaia isn't hesitating now. She reaches in.

Got it.

Now the other one. On her.

Justin motions toward Buff. Gaia reaches in his same pocket and removes his fob.

You're doing great, Gaia. Toss one over by me.

She follows orders, the fob bouncing off Justin's boot.

Now throw the other into the field.

What?

You heard me.

She flings the fob, not far off the road, not far out of sight, among rows of brittle cornstalks, like dead scarecrows.

That was a weak-ass throw, Justin says. I should kill you just for that. Get down on the ground.

Gaia sprawls on the asphalt, her left cheek pressed into rough gravel.

Meanwhile, Buff Cop stops convulsing. We all freeze for a moment, sneaking glances, then looking away, in our own way: Gaia calms herself with a breathing exercise; Thin Cop sobs; Justin gloats; and I hope to hell I don't die suffering like that.

Justin shoots a quick look at me, it's been about two minutes, so I kick the keys over his way. He keeps his assault weapon fixed on Thin Cop, grabs the keys, comes up behind me, well inside my unsafe space but right now there's not much we can do about that.

Relax, he says, I'm not infected.

He wriggles the key in the lock of my cuffs.

My homeless guardian angel, I whisper with a bite of spite.

He laughs.

You really think I'm homeless? I've got a PhD, mutherfucker.

He twists the key. Click. I massage my wrists, free of my binds.

Get your phones. I lift the cheap Cellina and pocket it. I consider leaving my blood-streaked LG on the ground but I have many recordings I haven't posted and it's been well over two minutes, must be safe by now, so I pick up my phone by the gloved tips of my thumb

330

and index fingers and toss it onto the passenger side floor mat. I rip off my gloves and toss them on the floor too.

Get in the truck, Justin says.

I can help.

Just get in the truck. I got this.

I climb behind the steering wheel.

Is the fob in there?

It's here, I say. I press a button. The truck turns on. Justin tosses the handcuffs over to Gaia.

Cuff her.

Gaia works the cuffs around Thin Cop's wrists. Justin leans his masked face close to the passenger window, still keeping the Sisters in his gunsight.

Who are you? I whisper.

Name's Troy. Justin Tyme is my handle.

You're an undergrounder?

I'm a chemical engineer. Fighting the good fight.

More like murdering.

How many brothers do you think that cop's killed?

Doesn't matter.

Sure it does. It all comes out in the wash.

Done, Gaia says.

Lemme see.

Gaia pulls on both of the cop's arms. The cuffs don't budge.

Good girl. Now get down on your stomach.

Gaia crawls away from the bloody gravel, closer to the truck.

Where you think you're going? Troy asks.

I'm not lying down near that mess.

331

She crawls far enough away, just a few feet from her truck, and lies down on her stomach. Troy picks up the cops' revolvers.

I don't suppose you know how to operate one of these.

He's not a very good shot, Gaia says.

What a shock.

He hands a dark gun to me through the truck window, I have no idea what kind, but it reminds me of the Glock that I shot target practice with a few weeks ago.

Always aim for their breasts. Should be easy enough, it's what we look at anyway. He gives me a once-over look of disgust, stepping back away from Gaia's truck: You better be worth it.

What about Gaia?

Never mind her, Troy says, his eyes focusing intensely on the distance, at the headlights from a dark vehicle cresting a hill, a half mile behind us, approaching at a good clip.

Go! he says.

I can't just leave her—

Troy pounds on the hood of the truck.

'the fuck outta here!

The dark vehicle speeds closer, a van, could be those Sisters In Black. Troy doesn't wait, he sprays gunfire at it, hits the side and a tire. The van swerves, bangs against a tree, crunching the side, but stays upright, turns back onto the road and races straight at us, wheel sparks grinding on asphalt, bullets answering back.

GO!!!

Bullets ping my fenders and shatter the front passenger window. I stomp on the gas pedal and peel gravel and hear a thump as I speed off in Gaia's yellow truck. Ohmygoddess I didn't just hit her did I?! But

I keep my head down, hearing the barrage of bullets fading in the distance. They're not shooting at me anymore, thank goddess, but I can't believe I left Gaia back there. Maybe even killed her. I beat the steering wheel with both hands, yelling, spit spraying: Get a grip, Bryan, get a grip!

I adjust my rearview mirror and see that no one, not the van, not the cruiser, nothing is following me. It's been two years since I've driven and I feel my left leg trembling—thank goddess it's not my right—as I press the accelerator, adding separation between myself and the massacre. I'm driving on adrenaline, muscle memory kicking in, for miles on these lonely roads, taking lefts and rights, trying to lose any possible tail, speeding until my paranoia slowly dissolves, backing my foot way off the pedal until I'm driving below the speed limit. Into Goddess's country. Dry cornstalks wave like paper dolls in the breeze. My leg tremors worsen, my left knee is bumping the steering wheel, but I can't think about stopping. I pull out my No Worries bottle, uncap it, don't bother with the dropper, I tilt my head back and shoot the tincture like tequila, swerving onto the shoulder of the road, then swerving back, overcompensating, gravel kicking up. I correct the truck's path, getting it back into my lane. Now I can think again about where I'm going, literally and metaphorically, breathing out the longest sigh of relief of my life. What the hell just happened? Shit, I know I am only a cog in the Sister Machine, but I have given life to so many young Sisters out there, and, man, it's just not right to do this to me. I pound the steering wheel. Fuck Miriam! Fuck Gaia! How could you both turn on me?! Drew and Miguel warned me. How was I so stupid? Fool me twice. I approach a stop sign, slow down, catch my breath, look all directions. No cars in sight.

How's the new batch? Gaia asks, her green eyes popping-up in the rearview mirror.

What the hell?!

I aim my gun at her.

Relax, Bryan. I jumped in during the shootout.

You turned me in!

Ohmygoddess, Bryan, I was trying to save your life. That's pretty much impossible now that your buddy murdered a cop.

Get out.

Bryan—

Out!

It's freezing.

I mean it Gaia!

Let me help you.

I hope that's a joke.

I grip the cop's pistol with both hands, just to emphasize. She snorts.

You're a terrible shot.

I think I can hit you from here.

Yeah, you probably can.

She swings her left leg over the truck's sidewall, straddles it, pauses, suddenly swings her leg back into the bed.

I think we both agree, she says, the killing needs to stop.

I point the revolver at her.

Out.

You can't keep my truck, they'll be looking for it.

Out!

I've got an idea.

I glare at her kneeling in her truck bed. It hurts how badly I wanna trust her, how badly I wanna trust someone, anyone, even someone who already has shown me I can't.

I swear to god, Gaia—

I mean it, Bryan. I put it on our friendship.

Not good enough.

I put it on my mother. I put it on every Sister I know.

I feel myself weakening, our past clouding my judgment. I'm Charlie Brown trusting Lucy with the fucking football. Again.

Show me your phone, I say.

She holds it up.

Toss it where you can find it later.

Why don't I just give it to you?

It's either you or the phone, I say.

She looks around, up at the rusted crossroad signs, gleaming in the moonlight—Elizabeth Township Road and Julia Township Road. Elizabeth and Julia, she whispers, memorizing them. She spots an ottoman-sized rock along the edge of the road, surrounded by dry brush. She tosses her phone into the brush just beyond the rock.

A'ight, I say, now what's this idea?

AMISH YOU

I drive the bullet-riddled yellow truck to the horse stables. It's evening and we're the only ones here as I park behind Magic's stall. Gaia jumps out of the bed and feeds a few oats to her reddish-brown Morgan. I suck on tincture.

You're doing too much of that.

Says the dealer to the junkie. Y'know, I haven't ridden since we were kids.

I remember. You squealed like a little girl.

I never wanted to get on the damn thing. I just wanted to impress you.

She kicks her boot into the flimsy door of a next-door stall, kicks a couple times, breaks the door in. Moments later she comes out with a bundle of clothing: overalls, flannel shirt, black overcoat and black felt hat. Amish winterwear.

Follow me.

She leads Magic behind another stall to a black buggy parked outside a round pen. She sets the clothes down on the buggy seat.

They won't be looking for you in this.

Whose is it?

A group of Amish families keep it here, as backup, just in case a buggy breaks down while they're in town.

She harnesses her horse with a flowing beauty. I pull out my phone and record her hurried instructions. I'm amazed by her tucking leather straps and tightening buckles with grace and precision. She doesn't mind the cold. Me, I rock back and forth to keep warm.

You paying attention?

I nod, my teeth chattering, my body shivering. I record her describing how to hook-up Magic to the dark buggy, running the shafts of the vehicle through the belly band, adding blinders to the head gear. I climb up into the buggy, store my pack in the back, sit on the cold bench.

Fuck it's freezing!

I shakily pull off my sweater and wriggle into the flannel shirt. It's impossible trying to button it with gloves on, so I peel them off with my teeth. Thank goddess the Amish wear jeans. I don't need to change those.

Gaia tosses a bundle of oats into the buggy, just missing my head. She tears a blanket with a knife, cutting off a strip six inches wide, the length of the blanket. She wraps it around a fence post.

What's that f-for?

Scarf. With that bird's nest on your face, there's no way you pass as Amish. Cover everything but your eyes.

I fluff out my graying week-old beard while she drapes the rest of the blanket over the fence. Might as well take that too, she says. She double-checks whatever it is you double-check on a buggy. I pull on the black overcoat and pop the wide-brimmed hat on my head. It's a size too big and sinks down over my eyebrows. Gaia snorts.

You should see yourself.

I'm glad I can still amuse you, I say, stuffing my sweater into the hat, again fitting it on top of my head. I tighten the chin strap.

Better?

It'll do, she says, holding a pair of loose reins in her hands.

These are called reins.

I know that.

Hold them in your left hand.

I turn my cell on again to record her.

Separate them between the 2nd and 3rd fingers, she says.

Okay.

Your left hand controls the speed and assists in steering. Rotate the reins backward to move left and forward to go right.

I practice it and eventually get her smile of approval.

Now pick up the whip.

That I can do, I joke.

Always keep the whip in your hand, up at a forty-five-degree angle. If Magic doesn't obey, you tap him with it.

Just tap him?

The more he disobeys, the harder you use it.

Do I crack it?

No. Gentle to medium.

She demonstrates, then shows me how to use both hands to handle the reins. The right hand—still holding the whip—pulls on the upper rein to turn right, the lower rein to turn left.

Never take your left hand off the reins, she says.

Left hand. Never. Got it.

If you need a sudden stop, reach forward and grab the reins with your right.

I practice that. Doesn't seem too hard.

Take him around for a spin. He'll move once you ease up the pressure on the bit. You can also say, tst-tst-tst.

On hearing that, Magic steps forward.

Whoa-shit!

I wasn't at all ready for that, nearly tipping over on my seat, but Magic knows what he's doing. I pull on the reins a little, he ignores me, I pull a little harder, nothing, so I yank and now he listens, slowing down. We cruise around, I don't have to do much, Magic turns when he needs to. I practice turning him the other direction and stopping. Gaia points out my flaws, of which there are plenty. I concentrate, trying to get every last instruction, slowly getting the hang of it. It's kinda fun in a Ben Hur way and I forget for a few minutes that I'm on the run. Then Magic jerks a hard left as if I'd hit the gas.

Watch your reins! Gaia says. Lighter touch!

I loosen up and guide him back on track, approaching the dangling scarf fluttering in a light breeze. I steer the buggy alongside the fence and pull back on the reins. Magic comes to a stop, close enough for me to reach over and grab the scarf and blanket.

I think I prefer the buggy over the horse, I say.

You would, she laughs.

I wrap the scarf around my face, leaving only my eyes exposed, as instructed, keeping them focused on Gaia, while tucking the ends of the scarf under my overcoat collar.

Any other questions?

If I do, I'll Google 'em.

It's a wonder how you brothers ran the world as long as you did.

She pulls a pad from her back pocket, jots down a couple notes.

339

Here are feeding and watering instructions.

She tucks the pad into a pocket on the side of the buggy, then sits on the ground and winds duct tape around her legs.

What are you doing?

CYA. I'll tell the cops you stole Magic.

Great, they used to hang horse thieves. I can only imagine what they do today.

I won't tell them about the buggy.

I must've made a doubtful face.

You got a better idea? she says.

No.

She tears off the roll of duct tape and tosses it into the buggy. I look ahead into the charcoal gray Ohio night.

Go down 97, she says, you won't hit much traffic. Get into Amish country. Don't tell me where, don't contact me, just get out of Sisterfield.

Got it.

When you're done with Magic, text me where you leave him. She pats Magic's flank and kisses the star on his forehead. You be a good boy, she says, glancing up at me too. She holds her wrists up, together. You need to finish this for me, she says.

I hesitate.

You want to sell this plan or not?

I take a deep breath and hold it as I wind tape around her wrists.

Not too tight.

She's going above-and-beyond and I want to give her a thank-you hug, but I can't, even if I could, she doesn't deserve it, this is the least she could do after snitching on me. I tear the tape, not an easy thing to do in this frigid cold.

Now my mouth, she says.

I look away and inhale again, deeply. I turn back around and wind duct tape around her head a couple times, covering her face from the bottom of her nose to her lower chin. I rip the tape. She shuffles away.

'ake 'are of 'im, she says, muffled.

I tip my hat.

Thank you, ma'am.

I grab the reins, make sure I'm holding them correctly, look to her for confirmation. She nods.

Giddy-up! I say, forgetting what the riding cue is.

Gaia shakes her duct-taped head.

Tst-tst-tst!

I loosen the pressure on the reins. Magic clop-clops, pulling me and the buggy away from the stables, away from Gaia. Good boy, I say every hundred yards or so as the crisp December air cuts through me and I look up, half-expecting to see my drone come zipping closer, spying on me, and it feels so good not to have that fucking thing following me everywhere. I pass a trio of concrete grain silos and small groups of cows huddled together to keep warm. Christmas lights twinkle on a farmhouse, reds and greens in swirling mesh. I remember growing up, my neighborhood lit up with displays: giant candy canes, blow-up Santas and Frosties. As a kid, I would bundle up in my thermals and parka, ski mask and gloves, delivering tins of my mother's cutout cookies to our neighbors on Christmas Eve. Many would invite me in, give me their own cookies to take back in return. Some would give me a sip or two of spiked Eggnog or toddy, winking

341

before sending me on my way. One neighbor smoked with me. In one form or another, I got buzzed on Christmas. I always looked forward to the holidays.

I ride underneath the I-71 overpass, past franchise row—Starbucks, Wendy's, Taco Bella—and then out into pure country. There is little traffic here, the steady clop-clop-clop of hooves on pavement as soothing as a heartbeat. Gaia was right, Magic knows what he's doing, but the buggy is slower and bumpier than I would prefer. It gives me too much time to think. I could use a little mindfulness right now, but don't have the bandwidth to stay that focused. I should've listened to Miguel, he's looking out for me. I am no longer an Appleseed, unwanted and wanted, dead or alive. A Sister who catches or kills me will be honored, just like in that computer game, The Hunt. In reality or fantasy, Sisters seem programmed to win.

The occasional passing car gives me a wide berth. Sisters check me out. The buggy is not inconspicuous but is common enough. Another buggy approaches, an Amish family of four heading toward town. The father drives, Sister Mother rides next to him, and two daughters rest their heads against each other in the back. The mother doesn't look my way, but the father checks me out, flashing a cheeky grin, lost in his thick dark beard. Is he on to me, am I that obvious? Maybe it's the scarf. I pretend to scratch my cheek and realize the cloth has fallen halfway off my face. As we pass, he nods and I dip my head in return.

I eventually hit State Route 39, following the red taillights that constantly pass me by, my bright red triangular reflectors making it easy for vehicles to see me, but I'm struggling to see where I'm going, into the largest community of Amish and Mennonites in America. Don't worry, I'm not pulling a Witness here.

EDITOR'S NOTE: Witness, the 1985 movie starring Harrison Ford, is about a fugitive cop that hides out in an Amish community.

I'd prefer to find a farm that isn't Amish or Mennonite, where I have at least a chance of finding liquor, although so far their chaste, sequestered lifestyle has protected many Amish brothers from The Y. Not because they are immune, but because they avoid town whenever possible, limiting exposure. Amish brothers may be the cockroaches of humanity, surviving this terrible plague and outliving us all.

I ride up and down the rolling hills, thinking how this will be good for me, most country folk are welcoming people, not the snitching type, and farmhouses are far apart. Far fewer suspicious eyes. I pass a couple farmhouses, some have lights on inside, most don't. Some have the forest green FF spray-painted on the front door. Most don't. It's so dark, I ride by, leaning out of the buggy to get a good look. Sometimes I park and climb out and walk up to the porch, shining my phone flashlight before I can make out the FF. I think of my aunt and uncle, Bert and Dorothy, they once lived in a farmhouse like this. My family seldom visited them, they rarely visited us. I doubt I could find their farm anymore. Wouldn't matter, they're dead, like all my uncles and brother cousins. Most of my Sister relatives have moved down to Columbus suburbs.

I climb out of the buggy, and walk across a yard, looking up at another dark door on a dark house, no FF spray-painted on it. I tap on

343

my cell flashlight, lean forward to peek inside. The door suddenly swings open.

Can I help you? A suspicious Country Sister says, her thick arms folded.

Is this the Johnson's?

Nope. Lost?

You could say that.

You might try using that phone in your hand.

I look at the flashlight.

No reception.

Sorry, nothing personal, I'd like to help you but you best be getting off my porch.

Yes ma'am, I say, as she closes the door between us.

I ride away, realizing I didn't fool her. I ride past a well-maintained home, full of Sister life, a Christmas tree shining in the picture window and Little Sisters twirling around the living room, pure joy on their faces. I hope the perfect home will appear over the next crest and I debate going back to the one with FF on the door. It won't have food, but I have Power Bars and nuts, I can get by tonight, can search better in the morning light.

I ride past a double-wide with laundry on a line, shirts and suspenders and frozen bed sheets with damp leaves stuck to the stiff cloth like they've been out on the line for days. Behind the house is a barn that leans like it could crumple if I spit at it. The house itself is eerily dark but country music calls out from inside, Luke Combs, I think. Cars are parked in the driveway, hoods up on two. This home is too recently vacated, death hasn't even left yet and despite freezing my ass off, I ride on. A mile or so down the road is a white, two-story, gabled-roof farmhouse with a huge tree—willow, I think—naked of leaves. A porch wraps halfway around the home. There's no FF on the front door but plenty of neglect. Withered vines cling to the vinyl siding, as if they died trying to choke the house. I park my buggy, pat Magic's neck.

Don't go anywhere boy.

I cross the lawn of tall, brown grass and step onto the porch, peeking through a window of tattered curtains. It's as dark inside as out. I step forward and my foot plunges through a rotted floorboard. I clutch a creaky porch column and pry my foot free. I tread lightly now, opening the screen door and knocking on wood. Flakes of peeling paint flutter down. I knock again. Nothing. I grab the front door handle, it's locked, so I push on it and the doorjamb wiggles. I pull the trowel out of my overcoat, wedge it in the door crack, twisting and pushing. The door pops open without much of a struggle.

Hello?

I try a wall switch. Nothing. The house is dark, dank, and creepy but far from empty. There are many silhouettes, four feet high, pods with curved heads. I freeze. What the hell? I tap on my cell flashlight. The pods reveal themselves, classic car and truck seats, buckets and benches, I'm guessing from the 50s to the 70s, rows of seats in every room, arranged by makes—Chevys, Dodges, Fords—the colors muted under years of dust. Cobwebs stretch between many. To the right, in the living room, nine bench seats are crammed together and above them, a painting of Jesus—the one with the Coppertone tan and long, wavy brown hair—looks heavenward, as if asking Goddess to protect this upholstery. The kitchen has only a couple of seats in

345

the center, like an island, allowing room to maneuver along the counters. I try a kitchen light switch. Nothing.

It'll do, I say to the house.

I ride the buggy into the dark barn, clearing an area among stacks of bumpers and fenders. I unhook Magic, tie him to a support beam, give some slack in the rope and keep the bridle and bit on him in case I need to evacuate. I shine my cell light, at steering wheels and hubcaps hanging on the walls. Sisters either don't know all this is here or don't care.

On the lawn between the house and barn is a well pump. I work the cold iron handle, water spitting, then heaving, then flowing smoothly. I slurp it up like I'd been lost in a desert, it's ice-cold and tastes like rust but I can't stop, until I think about stories of people who die drinking too much. I find an old bucket, fill it, give it to Magic. He laps up the water and then I feed him the bundle of oats that Gaia threw into the buggy, knowing enough about horses to know that won't last long.

Back inside the house, I sweep my cell light over the kitchen counters, onto a deck of cards, dealt into two curled piles, and a scoresheet and pencil, all left out as if someone was coming back to finish the game. I blow a thick coating of dust off them, rippling and fanning the cards across the counter. I set up the portable charger that Gaia brought me, lay the phone down on it. The charger has no charge.

Thanks a lot, Gaia.

I blow dust off the closest bucket seat, a black Pontiac, and plop down. I smell the stains of cigarettes, fast-food grease and beer. A spring snaps through the upholstery and pokes my hip. I'm too

346

exhausted to move, I just wriggle away from the sharp spring, smooshing myself onto that curved, burping vinyl. It fits me well. I wrap myself inside the blanket that spawned my scarf. I close my eyes, my entire body shivering, and I think about everything that happened today, but then tell myself not to think, and even with the biting chill in the house, it's not long before I'm in dreamland.

THE AUTO-PARTS FARM

I wake up to the distant alarm of sheep bleating. Rays of sunlight poke through the torn curtains, bathing a blue Buick bench in front of me. I slide onto it, the upholstery warming me, I wanna sleep longer, I lay down, could sleep all day, but my mind won't let me. I check my phone. 8:12 AM. I rise, look out the window, don't see another farmhouse in sight. I search the house, avoid the powerless fridge, nothing good can come from opening that. In the cabinets I find some bags of hardened flour and sugar, so old that not even ants or cockroaches bother with it. I dig through my backpack, find a Sister Power energy bar, tear off the wrapper, bite into it. The chocolate tastes like chemicals.

I search downstairs in the musty cellar. Rusty tools hang from hooks on the walls and jars filled with bolts and nuts and screws hang from the low ceiling, the lids nailed into the wooden beams. A cabinet is draped in cobwebs and inside I find a few mason jars of canned peaches, green beans, and raspberry jam, enough food for a few days. I blow dust off the jars. Dates are all in the early 2010's, old but not dangerously old, at least I hope not.

I grab a water pitcher, fill it at the well, chug. I re-fill the bucket, put it in front of Magic. He guzzles while I check out the barn, admiring the dark hewn beams high overhead. I search for bales of hay or horse feed, find nothing, just some tires and rims. The only farming here is of auto parts. I return to the house and empty a jar of green beans into a large bowl, feed that to Magic. He gobbles it down, while I slurp up some peaches, dribbling juice down the front of my overcoat. Bet you want these, don't ya? I stroke his flank, digging my curled fingertips into his hair. He works his lips to get the last of the green beans off his chompers and follows that up by lapping water greedily.

Back inside, in the daylight, I now see the debris—cigarette and cigar butts, empty beer cans, and one-shot liquor bottles swept into the corners of the floor. I search upstairs. The bedrooms are filled with auto hardware: chrome door handles, sideview mirrors and license plates. Mustang and Cadillac logos are spread across a lumpy brown mattress. Nothing up here I want. Back downstairs, I try out different bucket seats, most wobble or lean. The leather Mercedes are the nicest, molding around me. I drag a black one to the second row in front of the living room picture window, in the middle of the righteous sunlight. I recline, yank off my scarf and gloves, rub my scruffy face. I record my thoughts about yesterday, keeping an eye on the large porch window. I'm not sure what to say about the cop shooting but I decide to tell it all, keeping my Survival Buddy trowel at my side.

And then I fall asleep.

I open my eyes, check my cell: 3:23 PM. Nothing like sleeping out in the country, they say, and I yawn and stretch and—shit, someone's at the front porch window!—I snap awake. It's an Amish boy in black, peeking between the curtains. I don't move, hoping he can't see me, but a slant of sunlight still touches my seat. Busted. I raise my hand, give a little wave. He returns it.

349

What's your name? I ask loudly.

He doesn't answer, just stares through the window. I peg him for seven or eight.

My name's—I hesitate—Garrett. What's yours?

Josiah.

You live nearby?

He points up the road.

You wanna come in and look?

He nods.

I wrap the scarf around my face and open the door and step back into the kitchen. He enters, wide-eyed. A house full of car seats must look even cooler to a young boy, he's probably dreamed of coming in here, but being a good boy I bet he never broke in.

Try 'em out, kid.

He does, sliding his butt across vinyl benches with the logos of Chevy, Ford, Dodge. He stretches across a dusty aqua Chrysler bench.

Good choice, kid.

I enjoy watching him, it's been months since I've seen a little brother. I move closer. My Amish costume doesn't fool him and he reaches toward me like I'm a curiosity. I step back, startled, which then startles him.

Sorry.

He looks away, rubbing his little hands along the seat vinyl.

How did you know I was here, Josiah?

I saw your horse.

How? He's in the barn.

He points beyond the barn.

I walk to school.

Through the yard?

He nods and looks down at the floor, at the crops of cigarette butts, beer cans and tiny bottles. Something shifts in him and he seems to realize he should not be here, not with a strange, non-Amish brother. He leaps off his seat.

I gotta go.

It was nice meeting you, Josiah. Do me a favor, will ya? Don't tell anyone you saw me, okay?

Josiah nods. The boy's a nodder.

Come by again. I'll let you sit on any chair you want. Deal?

He smiles and swings the door open and jumps off the rotten porch, kicking through the tall dead grass on his way home.

I poke my head outside, look up at the milky-gray sky, the season has definitely turned, winter lingers in the silvery clouds. I can smell snow is near. Some people smell rain, I smell snow. I hide back inside and act like Josiah, sprawling on many of the bench seats, checking them out as if in a mattress store. I find the one I like, a red-and-white Cadillac bench seat, the longest one here. I wipe down the upholstery, tuck in my blanket, and layer some blankets that I found. I wedge a rusted butcher knife into the crack between the vinyl seat and back cushions. I lay my Survival Buddy trowel underneath the bench, my police revolver by my side. It's good to have options, Steven preached. Through the torn curtain, I watch the dull sunset, as if the sun were hiding too. I remember watching sunsets with Bernie as I eat some canned peaches. I try to get some shut-eye. The bench seat isn't bad, but every time I move the upholstery burps.

I live like this for another day. The snow hasn't arrived yet. I find a rusted Smokey Joe barbecue and a bag of charcoal briquettes. I light it in the backyard, warming my hands and heating a pot of water. I find a jar of old instant coffee, and scrape caked grounds into a dented thermos, filling it with boiling water, letting the metal warm my hands. I sip on the weak coffee until the sun is strong enough to take the chill outta my soul. I spoon half a jar of raspberry jam for breakfast. I feed more green beans and water to Magic then go back inside and do push-ups and sit-ups to keep my body busy. I let Magic prance around a fenced-in area for exercise. The horse farts up a storm as he runs, must be the green beans. I need to get him some real horse food. I return him to the barn, mucking the piles of manure, dumping them into a garbage bin.

For dinner, I chow down on green beans and peaches, wondering about Josiah, why he hasn't come back. I take that as a good sign. Another good sign: my left leg hasn't twitched since I arrived. I feel safer and more settled than I have in weeks, but in a few days I grow tired of mucking, tired of hiding, tired of sleeping on bench seats. The cold is getting colder, the nights longer, the fear stronger. If I didn't have my phone, I wouldn't even know what day it is. I'm ready to find a new place, ready to try something new. I'm not cut out for this.

***

I wake up to grit on my teeth and rotten breath trapped inside my scarf, haven't brushed in, what, two days? I have to pee badly so I shuffle into the bathroom, the blanket wrapped like a shawl around my shivering shoulders. I peer out a window over the toilet. Thick snowflakes flutter downward, a gentle white storm of tiny patterns landing softly, melting into droplets that slide down the glass. First snows always mesmerize me. I think back to my childhood days, how they told us no two snowflakes are ever alike, believing that was a lie, on the lines of Santa Claus, I mean, how can they ever prove that? I think about the billions of brothers, no two ever alike, not even identical twins, but the numbers are getting low enough now that they could probably test and verify that.

I turn on my phone. Power is down to five percent, the temperature 28 degrees. It feels even colder than that. A wicked wind sweeps off Lake Erie and sneaks in through the cracks in the windows of this wooden igloo. I need food, I need power, I need to make a decision. It's December 7, Pearl Harbor Day, as good a day as any.

I step onto a nice carpet of sparkling snow on the back lawn. I inhale the fresh scent, as if the ground were scrubbed white with Downy. I form a snowball with my gloved hands, flinging it at a fence post, missing by a foot. Try again, miss again. I give up and pump the well, filling a bucket with cold water. I dump the last jar of green beans into another bucket. Magic stares down at it, gives a little toot. I should start calling you Stinky Magic, I say, patting him. I light the last of the briquettes in the Smokey Joe and heat up a pan of water for coffee. French roast and espresso are my favs, but here I settle for crusty Folgers. I chip grounds loose from the clump inside the can. I look out the kitchen window, see something trudging through a patch of forest, short and thick, like a bear cub, but bears haven't been here for two hundred years. I smile, recognizing the little bundle, Josiah, carrying bags. My eyes scan the forest see nothing but snow, which he kicks through, waving. I wave back and step outside.

Going to school?

He nods and heads straight to the barn. I follow him, watch him open one of the bags and shake oats into the feed bucket. The horse gobbles them up. He tosses another bag of oats out of Magic's reach.

For later, he says.

Come join me, I offer, pulling the scarf higher around my face.

He warms his ungloved hands over the glowing Smokey Joe.

Gonna be a cold one, I say.

Yup.

My pot of water boils on the barbecue. I pour it into the thermos, creating wanna-be-coffee. I squeeze a dropperful from my nearly-empty tincture bottle into my thermos. We head inside. He slides his butt on different bench seats, chooses one, pretends he's driving, steering with his left hand, shifting with his right, stomping his left foot on an imaginary clutch, his right on the gas. I make a rumbling engine noise as he shifts and stomps. I feel a slight hope for brothers' future.

Do you know how to hook a horse to a buggy?

He nods firmly.

We head to the barn, where I watch the instructional video of Gaia on my cell.

Your wife?

Just a friend.

While I'm playing and pausing the video, struggling to learn what-goes-where, little Josiah is hooking Magic up, and before I know it, he's done. I thank him. I lower my brobot mask, rubbing my scouring-pad face between my thumb and fingers. How's it looking? I ask.

He squints like he can't see it and then gives me a thumbs-up.

I hafta go, he says, starting out into the field. I bend down and gather up a snowball, launching it at his back—it nicks his shoulder—

and he doesn't even flinch. He turns around. I flash him my biggest smile. He lowers his black mask and returns it, his teeth crooked and gaped. I catch a few snowflakes on my tongue. He copies me as he ambles through the snow to school.

Back inside, I look in a mirror, examine my scruff. I think I can almost pass as authentic as long as I don't open my mouth to speak. I pack the thermos and charger into my backpack, slap the car-bench dust from my heavy overcoat, and bundle-up for my first excursion away from the farmhouse. I loop my mask over my ears, wrap my blanket-scarf around that, and fit the black hat on my head. I head out to the barn.

C'mon, boy, I tell Magic, it's time to go. Can't keep living like this.

Magic's hooves stomp through the snowy white roads dirtied by bisecting black tread marks. Snowflakes tumble around the buggy even as the December sun cuts through clouds and I sweat a little in all this black. My left leg twitches, no one can see it, thank Goddess, as I ride into the nearest town, Millersburg. Sisters in blue-and-white bonnets and knit caps go about the day's business. I park the buggy and tie Magic to a hitching post outside the 150-year-old Holmes County Courthouse. A cupola and copper green clock tower loom over the quaint downtown, the time frozen at a minute before twelve. Next door is the library. I feel my heart beat faster. I step lightly onto the sidewalk in my Asics running shoes, trying to stifle my twitching left leg. I pull out my Gaia juice and squeeze a couple drops under my tongue. It's empty, I'm already dry.

Fuck.

A nearby Sister raises her eyebrows.

Sorry, Sister.

I enter the library, keep my mask and scarf on. I must look homeless, still wearing the same rumpled jeans and flannel shirt since Gaia helped me escape.

May I use a computer? I ask a Sister Clerk at the front desk.

Library card?

I shrug.

An ID will work.

Again, I shrug.

I'm sorry, she says, I can't assign a computer without an ID.

I leave the desk and browse the aisles, keeping my eyes on the computers in use: a middle-aged Sister watches a video; a teenage Sister surfs social media; a couple Amish Boys play video games in the bro-only section. Little brothers, what a delight. I hang near them, grabbing a book, pretending to read, eavesdropping on their talk of chores, computer games, and crazy teachers. Not much different than when I was growing up. Their enthusiasm seeps into my skin, a boyish osmosis. I feel connected.

The Teenage Sister stuffs her phone and makeup case into her purse and walks away from her computer. I quickly stand by it to block anyone who might try to sit there. I count the seconds in my head. One-thousand-one, one-thousand-two, one-thousand-three. . .

The library door opens, an Amish Sister enters, looks me over, heads to the children's section. I lose my count, start again, and after about a minute-and-a-half recounting—plus whatever I'd counted before I started over—I slide onto the seat. I plug my phone and portable charger into a wall outlet. I search The Sisterfield News website, scanning for stories about my escape or manhunt, slightly disappointed to find nothing, not even a news brief. I search up news about recent attacks or bombings, again I find nothing. I click on the Weather Channel, it's gonna stay cold for the next several days, highs only in the low 40's. I upload from my phone my videos and writings, posting on the dark *It*, knowing of the digital risk. One click could doom me.

The computer warns my time is almost up—even the computer knows my mortality!—and I unplug. I commandeer the bro-only single-person bathroom. I twist the lock, peel the scarf and mask off my face, and hold my hands underneath the warm flow of water for a good minute. Heavenly. I splash my cheeks. The water brings me back to life. I peel off my overcoat and flannel shirt, wash up my face and underarms, and warm myself under an electric hand dryer, the first time I have felt anywhere near comfortable in days.

The door bumps against the jamb. Knock-knock-knock.

Busy!

Whoever it is goes away and I wriggle back into my flannel shirt. I warm up my heavy overcoat under the hand dryer, shrug it over my shoulders. I fluff the scruff on my chin, loop on my mask, wrap the scarf around it, rub my gloved hands one last time under the dryer and leave my warm sanctuary.

Outside, the snow has stopped. A Holmes County Deputy cruiser rolls slowly down Main Street, coming toward me. I tense up as it parks in front of the courthouse. A Spunky Deputy Sister climbs out, walking with the swagger of a Sister not to be messed with. We make eye contact. She looks me up and down, her eyes stopping on my Asics. Boots, idiot, I need to buy boots. I nod and she tips her hat. I reach my buggy, unhook Magic, and climb in, looking back for Spunky Deputy. She's nowhere in sight.

357

A few blocks down Main Street, I park the buggy in front of the Millersburg General Store. Inside, I push a cart down the aisles, loading up on peanut butter, homemade Amish jams and breads, bananas, berries, coffee, two gallons of milk. I avoid fresh meats, anything that I have to actually cook, and stock up on some canned tuna, soups, and sauces. Quick and easy. Never know when I'll have to vacate.

I wonder what the boy Josiah eats. Can't very well have PBJs without pop and chips. I toss in two-liters of Fanta orange and cola, and a couple boxes of Froot Loops, and I grab myself some Honey Bunches of Oats. Trail mix, too, that's good, I grab a lot of that. I lift a couple bags of Queensford charcoal and a plastic bottle of lighter fluid, then push my cart over to the clothing. I pick two pairs of jeans and three flannel shirts, medium plaids. I inspect overalls and suspenders, but I'm just not feeling them. I find a pair of black snow boots in my size, they look Amish enough. I drop them into my cart. I grab a toothbrush, toothpaste, deodorant. Next, I find myself near the alcohol, no hard stuff, just beer and wine. I leer at it, wanting to buy some so badly, but I know I can't, the Amish don't drink.

Spunky Deputy stares at me. We lock eyes and I lift my eyebrows in a look of "Oh well." She grins.

You should be able, she says, to have it, you know, if you want. She leans in a little closer. Don't worry, I won't tell.

I laugh behind my mask and scarf. Won't tell on what, I wonder, the alcohol or my disguise?

Not from around here, are you?

Olivesburg, I say, stepping back, pretending to rearrange the groceries in my cart. Just use short sentences, I warn myself, short and sweet.

What are you doing down here?

Visiting my brother, Abe. His wife just died.

Spunky Deputy eyes the junk-food contents of my cart.

Not typical Amish cuisine, she says.

Abe's got lots of kids. I spoil 'em. You know Abe Yoder? (Yoder is the only Amish sir name I can think of.)

I know lots of Yoders. I can't keep 'em all straight.

Neither can I.

She smiles at me.

You have yourself a fine day.

You too, Sister.

Spunky Deputy carries a flavored water up to the counter. I relax, letting breath escape through a pinhole between my lips. I push my cart around, waiting for Spunky to pay and leave. After she does, I head up to the counter. A bored Teenage Sister Clerk scans my things one-handed while scrolling social media on a cell phone in the other. Every now and then, she peeks up, glances at me, refocuses on her scrolling.

Throw in four of those bags of feed, I say.

I motion to a stack of 'em outside along the front wall, visible through the window. She rings it up. I pull out my roll of $100s that are marred by the bullet holes, peel off three, place them on the check-out counter, so that my gloved hands don't have to touch her ungloved ones. She pays no attention to me, glances at the Benjamins with blackened holes through Ben's faces. She looks at me. I shrug. She is an *It* robot, a teenager with flat affect, as she fishes out my change—a $5 bill and a few coins—from the register, before resuming scrolling on her phone.

Keep it.

This gets a second curious look from her. I tip her not because of great service but because I don't wanna touch that germy money, even with my winter gloves.

Outside, I load my groceries and goods into the buggy and untie Magic from the hitching post. I ride out of Millersburg, my life a modern-day western. Black slush sprays up alongside the wheels as the buggy rolls past plowed fields sprinkled with snow. Halfway to my farmhouse, I pass Der Dutchman, an Amish family restaurant. I smell grease lingering in the air and can almost taste the beef and pork and poultry, smothered in gobs of gravy. I can dumpster dive there if I ever get desperate. I think back to our Thanksgiving meal at The Factory and I miss hanging with the Appleseeds, playing Euchre, watching Shawshank, tossing the football. I long to see mom and Emily and I miss Gaia and Miriam, although I shouldn't, not after both betrayed me. This sucks. I am an island. A fake Amish island.

Back at the farmhouse hideout, I change into my new Amish duds and boots. I eat a feast—a PBJ and bowl of Honey Bunches of Oats—and after lunch, I nap. Not a lot else to do.

777

Over the next few days the weather warms, the skies brighten, the snow melts. I tidy up, sweeping up the party paraphernalia from the floor, the dead roaches, beetles, and moths from the counters and cabinets. I feed and groom Magic. I like it here, could keep this routine going till spring, however, I see an SUV drive slowly past the house, a Sister behind the wheel, peering at the porch window. I back away into shadows, pretty sure she didn't see me. But I can't be too careful. Fuck. That's it, I'm so tired of feeling paranoid. I pull out the Cellina phone Miguel gave me. I type 777. It unlocks. I tap the only app, the **B** icon, and it opens, sending GPS coordinates, I guess, and then disappears. My screen is now blank. I remember what Miguel told me and I toss the cell onto burning coals in the Smokey Joe. The face cracks, the plastic bubbles, and toxic fumes rise. I should leave right now, but I just can't, not with night approaching, not again, I don't have it in me. I'll leave first thing in the morning. So I turn in early, sleeping sitting up on the red-and-white Cadillac bench seat, checking my weapons: my revolver next to me, the trowel underneath the bench, the knife wedged into the crack between the cushions.

I seldom dream—don't need to, reality's surreal enough—but I do have a recent, recurring dream: staring at myself in a mirror, I am a

Sister, an ok-enough-looking one, yet I feel like an ugly man. It'd be a no-brainer for Freud or Jung to analyze, but it gets me wondering if I were a Sister, would I be at all like I am now? Would I have any of the same interests, same sense of humor? How influenced are we by the make and model of the vehicle we're born in?

I awake from my nap. The sun hides, the dark creeps in like fog, the day so short now, less than two weeks to winter solstice. I smell an out-of-place scent, recognize its sharp sting but can't name it. I listen but don't hear a thing. I imagine Sister SWAT teams surrounding the farmhouse, me vowing not to be taken alive. Yeah, right. I sit up on the bench, look outside at the sky smeared with the last pink dust of dusk. I glance at my cell: 4:55 PM. Not asleep long. I hear a stirring, a creaking, a boot step on the front porch plank. . . ?

Josiah?

Another footstep creaks. Not so sure it's coming from outside, I slowly reach for the police revolver beside me—umph!—I'm taken from behind, strangled in a choke hold, struggling, flailing at where I think my attacker's head should be, striking ineffective blows on shoulders. I feel around the bench, frantically, but my hands come up empty. I reach between the cushions. My attacker clasps my wrist and pulls me away from the bench, wrapping a strong arm around my neck and, suddenly, rubbing the top of my head, giving me a noogie.

You sonofabitch!

I do a move Drew showed us, grabbing his noogie hand with both of mine, bending his fist forward, almost to the point of breaking it.

Ow! Jesus, B.B.!

Miguel lets go, wincing in pain.

Are you crazy?! we both say simultaneously.

I loop my mask on.

Relax, I'm negative, he says, I test every day. He massages his wrist. I notice he's dressed in Amish garb like me.

I don't care. I could've killed you!

Not likely.

He holds up the police revolver I'd been fumbling for. Then he nods toward my trowel, laying on a kitchen counter.

You missed my blade, I say.

The one between the cushions? Just couldn't get to it. Neither could you. He snoops around. Who's Josiah?

Nobody.

Miguel plops down in a black leather BMW bucket seat.

You got anything to eat?

I fix us PBJs and the last of the canned peaches and watch Miguel stuff his face.

I see you stole Gaia's horse.

Gaia loaned him to me.

Before or after she turned you in?

She's not the enemy, I say, trying to convince myself. I move around the house, peering out all the windows, looking for a clue. So how'd you get here?

Miguel wolfs down the last of the PBJ, attacks the peaches, moans ecstatically.

I can't tell you the last time I've tasted one of these.

A Sister is dead because of me, I say.

Better her than you.

I'm a dead man walking.

Aren't we all?

363

Is Troy dead?

He's okay.

You had him spying on me?

I knew you'd need my help. Eventually.

He murdered a Sister Cop. I watched her choke to death on her own blood.

Day wasn't all bad then, was it.

You've become ugly.

You know how many brothers I've watched die?

It's still not right.

In case you haven't noticed, morality is obsolete.

He jabs a peach slice with a fork and lifts it to his mouth, studies the golden curve.

How long you been here in this hole?

Four days.

That's too long, he says, chewing, peach juice dribbling down his chin. You can't stay here. First rule: you gotta keep moving.

That's why I contacted you. I'm tired of running.

You're tired? He slurps up the rest of the sugary juice. Got any more of these?

That was the last jar.

Got any cash?

I've got a roll of hundreds with a bullet hole in 'em.

He shoots me a quizzical look.

I can get more, not far away.

Good, let's go get it. And lose the dead cop's gun.

***

Stars break through the clouds and I dig a hole in the hard ground behind the barn with a rusty shovel I found. I wipe my prints off the revolver and bury it, covering the freshly-turned dirt with snow and branches and leaves and an old tire.

I'm giving you a chance here, Miguel says, but you have to step up. Sé un hombre.

What does "be a man" even mean anymore? It's that attitude that got us here in the first place.

You're brainwashed, my friend, that's like blaming slaves for slavery. He goes into his revolutionary spiel, you've already heard it, I won't bore you. Soon it comes around to this: Join us, now. Before it's too late.

I don't wanna run, I just want my life back.

Don't be freaked out by the new normal.

I'm a worrier, not a warrior.

Miguel wanders off into the bathroom, unleashing a torrent of piss.

Fuck fear.

I'm so tired of him, I tell myself.

Say it, he says.

Fuck fear. I say it with all the pizzazz of a sixty-year-old flight attendant asking if you want free peanuts.

We soon fade into sleep, each sprawled out on our own bench seat, mine the red-and-white Caddy, his a brown Vanagon bench, fitting, always the activist. During the night, I wake up twice, both times Miguel is sitting up, staring out through the ripped curtains in the porch window.

Go back to sleep, he says each time.

You expecting someone?

365

I'm always expecting someone.

I try to stay awake but sleep wins. Sleep always wins.

The next morning, I serve up Peet's coffee with a choice of cereals—Froot Loops or Honey Bunches Of Oats—and a couple slices of untoasted bread. Miguel doesn't complain, doesn't thank me, he just shovels it in.

If I were to join up with you, I ask, what's the next step?

You have to commit. We're a school of fish, BB, all of us moving as one brain, one heart, one soul. To act independently is to destroy what little we got.

A'ight, I get the analogy, but what does that look like?

He's paying me no attention now, rising quickly, spotting something outside, his gaze troubled. He places a hand on his weapon. Oh god, here we go. I grab my knife, my trowel, and peer out the window, at falling snow, wondering what he sees. Then I see it. I relax.

That's Josiah.

The boy in black kicks his way through snow and leaps up onto the porch, deftly avoiding the crater in the rotted floor. Miguel doesn't look too pleased as I open the front door.

Hey little brother.

Josiah stops in the doorway, startled to see that I am not alone.

It's okay, this is my friend M—

—Mickey, Miguel interrupts, fitting on his brobot mask.

We've known each other, I say, since we were your age.

Where's your mask, Josiah? Miguel says, giving me the eye.

The boy reaches in his pocket and pulls out his black one, fitting it over his face.

366

Miguel turns to me.

We need to talk. In private.

Sure. Hey little man, go ahead and pick out your car for the day.

Josiah browses, choosing a black Mustang bucket seat that almost swallows him. He pretends to buckle up and start it up. I sound a chug-chug-chug-chugchugchugchugchug, pretending to fire up a loud and powerful V8. VRMM-VRMM-VRMM-VRMM-VRRRRRRRM. When he shifts, I chuk-chuk; when he turns a corner, I squeal. Josiah giggles.

Cute, Miguel says, pulling me aside. Really fucking sweet. Está loco?

He promised not to tell.

You trust a child?

He's about the only one not proved me wrong.

Esto no es bueno. Vamos.

I like it here.

Ahora!

Josiah, I say, we have to go into town.

That's okay, I hafta go to school anyway.

He pushes in the clutch, shifts, brakes, and pushes the fake stop button. He has no idea old cars like these required a key. I make the sound of a dying gas engine—ping-ping-ping—ping—pinnnnggg. Josiah pretends to unbuckle and climbs out of his bucket seat.

Bye.

Bye Josiah.

He pulls the door open with his little hand. Miguel and I wave as he walks around the front porch and jumps down, kicking his way through the snow.

Miguel snaps a look at me:

What were you thinking?

He's a boy.

With Sister relatives. You got five minutes to pack up. Then he gets down to business, bagging some food. Guess I have to get serious too.

Thought you refused to be paranoid, I goad him.

This isn't paranoid. This is smart.

It's snowing again, a perfect, gentle flurry. I carry a stack of winter clothes in my arms, out to the barn to load the buggy and hook-up Magic. Miguel beat me to it. The buggy's loaded with food and horse feed, and Magic's already hooked up.

Gaia teach you that?

She taught me a lot of things but not that, he says, fully aware how that must hurt me. You're not the only brother to ever live among the Amish, he adds. Now let's go get that cash, he says, handing me the reins. You drive.

I'd think you'd wanna drive.

He points to the visible brown skin around his eyes. Miguel's right, he's too dark, the Amish look white as island sand this time of year, so he climbs into the back of the buggy. Magic hoofs it down the slushy street. We pass a truck and an occasional car, there's not much traffic on these country roads. Along the road up ahead, Little Josiah traipses on his way to school, catching snowflakes in his mouth, buoyed by just being a boy, walking through who-knows-what landscape he imagines in his head: maybe a field of sugar or a winter battlefield or an all-white planet in a galaxy far, far away. As we pass, he fires a snowball that thumps the side of the buggy. I love it, he was

368

ready for us, and I wanna stop and return fire in an epic snowball fight but I can feel Miguel's disapproving eyes on the back of my head, so I just give a gloved thumbs-up to the boy as we continue up and down this rollercoaster of a road. Magic's hooves clop-clop-clop-clop, hypnotically keeping time on the road. I can't help but smile, I am so fucking-in-the-moment. I blurt it out:

There's a vaccine!

Clop-clop.

No shit Sherlock. Everybody knows.

Those words flutter and settle like giant snowflake letters as we ride down Route 95 to Mohican State Park. Magic pulls us down the winding road into the river gorge, the forest white with snow, and down at the bottom is the dark covered bridge, its roof frosted. I wish I could just freeze this moment and hold onto it forever. The air smells cold, crisp and clean. I close my eyes and let up on the reins, let go of pretending I have control and even though my ass is freezing, I enjoy every second of that buggy ride down, very sorry that it ends.

We park next to the bridge and I recall the bittersweet memory of seeing my daughter, little Nev, but I do not mention that. I clutch my backpack and hop out of the buggy. Miguel stays put.

The hike would do you good, I say.

I've been running on empty. Think I'll just chill.

He hangs in the buggy so I hike the same trail I hiked before, in my black overcoat, jeans, and boots. On my right, the river flows gently, with a patchy skin of ice on top. On my left is the wooded hillside, a little elevation gain, maybe a couple hundred feet. Not a lot of wildlife out, a few robins and crows, but I do see two black beetles doing it on the trail, black-on-black surrounded by cottony snow, the

369

brother beetle on top, humpback style, lasting a long time, he should be proud. Sister bug keeps trying to kick him off but can't, her threadlike legs won't reach above and behind her. I wonder if this would qualify as insect rape. Instinctively, I feel sorry for the Sister bug, but then there's another part of me that roots on the brother bug, like she had it coming.

I pass the fifty-foot plunge of Big Lyon Falls—the flow is decent from snow melt—and climb up the steep wooden staircase to the right. I stop at the top for a moment to admire the simple beauty. I've always loved falling water and I fling a branch at the top and watch it tumble over, past dangling icicles, getting sucked up in the swirl, pummeled at the bottom, disappearing between rocks, before surfacing, broken and floating downstream. I leave the falls and hike onward, sidestepping piles of small brown scat, probably deer droppings. Not far away, I spot a buck, eight-point. It lifts its majestic head, sniffs my existence, unalarmed, resumes nibbling on a bush of wrinkled berries poking through the snow. With the wipeout of brother hunters, deer are proliferating. Many Sisters like guns but they're not so crazy about hunting animals.

Before I reach Little Lyon Falls, I see the coffee-cup-shaped stump and I reach down into it, finding the trowel I hid inside. I measure six feet out from the tree trunk, to the east, and then I dig. The ground is colder and harder than when I buried the backpack, it takes about fifteen minutes of chopping and scraping. I eventually stab it, digging firmly around, pulling out my plastic-wrapped pack. I undo the twist ties, open the double garbage bags, unzip the pack, and rummage through clothes and water bottles. I pull out a couple Power bars and the rolls of cash. I don't know what Miguel needs it

370

for—I'm afraid to ask—but maybe I can buy my safety. Certainly don't think my friendship is enough. Since I already have a backpack on, I don't wanna draw more attention, as an Amish brother hiking with two backpacks. I re-bury the bundle, covering the dirt with the usual forest fluff of leaves and twigs, stomping it down. I return the trowel inside the tree stump and hike back, a little more bounce in my boots, feeling good that I retrieved the pack so easily and that survival techniques do work. I follow the trail around a corner and see the covered bridge over the gently flowing water with its skin of ice—

I freeze in my tracks.

Spunky Sister Deputy is searching our buggy. I tiptoe backward up the trail and duck behind a group of boulders. I also see a Second Sister Deputy, snooping around the bridge and riverbanks. And no sign of Miguel. Don't fuckin' tell me he turned me in too. I power hike back into the bare woods, in my boots and Amish garb, stomping through the sparkling forest, hard to hide this time of year. I head uphill to Big Lyon Falls, scampering up the wooden staircase and along the trail, past the coffee-cup-shaped tree stump. A few hundred yards later, I come upon Little Lyon Falls, the trail skirting up to the left, leading to a walking bridge over the top of the falls. I leave the trail, clambering down over boulders and fallen trees, all mossy and slippery from the water splashing relentlessly. I slink over branches and rocks, working my way around the two-foot-wide falls and in-between thick icicles, scooching against slimy boulders. I'm a muddy mess in my black hat and overcoat, slithering through a damp crevice between boulders to avoid the falls itself. I squeeze into the "cave"— shallow as a bowl standing on edge, maybe twenty feet high by ten wide by ten deep. I've gotten wasted here a few times, even tripped

371

on acid once, back in college—thought I saw God, but that's another story—and it's too obvious a place to hide, I know, but I don't know where else to go, there aren't many choices here in the bare, white woods. I can't follow the river, Sisters will be doing that, so I wait here, in the shadows behind the waterfall, my left leg twitching, first time in days. I pull out my LG BFF 3, whisper into my best friend:

Fuck.

EDITOR'S NOTE: We have reached our opening cave scene.

I hear dogs barking in the distance—they say even the tracking dogs are bitches—coming steadily closer. I'm gonna have to make a run for it, but where do you run when you've got nowhere to go?

Water splashes my face. I should've kept running. Like that would matter, they got dogs out after me, I'm not outrunning them. Sisters, yeah, maybe. I back up into the cave, wiping water from my eyes, focused on the trail. I pull out my elixir, manage to squeeze out one last drop, let it swirl under my tongue. I pull my weapons from my backpack, unfold the Survival Buddy trowel in my left hand, grip the butcher knife in my right. I peer through the falling water. A German Shepherd makes her way toward the falls and me, sniffing back and forth, pulling along a Sister K9 Deputy, both eager for the hunt. Sure wish I had my cop gun, the one that Miguel made me bury, it's gone and he's gone and I'm screwed. The black-and-tan K9 traces my scent, zig-zagging closer, leaving the trail and clambering over boulders, straight toward me, seemingly confused by the tumbling water, now skittering back and forth, it knows the scent is around here, somewhere, the black snout sniffing around the rocks, poking up

372

in the air. Behind the silvery wet curtain of camouflage, my left leg trembles. I clamp my right around it to keep it still.

The German Shepherd heads up the hillside, sweeping back and forth, skirting the cave. I breathe a sigh. Listen for the panting and rustling sounds to disappear.

Thank you, Goddess.

I can't see what happens next but the dog must have caught a whiff or something, because it comes scampering down the hillside, focusing straight at the falling water with me behind it. I grip my knife and trowel, poised to strike like a crab with its pinchers, while the big dog scrabbles on the wet boulders, slipping, once, twice, not caring that it's getting drenched, it's on a mission and that mission is me.

What do you see, Molly? the Sister K9 Deputy says, playfully, a 'coon? Some teens getting' high? Or maybe one of *them*?

The German Shepherd's black nose pokes through the drape of water. I stand quietly in the shadow. Maybe there's still hope.

Nope. The beast growls, water falling around its head like a collar. Then it barks and I make my move, lunging forward, bursting through the waterfall, breaking a thick icicle, slashing the butcher knife, drawing blood that splatters in the snow and the dog howls and I kick it aside. The Sister K9 Deputy draws her gun from her holster—

Halt!

I fling the bloody butcher knife at her chest, it doesn't penetrate, the handle bounces off her shoulder, but drops, blade-tip-first into the flesh of her ankle. She grunts and wobbles and I lunge and slash with the serrated blade of my trowel, slicing her gun forearm. Blood flows. She clutches me and stumbles backward over a wet boulder, she won't let go, trying to pull me down with her. I lean back and kick my leg in her gut. She loses her grip and tumbles down the rocky hillside, coming to a stop against a tree trunk, her leg snapped, broken and bleeding but alive. I scurry away, onto the trail, running, faster without my backpack weighing me down—don't look back don't look back.

I hear the Sister K9 Deputy yelling, the German Shepherd yelping.

Crack-crack!

Bullets slice the air near my ears.

I plow through snow, sidestepping branches, scrambling on the hillside above the icy green river, away from the bridge until I can't run any more. I need to catch my breath. I hide behind a wide tree for a moment and scout the forest. A 2nd Sister K9 Deputy is tracking me on the other side of the river, another German Shepherd at her side, but she doesn't need the dog now, she can clearly see me, taking a shot across the water. The bullet lodges in bark, inches from my face. I hustle away, serpentining off-trail, crouching as low as I can, bullets ricocheting off rock and kicking up snow and leafy ground. I hyperventilate and turn a corner around a crop of rocks, too panicked to know what to do, do I surrender, do I kill myself? *Could* I kill myself? Doesn't sound like a bad idea. If the Sisters capture me, Goddess knows what they'll do to me now. I wish I had that gun, it'd be so much easier with a gun—

Something grabs me, pinning me against the cold rock. I raise my trowel, poised to slash—

BB, it's me!

Miguel shoves me aside and raises a snub-nosed assault weapon, spraying bullets at the K9 Sister across the water, and at Spunky Sister now running toward us on our side of the river. They take cover behind trees, returning fire, bullets flying back and forth on both banks, their revolvers mismatched against Miguel's assault rifle.

Wish I had my gun, I say.

He clutches my arm—C'mon!—and leads me up the hillside, between clumps of trees, bullets zinging past us. Suddenly we are totally exposed and K9 Sister has a clean shot at us, squeezing her trigger—

Miguel spins, unloads a hail of bullets that pin her backward against a tree. Her bulletproof vest saved her core, but blood trickles from holes in her head and limbs. She slumps to the ground, her German Shepherd circling her, whimpering, freaking out, nudging her to get up.

Spunky Deputy reloads her clip. Miguel faces her, aims—

No! I bend his arm down, sending bullets into the ground.

What the fuck?!

She's been cool to me.

He pushes me uphill and barks:

Get to the top. A ride's waiting. Andalé!

So I andalé up the hillside next to Pleasant Hill Dam, water spilling through a concrete channel into the river below. Miguel hangs back, engaged in a battle, bullets flashing back and forth. I crouch, trying not to look back, and near the top of the dam I can feel the power of the gushing water released downstream that will eventually flow under the covered bridge. I finally look back. Miguel's right behind me, much closer than I thought, pushing me uphill:

Keep going!

He stops and turns and unloads a barrage of bullets as I stomp up the rest of the trail, cresting the top of Pleasant Hill Dam, at a parking

375

lot, where a white Honda Shimai SUV zips toward me. Miguel is right on my heels.

That's us!

He sprints past me, blood dripping from his left forearm, he's been shot. I race behind him. The Honda pulls up alongside us. Miguel climbs in quickly and lays down across the backseat. I climb into the cargo area, pulling the cargo blind over me and closing the back door, folding myself small. The three of us are as socially-distanced as we can possibly be inside an SUV. We drive off, not in a flash, but in a leisurely crawl, so I poke my head up and pull back the blind. We are out of sight, as the road bends through some trees. I look back, get a glimpse of Spunky reaching the top, searching around the few parked cars on top of the dam. I feel a weird sense of relief that she's alive.

Do you think you could go any slower? I snap, lifting my head high enough to get a glimpse of our driver, a homely granny, but I can see it's a grandfather-brother in disguise, I see it in his eyes as he glares at me in the rearview mirror, not saying a word. We get a couple miles up the road, and come upon Three Sister Deputies beginning to set up a road block.

Stay down! Miguel orders me.

The Sister Deputies check out our approaching Honda. We creep along, with homely granny hunched over the steering wheel. The barrier isn't yet in place across the road, but we come to a stop anyway.

What are you doing? I whisper through clenched teeth.

The Sister Deputies smile and nod respectfully at homely granny driving herself, old-school in this age of self-driving vehicles. They wave her through, she waves back. A Busty Sister Deputy tips her

Stetson. As we drive away, homely granny speaks in a baritone voice, for the first time:

I'd tap that.

DIANE'S SPORTING GOODS

Hiding in the back of the SUV, I keep my head pressed against the rough charcoal carpet. The new car's chemical smell slaps my nose.

Your sweetie shot me, Miguel grunts as we hit a pothole.

After what feels like forever we pull into a nearly-deserted shopping center off Lexington-Springmill Road. The anchor store Target—exactly how I feel—is still open, but the other stores are shuttered, CLOSED and FOR LEASE signs plastered to the front windows. Granny brother drops us off in the back, behind Diane's (formally Dick's) Sporting Goods. Miguel and I climb out among dumpsters and a twenty-foot-high hill of patchy snow leading up to the back of a separate shopping center. Miguel holds his right hand against the blood-stained coat sleeve of his left forearm, manages to flash a V sign to granny brother who drives off, elderly-slow.

Peace or victory? I ask.

Vaccine, he replies.

He kicks the back door of Diane's. Moments later it opens just wide enough to let us slip inside. A brother wearing a dimly-lit headlamp closes the door behind us.

Leonardo, this is Bryan, show him around, Miguel says, wandering off into the store's darkness.

Leonardo flicks his headlamp down over his brobot-masked face, illuminating it in an eerie latex glow. Pale, effeminate, thirty-something, he must be gay, I think, but then I notice no Adam's apple below his mask.

We got everything you need here, Leonardo says, his voice both husky and frilly. Sleeping bags, guns, ammo, binocs, camp stoves, dried food, thermals. Take what you can, we won't be here long.

I grab a headlamp from a display case and look around at a carousel of knives, cases of rifles, a wall of assembled tents. Other brothers relax on the store's floor, inside tents, on air mattresses, or in hammocks, eating from packets of dried food. I do not talk to them and they do not seem too curious about me. I imagine everyone here has a story and it's all the same: survival.

I'm surprised you're able to hide out here at all, I remark.

You can always find a Sister on the take, Leonardo says, greed is genderless. Problem is, spots like this never last long.

He leads me through an aisle of stoves, kerosene burners and cooking tools. I can sense him reading the confusion on my face.

You just gonna stare at me like I'm a freak of nature?

What are you talking about?

He protrudes his tiny breasts like a bird displaying its plumage.

You're wondering about me.

Seems obvious.

Does it?

You're a Sister, I say, backing away.

Relax, I'm not a carrier. I was born a Sister, yes, but I transitioned. Well, mostly. If I was a crossword puzzle, I'd just be missing number six down and number two across.

I must really look confused now.

I can't get a doctor to finish the job. They could lose their license.

You have a penis?

A surgical implant. It's not finished. Wanna see?

No, that's okay.

Don't have much need for it these days.

Why not transition back? You still got the face for a Sister.

That's sweet, he says, but once you become Jack, you never go back. I've been kicked out of the Sisterhood. I'm a traitor. So, I'm stuck with you guys.

Welcome to the fucked club, I say.

Welcome indeed.

I see Miguel grimacing in a camping chair while a brother doctor removes the bullet from his arm. I toss the two rolls of $100s I retrieved into his lap. There's a long look between us that encompasses our three decades: the laughs, jealousy, indifference, hurt, desperation, it is all there in his eyes, sparkling under the doctor's dim headlamp.

I look away, grab a water purifier, stuff it into a pack. Across an aisle, Troy looks down at a map spread out on a display case of knives, plotting a next move with a couple brothers. His headlamp follows his finger on the map.

He's been waiting for you, Leonardo says.

Troy lifts his head. I expect a grin; instead I get a growl. And a dim but still blinding light in my eyes.

I thought you were dead, I say.

So did I. From now on you hold your own. We're not gonna keep saving your ass.

Fine. I don't need your shit, I say, grabbing energy bars from a bowl on a counter, stuffing them into my backpack, and stepping toward the back door. Brothers appear from behind clothes racks and kayaks, blocking my path. I reach in my back pocket, pull out my fold-up trowel. I hear some chuckles. Followed by the clicks of pistols and a rifle staring me down.

Talked me into staying, I say, pocketing my trowel.

It's us versus them, not us versus us, a guy behind one of the weapons says.

Brothers, relax, Miguel says. Come here, BB.

Stitched and bandaged, he leads me to a group of dudes stuffing survival backpacks. Not that much different from what I've assembled myself: warm clothing, thick socks, water bottles. I join them, helping stuff packs until we run out, we must have stuffed at least fifty. Under darkening skies, we load the packs into a white Femme Floral van parked out back. Back inside the store, I massage my shoulders, sore from all the repetitive motion.

Get a good night's sleep, Miguel advises, and be ready to leave like a Minuteman.

It's cold in here, a thermometer reads 42, but at least it's warmer than the farmhouse. We chew on Sister Power Bars and freeze-dried food. I wish I was back in my farmhouse. Hah, that's rich, *my* farmhouse. Nothing's mine anymore. At least here I'm not alone, I count eleven of us. One is in Amish garb, like me. I look for bedding. There are no air mattresses left, they've all been claimed, so I spread out blankets on some exercise mats, grab a sleeping bag, unfurl it, cocoon myself, and wrap the floor blankets around me. If I'm gonna

381

be on the run, the least I can do is be cozy. I get some looks from the other brothers and can hear their mumbles:

Hey sperm boy, want some candles and R&B?

He'll never survive.

I give him two days, tops.

I hope we have a plan B.

Plan B? What is my role in all of this, I wonder, as I listen to their conspiracy chatter and rude comments about Sisters. What I don't hear is talk of wives, girlfriends or daughters.

A whisper soon travels through the store: Lights out.

Brothers hunker down far from the front windows plastered with CLOSED signs, blocking much of the parking lot lamppost light. There's no power in the store, so no little orange, red, or blue charger lights glowing. We're like a group of boys camping out in the retail wild. All we need are the s'mores. Brothers take shifts standing guard, two at a time, one by the front check-out counters, the other by the back loading dock door. I am not asked to take a shift.

Sleep comes slowly, in the form of my recent recurring dream, this time staring at a mirror in a gas station restroom, now I'm a beastly Sister with bulging eyes, hairy lips, pointy ears. I wake and wanna record the details but not with all these other brothers around. I close my eyes and breathe.

In the morning, Leonardo shows me a display of weapons that would make a paramilitary soldier shoot his wad. I choose simplicity, a silver 9mm Glock, similar to the one I fired at the shooting range. I fondle the pistol, make best friends with it. Leonardo gives me a box of ammo and a firearm lesson.

I pretend to shoot at a kayak.

Leonardo sits me down at a laptop, teaches me how to hack the hell out of Sisters' servers, mainframes and SisCloud. Cody would be proud of me. Don't really know what I'm doing, but I'm a fast typist and they've scripted it all out.

This is how I become a reluctant undergrounder, hardly talking to anyone except Miguel, Troy, and Leonardo. I think the other guys resent me. We all have so little emotional energy any more, we're zombies, stripped of dignity, so why waste any energy on someone like me.

At night I hear a frustrated Miguel receive bad news on his cell. He looks at me blankly, won't tell me what happened, all he says is:

There are some bad bitches.

Moonlight streams through the large front windows, shadows crawling across the displays of balls, sticks, skateboards, and snowboards. I drift to sleep for what feels like a minute. A brother shakes me awake with a whisper: Evacuate. The command spreads through the aisles.

A Security Sister peers into the storefront windows, shining her flashlight, the beam bouncing off the glass, back at her. She pulls on the front door, it's locked. We are deep enough inside, back in the camping, that we can't easily be seen, crawling slowly, our weapons drawn. I follow the others, slinking through the shadows, converging at the back door. Leonardo opens it, blocks us with a stiff arm. I look through the doorway crack, there's a security vehicle approaching, headlights illuminating the parking lot. Leonardo slowly pushes the door closed.

You must have greased the wrong palms, I say.

In the front, another cruiser—this one looks like county—creeps toward the store, its headlights flooding the front windows.

Don't worry, brothers, a voice calls down from a second story of overstock boxes, I got you covered.

I know that voice. I gaze up.

Steven?

I see him behind some boxes, up in the shadows, in a sniper position. He gives a single wave down to me.

I quit beating off, he jokes, this is what I live for, this right here.

I hide behind a ski jacket display, standing almost directly underneath him.

That trowel helped saved my life, dude, I owe you.

You sure as hell do, brother. Now get outta here!

To the crossbows! Miguel orders.

No one questions him, doing as we're told, like good soldiers. I follow the others to a back corner of the store.

The front door batters open. Sister Deputies and Cops rush in, armed. Steven sprays a staccato burst of bullets. The Uniformed Sisters duck behind counters and display islands, returning a volley of gunfire up at Steven, a battle between upstairs overstock and the checkout counters below. A couple other brothers take up positions around the camping section and return fire. Bullets zing back and forth, shredding aisles of clothing and knocking running shoes and baseball gloves off of shelves.

Miguel and Troy splash lighter fluid over the floor and clothing racks, knocking the racks over. Leonardo sprinkles bullets over that as Miguel lights a long match and flicks it at the rivers of lighter fluid. Whoosh! Flames spread from the camping section to the clothing to

384

the snowboards and skis. In mere moments, the store is half-ablaze. The Sister Cops and Deputies flee back out through the front door.

I join the others huddled together, as two burly brothers slide a cabinet of crossbows a few feet to one side, revealing a hidden passageway that we enter in a single-file evacuation of brothers. Miguel shoves me forward into the tunnel.

What about Steven?!

Behind us, the burly brothers roll the crossbow cabinet back across the doorway and join us in the tunnel. Moments later we emerge from behind a full-length mirror, swiveled away from the wall, into a dark dressing room with hooks and mirrors on the walls. We spend a few moments collecting ourselves, double-checking our revolvers and assault rifles. I grip my Glock, the sleek metal cold and smooth in my hand.

Staying alive is a full-time job, I say to Leonardo.

Prey always have to work harder than predators.

I follow the others scurrying through Target. Floodlights sweep through the windows, we stop what we're doing, one step ahead of the light, hiding behind displays or posing as mannequins, like we're in a fucking sitcom.

Don't Targets have alarms? I whisper.

We cut power to the entire shopping center, Leonardo replies, frozen.

What about backup generators?

We disabled them.

Wow. You guys are good.

We've had lots of practice.

The floodlights quickly lose interest in the quiet of Target, fire engulfing the store next door, the parking lot overrun by flashing lights and wailing alarms. Sister Firefighters rush forward, hook-up hoses and shoot water at the flames. Then something extraordinary happens. The fire sparks the ammo that Leonardo scattered, sending bullets flying in firecracker-bursts, shattering the sporting goods store's windows, spraying across the parking lot, ricocheting off the pavement, pinging off the cruisers and firetrucks and ambulances. Sisters scramble for cover, backing their vehicles out of harm's way, watching the store burn, along with the brothers they believe are still inside. Steven still is.

Troy leads us to the back, cracks open a door, peers outside. Two police cruisers back out of the narrow parking area, away from the wild and sporadic gunfire spitting out of the windows. The cop cars park at the other end of the shopping mall. We hurry out into the loading-dock darkness, dodging random bullets, to the short but steep hill, patched with leftover snow.

Stop!

Two Uniformed Sisters peer out from behind a dumpster, their revolvers fixed on us. Miguel raises his arms in surrender, still holding his assault rifle, and we follow his lead.

Drop your weapons!

Miguel holds his left palm out, the universal hold-on sign, and he lowers his rifle, then cocks his right elbow and fires and we all follow suit. Bullets crack back and forth, sending the Uniformed Sisters hiding behind the dumpster. We scatter. Bullets fly everywhere, from us, from them, from the fiery windows inside the store. A brother— don't even know his name—is hit and crumbles to the pavement, writhing in pain. A Uniformed Sister aims right at me. I fumble with my Glock.

Ptu-ptu-ptu! I flinch at the flashes that come down from the fire glow in a second-story window. The Uniformed Sister collapses on the pavement, screaming. The Other Uniform takes aim at me—

Ptu.

She drops to the ground, blood splattering from a bullet hole in her forehead. I look up.

Damn, Steven!

Vamos! Miguel orders.

We crawl up the short, steep, snowy hill into a parking lot in an adjoining shopping center, where two Femme Floral delivery vans await. I crouch down at the crest of the hill and look back at Steven, in an upstairs window, a bandana dripping-wet around his face to cut the smoke. He's drawing fire from Sister Cops that come running around the corner of the building, tending to their fallen. They seem unaware of us, hidden atop the crest of the hill. Smoke engulfs the back of the building and I can't see Steven any more.

A Security Sister examines our footprints in the snowy patches on the hillside and pretends not to look up our way, but she gets on her radio in one hand, raises her weapon in the other. A Sister Cop comes running, joining her, gun drawn.

Steven leaps through the upper window—

You daughters of bitches!

Flames shoot off his back as he sprays bullets into the Security Sister, shredding her, Rambo style. Steven hits the pavement and rolls, flames flickering off his flesh, smothering them in the snow. Assault rifle still in hand, he tries to stand, crumpling, one leg broken underneath him. A Sister Cop approaches, takes careful aim at his smoldering body. She puts two bullets into his head.

Thwup-thwup.

Blood and bits of brain spark in the flames burning away his face.

Steven!

Shit, I said that too loudly, the Sister Cop looks around the parking lot, I crawl away on the top of the hill, out of sight.

C'mon, Miguel says, leading me to the back of a delivery van, shoving me inside, climbing in behind me. Everyone else is piled in already, waiting on me. The doors shut quietly. Troy is in our driver's seat, starting the engine, fitting a curly black wig over his head. Five of us are seated in the back, on benches along both van walls, a stack of undelivered survival backpacks between us. We're forced to sit more confined than we should, breathing as little as possible, tightening our brobot masks as we pull away and around the front of the Femme Floral shop. In the other van, Leonardo is behind the wheel, wearing a brunette wig, looking like the Sister she was born as. In the background, rainbows of water douse the burning sporting goods store.

Steven's dead, I mutter.

Who isn't? says a brother I don't know.

There's little traffic at 2 AM but we keep under the speed limit, turning left on Park Avenue, heading downtown. I stare at the stoic faces sitting across from me, their eyes infused with the lust of violence and fearful passion. I can't shake the image of Steven burning on the ground, assassinated by a Sister. My left leg goes shaky-crazy. I gaze out the back windows, focusing on a church cross that glows Christmas-red, but it might as well be blood, the way we are all being sacrificed. And down the street, atop the Richland Bank building, a Christmas tree looms, half its bulbs dark, no one really caring enough to keep Christmas fully lit.

We pull up to the Farmers Bank building, drive down into the empty underground parking garage, emerging from the vans, guns drawn. Power is on, that's a relief. Miguel leads half of us into the elevator, the other half wait for the next trip. The ride up eleven floors gives us the opportunity to wind down a little, trying not to breathe much, lost in our own heads but hyped with testosterone, our collective sweat steaming up the LED floor display. Someone pounds on an elevator wall.

We reach the top, the doors open onto an office suite that takes up half the floor, a maze of cubicles, with red and blue lights dotting the darkness, power indicators on computers, copiers, and other office equipment.

Pick a cubicle, Miguel says, but don't turn on any lights.

We use the screen glows from our phones to look around the office, at abandoned desks and swivel chairs, computers and calendars, and brother paraphernalia: Nerf footballs and basketballs and a calendar from 2031 with a bikini-clad female leaning over a classic car, her cleavage practically polishing the hood.

I look out through tinted windows, south across Park Avenue, at the sandy spires of St. Peter's Cathedral.

Sister Beth, I whisper, I could use that prayer right now.

Below, to the west, is the old, restored Renaissance Theater, one of the city's jewels. The marquee flashes:

SUPER SISTERS: THE PLAY
FRIDAY THRU SUNDAY

The marquee swipes to:

CONNECTIONS

SISTERS COMMUNITY CENTER

OPENING DEDICATION

TOMORROW

1 PM

To the east, I see the downtown square, the dry, coppery-green fountain, the statues of Sisters, the one still-standing brother memorial, to MLK, Jr., from the waist-up, rising out of the ground.

I got a good feeling about this place, Miguel says, placing a hotspot on a central desk. We claim cubicles, pull out our devices and plug in. I pick a window cubicle on the east end, so I can look out in the direction of my childhood home, four or five miles away. I can't actually see it, but I know it's there, just like the past. My cubicle belonged to Randall Reed, assistant manager of Software Analysis. Magnets from all over the world stick to the metal filing cabinets. On his desk, is a moldy coffee cup. This is a ghost biz, one of millions around the world, places where everyone went to lunch and never came back.

C'mon, Mr. Jack-Off, follow me. Miguel leads me into a conference room and closes the door.

This place feels too good to be true, I say.

Your money is paying-off a Sister, he replies. Look, I need you to do something. I need you to talk to the mayor.

I knew it, I tell myself, but don't say. What I do say is: I don't have access to her anymore. She turned me in.

Of course she did. But she can get us the vaccine.

She says she can't.

390

She lied.

He props up an iPad on the conference table. On it, he shows me a video of three ladies—Miriam, a Council Sister Rebecca something-or-other, and a Sister I don't recognize—all entering the bland, single-story Sisterfield Medical Center. The video is time-stamped 2:13 AM.

So?

What do you think she's doing in there? Pulling out a splinter?

Time-lapse on the video shows them emerging at 2:24 AM. The Sister I don't recognize is holding a small case.

Word is the Cleveland Clinic created the actual vaccine, months ago, and sent it to other clinics for trials. Check this out. He cues up a video, a Sister leading three young boys into the dark clinic, again after hours. They're inoculating Appleseed recruits, he explains, and not giving a flying fuck about the rest of us.

I feel his words seep into my skin like a bitter oil of betrayal. Miriam might as well have waved the vaccine in my face.

What do you expect me to do?

She's dedicating the new community center tomorrow.

She won't talk to me. She tried to have me killed.

You just need to deliver a message, he says, opening the conference room door.

What's the message?

More like an ultimatum.

You want me to threaten the mayor?

We need to scare her.

Why don't we just break into the medical offices?

It's guarded and alarmed and we don't know what we're looking for. We could grab the wrong vaccine or worse, another virus, and god knows what might happen then.

We could kidnap a medical staffer.

We don't know which staffers know what. If we mess that up, we tip our hand.

Why don't we hack our way in to get the info?

We've held city data hostage more times than I can count. They have safeguards, multiple backups, backdoors, it's cat-and-mouse bullshit. Every time we succeed, they shut us down. We need more than a digital presence. The mayor has access, you have access to her. You just need to convince her.

And when she refuses?

Tell her the truce ends on winter solstice.

That's only four days away.

Tell her if we don't get the vaccine, the carousel will look like kids' play.

Back at my cubicle, I curl up on the floor, a stack of file folders as my pillow. I pull out my phone and record all that's happened tonight. I nod off. Way too soon, I wake up to the smell of strong coffee and the sweet industrial scent of microwaved freeze-dried food. I think I even smell popcorn. I look up at Miguel standing over me.

The vaccine for peace, he says.

And if she still says no?

Then tell her no more Mr. Nice Guy.

ALL I WANT FOR CHRISTMAS
IS THE VACCINE

The sun is bright, the air apple-crisp, the snow all melted, except for scattered mounds of black slush along the streets. I'm standing alone, just an Amish man on the square, scarf around my face, well away from a small group of Sister Dignitaries—including Gaia, her hair shining bright red—listening to Miriam dedicate Connections, the new Sisterfield Community Center. Miriam wears a bright red pantsuit, furry coat, snowflake necklace, and silver bell earrings. I like the look. Life is all about connections, she speaks, connections with family, with community, with the world.

She snips the big ribbon cleanly with supersized scissors, an old pro. She shakes hands, poses for selfies, gives a short news interview. As Sisters disperse, the news crew loads up their van, and Miriam and Gaia share an animated conversation. They hug and Gaia walks away toward her store, two blocks north on Main. Miriam excuses herself, wanders off alone, bossing someone on her phone. She looks over my way, sees me in my Amish getup, looks right past me and walks around the gazebo. I move closer, the gazebo between us, until she gives me another look, recognizing my eyes this time.

I gotta go, she says, disconnecting but keeping the phone up to her face, pretending to talk into it, not to me.

I see you're okay, thank goddess.

No thanks to you.

I couldn't see you. I was sick.

They shot at me.

They were supposed to just bring you in.

Why?

I feared you'd run off and do something stupid.

I didn't kill any Sisters.

I know.

Call the dogs off.

Just because there's a "truce" doesn't mean there's a truce, if you know what I mean.

Always a politician.

I'm the mayor of a city of Sisters under attack by brothers. You do that and try to be all warm and fuzzy.

I see her bodyguard, Bulldog Sister, drifting over our way. Miriam waves at her like it's all good. Bulldog Sister stops, in close range, keeping an eye on us. I pretend to study an American Daughters of the Revolution plaque while Miriam pretends to talk into her phone.

I could turn you in right now, she says.

So why don't you?

She wants to tell me why, I catch a glimpse of the struggle on her face.

What is it you want, Bryan?

We just want twenty doses. And the formula.

She smirks.

The vaccine for peace.

Catchy, she laughs, but you're hardly in a position to negotiate.

If you don't give it to us, the carousel will look like kids' play.

Your words or Miguel's? That's ballsy, for any brother.

Bulldog Sister looks ready to draw her weapon. Miriam shakes her head subtly.

I think we're done here.

Give us the vaccine and we'll go away quietly.

She gives me a "Wish I could" look that almost looks sincere. Go, she says, tapping her screen, before I'm forced to turn you in.

I tip my black hat and walk toward the MLK, Jr. statue.

Wait.

I stop. A long silence separates us.

I miss you, she says. I hope you know that.

She opens her mouth to say more, I can sense it, but no words emerge. Bulldog Sister struts over our way. Miriam turns her back on me, still pretending to talk into her cell. I walk away.

Back at our penthouse HQ, Miguel is not surprised by my report. He stands at the wall of windows, looking out over Sisterfield, planning his next move. No one else talks to me, not even Leonardo. I have let everyone down.

***

The next morning Miguel and I sit in the back of the Femme Floral van, Leonardo behind the wheel in a Delivery Sister wardrobe: matching brown slacks and blouse, curly brown wig, rouge on his cheeks, a name tag that reads Layla. We drive out of the underground parking lot, down Mulberry Street. I have no idea where we're going.

Let me get this straight, I say to Leonardo, you were a Sister.

A Born Sister.

You're not a carrier.

One of the lucky few.

Like Miriam.

We turn right onto 6th Street.

And now you're a brother.

Seventy-eighty percent there.

We take another right onto one-way Main Street. Leonardo parallel parks in a space across the street from Gaia's store, 'Round & Ground. I glare deep into Miguel's eyes.

What are we doing here?

Plan B.

Which is?

Going after collateral.

Gaia?! Why?

Seriously? You don't know?

Know what?

Leonardo climbs out of the van, rolling his eyes. Miguel takes his place in the driver's seat as Leonardo opens the van's back doors.

They're fuck buddies, Miguel explains.

Who?

Miriam and Gaia.

What?!

On-and-off every couple years. Right now they're on.

No way.

Oh yeah, we've spied on them.

I collapse hard on my bench seat, watching Leonardo grab a basket; a colorful fall bouquet of purple asters, orange mums, and peach pansies.

I assumed you knew, Miguel continues. 'the fuck you talk about with them?

Not that. I want no part of this.

You should. She snitched on you.

But then she helped me. Jesus, Miguel, not Hermione.

Forget who she used to be. She's a Sister.

No way, I'm not down for this. I love her. You did too.

You think I give a fuck about Gaia, if we can save millions of brothers? You and me included.

Leonardo checks himself in the sideview mirror, adjusts the Layla name tag on his blouse, dabs gloss from the corner of his mouth.

There's gotta be another way, I say.

I'm all ears, Miguel replies.

But I've got nothing. My left leg shakes like an unbalanced washing machine, a shitty time for my nerves to kick in. I'm all out of tincture.

I'll grab some of your special sauce while I'm in there, he says. Relax, we're just borrowing her. It'll all work out, you'll see.

I've never heard him sound less confident about anything.

Leonardo carries the bouquet past Sister Customers sipping coffees at outside tables underneath tree-like space heaters, while working on their devices. I think about running into the store to warn Gaia, but I can feel Miguel's eyes on me.

If you do, I'll kill you, he says.

I smirk. He doesn't.

397

Leonardo enters the store, delivers the flowers to Gaia behind the counter. She's bundled in an emerald jacket, her hair bright red, standing in front of a space heater, the folds of fabric rippling like a field of grass in a breeze. She signs the delivery receipt. Leonardo bounces up and down on the balls of his feet, asks a question, she points to the back. He wanders off in that direction, to use the bathroom, I guess. Gaia reads the card, smiles, smells the flowers, then returns to her work.

Miguel shifts into drive, jerks the van forward, pulls a left on Fourth Street and then another left into the nineteenth-century alley, parking in an empty brick courtyard behind the 'Round & Ground.

Get behind the wheel, Miguel says, hopping out. You're our getaway driver.

Fuck that.

He makes sure I see the wicked weapon underneath his coat, so I reluctantly climb behind the wheel. Leonardo opens the back door; Miguel slips inside. I wanna drive off in the van, but then what? I'd be hunted by Sisters *and* brothers, worse off than when Miguel found me. Besides, I can't abandon Gaia. I settle in, check the rear and sideview mirrors, hoping no one is sneaking up behind me. I drum the steering wheel, nervously, resigning myself to this new life of crime. Unbelievable, I think, Gaia and Miriam? Could that really be true?

Two Sisters Holding Hands walk past the alley entrance behind me and then out of view—

Bang!

The store's back storm door flings open. Leonardo hustles Gaia outside, her head hooded in a cloth book bag, her hands twist-tied behind her back. Miguel follows on their heels, holding a box, flinging

398

open the van doors and climbing in. Leonardo loads Gaia into the back, guiding her to a bench at the far end, away from Miguel. Born a Sister and completely immune, Leonardo can touch Gaia all he wants. I'm so jealous. Gaia jumps up, squirrely, heading for the doors, a tantalizing lavender scent wafting around the van. Miguel kicks her back down onto the bench.

Get in the back! Leonardo orders me. He climbs behind the wheel, shifts into gear. I slide onto the bench opposite Gaia, both my legs shaking now, alternating, like pistons. Miguel digs into the box, pulls out a tincture bottle, sets it down on the bench.

Is that what you wanted?

Gaia's hooded head snaps in his direction.

Miguelito?

He bristles at the old nickname—Little Miguel—while Leonardo drives us casually around the downtown streets in four-five-six block circles, lots of lefts and rights, all to confuse Gaia about how close our HQ actually is to her store. I catch a glimpse of the bottle label—Chill-Bro—but need to wait—2-10—although we are definitely not observing the social distance.

HELP! Gaia screams.

Miguel kicks her back against the van wall.

Stop it! I yell at him.

Gaia's head turns toward me, slowly, as a plant turns to the sun.

Bryan?!

I pick up the bottle, sooner than I should, twisting off the dropper, squeezing out a dropperful.

Why are you doing this?!

Calm usually spreads through my body after a couple drops of Gaia's concoctions, but not now, not while sitting across from my childhood-friend-turned-hostage.

***

Back at HQ, Leonardo wraps computer cables and electrical cords around Gaia, tying her to a swivel desk chair.

Is this really necessary? Gaia asks underneath her book-bag hood.

It wouldn't be, Leonardo says, if you Sisters just cooperated.

He double-checks his knots. Satisfied she's not going anywhere, he clears everything personal from the cubicle: all identifiable signs, pictures, magnets, and penholders, dropping them into an empty copier paper box. He yanks off his wig, rubs off his makeup, wipes away all obvious traces, renouncing Sisterhood in Gaia's presence. He leaves her alone with me.

Don't freak out, I say, I'm gonna remove your hood.

I reach over, lift off the book bag, and back away from those gorgeous green eyes squinting underneath her red hair.

Better?

It's a start. She wriggles to free herself. What the hell, Bryan!

We don't want you, you're just bait.

Well that makes me feel so much better.

I won't let anything happen to you. I promise.

She slowly swivels around to get a 360-degree look, trying to find something to identify where she's at, can't see much above the cubicle walls, other than the office ceiling.

Let me go, Bryan, I won't say anything.

I can't, not until Miriam gives us the vaccine.

400

That's a pipedream. She won't help you.

That's what I've been telling them.

So let me go. We'll call it even.

I trusted you.

And I helped you escape. She squirms, a fruitless effort to get more comfortable. You're angering me, Bryan.

I smile at her gerund.

Guess I can't count on you publishing my stuff.

Not like this.

I need to ask you something. Are you & Miriam. . .

Are Miriam and I what?

Are you a thing?

A thing? She laughs. You kidnap me and you want to know if we're a thing? Yeah, she stops laughing, we're a thing.

I squeeze another dropperful of tincture under my tongue, letting it and her confession seep in.

Were you seeing her when I was with her?

No, she's not like that. She prefers men. She only hooks up with me until she finds another guy, which is hard to do these days.

Miguel approaches, stopping outside the cubicle doorway, tightening his mask.

At last, he says, the Golden Trio back together again. The first time in, what, twenty years.

Let me go, you bastard.

Get over yourself, you fascist Sister.

This is going well, I say, trying to defuse the tension. Hey, remember all our dreams as kids? I was gonna be a rock star. Gaia, you were gonna be a world champion rider. And Miguel, you wanted to change the world.

Looks like we all struck out, she says.

I haven't, not yet, Miguel says.

An understanding of truth passes between the three of us.

How does it feel to be so disenfranchised? she says. Not so fun, is it. At least we always had the strength of motherhood. What have you got? Sperm?

Fuck you, Gaia! Miguel pounds the cubicle wall. It wobbles. Give us the vaccine, he demands, and we'll start our own new world somewhere else.

What vaccine? she says. Conspiracies are the muse of imagination.

Puta!

She scowls at him, perhaps condemning him with a curse.

What happened to Sisters? I say.

I admit we've gone too far, she says. Call it an overcorrection.

We will rise and reclaim our place, Miguel proselytizes.

And put us back in ours?

If we have to.

The revenge of the dinosaurs, Gaia says. Now if you'll excuse me. She closes her eyes, focuses on her breathing, smiles.

What's so funny? I ask.

I'm remembering when I tried to teach you two how to meditate. Neither of you could sit still or stay quiet. You were so focused on my breasts.

Miguel and I share a brief, fond remembrance.

Brothers are so insecure you can't even be comfortable in your own minds.

Gaia, I beg, just help us. You know it's the right thing to do.

Do you mind? she says, still trying to meditate.

We leave her to her inner peace. I notice the Om bracelet around her left wrist, her chipped red fingernails, the silver roots in her red hair. Miguel snaps a series of photos of her. She opens her eyes.

I want delete rights.

You have no rights now, he says, just like us. He stares down Gaia.

What? she asks.

We thought climate change or nuclear war would do us in, he says, but turns out it's you. All of you. The goddamned weaker sex.

***

I promised to protect Gaia, so that night, I sleep—well, I attempt to—in the next cubicle.

Bryan? she whispers.

Yeah?

You've aligned yourself with the devil.

I know. But the devil just might get us the vaccine.

Sometime later I awaken to a slow steady squeaking. I rise and peek over the wall. Gaia's cubicle is empty. I loop my mask over my ears, tap my cell, aim the flashlight in the dark, follow the squeaks. Not far away, I find Gaia, blindfolded, in her office chair, in the lobby, creeping toward the elevator.

Nice try.

403

I grab the headrest and drag her back to her cubicle. The rest of the night, I camp outside her doorway. She'll have to roll through me first.

In the morning, Leonardo hooks eight bungee cords to her swivel chair, radiating away from her like spokes. The other ends are hooked to the desk, filing cabinets, and cubicle walls. All the bungees have just enough tension in them to keep her in place, stuck in the middle of the space, like the axle of a spoked wheel. She tries twisting out of her predicament, but no matter how she wriggles her chair, kicking at the ground in all directions, the bungees keep her rigidly in place.

BACK AT THE SHACK

It's 5 AM, Thursday, December 16. Leonardo—dressed as Layla the
delivery lady—drops off Troy and myself at the Sensitive Estates.
Leonardo will wait here in the van, a Fix-It Sisters sign now covering
the Femme Floral sign. Troy and I hike uphill in bitter cold. Under our
bootsteps, everything is icy brittle—twigs snap, frozen leaves crunch.
Our breaths feather through our masks and scarves. The full moon
casts a horror-movie glow behind the cumulus clouds crawling across
the sky. Troy grips his pistol.

What is that? I ask.

A Beretta 92FS. Fifteen rounds a clip.

Cool, I say, fingering the Glock in my pocket. If my brother Tommy
could only see me now. . .

You sure she's gonna show? I say.

She's been meeting Gaia the same time every week since you
two stopped.

Sounds like her. She hates rearranging her calendar.

We reach the mansion grounds, slinking in the shadows, in case
Miriam is tracking the security camera, but my guess is she's probably
not. She's not a Big Sister, even though she works for them. I sure
miss our hook-ups, they kept me grounded, gave me hope. I feel so
adrift these days without my weekly dose. Even after all that has

405

happened, I still love her for what we shared. She controlled our relationship, but I will never be intimate like that with anyone again.

Troy and I approach the Shack's kitchen door. I type in the alarm code, the red light blinks green, good, the code hasn't changed. Big Sister must've assumed I wouldn't be around to use it again. I light the bundled wood in the fireplace, pop a breath mint from the mantle, flop on the couch. Troy searches the other rooms. As usual, Miriam is late, but I welcome this time to rehearse. I squeeze a few drops of tincture under my tongue, pace the guesthouse, planning what to say. One thing I know, I need to be totally focused, can't let any of my feelings cloud my assignment. It's all about the vaccine. Don't appear weak, I tell myself, Gaia's life is on the line, all brothers' lives are on the line. Be strong, stronger than I've ever been. Don't put up with Miriam's denials anymore, that's for sure, she is the enemy now. I kneel and poke at a log. Orange sparks shoot out and I flinch backward on the rug. I can smell Miriam in the plush fabric of Southwestern motifs and feminine symbols. I attack the log with the poker, stabbing as if it had stolen from me, ripping off charred bark, like skin, leaving the dried woody flesh to burn. In the coals I see Steven, I see Bernie. Dad. God.

Then I hear humming. Beyonce's Halo.

Miguel, I say softly, it's showtime.

I'll wait in here, he says, you talk first.

I put down the poker and stand, my back to the fire, feeling a blast of heat. The kitchen door opens. I listen for the sounds of her usual testing routine, wait for the little moan as she pricks her skin. But there is no need for that anymore. Miriam enters the living room, surprised.

What are you doing here?

We've got Gaia. I tap my cell screen, turn it toward Miriam to show a live stream of Gaia bound to the office chair.

Ohmygoddess, Gaia! You okay?

Miguel's nervousing me, she says, more terror than I've ever seen in her soft green eyes. He's threatening to kill me.

He better not have touched her, I think, amped up.

Where are you? Miriam asks.

I don't know, an office—

Let's get to the point, Troy says, emerging from the bedroom, pointing his Beretta. Give us the vaccine.

Miriam shoots me a look. My left leg trembles.

I didn't wanna do any of this—

Shut up, Bryan! We'll trade you, mayor. Gaia for the vaccine.

First it was peace, Miriam says, now it's Gaia.

Now it's both.

How many times do I have to say this—I can't get the vaccine.

You're going to have to, he says, nudging his gun barrel at the indentation in Miriam's neck, just below where an Adam's apple would be, tracing the barrel down to the beginning of her cleavage. Otherwise, he says, we'll have to kill both of you pretty Sisters.

No, Miriam answers, that's not the way we're going to play this. What you're going to do is put your toy away—

Shut the fuck up!

She stiffens.

Give me your gun, he says.

What gun?

Do it, Miriam, I say, he'll kill you, I've seen him do it.

407

She engages Troy in a stare-down. Reluctantly, she reaches into a pocket in her sweats, pulls out a SisPistol, small and easy to conceal. Troy snatches it.

How long have you carried a gun?! I ask.

I've always carried a gun.

Troy shakes his head at my cluelessness.

Now yours, he points to me.

Why does everyone keep taking my guns away?

I don't trust you.

I hand over my weapon. Grudgingly.

Squealing tires signal we've got company. Through the bay windows we see two pairs of headlights zig-zagging up the winding road.

What's happening? Gaia asks, panicky on the phone. I pocket my cell but leave it turned on so she can hear, just not see.

Leave now, Miriam warns me, before it's too late.

Why will you not help us?

I'm trying.

The ominous vehicles roar like dogs onto the driveway.

Give up, Miriam says, it's the only way you're leaving here alive.

Troy closes every curtain and turns off the lights, but the fire still illuminates us in a flickering golden glow. Two SUVs pull up, headlights and spotlights bathing the exterior in blinding white. Car doors swing open. Four Sisters In Black kneel behind them.

Mayor, you all right in there? a Sister's bullhorn voice asks.

Troy fires bursts of bullets through the bay window, piercing car doors and cracking windshields. I pull Miriam to the floor behind the sofa, covering her like a blanket, face-to-face, my leg trembling on top of her. Surrender, she whispers in my ear, I can't let you die. She clutches me, intimately. I feel myself weakening, wanting to be with her again, Romeo and Juliet shit, but I catch myself and suddenly realize Miriam is holding me on top of her as a human shield. Or am I using her? They won't shoot at me when I'm on top of her. Either way, true romance.

I wish you had listened to me from the start, she says, none of this would have happened.

Advice that could apply to generations, I think to myself.

More bullets fly out the window. Troy clicks another clip into his gun. He squeezes his trigger. Pop-pop-pop-pop! A grunt is followed by the clank of a gun on the driveway and the wailing of a wounded Sister.

Get up, Troy orders us both. We rise and he moves behind Miriam, wrapping one arm around her neck, pressing the gun to her temple, leading her to the bay window.

Drop your weapons now or the mayor's dead!

The Sisters don't act, remaining behind their cars, their rifles and revolvers aimed at the window, not shooting, not dropping their weapons, just waiting. I reach into my overcoat pocket and pull-out my fold-up Survival Buddy, opening it, palming it in my hand, running my index fingertip over the serrated saw edge.

Do what he says! Miriam orders.

One by one, weapons clatter on pavement.

Stand up! Troy orders them. They obey. Hands up! Lock your fingers behind your heads.

Again, they obey.

Step away from the vehicles!

409

They look to Miriam. She nods. They back away from their cars.

Keep going, Troy says.

They take steps back.

That's good, he says, calmly unleashing a hail of bullets that dig into bulletproof vests but also hit heads and shoulders and biceps.

No! Miriam cries out, struggling to stop him.

Each of the Three Sisters crumple to the pavement before they can get back to their weapons. One Sister crawls toward her vehicle, leaving a smeared trail of blood on the driveway. Troy squeezes his trigger. Click. He shoves the empty gun in his pocket, pulls out my Glock and puts a couple more bullets into the poor Sister's shoulders. The bloodbath is over quick. Four Sisters In Black, all down on the driveway, blood streaming in rivulets. Moaning pierces the moonlit air.

You're never getting the vaccine now! Miriam screams.

He pushes her away and aims my Glock at her head, tilting it gangsta style.

Yeah, I realize that.

I lunge at him, he spins toward me, I slash the saw-edge of the trowel across his neck, blood spurts. I shove him into the river rock fireplace. My Glock tumbles from his hand into the flames. He gasps and gags, his blood squirting into the flames, but that doesn't stop him from grabbing me by my neck and squeezing my windpipe.

Whose side are you on?! he growls, intent on choking the answer out of me with his right hand, his left reaching into his overcoat for Miriam's SisPistol. I grip his left wrist with both hands, while he squeezes the life out of me with his right, intensely strong, a rush of dying adrenaline, even with the blood draining out of him. I feel faint, I see stars, I'm gonna black out. Out of the corner of my eye, I see

Miriam grab the fireplace poker, rear back and spear Troy through his lower back. His eyes bulge. His strong dark hand slowly loosens from around my neck, his body slumps to the blood-splashed rug, the same rug Miriam and I made love on so many times.

Miriam pulls the poker from Troy's gaping wound, holding it over him with both hands, ready to strike him again. There's no need, Troy is clearly dead. She drops the poker. We embrace, sobbing and shaking, until sirens blare and lights flash from deputy cruisers and emergency vehicles rushing onto the scene. The kitchen door bursts open and a wave of Uniformed Sisters flood in, weapons drawn, surrounding the three of us, Troy lying dead on the rug at our feet.

I don't wanna let go of Miriam but I raise my blood-splattered gloved hands as high as they'll go. A Tough Sister Deputy grips my arms and cuffs me, shoving me toward the door.

Do not hurt him, Miriam says, he saved my life.

Outside, Sister Paramedics try to revive the Four Dead Sisters, pumping on chests, pressing on wounds, breathing into mouths, performing four separate CPRs at once. The Tough Sister Deputy cups my head and folds me into the back of a waiting cruiser, intentionally bumping my head into the top of the doorframe. Sitting in the front seat, she and her Sister Partner discuss what to do with me, no masks, no social distancing, not that it much matters anymore.

Still, I ask: Do you mind wearing masks?

They curse and ignore me. I look back at Miriam standing at the shattered bay window, watching us drive off, with the same mix of horror and sadness on her face that I feel on mine.

SHAWSHANK

Riding handcuffed and unmasked in the back of the cruiser, I look out at a black billboard with stark white letters:

Don't Make Me Come Down There

— ~~God~~ Goddess

We approach the Ohio State Reformatory, the gray castle-like behemoth of a building hewn from rough stone, once featured in Shawshank Redemption, the film we Appleseeds watched many times. The prison has been a museum my entire life, the number one local tourist attraction, but Sisters reopened it after the carousel attack, making a statement putting us brothers here. Inside smells like stale death, the stench permeates the stone, and I can imagine my fingernails ripped off one at a time or being stretched on a rack until my limbs are torn off, or my flesh gnawed at by hungry rats.

In the lobby, where tourists pay to enter, a Sister Guard processes me from behind a carved wooden wall, cracking raw vegetables with her teeth. She asks me a couple questions: name, address, other irrelevant things. Behind me is a gift shop that's closed since it's barely dawn. I'm being imprisoned in a fucking museum.

A tall guard frisks me with her enormous man-hands, squeezing my junk. She confiscates my tincture bottle then leads me to the showers. She uncuffs me, tells me to strip, watching me with deadly cold and angry eyes. Word is obviously out about the body count.

I didn't kill any Sisters, I say, sounding like Andy in Shawshank.

Sure you didn't, Sister Man-Hands says, grunting.

The water is freezing. I scrub and shampoo as fast as I can, dried blood flowing off of me, a brown-red swirling down the drain. Man-Hands tosses me a towel and a bundle of warm, comfortable clothes: Eddie Bauer sweats, L.L. Bean slippers. She escorts me into the east cell block of massive stone walls and six tiers of iron bars, rusted and corroded. A good pair of bolt cutters could break one out of here. Multiple layers of paint—grays, dirty whites, and creamy yellows— dangle like peeled rinds, the sizes from sleeping pills to sheets of copy paper, generations of death peeling away from the skin of this beast. The only saving grace is the tall, barred cathedral-like windows on the other side of the corridor that let the morning light stream in.

Sister Man-Hands mumbles to herself, her bootsteps echoing as we pass empty cells, but every third or fourth one houses a very depressed brother prisoner sprawled on a cot. No whistles or catcalls at me like in the movies. Sister Man-Hands stops at an open cell, away from any other brother.

Home sweet home, she says.

I fight the urge to flee—a ridiculous thought since she is armed and large and I am neither—as she shoves me into the eight-by-twelve-foot, stone-walled cell. She clangs my iron door behind me, the rusted lock clicks, and little flakes of iron sprinkle to the floor in rust-colored rain. Man-Hands looks me up and down, reaches into her pocket, and rolls my bottle of tincture at my feet.

Yes! I get down on my hands and knees on this freezing gross floor, wanna scoop up my bottle, but I must wait—2-10.

Could I get a pen and some paper?

Man-Hands walks away without a word, her boots clicking on the concrete floor, echoing, drifting, teasing me with their staccato freedom. I look around at my digs: a cot, dirty mattress, thick striped blanket, brown-stained ceramic sink on top of a blackened toilet—both of which were once white—and a smell that would turn away a skunk. A quarter-sized paint chip bounces off my ear, falling to the floor. A fat roach scurries over, feels it with its many legs, decides it's not edible, and retreats into a shadow.

I snatch up my tincture bottle, suck on my dropper. They locked me in here, straight up, no phone call, no lawyer, just left me alone. I think of Troy, the brother who had saved my life. I had to do it, I keep telling myself, he would've killed Miriam. And there's the rub. I killed a brother to save a Sister, maybe two. And I have no idea what's happened to Gaia. I promised to protect her. My head burns with the twins grief and guilt, locked up like an animal with my cocktail of rage. I rattle the bars on my cell door, shaking rust dust to the floor.

Fuck!!!

My curse echoes. A raspy giggle echoes back. I'm gonna die in here, a slow, painful death, like most brothers. I pace my cell but for only three steps before I have to turn around, over and over, until I get nauseous. I turn on the rusty faucet. Nothing happens. It's for the best, wouldn't wanna drink what comes out of these pipes. I plop down on the stinky, stained mattress. I close my eyes, squeeze a couple more drops under my tongue. Better slow down, at this rate I'll run out of my nervous juice before nightfall.

414

I hear boots tapping on the hard floor, this time softer, a Latina Sister Guard on her rounds, walking along the tall wall of windows, bathed in sunlight, as far away as she can be from us in this corridor. She is chunky, with dimpled cheeks. I read her name tag.

Belica, what a cool name, I say. What's it mean?

She stops.

It means beautiful.

I just love it when they get a name right.

She smiles, moves on.

Belica?

Hmm?

I could sure use a pen and some paper. I'm working on a book.

Oh you are, are you? Aren't there enough books by brothers?

I could put you in it, Belica, I say as she walks away.

And as if prison weren't humiliating enough, Sister tourists wander through. I took the tour years ago—it's cool but over-priced—and now I'm a museum prop, one of several on display, brother inmates in our row of cells. Tourists gawk at me like I'm a circus freak; some merely curious, some spiteful.

What are you looking at?!

I grab the cold, corroded iron bars, giving them a good shake. The Sister Tourists are hustled away by their Bored Sister Guide who's seen far worse than me, I'm sure.

There's a vaccine! I yell at their backs. And they're keeping it away from us!

Free the vaccine! I hear an inmate yell back.

I feel proud that I stirred that, until I hear a giggle and I realize I'm being made fun of. Sister Man-Hands comes out of nowhere, whipping out a can, shooting pepper spray in my face.

Aaah!

She raps my knuckles with a Billy club. I stumble away from the bars and fall onto my cot, my eyes stinging like a thousand tiny needles pricking my corneas. I rub them with my rust-stained hands and that makes it worse, I can't see, tears streaming down my face.

What happened to having a heart, Sisters?

Suck my dick won't you, Sisters? a brother prisoner mocks me from his cell.

Sister Man-Hands makes her way down the line, boots clicking, pepper spraying. "Don't!" and "You missed!" and "Fuck!" follow her. I sure know how to endear myself to my fellow inmates.

My eyes are blazing, with no running water, nothing to relieve them. Great, now I'm blind too. This must be my karma for killing Troy. I, Bryan Bowman, *blind* Bryan Bowman, a nobody, took a man's life— an asshole, really—but there's something to be said for killing: it's mindfulness to the extreme. Yoga and meditation gurus should kill and then tell us about being present, about living in the moment. But in here I feel too present, it's exhausting. Shit, I'm gonna go crazy; just when I think there's nothing left for Sisters to take, they steal my sanity too.

Hours later, I hear those soft, swishy bootsteps. I open my crusty eyes, the sunlight from the tall wall of barred windows blinds me, but I can make out a vision of Belica's silhouette standing outside my cell.

Here you go.

Through the bars she slides a bottle of water, a dull, chewed-on pencil with the eraser long gone, and a wrinkled pad that looks like it's weathered a storm.

Sorry it's not nicer. That's all I'm allowed to give you.

I look up at her silhouette in the streaming light. A plump angel.

Thank you, Belica.

I let the bottle set for two minutes—true torture—and then I grab it and splash water on my eyes and down my parched throat. My eyes soothe slowly, I can crack them open, one at a time. After the pain is gone, I separate the sheets of paper that are stuck together, smelling sharp and distinct. Urine. I crinkle my face but force myself to write all that's happened these last twenty-four hours.

Meanwhile, inmates chatter like happy hour and I eventually introduce myself and tell them I'm writing a book.

Tell the truth, brother.

Truth, hah!

Fuck truth.

They tell their stories, I take a few notes, TBH I can't get caught up in all their drama.

On every tour, Volunteer Sister Guides explain how the city and county jails house Sister inmates and it would not be safe to house us there. So we are kept here. I take notes as the Guides give history lessons on the Reformatory itself. It opened in 1896, an imposing mix of Romanesque and two Victorian styles—Gothic and Queen Anne. The doors closed in 1990, two years before I was born. This block of cells is six tiers high, the tallest prison block still standing in the world. Back in the day, the goal was to reform incarcerated brothers with things like crafts and woodshop. Thus, the Ohio State Reformatory.

417

A Preppy Sister Guide lowers her voice, as if we couldn't hear her perky echo in this cavernous structure: Lot of good it did reforming them. The Sister Tourists chuckle. We've been trying for decades, she resumes, to raise the millions necessary to clean the building, to bring in boutique shops and restaurants. I think a blues bar would fit in nicely, don't you? But for now, you can feel what it was like. What better way—she sweeps her arm like a game show model—than with real-life prisoners.

I can think of one: let them spend a night in here. But I keep quiet and give them the expected surly look as they filter past.

***

I don't have a clue what time it is in here. All I know is that it is night. My tremors begin again and I squeeze drops of Chill Bro, looking out at the barred windows across the corridor, at clouds parting and bright silver moonlight streaming down into my cell. I lie on the cold floor, scribbling under the ray of light, filling every spot on the crinkled urine-stained page with tiny handwriting, constantly peeling off wood shavings to expose the graphite tip. I massage my wrist. Clouds soon obscure the moon, again, and I lose my nightlight. I struggle on, writing with my face inches from the foul-smelling paper. From a cell off to my right comes that raspy smoker's voice.

Whaddya in for, bro?

Murder of several Sisters, I've lost count, I say proudly if falsely. Well I didn't murder them, I admit, someone else did, but I was there. And then I can't believe I tell him about Troy. Killing a brother is the worst offense a brother can commit. Yet I figure, what the hell, I'm not heading anywhere but to an incinerator, and this could be my last confession.

I killed a brother. To save a Sister. Go figure.

Is that right?

I had to, I add.

I hear a jet stream of spit—snuff, tobacco, pure saliva?—splat against metal, a spittoon, I assume.

Shee-it, I done lost track how many brothers and Sisters I killed. Don't let it eat at you, bro, guilt is useless. We're survivors, plain and simple. We done outlasted most of the brotherhood. Ain't nothin' to be 'shamed of.

Splat.

His words surprise me. I scooch over to the wall closest to his cell and press my back against the cold concrete.

Whoever you killed, the raspy voice says, he lived longer than most.

Splat.

We make microscopic talk about the food, the weather, the guards, and then the sweet scent of weed sneaks into my cell.

Y'know, they say we experience three deaths, this spitting philosopher says. The moment we pass, the moment we're buried, and the last time sum'un speaks our name.

His tobacco-stained words soak into my soul.

So, keep sayin' the names o' all the bros you've done lost. Keep 'em alive as long as you can.

I like that, muttering names to myself: my brother Tommy, my father William, Bernie, all my relatives, and Steven, even Troy, keeping them all alive, as long as I can. As I do so, I hear a scratching on the cold, hard floor. I look down. A skinny rodent crawls between

419

my cell bars, an emaciated rat, no surprise, it's prison, but what I don't expect to see is smoke rising from its back. I leap up onto my cot.

Guard?!

Relax man, that's Ben.

I look closer at the bony back. What's smoking is a fat spliff that'd make a Rastafarian proud, attached by a clip to a wire harness on the rat's back. The critter stops short of my cot and waits, trained, the joint burning, ashy end facing away from the coarse hairs. I'm standing on top of my mattress, my leg quaking. A putrid mix of skunky smoke and singed rat hair fills my cell.

He's clean, I'm clean, too, but you go 'head 'n wait a couple minutes, it'll keep burnin'.

I look closer at the joint. It's not only fat, it's tight. Impressive.

Ben's my boy, he'll wait 'til you take the j or 'til I call him back.

I think I'll pass.

Don't sweat it. Guards let us smoke at night. Not durin' museum hours. Can't do nothin' durin' museum hours, but afterhours knock yourself out. Go on, try it.

I stare at the thick joint on the back of the rat. I've had weed delivered many times in my life, delivered some myself, but never by a fucking rat. I reach down for it, slowly. Ben's nose and whiskers twitch. I flinch. Then I lightly tug the j out of the clip. Ben turns and wriggles between the bars on my cell door, disappearing down the corridor. I sample it with my first hit.

Saw a rat deliver cigs in a prison movie, Papillon, I think. I tried it. Blew smoke in his little freakin' face. He loves it, he's the most mellow rodent you'll ever meet.

I flick ash into my blackened sink, exhale a cloud of smoke, and guzzle from my water bottle, coughing it out onto the floor. I'm such a lightweight. I swig and cough again and manage to string a few words together: Seriously—cough—they don't do anything—hack—about us smoking?

Naw, they encourage us. Compassionate 'prisonment they call it. Oxymoron bullshit ain't it?

I take a small hit this time, already feeling a tingly rush coming on, much needed since I'm nearly out of tincture.

They wanna keep us happy for their dog and pony show, he says. If we die, who's gonna replace us? Ain't many dogs or ponies left. By the way, my name's A.J.

Bryan, I say, taking a last swig of water. A.J. stand for Anthony Junior?

Naw, he says. Stands for awesome joints.

Splat.

I feel a smile warm my face.

Thanks for the smoke. It's been awhile.

Good shit, huh?

I can't finish the joint, so I snub it out on the concrete floor and look around for somewhere to hide the roach from roaches and I giggle at the thought. I stuff the roach into my sweatpants pocket. A.J. and I trade ideas, like soloists trading riffs, of how to break-out and fight the Sisters or retire on a farm or go traveling around the world. We say brilliant things that I declare I must write down, but I don't, and that I must remember, but I won't.

So this is my life, being a prisoner and playing one for the tourists. It's just above freezing in here, and at night the guards place orange-

421

coiled heaters outside our cells. Problem is the heat rises up this tall cellblock. The walls and bars and mattress springs are all icy to the touch. I can't ever shake off the chill. A.J. tells me I will have a cold once-a-week shower to look forward to, but I have to wait three more days for the next scheduled one. The Sister Guards—either Man-Hands or Belica, it's always one of those two—they bring us food three times a day. Stale cereal and toast for breakfast, soup and bread for lunch, pasta and wilted salad for supper. For evening dessert, A.J. and I get wasted. Guess it could be worse, I could be sober.

What are the others in here for? I ask A.J.

Most for murder, like you and me, his raspy voice replies. Insane, right. "Charging someone in war with murder is like passing out tickets at the Indianapolis 500." You know that film, right, Apocalypse Now?

I know of it.

Sisters are like Kurtz. Gone off the deep end. Most of these clowns in here have no idea what I'm talkin' 'bout, they never heard of the film. And that's a cryin' shame.

Splat.

We talk about things like that from the past, movies and muscle cars and a brother culture that has vanished right before our very eyes, things that once meant something. I realize how reminiscing, even with someone you don't know, comes pretty easy in here.

The telephone booth, A.J. says, you had some privacy when you talked on the phone. Now all these smart phones everywhere and no booths, not a one in sight. We giggle at his idea of a bubble that inflates around you when you're talking on your cell, a booth in essence, so the rest of us don't have to listen to your brainless chatter.

How old are you? I ask.

Not nearly as old as I feel. And older than I thought I'd ever be.

***

After three days I've got a routine down, writing and taking hits off joints delivered by Ben. When I run out of paper, Belica kindly brings me fresh, clean sheets this time. I ask her if I could speak to a lawyer.

Ain't no need, A.J. says, eavesdropping, you're a brother and for that alone you're guilty.

To pass the time, I mess with the tourists. I might lunge an arm toward a Curious Sister who strays too close, scaring her, before busting out my sweetest grin. Or I play dead on my cell floor, sprawled out, a leg at a funny angle. I try not to snicker as I wait for the inevitable question:

Is he dead?

And then I belt out Roxanne just like Eddie Murphy did in jail in the movie 48 Hours. The Sister Tourists don't get it, they just scurry off to their next tour stop, though it always gets a laugh out of A.J. But I never goof like that when Man-Hands is on the block.

One afternoon, Regina, the bigger-than-life African American Sister lawyer I visited a few weeks ago, saunters past in a yellow pantsuit, bracelets and necklaces jangling.

Regina?

She stops, backtracks, looks me up and down.

You again? How ya doing?

Can you help me?

She laughs.

Can I help you? Oh, that's a good one.

She saunters off, still laughing. Nothing much worse than an echoing laugh at your expense, in prison, especially from a lawyer.

***

I'm sitting up in bed, writing, so lost in my head I don't hear the clicking bootsteps of Sister Man-Hands until they're almost to my cell. She's humming Mariah Carey's All I Want For Christmas Is You. Didn't see that one coming. She stops, a towering presence, her long shadow breaking my soft ray of moonlight. Then, stepping out from behind her is Miriam in a Christmas parka, she's the one humming. I rise, surprised to see her.

They haven't released Gaia, she says.

And they won't, I say.

We've negotiated a deal. I'm releasing you. You're not part of the deal, don't get the wrong idea, but I can't trust any other brother. If you help me get Gaia back, I'll give you the vaccine.

And my freedom?

You always had that. You chose to run.

How strange this now is, I reflect, I'm behind bars, but for the first time in years, I feel like I've got some real fucking power.

I wish to sign him out, Miriam tells Man-Hands.

Are you authorized?

I'm the mayor.

I realize that, but—

Release him.

Yes, Sister Mayor.

I gather my papers. Man-Hands unlocks my cell and gives me a steely-eyed glare.

You two have a good time.

Miriam and I walk past the other cells. A tattooed arm reaches out between the bars of one, waving toward me. Miriam and I keep to the wall of windows across the corridor.

Bryan, it's A.J., take me with you.

I look to Miriam. She shakes her head.

C'mon, bro, the raspy voice begs.

I feel horrible leaving him here, I truly enjoy talking to him, but I'm taking his advice, trying not to feel guilty, as we walk out of the cell block, to the rattle of bars and an extra-loud:

Splat.

In the visitor's lobby, Miriam signs me out. Evening, Charlotte, she chats with the front desk guard. How's the baby?

Tamara's precious as always, thanks for asking.

Sister Charlotte hands me my bundled Amish clothes. I fit on my black overcoat while she shows Miriam a baby photo on her computer. Miriam is taken aback.

Is something wrong, Sister Mayor?

No, no, she's absolutely lovely. She just reminds me of somebody. You take care of that little girl.

Oh I am, Sister Mayor, I am.

Sister Charlotte pushes a button. The front door opens.

What did you see? I ask.

Miriam gazes at me.

Your eyes.

I look back at Sister Charlotte. Wow, her too?

425

WINTER SOLSTICE

We step outside onto snow sparkling under lampposts.

What time is it? I ask Miriam.

Almost midnight.

What day is it?

The nineteenth.

Almost winter solstice, I think to myself, Miguel's deadline, as we climb into her gold Lexus sedan.

Aren't you risking your political career?

I can get back into the medical field. She turns, faces me: What happened to you and all your friends, I'm sorry I didn't act sooner.

She starts the car. I sense there's more to her change of mind, but don't push it, instead I melt into the warm leather seat that embraces and caresses me. Seat warmers gotta be *the* greatest invention. Other than the vaccine, of course.

So tell me about you and Gaia, I say.

There's not much to tell. She gives me comfort.

She taps a button on her steering wheel. SysPop surrounds us with smooth, mindless sound. We don't move, just sit here in the parking lot in her warm, gold Lexus surrounded by the sparkling snow.

I'm pregnant.

And just like that time stands fucking still. The word swells in my brain and I look down, only now noticing her slight belly bump.

What?!

Why do you think I gave you that extension? And why I let you see one of your daughters?

So you've known for a while.

I didn't know if I was going to keep it.

I'm definitely the father?

She shoots me a bitter look.

Ohmygod, this is crazy.

I want my baby to have a father, she says, clutching my hand.

I look out at the beautiful snow. Here I am, forty, I'm having a child, the last thing I had ever wanted, what I already have thousands of, but now a child I can know. This is so bizarre I can't wrap my brain around it. I squeeze Miriam's hand. She squeezes back.

What do we do now? I say. We can't legally get married.

We wouldn't anyway. I want a father for our child, not a husband.

Then run away with me. We can make a new start.

I wish we could.

We can.

We can't. This is no happily-ever-after. But I've arranged a sweet setup for you, a bro-condo in Florida, you'll love it. We can come visit, maybe spend winters there. You know how we Buckeyes love Florida.

So you weren't lying about retirement.

I lie to the public. When I have to. But not to you.

You lied to me about the vaccine.

I had no choice. In that case, you *were* the public.

427

She reaches into her glove compartment, pulling out a small, sleek, black .38 caliber SisPistol.

How many guns have you got? I say, reaching for the petite pistol but she pulls it back.

Think you can handle it?

Why does everyone say that?

She hands it over. I bury the gun in my overcoat pocket, don't wanna seem too eager. She reaches under her seat and removes a silver SisPistol for herself.

You come well-prepared.

Sisters usually do.

Then she reaches behind her seat and produces a padded black case a little smaller than carry-on luggage.

Is that what I think it is?

Your Holy Grail.

Is everything in it?

Everything Miguel asked for.

She hands me the case. I hold it on my lap—is it on my lap or in my lap? I'm never sure—and both of my legs are shaking underneath it. I'm holding hope. That's fucking scary.

How long have they had it?

Awhile.

You bitch, I think to myself, you lied to me for how long? Miriam shoots me a sharp look. Shit, turns out I must've whispered it.

May I? I say, not waiting for an answer. I unzip the padded case. Inside, packed in pre-cut gray foam, are twenty vials and twenty syringes. I leaf through the paperwork: chemical formulas, dosage directions, and a list of possible side effects. Fever, headaches,

428

nausea, rash or swelling, decreased libido. I'm hoping for some others: reduced nihilism, loss of existential angst, renewed libido. A brother can dream, can't he?

Just know it isn't yet FDA-approved, Miriam warns me.

But it works?

It appears to.

I zip up the case, wrapping my arms around it. Miriam drives away from the prison, rather than engaging auto driver, as most Sisters do.

I need to make a call, I say.

Go ahead.

They took my phone.

Call, Miriam tells her dash screen, as I punch in the number and after a ring or two, Leonardo's face appears on the dash screen.

We got it!

Okay, um, good.

You all right?

You need to see this, Leonardo says, swinging his cell phone around, until the camera looks down over a cubicle wall, at Gaia, fear in her green eyes, still tied to the desk chair, bungeed all around. Miguel stands in her cubicle doorway, terrorizing her with his masked glare, like he wants to kill her, like he *will* kill her if there's any hitch in his grand plan. Gaia has always been strong in a sinewy hippie way, and she grimaces stoically. But a tear trickles down one cheek.

He's been like this for an hour, Leonardo says.

Miguel, this is Sister Mayor. Back off now or the deal is off.

Miguel's stare intensifies, like he wants to rip his hostage—his long-ago-ex—apart with his bare hands.

Stop! I shout helplessly at the dashboard screen. I've got the vaccine!!

Miguel's head turns toward the camera, squinting at it.

You certain?

Meet us at the lake. One o'clock.

Miguel shifts from angry to busy, yelling off-screen: V-Day is here, brothers!

Gaia slumps in her chair.

This'll all be over soon, Gaia, I say. I promise.

Leonardo's face fills the screen.

Stay with her, please, I beg him. And make sure you're at the exchange.

I wouldn't miss it.

I end the call. Miriam squeezes the steering wheel, pissed like I've never seen her. We're lucky she isn't turning the car around and calling this whole thing off. What the hell was Miguel thinking? Goddess, I wish I had some tincture right now, I'm bone dry. I wrap my arms even tighter around the case. I pull out my last blank sheet of prison paper, using the padded case as a writing surface, not ideal, the pencil tip tears the paper. I discover the proper pressure and the pencil starts to scrawl on its own: Kill Miguel. Kill Miguel. Kill Miguel.

I look out on this very cold night, heading east on Route 30, the snow along the highway sparkling like fields of white diamonds. Christmas lights twinkle and trees glow at a few distant homes.

I'd forgotten that it was almost Christmas, I say.

She takes my hand and places it on her belly, the incubator of my seed. This is the first time I've gotten to be so close to a little me, and I worm my hand underneath her coat and sweater. I can feel the new stirring of life, not so much kicking but swaying ever so slightly

430

underneath my hand. I twirl a slow groove around her belly button. My shoulders shiver with goosebumps.

I haven't told you everything, she says.

Whaddya mean?

About our baby.

The seriousness on her face worries me.

I had an ultrasound yesterday.

Is there a problem?

More like a complication.

Downs? Bad heart? What is it?

She bites her lip. Her face softens.

It's a boy.

A boy?

The word sinks in. And then the implication. That's why she got me out of prison—if it were just another girl I'd probably be left to rot in that fucking cell—but then, you know what, I don't care, the thought is swept away by a tsunami of well-being. I'll be damned. I've got the vaccine. And I'm gonna have a boy. I'm so afraid that if I look away from her, this moment will forever vanish. I try to hold onto it, but we've got the most intense meeting of my life coming up, I have to be on top of my game, not all gaga-eyed like I am now, driving through the white countryside with Miriam, listening to her hum along to the SysPop, my boy growing inside of her. *My* boy.

Wow.

Miriam's brown face glows like polished walnut, her ebony hair cascading over it. I keep my left hand on her belly and my right goes crazy scribbling down all the details that've happened this evening, all my thoughts and feelings.

431

Five miles east of Sisterfield, we turn right on rural Route 603 and coast behind a parked sedan.

What are we doing? I ask. This isn't the meeting place.

The mayor's bodyguard, Sister Bulldog, emerges from the other car in a long, dark overcoat. I feel my wave of well-being crash.

Get in the back, Miriam says.

I clutch the case of vaccine, climb outside and into the backseat. Sister Bulldog climbs in front with Miriam. I tighten my mask.

Relax, Bryan, she's not infected.

Sister Mayor, Bulldog says, permission to speak to the brother?

Of course.

Bulldog gives her head a quarter turn, her face in profile.

I test every day.

That's it, she faces forward again, a Sister of few words. I wonder why Sister Bulldog's not vaccinated, she must not be if she tests every day. I wonder who is and who isn't allowed what I hold in my lap. And what about Miriam, she's vaccinated, she's gotta be, right? Taking all those tests was just a charade or maybe an extra precaution because she loves me. Jesus, what a night. I look up at the spray of stars and three-quarter moon peeking through a few high clouds. Won't need flashlights tonight, as if Mother Nature wants to be sure we can see what we're doing. The fact that we're not driving away, just sitting here, is, as Gaia likes to say, anxiousing me.

This isn't the meeting place, I repeat.

I know, we're early.

Not really, I think, glancing at the dashboard clock—12:53 AM—but I keep quiet. I scrawl more notes, last thoughts. My hand is shaking now, joining forces with my leg.

I'm gonna have a boy! I scribble, trying to bring peace to my quivering. Miriam opens her door.

I have to pee.

She wanders off into nearby woods, leaving me alone with Sister Bulldog sitting silently in front of me.

Happy winter solstice, I say.

No response.

Did you get the Mayor anything for Christmas?

Again, nothing, so I gaze out the window.

Did you enjoy *your* present? she speaks, finally.

It takes me a moment to make the connection:

That was *you* who left it at the guesthouse?

Again, we sit in silence. Bodyguards are good at that.

Do you know what's in here?

Sister Bulldog twists her thick head around, looks down at the case, then at my face.

I can guess.

The trunk pops open. Miriam pulls out a bulletproof vest, strapping it on.

You got one of those for me? I ask.

Sister Bulldog snorts. Miriam climbs back in.

Everyone ready?

She doesn't wait for an answer, pulling the car back onto Route 603. The clock reads 1:04. We're already late. I roll my window down a crack so I can smell the solstice, a mix of old autumn and fresh new winter snow. We drive a lonely mile in complete quiet, then turn onto Route 430. Miriam pulls the Lexus toward a small parking lot along the shore of Charles Mill Lake. The delivery van is already here, idling. The sign on the van now reads: Seven Sisters Caterers.

Here we go, I whisper to my frosty window, as we turn into the lot, my upper lip twitching underneath my brobot mask.

THIS IS HOW IT ENDS

EDITOR'S NOTE: This is from my recollection. For consistency, I retained Bryan's first-person voice. Moments that I was not privy to are recreated.

So here we are at Charles Mill Lake, my go-to getaway, the place where Orange Eyes haunted locals long ago, and where I played Nirvana for the dying fisherbrother. I've never been here this late at night, it's got a rural noir feel, the not-quite-full moon glows on the still, gray water and casts long, thin shadows of the bare trees. No homes nearby, we're away from people and cameras, close to three highways and the 71 Freeway. We could flee quickly up to Cleveland or down to Columbus or over to Wooster. I suggested the spot and Miguel agreed, which surprised me. Growing up, we never agreed on anything. I liked Cleveland sports teams; he rooted for Cincinnati. I was a moderate independent; he was a radical conspiracy freak. The only thing we agreed on was Harry Potter. And Gaia.

Miriam circles the Lexus around the parking lot, in super slow-mo, before settling on a spot facing the van, the snowy pavement between us. Behind the wheel of the van, Leonardo sits, dolled up as Layla the delivery lady, looking like the Sister she once was.

435

In the seat in front of me, Sister Bulldog pulls a scary-looking weapon from under her overcoat.

What is that?

AK-12, she snarls.

I suck in a deep breath and open the door. Sister Bulldog reaches back, grabs the padded black case. We tug-of-war, but she is stronger, ripping it out of my hands.

Careful!

I shoot a look at Miriam.

I can't walk over there without the vaccine.

You'll have to. I need to see Gaia first.

Can you at least put it up on the dash so they can see it?

Miriam nods. Sister Bulldog wedges the case against the front windshield, in moonlit sight.

We're not pulling any tricks, Bryan.

We're not either. (I hope my words are true.)

Remember, Gaia first, Miriam reminds me, as I climb out, bounce on the balls of my feet, cold and fearful. I meant what I said earlier, she adds.

I'm not sure which earlier she means and with Sister Bulldog eavesdropping, I let the comment go unanswered. I walk very deliberately across the parking lot. No walk in my history of walks ever felt so long: not across my graduation stage, not to the altar, not even to my prison cell. I feel tremors all over my body, little ones, as if I'm a walking, vibrating chair. Leonardo gives me a WTF glare from the driver's seat. The van's back doors swing open.

Where's the vaccine? Miguel snaps, behind a BLM—Brothers Lives Matter—sticker on his brobot mask.

I refuse eye contact with him, climbing inside and sitting on the bench opposite Gaia. Her wrists and ankles are still bound by computer cords and cables, her eyes closed. She appears to be meditating.

Where the fuck is it?! Miguel demands.

I rest my hand in my Amish overcoat pocket, my fingers wrapping around the SisPistol inside. I wanna pull it out and put a bullet between Miguel's eyes.

It's up on the dash, I say, you can see it.

'Fuck it's doing there?

She wants Gaia first, what else?

No way, Sister Lover. I told you, the vaccine first.

Miguel is as pissed-off at me as I am at him. I gotta guess he knows I killed Troy. Shouldn't matter, I've come through with the vaccine.

Meet in the middle, Gaia says, her eyes still closed.

Miguel moves to the front of the van, whispers with Leonardo. I whisper to Gaia.

Don't worry, I seethe through my mask, I'm gonna kill him.

Get in line, Gaia and Miguel say at the same time.

Guess I should tell you, she says, I've been editing your posts.

I feel a wave of well-being.

When this is over, she says, we can work on it together.

The wave grows bigger.

And I'm glad you're getting the vaccine, she says, you deserve it.

The wave is huge, curling.

Here's what we're gonna do, Miguel says, facing us, fitting a red ski mask over his brobot mask.

437

And the wave crashes.

Leonardo will stay in the van, he says, and watch over us with his Little Sister—Leonardo waves his own assault rifle—while BB, you and I escort Gaia to meet the mayor and her dike. Halfway.

I think she'll accept that, I say.

She sure as hell better, Miguel says, gripping his nasty Uzi. Where's your piece?

They confiscated it when I was arrested, I half-lie.

Miguel snorts at my lame manhood. I can visualize it, clear as day, one bullet right between his eyes.

Leonardo helps Gaia out of the back of the van. She stutter-steps in the snow, her hands and legs wrapped in cords and cables, her hands behind her back. Leonardo climbs back into the driver's seat, pointing the barrel of his Little Sister out the driver's side window, with a clear shot at anyone he chooses.

I accompany Gaia across this snowy no-man's land, toward the Lexus, maintaining social distance, our walk dreadfully slow, micro-steps, with Miguel following three steps behind, pointing his Uzi at our backs. Now *this* feels like the longest walk ever.

Got any tincture on you? I joke to Gaia.

Miriam and Sister Bulldog climb out of the Lexus. Miriam clutches the vaccine case and her SisPistol. Sister Bulldog fixes her AK-12 on Miguel and myself. The only one unarmed here is Gaia, ironic since she's probably the best shot of all. With each tiny step we take, my legs tingle. The bare tree branches sway, as if waving goodbye. I swear I can smell their sour pheromones.

Gaia and I are halfway to Miriam and the vaccine. Time crawls like Gaia's tiny steps across the snowy pavement. Strange, the

438

thoughts that seep through my brain cells, I think of Bernie and how I wanna capture this heightened awareness, bottle it as a new elixir: The Moment. That's all we've got, the moment, there is no afterlife, not even digitally if no one clicks on your posts or pictures, since we're always bombarded with newer things to click. Nostalgia is obsolete.

Gaia stops, so I stop, ten feet apart, and another ten feet from Miriam and Sister Bulldog. Miriam steps forward.

Gaia, are you okay?

She's fine, Miguel says, his Uzi fixed on us.

I'm talking to *her*.

Miguel's eyes blaze through his ski mask.

I'm well enough, Gaia says. *Most* of them were gentlemen.

Miriam starts the proceedings, scanning all the nervous fingers on triggers: Okay boys, first off, let's not use any of these toys. We're both getting what we want here. Let's just do the exchange and go. Nobody shoots, nobody gets hurt.

We shiver and mumble agreements.

The vaccine first, Miguel orders, then you get your precious Sister.

Okay, no, Miriam replies calmly, this is how we'll do it. Bryan, you bring Gaia forward. I'll give *you* the vaccine. Then we go our own ways.

I look to Miguel. He nods reluctantly, training his Uzi on the three Sisters: Gaia, Miriam, and Sister Bulldog pointing her own AK-12 at Miguel.

At least it's a worthy ransom, Gaia says, taking a tiny step forward. I move with her. Miriam steps toward me, the black case plastered to her bulletproof-vested chest, the SisPistol gripped in her

439

hand. Fingers tighten on all triggers. Miriam smiles at Gaia as they pass, that Sisterly smile a brother can never replicate. Gaia continues on toward the gold Lexus. Miriam takes her last steps toward me.

Merry Christmas.

She hands me the case. I let go of the SisPistol hidden in my coat pocket. I unzip the case, check the contents.

Looks good, I say, zipping it up. I look at Gaia: I'll see you around, Hermione, my words sounding much sadder than I intend.

Gaia looks back over her shoulder: Be well, Ron.

We all back up toward our respective vehicles, weapons fixed and focused, fingers curled around triggers. With every cautious step backward, I hyperventilate with happiness, mentally listing what I will do after I'm vaccinated: hug mom and Emily, take mom on a drive to look at Christmas lights, then after the holidays leave Sisterfield, head down to that bro-condo in Florida.

A buzzing grabs our attention, like a giant insect, a sound easily recognizable, a drone, hovering dark against the bright night sky. I recognize the model, it's the same as Drew's, the size of a raven, the one he joked gave me drone envy. Leonardo aims his Little Sister out of the van's window, spraying bullets that flash in the moonlit sky. One connects and the drone sparks and tumbles to the pavement. It cracks and sputters and dies. No one even notices my fellow Appleseeds, Drew and Cody, emerging from the bank of the lake, masks on, guns drawn. Drew rushes behind Sister Bulldog, jabbing a revolver at the back of her head and Cody pokes a pistol in Miguel's back.

Drop it, Cody says, behind his brobot mask.

Are you shitting me?! Miguel exclaims, relinquishing his Uzi.

440

Thank you very much, Cody says, snatching it, backing away, giggling with boyish delight.

Now your turn, Drew says, choking Sister Bulldog in a wrestler's headlock. She refuses to surrender her AK-12.

What the hell are you guys doing?! I yell.

Don't try to be a hero, Bryan, Drew says, heroes die.

I'm clutching the case of vaccine, like robbery loot, in one hand while my other grips the SisPistol in my pocket that only Miriam knows I have.

Drew presses the barrel of his revolver deeper into the back of Sister Bulldog's head.

Give it up, Sister.

She has no choice, reluctantly releasing her grip on the AK-12. Drew clutches her weapon, turning it on her, poking the barrel between her shoulder blades. Meanwhile, in the van, Leonardo tries to fix an aim on either Drew or Cody, but he can't shoot without risking Miguel or myself or the mayor, all in his line of fire. Fingers itch on all those triggers.

Drop your gun, Sister Mayor, Drew orders.

Miriam hesitates.

Now!

She lays her SisPistol on the white pavement.

Kick it over here.

She kicks the tiny gun, sliding it across the pavement, leaving a trail in the veneer of snow, coming to rest near Drew's feet.

How did you know about this? I ask.

I hacked into the mayor's GPS, Cody says, flickering his eyebrows proudly. We didn't, like, know *you* were going to be here.

441

Don't do this, I plead, holding the case up. One of these is for you! Both of you!

Why should they get one? Miguel complains. We did all the work.

Put the case on the ground, Drew says.

I assess the situation, searching for alternatives. Drew sprays a few bullets at my feet, leaving pockmarks in the snow. He makes a solid argument.

Okay, okay! I set the case down and step away.

Everyone back to your vehicles, Drew says, drive away and no one gets hurt.

Without even thinking, I join Miriam and Gaia at the Lexus. Miguel glares at me.

Too much happens too quickly to describe. Here is what I can remember:

Sister Bulldog shoves her elbow up hard into Drew's jaw—crack—jarring the AK-12, sending bullets spraying like shooting stars. She and Drew wrestle for control of the weapon—

Miguel spins and tackles a distracted Cody, grappling for the Uzi. Cody is younger, Miguel stronger—

Leonardo fixes his Little Sister on everybody, fidgety, it's never clear when or who to shoot—

Sister Bulldog flips Drew, slamming him to the pavement, the AK-12 wedged between them—

Miguel snatches control of his Uzi, jabbing the end of the barrel up one of Cody's nostrils. You're lucky you're a brother, he says, Uzi-whipping his head, delivering a blow to the temple that knocks Cody unconscious. He collapses—

I help Gaia into the Lexus backseat, frantically working to undo the many cords around her wrists while Miriam climbs behind the wheel. You got a knife in here? I plea—

Drew uses an old wrestler move, flipping Sister Bulldog off him, the AK-12 slipping to the pavement. They untangle and crawl toward it, each clutching the weapon with one hand, clawing at each other's faces with the other—

Miguel aims his Uzi at the wrestling tumbleweed of brother and Sister—

My hands shake trying to untie the cords and cables around Gaia's wrists. Miriam hands me nail clippers. I glare at her: You gotta be kidding me—

Leonardo sits petrified in the van, too confused to shoot—

Sister Bulldog tears the AK-12 away from Drew—

Miguel seizes the moment, squeezes the Uzi trigger—

Bullets ripple Sister Bulldog's back, shredding her bulletproof vest, and her shoulders and thighs. One pierces the back of her head. Blood splatters Drew—

I snip at the cords around Gaia's wrists as Miriam pushes the START button—

Drew props up Sister Bulldog's dead body as a bloody shield—

Miguel grabs Cody off the pavement, using him as a human shield too. Drew can't shoot at Miguel, not with Cody in front of him. It's a standoff—

Setting undisturbed on the snow is the padded black case.

Miriam shifts into drive and stomps on the gas—

Miguel spins and aims his Uzi at the Lexus barreling toward him—

Noooo! I yell—

443

Miguel lowers the Uzi barrel, firing bursts at the tires, flattening them, riddling the front grill. We coast to a stop—

I finally snip my way through one cable around Gaia's wrists. We hustle out of the murdered Lexus. Gaia is hopping along—her ankles still bound in cables—and we stumble away from the shootout, with nowhere to go but toward the water, into patchy woods of thin, bare trees the width of my skinny arms, too narrow to hide behind. If we dare swim away in the muddy-gray Charles Mill Lake, we'd be picked off like floating ducks at a carnival game. Plus there's no way Gaia can swim tied-up. And then there's hypothermia.

Miguel and Drew assess their standoff.

Join us, Miguel says, we need to be united.

Drew hesitates. Leonardo aims at him but Miguel is standing in the way.

I finally snip through the last cord, freeing Gaia's wrists from behind her back.

Give me your gun, she says, you can't shoot worth shit.

I hand over the SisPistol. She returns both hands behind her back, as if still tied.

We'll let them wipe-out each other first, she says.

Miguel decides he's done waiting. He unleashes hell, a barrage of bullets into Sister Bulldog shield until one or two connect with Drew. He falls to one knee, returns his own hell, bullets flying everywhere, like a Tarantino shootout. His aim is erratic, the weight of the dead Sister Bulldog in his arms, the pain from multiple gunshots, the splattered blood in his eyes, all taking a toll. Miguel readies to finish Drew off, squeezing the last couple bullets out of his Uzi—click—it's empty. The forest suddenly quiets, as if a group of locusts have ceased screeching. Drew shoves his cumbersome shield, Sister Bulldog, aside and aims at Miguel and smiles and clicks his mouth—

A flurry of bullets zip from behind Miguel, past him, perforating Drew. He crumbles to the snowy pavement. Blood trickles, dotting his body red, his arms and legs bent in every direction.

Miguel looks back over his shoulder at Leonardo in the van. The barrel of Leonardo's Little Sister rattles against the door frame, mascara running down his ghostly cheeks.

I killed a brother, he mumbles numbly.

Miguel drops his emptied Uzi and hurries over to Drew, kneeling down and prying the AK-12 from his stiff grip. He also pockets Drew's revolver, then rises, kicking his limp body, making sure he's dead.

Guess you won't be needing that vaccine after all.

Miriam, Gaia, and I try to hide behind the thin trees.

Shoot him, Miriam whispers.

He's too far away, Gaia whispers back. If I miss, we're dead Sisters.

Without my gun, I grip the empty tincture bottle in my coat pocket, working it like a talisman in my gloved fingers.

Miguel points that terrifying AK-12 in our direction. He stalks toward the black vaccine case, shadows from the thin trees striping the white ground before him like a moonlit barcode. Miriam, Gaia, and I are trapped between him and the dark freezing water a few steps behind us. I hope he takes the case and walks away and then Gaia shoots him in the back, because that's a helluva lot better than other scenarios I can imagine. Miguel does pick up the case, holding it to his chest as his own bulletproof vest. He steps forward to the very edge of the thin forest, fixing his AK-12 at us. We back up behind the

445

last of the skinny-ass trees, the lake licking at our heels. Adrenaline rushes through the three of us, waiting to see what Miguel's gonna do. Gaia keeps her hands behind her back, as if still tied, gripping the SisPistol.

Let us go, I beg, you've got the vaccine.

Get your ass over here.

No one will snitch on you. You have my word.

Step away from the Sisters, Miguel demands, or I'll kill all three of you.

We've seen what he can do and since only Gaia is armed, a simple SisPistol versus that beastly AK-12, there's just one thing to do:

I step away from the Sisters.

There are many moments in life where the only option is to back off and obey. I decide this is not one of those moments. Shoot him when you can, I whisper to Gaia from behind my mask, as I raise my hands high and step around the naked trees.

Okay! I'm coming!

Miguel trains the AK-12 on us, keeping me in-between himself and the Sisters. He wedges the case under one armpit, and one-handedly opens the cylinder of Drew's revolver, emptying four bullets from the chambers. I come within a few steps of him. He tosses the revolver at my feet.

I left you two bullets. Prove you're on our side. Put one in each of their heads.

No way! I say, trying to sound strong, but feeling so fucked, ordered to shoot the mother of my child and our oldest, dearest friend.

The deal was the vaccine for Gaia, I plead.

446

I've amended the deal, Miguel says. If you can't kill a Sister, you're not a true brother.

This isn't right, Miguel.

I can kill all three of you if you prefer. Now pick it up.

I bend down.

Unh-uh. Turn around first.

I turn my back to him, my left leg pumping like an oil well.

He aims the dark barrel point-blank at my back.

I imagine you won't try taking on this bad boy.

If I was a true hero I would, I tell myself, as I scoop the revolver out of the snow.

Now walk back to them, he instructs, and put a bullet right between each of their eyes.

There's got to be another—

Do it!

I wish I was that hero I dreamed of as a boy and that I would spin around and fire those two bullets point-blank into his fucking head and we could all go home. But I know that's suicide. I wish Gaia had just shot him earlier, she can't now, I'm in the way. So I return to the patch of forest, toward two Sisters I love. My entire body quakes. Miguel is not far behind me, itching to shoot any and all of us.

Who's first? he asks.

From behind my mask, I whisper to Gaia: Wait for my signal.

Choose! Miguel barks, Or I choose for you.

I face Miriam, nudging the barrel of the revolver into her forehead.

I knew you'd pick me, Miriam says, loudly, spitefully, playing her part, perfectly.

Shoot! Miguel shouts at me, like he needs to see another sacrifice tonight, like there hasn't been enough blood spilled.

I'm sorry, I tell Miriam.

I'm carrying your child!

I pretend to be surprised.

Even better! Miguel brags.

It's a boy, you asshole! Miriam yells at Miguel. You'll be killing a little brother!

I don't care if it's Jesus Christ, Miguel spits out. Now you can see what it feels like, Bryan. Right, Gaia?

I look back at him, confused.

Oh, you still don't know, do you. Back in high school, she aborted my child. I didn't even have a say.

I didn't want to end up like my mom, Gaia yells at him.

You didn't want a Honduran baby.

I didn't want *your* baby!

I take a long, deep breath that I wish could sustain me until I think of a better plan.

Now!! Miguel orders me.

Okay, okay!

My fingers reposition around the trigger. Here goes. I push the muzzle into Miriam's forehead. I whisper one word:

Now.

Gaia whips her SisPistol from behind her back, leans around a tree, squeezes the trigger, shooting one-two-three-four bullets at Miguel. One finds the corner of the case, another finds his right upper thigh. He goes down to one knee, dropping the padded case. I pull Miriam away as Miguel fires a barrage toward Gaia. Bullets tear into trees. Miguel wobbles, blood flowing down his leg. He looks back at shellshocked Leonardo in the van.

Shoot them!

I can't shoot anyone else, Leonardo whimpers to himself.

Gaia aims, squeezes the trigger—pop-pop-click. She's empty. She collapses against a tree, blood dribbling down her emerald jacket. She folds to the ground. Miriam and I rush to her side.

Gaia!

I knew you couldn't do it, Miguel spits his words at me, you Sister-lover!

I press my hand against Gaia's wounds, two in her gut, feel the heat rising out of her.

Hang on, honey, Miriam begs, cradling her, touching her face with a Sisterhood intimacy. Miriam pulls out her phone.

Put that away! Miguel yells, wincing, still down on one knee.

It's not that bad, I lie, pressing on Gaia's wounds.

Go, she says, spitting up blood that we both know will kill me.

No. I'm not leaving you.

I'm not either, Miriam adds, squeezing her hand.

Blood drips from the corner of Gaia's mouth, her lips curling into a faint smile.

Be well.

I can feel her energy escaping her flesh, sweeping by me, chilling me. I channel my fury into her, pumping on her chest—one-two-three-four-five-six-seven. I rip my mask off and bend over, pinching Gaia's nose and blowing a long, steady breath into her mouth, the first time our lips have touched since our carousel kiss. I pump her chest.

Let me do that, Miriam says, taking over blowing oxygen into Gaia's lungs.

Don't give up, Gaia, I beg, pumping on her chest.

You're going to make it, Miriam adds, inhaling a breath that she exhales into Gaia.

I pump, Miriam blows, it's useless, we both know it, but we keep doing it. I look over at Miguel. He rises, wobbling, his face twisted in pain, yet taking pleasure at me grieving over Gaia. I hate myself for ever being friends with him. Each time I pump on her chest I see myself shooting Miguel.

Miriam pulls me away.

Gaia's gone.

I wanna keep trying, gotta keep trying, but Miriam won't let go of me. We rise in each other's arms.

I'll give you one last chance, BB, Miguel says. Step aside.

But I stiffen in front of Miriam.

If that's the way you want it, he says.

Miriam pushes away from me. She darts between the narrow trees.

Where do you think you're going? Miguel says, squeezing a few rounds at her. She dodges errant bullets, then one strikes her back, lodging in her bulletproof vest, knocking her forward, almost onto her knees, but she reaches the shot-up Lexus, hiding behind the back bumper.

Miguel limps furiously toward the car, spraying bullets. I rush him, gripping the revolver he gave me. Miguel turns, faces me, I fire. The first bullet lands nowhere near, the second barely misses. He laughs maniacally, knowing that's it, I'm out of bullets. He takes great pleasure aiming, wrapping his finger around the trigger.

Goodbye, Sister Lover—

A softball-sized rock thunks Miguel's temple—thrown by Miriam, the softball shortstop—and he stumbles backward, stunned. I lunge at him, knock his AK-12 aside, grab his good leg, and tackle him in a single-leg takedown—I sometimes paid attention to Drew—getting Miguel in a half-nelson around his neck. He reaches for something in his boot, twists and stabs me in my upper chest. I gasp.

Miriam clubs him over the head with a broken branch.

Die you bastard!

I crawl away, toward the AK-12 on the snow, the knife handle protruding from my chest. Miriam raises the branch again, swings it down but Miguel rolls to the side, avoiding the blow, grabbing the branch, pulling her to the ground. I clutch the warm AK-12, lift it, don't have a clear shot, Miriam's in the way, Miguel wrapping one hand around her neck. She's flailing at him but he grabs the side of her head, ready to twist and break her neck.

I lunge, poking the barrel past Miriam and into his lower gut, jabbing him, nudging him away from Miriam. I squeeze the trigger and I can feel him convulsing from the one-two-three-four-five bullets I pump into his body, squeezing the trigger until the gun clicks empty. Miguel's eyes flash with a final intensity as blood seeps from his wounds and trickles out from underneath his mask. His body slumps onto the snow.

I didn't miss this time, you sonofabitch!

I toss the empty AK-12 aside and sit back against a tree trunk. Breathing is hard, I'm wheezing, the knife punctured my right lung, but

451

at least it's not bleeding much. I can survive this, I think, and I grip the handle and grunt.

Leave it in! Miriam says, dialing 9-1-1, It'll make it worse if you take it out.

I obey, as always, gasping for breath, surveying the carnage, blood everywhere, five dead bodies on the ground, almost in a pentagram, the vaccine case in the middle. I look at Leonardo in the van, shaking with terror and guilt.

There are multiple casualties, Miriam tells the 9-1-1 dispatcher. Hurry!

She takes my hand and places it on top of the bulletproof bump over her swollen belly. I'm shaking all over.

I got a blanket in the car, Miriam says, rushing over to the sedan, popping open the trunk. I stare at the bright moon almost directly overhead. I fish the tincture bottle out of my pocket, open it, raise the empty dropper to my lips, letting it dangle like a cigarette and even though it's empty, suddenly I don't feel the chill anymore, I feel my warm blood coursing through me, my own energy, ready to live on, to take that vaccine, to see my son grow up and re-populate our gender. Miriam rushes over with the blanket, spreading it open—

Pop-pop-pop. I open my heavy lids and see Miriam spun around from the impact of bullets into her bulletproof vest. Blood splatters from the back of her left bicep.

Gotcha bitch.

Cody! He's splayed out on the ground, on his stomach, all-but-forgotten, like in a fucking video game, taking aim again, squeezing his trigger, pumping a bullet into her upper vest. I rise, bent over, charging at him, possessed, the knife still in my chest. He turns his

452

aim on me. I juke, stumbling, like we were playing football, he shoots, misses. I bounce off a tree, he aims, I zig, he misses, I zag, and hear another pop and feel a stinging in my gut as I slump on top of him, each of us with a hand on the revolver now wedged sideways between us.

Why? I plead, clenching the dropper between my teeth.

We had to do it. Drew, like, just got The Y.

Cody is younger, stronger, and gaining the upper hand on the gun. I grab the dropper from my mouth and grip it at the tip of Cody's left eye, starting to push it in—

Not my eyes!

He lets go of the gun.

I can't kill Cody, so I roll off of him. Clutching his gun, I lie there, dying. Cody's crying. Miriam approaches, grimacing from the gunshot in her own arm, leaning down and cradling my head with her other arm, screaming at the dispatcher's voice in her cell:

I've been shot too! Hurry!!

She wraps the blanket around me, applying pressure to my bullet wound.

Help Cody, will ya? I ask.

I feel myself clutching her forearm. Then, I'm not sure if I say this or just think it:

And tell our boy I love him. Every day. Tell all my children.

You're not going to die, she says.

Tell him. . .to be. . .a good man.

And that is that, I feel myself draining out of this body, and I try clinging to my limp flesh, my essence seeping out through my fingertips, my toes. I hear the 9-1-1 Sister Dispatcher's voice on Miriam's phone:

Hang on, EMTs are almost there.

Miriam holds me and I wanna tell her I'm not dead yet but I know it's a lie, I feel myself pull completely away from my flesh and bone, like I'm slipping from one world to another. I watch from a few feet above as Miriam cradles my old vessel. She doesn't perform CPR, as if she knows, instead she looks heavenward, back and forth above myself and above Gaia, tracking both our spirits. I wanna reach for her but I can't, I wanna tell her I am still here, hovering like a drone, but I don't. I feel like I should weep, but that's ridiculous, I have no eyes to cry with, and I wanna dive back down into my flesh, refilling it with my spirit like liquid into a mold, yet this all feels somehow oddly natural. I rise higher and higher, losing the desire to return.

Miriam lays my head down on the snow. She wipes her eyes and pries Cody's gun from my stiff grip and walks past Cody.

Don't move, she orders him.

She steps toward Miguel's perforated body, rears her leg back and kicks him in the balls. A ripple pulses through his dead body and I feel laughter vibrating through my spirit, and it's nice to know I will still have that as I rise higher, floating far above the tree tops. Then Miriam walks over to the black vaccine case—with a bullet hole in one corner—and lifts it off the pavement. She carries it to Leonardo in the Seven Sisters Caterers van.

You know what to do with this?

He nods his mascara-streaked face, too shaken to speak.

Good.

She hands the case through the open driver's side window.

454

Tell your people everything they need is in there.

Leonardo starts the van.

Wait, she says, unzipping the case, and removing a vial and syringe. Then she backs away as Leonardo shifts into drive and the van creeps out of the parking lot.

Miriam walks over to Cody's side, she preps the syringe, draws fluid into it from the vial, taps the needle. Cody pulls off his jacket and rolls up his left sleeve. Miriam jabs him below the shoulder. Without a word, she returns to my side, sits on the pavement, and presses her palm against her own bloody bicep. I am doing my best to hover, not so much because I wanna stay, I know it's time to go, rather because I wanna see how it plays out. The flow of energy is pulling me away, however, and I watch the red taillights of Leonardo's van's cross a bridge over the water, before fading in the distance. Ambulances, fire trucks, and deputy cruisers rush to the scene, lights flashing and sirens whining. My attention drifts upward into the star-dotted sky. I don't know where I'm going but I like the fact that I'm going somewhere and I feel joy that this is happening and that some form of afterlife is not so far-fetched after all.

EPILOGUE

EDITOR'S NOTE: Gaia had edited most of Bryan's posts, but since she is gone, rest in peace, I had to write the ending. I added a little New Age pizzazz as I imagine Gaia might have. I debated changing the outcome, there is way too much blood and death for my taste. But I didn't. Brothers probably won't mind.

After the Massacre at Charles Mill Lake, peace settles over Sisterfield. The Golden Trio, along with Leonardo, become known as the S.O.B.s: Saviors of Brothers. (The word Brother is now capitalized like Sister.)

Miguel is cremated two days before Christmas, no service, no fanfare, his ashes rumored to be spread somewhere over Honduras.

On Christmas Eve, Gaia receives a beautiful funeral service, with every available flower in Sisterfield on display and thousands of Sisters paying their respects. A bronze statue of Gaia is erected on the Square—next to Kamala Harris—and she stands in flowing clothes, holding a book, looking off to the distance, Lady Liberty-like. Two blocks away, her bookstore is a shrine, packed now, mostly with Brothers. Her ashes rest in a carved mahogany urn on a bookshelf in my home office.

Bryan receives a small service the day after Christmas. Sister Beth delivers the eulogy, laughing about how he caught her drinking in church and how he didn't believe in prayer but wanted one anyway. His mom attends in a wheelchair pushed by his Sister Emily and his niece Emma. Also there are André, Kimchi, and even Selfie shows up. Kimchi composes and performs an electronica requiem. After the service, we all take his mom to see Christmas light displays, so in a way Bryan made that happen for her.

His ashes rest in a bronze urn on my shelf, next to Gaia's.

I resign as mayor, too disgusted by the gender politics, and am now a consultant for the medical industry, which gives me more time with our three-year-old son, Bryan, Jr.

Cody survives, vaccinated, playing Bryan's guitar in a prison cell. Word is he has become quite good.

Leonardo delivers the vials to surviving undergrounders and Appleseeds and Brother Scientists. André—like Steven, a closet undergrounder—gets the formula to his uncle, a former scientist. Known simply as The Vaccine, it is replicated, mass-produced and distributed at no cost to Brothers. Hardly a single anti-vaxxer in the bunch.

A lawsuit goes to the SEW Supreme Court over ownership rights and theft of trademarked property, but Sister Justices side with Brothers and mandate government-funded vaccinations.

Mother Olsen announces that The Vaccine was invented almost a year before the Massacre at Charles Mill Lake, but was kept secret under the guise of safety testing. Brothers demand her removal, protesting outside the White House, but she remains our leader. She and I are no longer friends.

Winter solstice becomes a national holiday—Vaccine Day, the gift that keeps on giving—threatening to dethrone Christmas from its holiday perch.

Some rebel Brothers still hide out, far off the grid, in the rugged mountains of Afghanistan, the remote jungles of Africa, and the expansive plains of Montana. Small skirmishes erupt every now and then, and the survival of Brothers is far from certain, but the pendulum of history—a very lopsided pendulum—is swinging back their way. Congress approved the Brothers Bill of Rights and it's up for ratification in all 50 states. A national Brothers Monument breaks ground in Washington, D.C. And laws forbidding inter-gender marriage are rescinded. Now, hundreds of thousands of baby Brothers are born in America each year. A re-population program engineers gender at conception under a new Two-For-One Law—two boys born for every girl. Your first child must be a boy. The second can be a girl. The third, again, a boy.

Impromptu cement statues of Bryan, Miguel, and Troy go up in Brother Town, the former slum now undergoing a renaissance of restorations. Brothers are left alone there, autonomous, like the Amish in their communities and Native Americans on their reservations. I bring Bryan, Jr., to see his father's statue. A few Brothers hang around—masks are no longer necessary—paying their respects. Some thank me for my role. I don't have a statue yet, neither does Leonardo, I guess since we're both still alive.

Bryan, Jr. gazes up at his concrete dad. A guitar leans against one leg, a syringe held in one hand. I think a tincture bottle should have been in the other.

That's your daddy, I say, you have his name. Not much of a musician, really, but he and mommy and our friend Gaia helped save millions of Brothers' lives.

Wow. Mommy?

Yes, Bryan?

What's millyuns?

***

One last thing: a divide unfortunately still exists between the genders. As feared, Sisters are developing synthetic sperm. And Brothers are working on artificial wombs. The way we're going, one day no Sisters or Brothers will be required to procreate at all.

As Bryan might say: What the fuck?

Miriam

EDITOR'S EDITOR'S NOTE: The opinions expressed in this book do not reflect the opinions at Fertile Publishing, but we pride ourselves in bringing alternative views to print. We decided to end with one of Bryan's last postings, handwritten from prison on Dec. 18, 2032, two days before his death:

Even though I'm locked up in this hellhole, I feel freer than I have in years. Free of the tyranny of the sperm. Sisters rule now and probably always will, but I believe one day we will retool and rebrand ourselves. We will finally, truly change. I'm not naïve, we won't rule the world, not like we used to, that won't happen again, for good reason. Like it or not, powerful or not, we brothers are and probably always will be. . .

Obsolete.

ACKNOWLEDGEMENTS

I'd like to thank friends and family for keeping me from becoming obsolete. Thanks to mom for inspiring my love of reading and to dad for all his support. To Paula Kimes for her early readings. To the book group: Michael Beck, Linda Goulet, Peter Shaw, Kathleen Kitch, and Jennifer and Rob Weiher for their suggestions. To Fernando Garcés for inspiring my music. To my dog Mugsy for being at my feet for all the drafts. And to my wife Paula Donnelly for her input, support, and putting up with the hundreds of hours I sat hunkered down in front of my laptop. And, mostly, for all her love.